P9-DFU-426

# THE ROAR OF THE DEAD DRAGON

Above their heads Pelmen the powershaper and the blue-blinded Tahli-Damen heard the double-throated roar that had chilled men's blood for centuries. It thundered down upon them as palpably as an avalanche. Tahli-Damen knew that roar. It came from Vicia-Heinox. The two-headed dragon hovered in the air above them.

The scream stiffened the hairs on the back of Pelmen's neck and knotted his body with tension. But he didn't cower from it. He turned his eyes up to stare at the monstrous beast.

"But Vicia-Heinox is dead!" Tahli-Damen wailed.

"Yes," Pelmen muttered. "The dragon *is* dead. I killed it."

Above them, vast jaws opened as one head shrieked in fury. "Who dares to trespass on my domain?"

Slowly, the huge beast began to descend upon them.

Also by Robert Don Hughes
*Published by Ballantine Books:*

THE PROPHET OF LAMATH

THE WIZARD IN WAITING

# The Power
AND
# The Prophet

Robert Don Hughes

A Del Rey Book

BALLANTINE BOOKS • NEW YORK

A Del Rey Book
Published by Ballantine Books

Copyright © 1985 by Robert Don Hughes

All rights reserved under International and Pan-American Copyright Conventions. Published in the United States by Ballantine Books, a division of Random House, Inc., New York, and simultaneously in Canada by Random House of Canada Limited, Toronto.

Library of Congress Catalog Card Number: 84-91701

ISBN 0-345-30353-9

Manufactured in the United States of America

First Edition: April 1985

Cover art by Darrell K. Sweet

for my parents,
who pointed me to the Power

# Contents

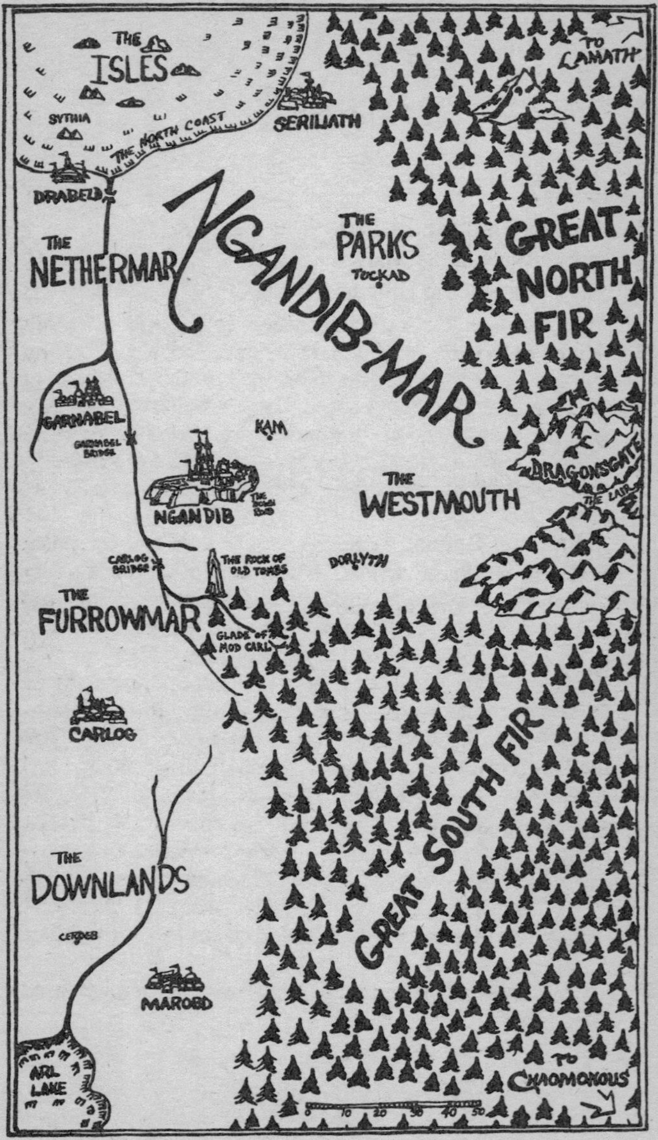

THE ISLES
SYTHIA
THE NORTH COAST
SERILIATH
DRABELD
TO CAMATH
THE NETHERMAR
NGANDIB-MAR
THE PARKS
TOCKAD
GREAT NORTH FIR
GARNABEL
GARNABEL BRIDGE
KAM
NGANDIB
THE WESTMOUTH
DRAGONSGATE
THE LAIR
CARLOG BRIDGE
THE ROCK OF OLD TOMBS
DORLYTH
THE FURROWMAR
GLADE OF MOD CARL
CARLOG
THE DOWNLANDS
MAROBD
GREAT SOUTH FIR
ARL LAKE
TO CHAOMONOUS
0 10 20 30 40 50

PROLOGUE

# The Power's Gateway

THEY WERE mined from the finest veins in the Mar—six huge diamonds, each the size of a giant's skull. A company of warriors, sworn to secrecy, bore them by horseback around the treacherous southwestern route. They wouldn't dare enter Dragonsgate with diamonds of this size, for Vicia-Heinox would claim them for himself. These stones were destined to be the dragon's bane, and that would end the conspiracy at its beginning.

The Mari warriors bore them to the scholars of the south, surrendering their treasures in the heartland of their hated foes. All men were allies now, for there was dragonburn on the land. In the hallways of the craftsmen, under the learned eyes of the wise, each diamond felt the chisel. Six three-sided pyramids were carefully cut—six slivers of crystal, each tapering gracefully to a point, each calibrated to fit precisely with every other. Then the wise men summoned the powershaper to meld by his magic the six sharp shards into a single diamond thorn.

There was a human failing. The cost proved too high. Unwilling to pay that price, the sorcerer improvised. He attacked the dragon alone, wielding the sparkling weapon in his bare hands. The battle—visible from distant mountaintops—left the shaper destroyed and the crystal object shattered once again into six three-sided pyramids. They all were lost for a millennium.

Now, a thousand years later, three had been rediscovered.

## CHAPTER ONE

# Pilgrims Through the Pass

AN AUTUMN wind stirred the grasslands of the Westmouth Plain, billowing Pelmen's robe out before him. He walked briskly toward the east, his head up, his eyes fixed on the jagged peaks of Dragonsgate. He could have flown. He was, after all, a powershaper; in his altershape, he took on the form of a falcon. Yet Pelmen was tired of flying. He'd done little else for days. And he was certain the one he sought would be on foot—*if* she was free to travel at all. Once again, Pelmen searched for Serphimera.

Something caught his eye. On the road above him, up in the foothills of the ancient pass, he saw a flash of powder blue. He knew instantly what it was, and it amazed him. "A sky-faither? Here?" he murmured and he speeded his already quick pace. His gown was of the same brilliant color, but he'd never before seen another like it here in this ancient land of warfare and wizardry. It wasn't his wandering lady—she still wore the midnight blue of the old Dragonfaith. But it was *someone* who shared his belief, and, by the Power, Pelmen wanted to know who.

By the Power! So much of what Pelmen had done in the past few years had been by the Power. Time and again he'd been summoned to lay down his personal concerns and take up cosmic responsibilities. Was Serphimera's disappearance a prelude to yet another such adventure? He could hardly tolerate the thought. Yet if Serphimera's prophecies were true—and she'd never been proved wrong yet—a new burden was even now being placed on Pelmen's shoulders. Because of who and what he was, Pelmen Dragonsbane could do nothing other than bear it.

He could see the figure above him clearly now, and his curiosity grew. The man clothed in skyfaither blue slowly angled off the road toward the north. Pelmen glanced that way and frowned. There was a path there, but it led only to a blind canyon. Was this skyfaither camped there? When Pelmen's gaze flicked back to the blue-clad figure his frown deepened with concern; the man tripped and fell.

He didn't throw out his arms to cushion his fall. Instead, he clutched them to his chest, as if he shielded something within his robes that was above value and that must be protected at all personal cost. Pelmen would have raced up to help him then, but there was a shout from the canyon above. Almost without thought Pelmen drew a shield of invisibility around himself, a spell shapers referred to as "the cloak." He disappeared.

There were boys among the rocks, playing at being men. They shouted back and forth, proving themselves upon one another—a harsh process that could make the mildest of lads brutal for an afternoon. Suddenly the noise died as they spotted the blue figure climbing toward them. They took his presence as some kind of challenge. "Halt!" one of the larger boys commanded. When the bluefaither kept on coming, a ring of lads quickly closed around him. Pelmen felt the threat of violence charge the atmosphere and he drew near to help. He soon realized he didn't need to bother; as one boy whirled the skyfaither around and drew back a fist to strike, the man opened his eyes. There were no pupils there, no irises, no whites. There were only two blank balls of powder blue. The boys all saw it together, and it sent them shrieking past the invisible Pelmen and down the mountainside. The man threw back his head and laughed. As the echoes bounced eerily off the canyon walls, Pelmen remembered. He thought he knew who this might be. He shed his magical cloak of invisibility and spoke.

"You dealt with them easily enough. I shouldn't have worried."

Tahli-Damen grunted in shock and whirled toward Pelmen's voice. "Who are you?" the blind man demanded.

"A friend."

"All my friends have names," Tahli-Damen growled, his forehead wrinkling in suspicion.

"Where are you going?"

"What's that to you?"

"I'd like to help you."

"Then name yourself!" Tahli-Damen snapped.

Pelmen didn't want to do that just yet. If this man was the one he thought, then Pelmen bore some responsibility for those hideous powder blue eyes. "That isn't important."

"It is to me!" Tahli-Damen snarled. "Did Wayleeth send you? Well, I'll not go back! You can go tell her to forget about me! I'm never going back there again!" Tahli-Damen crossed his arms protectively across his chest. He was obviously concealing something within his robes. In his blindness, he was unaware of how strongly that gesture directed Pelmen's attention to the very object the man was trying to hide. Pelmen knew at once what it was. "Don't try to block my path!" Tahli-Damen shouted and he started backing away.

"I won't," Pelmen responded quietly. "But the mountain will."

"What mountain?"

"The one you're walking into."

Tahli-Damen set his jaw. "I'm climbing into Dragonsgate."

"I'd guessed that. Tell me. Have you encountered any passing traffic?"

"There's been no traffic through the pass for a fortnight," Tahli-Damen grunted.

This news surprised Pelmen. It also caused him concern. Since he'd killed the great two-headed dragon, Vicia-Heinox, the pass had been blocked only once—by the villainous Admon Faye and a company of slavers. Did cutthroats once again control Dragonsgate? He glanced back at Tahli-Damen's suspicious frown and thought of another argument to convince the man they weren't yet in the pass. "Tell me this. Have you ever known lads—even the bravest or most foolhardy of Mari boys—to stray so deeply into a pass frequented by slavers?"

Tahli-Damen dropped his head and thought on that for a moment. "No," he grumbled sourly.

"I'm on my way through Dragonsgate myself, and your news startles me. Perhaps we can be of mutual assistance."

"Mutual assistance!" Tahli-Damen snorted derisively. "I can't even take the right pathway!"

"I disagree," said Pelmen quietly. "The color of your robe tells me otherwise."

Shock registered on Tahli-Damen's face, and he leaned forward, as if to peer through his personal fog. "You know the significance of this color?"

"I'm gowned as you are. But tell me, how did *you* learn what it means? Are you from Lamath?"

Tahli-Damen sighed. "I've spent time in Lamath. I've lived in all three lands. I used to be a merchant, back in the days of the dragon—a trading captain. I saw this robe occasionally there. Not very often."

"We were few then," Pelmen muttered.

"And," Tahli-Damen continued, "I learned a little about the Power. Didn't believe it then, of course."

"But now you do?" Pelmen said, asking by his inflection why the change had come.

"I got in trouble with some wizards. It cost me my sight. That plunged me into depression. Wayleeth—that's my wife—did all she could to make me feel better, but nothing could penetrate this blue fog that surrounds me. Then I had the strangest experience. I felt that something wonderful and powerful was suddenly coming through me, as if I was—" Tahli-Damen broke off, and he turned his head in the direction of Pelmen's voice. "Are you sure Wayleeth didn't send you?" he demanded. His harshness had returned.

"I don't even know your wife," Pelmen responded. "But it sounds as if she cares for you very much."

"Too much," Tahli-Damen grunted. "She thinks too much of me. That's partly why I'm leaving. She'll be better off without me."

"What's the other reason?" Pelmen asked.

Tahli-Damen shrank back from him, clutching his arms across his chest once again. "Who are you?" he demanded. "Are you from Flayh?"

Pelmen's eyes narrowed and his jaw clenched. That name bore bitter memories. "No," he growled. "I'm not from Flayh." He relaxed then and went on more calmly. "If I'm from anyone, you may believe I'm from the Power. I think it's possible that I'm here to help you by the Power's design."

Tahli-Damen's uncertain frown twisted his features as he barked, "But how can I be sure?"

Pelmen had faced that question himself many times. He had an answer ready. "You can't. But then you can't be sure there's any value in that robe you wear. You still wear it. That's why they call us 'faithers.'"

"You expect me just to trust you?" Tahli-Damen asked.

Pelmen thought a moment, then simply said, "Yes."

Apparently his conviction and sincerity were persuasive. After a brief pause, Tahli-Damen said, "Very well then. Where's Dragonsgate?"

Pelmen took his arm and guided him back down the steep incline. Few words passed between them. Tahli-Damen focused his attention on not stumbling. Pelmen pondered the irony of this situation. He had interrupted his quest for the woman who had deserted him in order to help this blind man desert a loving wife. At least, he guessed Serphimera had deserted him. Wrenching as it was, he could tolerate that explanation better than the other possibilities that had plagued his waking hours.

Pelmen and Serphimera had spent an idyllic summer. They'd explored the dirt roads of Chaomonous, lodging with peasants in pleasant cottages or resting beside quiet pools of crystal-clear water, engaged in a single, endless conversation. She'd told him her whole history—her girlhood, her growing fascination with the dragon cult, those first frightening moments when she'd sensed a responsibility being laid upon her, and the day she'd felt a new kind of power surge through her soul. Naturally she'd attributed it to the dragon, and that had intensified her devotion. Pelmen had listened sympathetically, his eyes gentle with understanding love. And he in turn had disclosed more secrets than he'd ever revealed to anyone else. She knew him better now than did the prophet Erri, better than his acting companion Yona Parmi—better even than did Dorlyth. She'd listened in rapt attention, laughing in the appropriate places, weeping a time or two. The bond of physical attraction forged between them by competition had been tempered by this intimacy into love. At last they'd declared it to one another.

But one barrier had remained. "We're not finished yet," she had constantly reminded him. "Neither of us. I've seen it."

Pelmen knew it was true. Throughout the summer he'd acknowledged to himself that he would have to confront the wizard Flayh. Even so, he'd seen no reason why that should separate them.

She'd left him resting beneath an oak at the edge of the Great South Fir, saying she was going to hunt berries. He'd waked hours later to find the daylight departed and Serphimera still gone. He'd started his search calmly; but as the long hours of evening passed into dark night and on toward dawn, he'd lost control of himself and grown frantic. He'd taken his falcon form and, for the next three days, had swept back and forth over the dense forest on the wing, punctuating each long turn with a sharp, fierce cry of frustration. Despite his enhanced vision and the advantage of flight, Pelmen never found a trace of her. It was as if she'd vanished—and no one could disappear except through the intervention of a powershaper!

These thoughts led him back again to the dark door of Flayh. What could the man do now? Clearly Flayh's powers exceeded those of all the shapers Pelmen had ever known. What were the man's limits? Had Flayh even found them himself? Was Flayh somehow responsible for this new blockade of Dragonsgate? As they headed up into the pass Pelmen probed his companion for more information. "You said there's been no traffic through here for several weeks. Have you heard any rumors to explain it?"

"*Only* rumors. The men of the House of Uda pride themselves on being cautious. They prefer that fiction to admitting their own cowardice."

"Yet you show little cowardice yourself, braving the legendary Dragonsgate alone and without sight."

"What do I have to fear?" Tahli-Damen murmured bitterly. "My House thinks I'm crazy. I've lost all honor there. My wife treats me as an invalid, smothering me with affection. I've lost my sight, so I judge myself poor material for slavers. You have more to fear from them than I."

"Perhaps," Pelmen acknowledged, the deadly tone in his voice making clear his opinion of slavers. "Yet I wonder if it's those whom we'll encounter. Cutthroats have blocked the pass before, but they never cut traffic off entirely. They make more money by controlling passage than they could by stopping it. Evil as they are, I'm expecting to meet something more ominous than slavers."

"But what could be more—"

As if in answer to that unfinished question, they heard above them the double-throated roar that had chilled men's blood for centuries. It echoed off the canyon walls. It thundered down upon them as palpably as an avalanche. Tahli-Damen's boasts about his total lack of fear melted away, and he crumbled to his knees in terror. He'd been a trading captain. He knew that angry scream. Vicia-Heinox, the two-headed dragon, hovered in the air above them.

The scream stiffened the hairs on the back of Pelmen's neck and knotted his body with tension, but he didn't cower away. He turned his eyes up to stare at the monstrous beast and said, "Who would have guessed it? The dragon."

"But Vicia-Heinox is dead!" Tahli-Damen wailed.

"Yes," Pelmen muttered. "The dragon *is* dead."

Vast jaws opened as one head shrieked in fury, "Who is this who dares trespass my domain?"

"Speak!" the other head demanded. "I asked you a question!"

"And I shall have an answer!" finished the first.

Pelmen propped his hands on his hips. "Why is it so important that you know our names?"

"What?" one head thundered.

"You dare to answer me with impertinence?" the other roared.

"Please don't anger it!" Tahli-Damen begged. "I know this dragon! We'll be eaten!"

"I very much doubt that," Pelmen muttered. "Stay close to me," he told Tahli-Damen, but his words were drowned by the dragon's bellow.

"I *always* learn the names of those I swallow! It adds piquancy to the flavor!"

The other head seemed suddenly puzzled, perhaps even annoyed. "Pardon," it mumbled, "but I think I recall that *I* am to swallow the next morsel!"

"But of course I am!" the first head snapped. "I always get the next morsel!"

"Why are you haunting this pass?" Pelmen shouted. "Begone!" He noticed then that the blind bluefaither was crawling away on his hands and knees.

"Haunting the pass?" one head sniffed.

"Begone?" the other snarled.

"I live here!" the first trumpeted.

"You don't live anywhere. You don't live at all. You're dead, Vicia-Heinox, and I want you to stop pretending otherwise!"

"*I* am *dead*?" the two heads chorused in unison.

In that moment something happened to Pelmen that both frightened and elated him. He was seized from within by that which he knew as the Power. All shaper abilities drained from him, replaced by that incredible sense of being shaped. Guided from without, he reached down to grab Tahli-Damen by the collar and hoisted him to his feet while calling aloud, "Yes! You're dead!" Quickly he bent to whisper in Tahli-Damen's ear. "Stand up, spread your legs and throw your arms out wide. When I say fall, fall backward."

"That's the most ridiculous statement I've ever heard!" the head named Vicia howled.

"And I've heard all the ridiculous notions of a thousand years of men!" Heinox added noisily.

"Nevertheless, it's true. You were divided by Pelmen the player, and slain by Pelmen Dragonsbane!"

"Pelmen!" both heads screamed with deadly malice and they struck.

"Fall," Pelmen ordered, but he needn't have, since Tahli-Damen was already falling backward in a dead faint. There was a sudden rush of wind off the plain behind them, and the two bluefaithers were suddenly sky-born.

"Pelmen!" the heads howled again, this time from a hundred feet below them. But the dragon didn't give chase. Pelmen thought he knew why.

"Wake up. We need to be moving."

Tahli-Damen opened his eyes to face the eternal blue fog. He had no idea where he was, the time of day, or who was speaking. He could feel a brisk breeze on his face, but that told him little. His sense of smell was dominated by the aroma of meat roasting over a fire. A warm, dripping chunk of it was thrust into his hand, and he brought it to his mouth without a thought. He was hungry, and it smelled delicious. The taste did not disappoint him. He swallowed with a gulp and grunted, "Where are we?" His mind had cleared enough to remember the stranger and his assistance through Dragonsgate. Suddenly the memory of that shocking encounter in the pass flooded his thoughts, and he trembled as the man answered his question.

"We're several miles within Lamath, at the edge of the Tellera Desert."

"The dragon! What about the dragon!" Tahli-Damen shouted.

"What dragon?" the other man replied calmly.

"Vicia-Heinox! If it spots us from the sky—"

"The dragon is dead."

"But—but we talked to it!"

"We talked to something. Or someone. But I have it on good authority that the particular beast you mention is very dead. There are more important things to worry about than being spotted by a dead dragon."

"How did we get past it?" Tahli-Damen quailed. His terror didn't prevent him from gobbling the chunk of meat. As soon as the last of it disappeared into his mouth, another slab was shoved into his hand.

"Do you believe in miracles?" the relaxed stranger asked him.

"I . . . guess I could," Tahli-Damen admitted.

"Then that settles it. There's plenty of that meat here for you. Eat all you can—we've got a long walk ahead of us."

"The desert," Tahli-Damen mumbled as he chewed.

"A seven-day walk, at least. Or seven nights. Even in autumn I prefer to take the desert when the sun's gone elsewhere."

Tahli-Damen nodded grimly and swallowed. Crossing the desert had loomed as a far greater obstacle than had Dragonsgate. But then, he hadn't been expecting a dragon.

"Of course, we could make it in two and a half days on horseback."

Tahli-Damen was shocked. "A bluefaither? Riding?"

"I don't recall the prophet forbidding it," his companion said breezily.

"I've . . . just never thought of that before," Tahli-Damen admitted.

The stranger laughed. "Then think of it, by all means!"

"But where can we—"

"You mentioned your House and your cautious kin. I know you say you've lost honor there, but surely not so much that they would deny you a pair of ponies. Your Lamathian waycastle isn't far—why not go ask?"

The idea made splendid sense. Tahli-Damen didn't really *want* to walk across the desert. "Lead me to it."

They found the castle within the hour, and Tahli-Damen walked inside the gates alone. His relatives suggested that he at least stay the night, then tried to constrain him when he refused, but at last they let him go, along with a couple of horses. In fact, they were relieved when he left. His blindness made them uncomfortable. After all, he'd lost his sight by meddling with sorcerers, and merchants took a dim view of that sort of thing. Besides, he was crazy. His ridiculous blue garment proved it.

"Ah," the stranger greeted him pleasantly as he led the horses out the gate. "I told you we could be of some mutual benefit."

"I hardly see why you need a horse," Tahli-Damen said, a bit suspiciously. "Why not just ride the wind?"

"You know, that's the trouble with miracles. They're great when they happen, but you just can't depend on them." He helped Tahli-Damen climb astride his steed.

The blind merchant grunted. "I had thought it more magic than miracle."

"You take me for a powershaper?"

"I don't know what to take you for—except a friend. You've proved yourself to be that. But should you be a powershaper, I'd rather not travel with you. My experiences with shapers have not been good."

"I see," the other man said as he climbed onto his horse.

"I *don't*," Tahli-Damen said pointedly, "and powershapers are the reason. That one you mentioned, Pelmen, for all his heroics, has proved himself nothing but a menace!"

"You'd be surprised how many times I've heard those very words," the other man muttered as he took Tahli-Damen's reins and gently nudged the flanks of his own mount.

"He's the man who caused my blindness!" the merchant called as they cantered forward, then broke into a gallop.

"Perhaps he would change that if he could," his partner called back.

Tahli-Damen clung to the saddle horn and gazed ahead into the blue. He didn't respond for a while. At last he shouted, "I'm not sure, now, if I'd like my sight back. I learned so much by losing it."

"Well, as I said before: You can't count on them, but there *are* miracles."

The desert breeze, raised to a wind by their riding in the face of it, chapped Tahli-Damen's lips and watered his sky blue eyes. He closed them and clung more tightly to the saddle.

He said no more, and his companion offered no further conversation. He imagined the nighttime sky above them as their mounts carried them deeper into the Tellera Desert.

There was something reassuring about the emptiness of this place. He'd remarked on it every time he'd crossed it and he'd made many trips in his years as a captain of caravans. He liked the desert's brooding silence and the way the flatness of the distant horizon added stature to the horse and rider. He found a peculiar grandness in being the tallest object visible between the earth and the open sky. While he couldn't see the horizon, he knew it was there, stretching out before him like a sandy ocean, as flat, as empty as—

The blow knocked him from his saddle, hurling him to the ground with a crunch. His scream never had time to form. There was the odor everywhere of desert dogs, of fetid breath, and of terror. One beast leaped astride his chest and slavered in his face as another ripped at his gown. Still another batted his head with a heavy paw. He'd been mauled by a dog before and thus had a horror of them already. But these were no ordinary dogs. "Show!" one growled in his ear. "Where!" another barked. "Now!" a third bayed at the sky, and the word turned into a horrible elongated howl. He fought them off, flailing his arms and rolling onto his stomach to shield his treasure beneath him. This only incensed the pack, and some began to burrow under him, raking his sides with their claws. Others ripped savagely at his back. Now he screamed, screamed again, and screamed yet a third time as the high, fierce screech of a fast-approaching bird of prey shattered the desert peace still further. He'd already given himself up for dead and was bewailing the injustice of dying as the dinner of a pack of desert dogs, when the whole pack scattered at a run. He heard the falcon screech again, at some distance now, then heard the fast beat of powerful wings churning toward him, over his head, and away in the opposite direction. The Tellera resumed its placid, silent character as if nothing out of the ordinary had happened.

Desert dogs—real desert dogs—did not attack human travelers. Tahli-Damen doubted these were dogs at all, and the thought terrified him. But his dread and dismay rested not upon the attack of these weird dogs alone, but also on the shape taken on by his rescuer. He had suspected it earlier, but forbade himself to believe it. Now he knew with certainty the identity of his traveling companion. He couldn't move from the place where he'd fallen. Had he been able, he would have burrowed into the sand.

"Let me help you up," his companion said quietly.

Tahli-Damen made no move to respond. "You're Pelmen."

The stranger sighed. Instead of hoisting up the blind bluefaither, he sat beside him in the sand. "Are you surprised?"

"Not surprised," Tahli-Damen mumbled into the earth. "Just terrified."

"You'd thought taking the sky blue robe would free you from the influence of powershapers."

"I had hoped," the blind man said mournfully.

"Hmm." Pelmen nodded. "I thought that too, once. But as long as there are powers to shape, then shapers will use them to their selfish, evil ends."

"So you battle powers with powers," Tahli-Damen said bitterly. "And I am, again, between you!"

"It's either be between us or be alone with the dogs of Flayh. It wasn't me they attacked. It was you."

"To get at you," the merchant said evasively.

"No. To get that pyramid of crystal that hangs around your neck."

Tahli-Damen clutched the object to him. "So now you'll take it away, instead."

Pelmen snorted. "If I'd wanted it, I would have it already. You slept for several hours this afternoon, remember?"

"Why didn't you take it, then?"

"I supposed that the Power we serve has given you some instructions concerning it. Am I right?"

Tahli-Damen responded grudgingly. "I've been sent to give it to the Prophet Lamath."

"Then I suggest we be on our way. If we stay here, those doglike demons will be back—and not even a powershaper has limitless energy."

Tahli-Damen felt himself being pulled to his feet and was led across the sand. He was relieved to hear the stamping of his horse and to feel the animal's strong back come under him as Pelmen helped him up. He'd feared that the horses were lost. After a moment of silence, Tahli-Damen got up the nerve to ask a hesitant question. "Do you know the Prophet of Lamath?"

"You might say that," Pelmen muttered. Then he grabbed the reins of Tahli-Damen's pony, and they were off again through the desert.

By the time the sun rose on their third day of travel, they'd left the high desert behind and descended into the region of the rivers. Here the moist air gave welcome relief to their dust-encrusted lungs. They began to encounter trees, first singly, then in stands of six or eight. At last they were into the deciduous woods that lined all the tributaries of the mighty Lamathian River. These were not tall, dark forests like the massive Great Firs. They were, instead, comfortable parklands where boys could stage adventures and young lovers could stroll in safe semi-privacy. The woods were interspersed with fields, and these were crisscrossed with rows of yellowing stalks and withering vines. The summer's warmth fled before the sharp, cool breath of autumn, and the crops stood waiting for the reaper. Already some of the trees had changed hues, as maturing leaves tired of youthful greens and experimented with the gaudy colors of fall. It was a beautiful, if forbidding, sight, and Pelmen appreciated it. He felt in the same moment a sadness that his companion was missing all this. He tried to restrain it, but a lingering guilt remained. Tahli-Damen was right. Pelmen shared responsibility with Flayh for the bluefaither's blindness, and it bothered him.

He'd hoped to hide his identity a while longer. While not a Mari, Tahli-Damen had lived in the Mar long enough to have a feel for events. Pelmen needed to update his knowledge; he'd been totally absorbed in his quest for Serphimera. But his meeting with the pseudodragon and the encounter with the dogs of night had convinced him that he could no longer ignore the menace in the land of mountains and mines. A mongrel sorcerer of incredible might inhabited the High Fortress of Ngandib. Flayh had brought that ancient tower to snarling, snapping life in a phenomenal feat of shaping. Now his potency increased, stretching beyond the borders of the Mar to the edges of the other great nations. Pelmen wondered if it reached to their heartlands as well.

That was something Pelmen would soon discover for himself, for they rode now to the kernel of the land of Lamath—to the capital city itself. At this rate, they would arrive by midmorning.

The ride was easy, and the surroundings pleasant. The people they passed, farmers mostly, were men of simple appetites and open faces. The relaxing sway of the saddle combined with the long night's ride to lull him almost to sleep. Pelmen fought it, stretching his arms, twisting his shoulders from side to side, and shifting his weight from one aching buttock to the other.

He almost missed seeing the little chapel nestled in a grove outside a village. When he did see it, the vision brought him awake with a shiver. The weeds had been cleared away from the door. It had been newly painted a glossy midnight blue. And over the arch hung the terra-cotta figure of a double-headed dragon.

"Come on!" he snapped to no one but himself, as he kicked his horse's flanks sharply and jerked on Tahli-Damen's reins.

The merchant came awake with a shout. "What is it! What's happening! More dogs?"

"No," Pelmen snarled bitterly as their tired steeds finally got the urgent message and struggled to produce a gallop. "More dragons!"

"Where!" the blind merchant cried, automatically throwing his head back, expecting to search the sky.

"Not there. In Lamathian hearts. Oh, how I wish it were just in the sky!" Pelmen saw no more of the landscape. He brooded the rest of the way.

They entered the city unchallenged; but as soon as they passed the outer gates, they were joined by a contingent of riders in sky blue gowns. Hearing the hoofbeats, Tahli-Damen grew more concerned than ever. So distracted was Pelmen by the sight of the shrine that he didn't take the time to explain. They clattered down the broad, cobbled avenue to Lamath's vast central square, and across it to the door of the dungeon. Pelmen was off his horse in a moment and went quickly to Tahli-Damen's side to help him down. Then he wrapped the merchant's shoulders in a firm, friendly grip, and guided him inside.

"Prophet!" a voice called in a warm, raspy bass. "The Power has answered my petitions! I've longed to see you, and it's none too soon! Sit!"

Tahli-Damen was puzzled. "Who's he talking to?" he mumbled to Pelmen.

"I'm talking to the Prophet of Lamath," Erri said. "The one who accompanied you from Dragonsgate."

"That's not me, Erri," Pelmen grumbled. "I threw that mantle on you."

"And the Power keeps shoving it back toward you! I'd be delighted if you could get that through your skull and accept the responsibility!"

"Then—Pelmen is the Prophet of—" Tahli-Damen began.

"Pelmen is *not* the Prophet of Lamath anymore," Pelmen snapped. "He's not the prophet of anything. *This* is the Prophet of Lamath, the former Erri the sailor!"

"Let's not confuse the man, Pelmen," Erri muttered, acquiescing to the title. "Sit. Please."

Pelmen finally looked around the room. "Chairs? At last?" He smiled at his short, wiry friend.

Erri hung his head. "While I was in Chaomonous marrying Bronwynn to Rosha the brothers came in and took away my straw. Burned it. When I got back, *these* were here. They said they did it to ease my aches and pains, but I think they were just tired of sitting on the floor."

"Good for them." Pelmen nodded, his eyes sparkling. Then they softened, and he looked over at his traveling companion, who was gingerly lowering himself into a seat. "And this is Tahli-Damen—lately a merchant of Uda, now a bluefaither."

"Oh, I know him." Erri shrugged.

Tahli-Damen's forehead creased. "Have we met? Since I can't see your face, I—"

"Only in dreams, my friend. Vague visions. I saw you coming."

"And I . . . heard myself called . . ."

"Which may serve as some reassurance that you're in the right place." Erri's voice conveyed many things, among them being warmth, honesty, and a confident authority that could both inspire and challenge.

"It . . . does," Tahli-Damen replied. He'd imagined this meeting over and over in the past few days. In each version he'd made a wise, prudent speech before presenting the object. But the humility in Erri's manner pointed out to him his own pride. He said no more, but just thrust his hands into his robe and pulled out the velvet bag that had hung around his neck for days. He drew its golden braid over the top of his head and held the object out before him. "I was sent to bring you this."

Erri got up from his stool and walked over to accept it, his sandals slapping on the stone floor. As it left his hands, Tahli-Damen's shoulders slumped. He'd rid himself of a great burden. He'd also forfeited the purpose that had kept him going.

Erri sat the bag on the table, opened it, and disclosed its contents. "So this is one of the precious pyramids." The crystal glowed with an azure iridescence.

"Don't stare into it," Pelmen warned. "I've told Bronwynn not to handle the one she has, but she's a queen now, and can be trusted to follow her own counsel alone. Should she and Flayh happen to be examining their pyramids at this moment, you could find yourself locked in a most unpleasant confrontation."

Tahli-Damen shivered at that. He'd viewed such a confrontation through this very crystal. That had been the last thing he'd ever witnessed.

Erri bagged the object with a look of distaste. "I've no stomach for that. I'm confronted with problems enough already."

"The rebirth of the Dragonfaith?"

"You've seen their reopened shrines?"

"Only one—in a small village to the south—" Pelmen stopped. Erri had laid a hand on his arm to still him, and now turned to the merchant again.

"Forgive us, my brother Tahli-Damen. We are old friends, with much to discuss that probably will not interest you. A meal, a bath, and a bed may be far more to your liking and these can be provided." Erri clapped his hands, and a pair of initiates popped their heads inside the room. Erri tugged on the former merchant's arm, bringing him to his feet. Strolling with him to the door, Erri told him, "These two brothers will tend to your needs. Tahli-Damen—"

"Yes?" the blind man asked earnestly, turning his head toward Erri's voice.

"We can also provide you with other things here. Healing for your eyes is available. So, too, is a new purpose. But it seems, at present, not both."

Tahli-Damen listened intently, and then nodded. He didn't reply.

"You're a wise young man, Tahli-Damen. Think it over well." Then the blind man left Erri's small, bare cell and was led away to more comfortable rooms on the upper floors of the old palace. Erri looked at Pelmen, and raised an eyebrow. "What about a walk on the wharf? I'm tired of these walls!"

Pelmen wrapped an arm around his short friend's shoulders and they walked out under the darkening sky.

## CHAPTER TWO

# Murmurings in the Mar

THUNDER GRUMBLED in a sky turned sullen. Pelmen and Erri walked along the band of the gray-green river, pulling their cloaks tight against the cold. Pelmen cast occasional glances at the threatening sky, but his short companion ignored the mumbled warnings. The somber clouds wrestling silently above them matched his mood. "This Dragonfaith," Erri said. "Can it be killed? I thought it dead, but now I hear daily reports of chapels being reopened and new initiates donning its dark blue habit." Erri abruptly stopped, and sternly fixed his small, dark eyes on Pelmen's face. "do you know the whereabouts of Serphimera?"

Pelmen sighed and turned away. A cool drizzle began, and he watched the river drink it in. They heard the roar then and both danced nimbly under an awning as the curtain of rain swept over and around them. The wind tore at the canvas momentarily, then raced onward, leaving behind a thick, murky downpour. The awning sheltered a tackle shop that had been shuttered up. There was no one around to overhear their conversation as they shouted to one another over the rooftop roar. "I did know! Up until last month we were together!"

"Where?" Erri shouted back, shivering in his cloak.

"In Chaomonous, near the Great South Fir."

Erri nodded. "What happened?"

"She disappeared!"

Erri frowned, and nodded again. "I've heard from the northwest, from the Lakelands. A Unionist monastery just reopened there. Worse," he added, "there've been reported sightings of the dragon."

"I wouldn't doubt it," Pelmen grunted, and Erri jerked around to stare at him. "I've seen it too."

"Then it's true?" Erri gasped. Their ears had grown accustomed to the backdrop of the rain's din and filtered it out. Enclosed within a dry box in the midst of a torrent, they forgot their surroundings completely to concentrate on the exchange of information.

"It is, and it isn't. It's true that the dragon has appeared again. But though it wears the form of the dead serpent, it's not the same beast."

"*Another* twi-beast?"

"No. There was only one Vicia-Heinox and we must beg the Power to keep it so. There is a clever imitation, however. The monster is being impersonated by an immensely powerful wizard."

"Flayh?"

Pelmen nodded. "The man has stumbled upon an incredible book of spells. It's given him a control over the powers unmatched by any present-day powershaper."

"Not even by yourself?"

"Perhaps not even by all the best of us combined."

Erri's bushy eyebrows laced themselves together over the bridge of his hooked nose. "Then you mean he's somehow changed his altershape to the image of the dragon?"

"No." Pelmen smiled at that notion. "A powershaper can't change his altershape any more than you could change the color of your eyes. Flayh is still the sharp-fanged dog. He's just learned to imitate the appearance of the dragon."

"That distinction is lost on me."

"You could disguise yourself if you so wished and could possibly maintain that fiction for some time. But you couldn't change your essential character. No shaper chooses his altershape. It manifests itself in a moment of magical passion and reflects the shaper's personality, for good or ill. Flayh is neither as stupid as Vicia-Heinox was, nor—I hope!—as dominatingly powerful."

Erri unconsciously scratched under his chin, mulling over Pelmen's words. "Do you think Flayh might have anything to do with these dog packs that keep harassing our borders?"

Pelmen grunted. "Those aren't dogs," he muttered.

"They certainly bite like dogs!"

"Have they attacked you?"

"No, but I've seen several torn habits and a mauled hand and arm!"

"They're not dogs. They're powers who have used Flayh to cloak them in flesh."

"Demons, then?"

"So some would call them." Pelmen nodded solemnly. "How many attacks?"

"Too many to number. And all on bluefaithers. I had assumed that the packs were trained by these new Dragonfaithers to go after anyone in a sky blue garment."

"I fear the dogs and the Dragonfaith are connected. Flayh is clever enough to realize that the best means of threatening Lamath is to make use of its own superstition. His imitation of Vicia-Heinox has renewed serpent worship. These dog attacks on skyfaithers seem to be aimed at convincing Lamathians it's foolish to trust anything but the dragon." Pelmen shook his head. "Flayh's not changed. His purpose is still to control the three lands. It's just that this time he has the power to accomplish it."

"No!" Erri snapped, stamping his foot. "By faith we shall resist him!"

"Indeed we will," Pelmen agreed. "And we'll make use of some other tools as well."

Erri looked at him sharply. "What tools?"

"We're not helpless."

"Certainly not," the small prophet grunted. "We have the Power. You're not thinking of using some other means, are you? More magic, perhaps?"

"Well of course I—"

"Don't," Erri ordered. "It would cost you your life."

Pelmen peered at him. "You know that?"

"I do," the prophet answered with a curt nod. "Now then,

if we know these things are related—the dragon's reappearance, the strange desert dogs, possibly Serphimera's disappearance—"

"There's no proof of that," Pelmen quickly interrupted. "Serphimera often disappears on business of her own."

"And it almost always has been related to the dragon."

"But she's changed her views! We've talked about this at length!"

"The nation of Lamath had changed its view!" Erri argued. "Or so I had thought. Now it appears I was wrong. Perhaps I wanted too much to believe so?" he asked shrewdly, gazing at Pelmen evenly to force home his point. The powershaper turned his head away, refusing to take it. Erri sighed. "We'll leave that. I was going to ask if you think all this is related to my other problem."

"Which is?"

"The Lamathian royal family. The old king is dead. His heir has decided he wants more power."

"I thought the son was a recluse like his father."

"He is. But he's apparently an ambitious recluse."

"Armies forming?"

"Not yet, I think. Just insistent letters from the vizier explaining the young man's views. You think Flayh's behind that as well?"

"He wouldn't discourage it. But ambition is usually born inside a man, not outside. Is the son capable of ruling?"

"I've never seen the boy. I don't know if he's capable of anything. I do know his advisors are urging him to embrace the Dragonfaith. So it appears the problems are all of one piece and are all related to this sorcerer in Ngandib-Mar."

Pelmen nodded. The implications made him weary. "What do you plan?"

"Plan? Why, the same plan I've held to since you thrust this task upon me. The lies must be exposed, the truths explained, and the battle won in the hearts of men."

"More missionaries?"

"More missionaries—sent to the heart of the Mar."

The heart of the Mar was the city of Ngandib. It stood in the geographical center of the country and, from its commanding height, dominated the surrounding highlands. It sat on a lofty plateau that was often ringed with clouds, so at times the High City seemed to float above the earth, a heavenly city detached from earthly cares.

That illusion passed swiftly for any visitor unfortunate enough to labor from the valley floor to the top of the Down Road. At one time Ngandib's streets had been tidy and well cobbled. Now they were more mud than cobblestone, and garbage often obscured the roadway entirely. Its people had once been the proudest of a proud race. Now they hung their heads and kept mostly to themselves, for the city was owned by brigands, one of whom had inexplicably been made the head of the city's defense force. Soon others joined him to celebrate his good fortune—and to steal for themselves what fortunes they could. Men who had once been hunted as outlaws by the Shurls of the North and South Firs now swaggered arrogantly about, picking fights with the locals and invariably winning. As many as eight or nine bodies a morning were ritually cast off the northern face of the plateau into the Burial Valley.

The problem daily grew worse, yet the king did nothing to stop the carnage nor to punish these loathsome intruders. The people of the city were hardly surprised. They knew their king well. Pahd mod Pahd-el spent most of every day in bed, resting up in preparation for a good night's sleep. "When Pahd wakes" had become a euphemism for the end of time. Privately, many citizens worried that King Pahd no longer had the power to do anything and that he'd fallen prey completely to the evil manipulations of the mysterious Flayh. They said nothing about it, however. Those foolish enough to criticize Flayh publicly had all disappeared, and there were reports of horrible screams from the vicinity of the High Fortress.

The High Fortress of Ngandib dominated the city as the city dominated the Mar. Built upon a towering spur of granite that rose many hundreds of feet above the plateau, it was obviously impregnable. There was no such citadel anywhere else in the world. It had never been stormed in war. In fact, no one had ever been fool enough to try.

The Maris who dwelt in the city had always been conscious of the castle's lofty mystery. Since Flayh had come, however, men swore that the fortress had assumed a distinctly malevolent personality. It was as if the castle lived and regarded mankind with a permanent snarl of contempt. Those who had once relaxed in the safety of the great tower's shadow now sought dwellings toward the plateau's edge. They preferred the precipitous drop-off to the feeling of living constantly under the gaze of a brooding, evil presence. Some had even tried to leave the High Plateau to seek a new life in the Mar proper, but they had been arrested at the top of the Down Road and marched back through the city to the fortress. None of them had been seen since.

Despite the ominous cutoff of downward traffic, men continued to make the harrowing climb up the steep road from the valley. Most of these were themselves cutthroats, coming to join their fellows. Among them was a small, feisty outlaw named Tibb. He carried with him a small bundle of personal possessions, a much-used sword, and a concealed dagger. Tibb had not come seeking fortune, fellowship, or a merry time at the expense of the townfolk of Ngandib. Tibb had come for revenge.

When he reached the top of the Down Road, he was challenged by a cluster of ugly thugs. "Stand, rascal, and give us your name!"

"Tibb, varlet. And yours?" Tibb snarled.

"You call me varlet?"

"I do, indeed, and will again!"

"Perhaps you'd like to tumble off this cliff?" the cutthroat threatened.

"Perhaps you'd like your guts tickled by my blade?" Tibb spat back, his hand on the hilt of his battered sword.

This exchange of unpleasantries set the rest of the small cadre to cackling, and now one advised his belligerent friend, "Hold, Naph. I think he believes himself one of us!"

Naph sneered. "Is that true, squirrel?"

"It's true enough," Tibb acknowledged modestly.

"Then why don't I know you?"

"I don't know." Tibb shrugged. "Because you're as blind as a cavern slug?"

Someone caught Naph's fist and shoved the angry man away while another outlaw squared around to face Tibb. "Here, then. If you be one of us, tell me where you've fought?"

Tibb's eyes gleamed. Wickedness? Savagery? The other brigand couldn't tell as Tibb grunted, "I wrestled in the darkness beneath the Imperial House."

There were several grunts in response and a low whistle. "And escaped?" someone asked stupidly.

"I'm here, aren't I?"

Naph, cooler now, shook off the arm that held him and came back to stare at Tibb's face. "Could be," he muttered.

"One way to check," somebody said.

"Yes." Naph nodded. "Let's go talk to the chief."

So Tibb was escorted down the main street of Ngandib-Mar by a quartet of murderous blackguards. If he drew any pitying glances from the city's cowed inhabitants, he didn't notice. He strode along casually, at home with this roguish company. He felt no fear, nor any need for concern. He'd told no lie. He *had* fought in the treacherous battle beneath the royal castle of Chaomonous. And though he couldn't be certain, he felt he knew who this chief scalawag would prove to be. He hoped he was right.

One could only enter the High Fortress from within. In the wall of rock a cavern had been cut, which served as the royal stables as well as the entryway into the castle. There was a wooden staircase that could be raised or lowered from the landing many feet above, but at the moment it was up. The only access was by way of a rope ladder, lowered through the gaping hole in the stable ceiling. Naph gestured roughly toward it, and Tibb quickly scaled it and climbed onto the landing.

He was greeted there by a stern-faced slaver he vaguely recognized. Naph and another joined Tibb and explained their business, and the slaver nodded curtly toward the top of another ladder some distance away. Then he went on about his work, making no secret of his belief that this was a waste of time and that Naph was a fool. Tibb strolled to the mouth of the new pit and started to descend.

He knew from the latrine stench that assaulted his nostrils that this was the dungeon. Then he heard a scream, the first of many he expected to hear today. It didn't slow him. Tibb was at home with such. The place was dark as pitch. He knew he'd reached the floor when his foot slid in the slime. He backed away from the ladder quickly to avoid the downward plunge of Naph, who seemed disappointed he'd missed the chance to mash Tibb's fingers. "This way," Naph grunted, and they followed the sound of the shrieks.

They turned a corner. A candle burned in a small alcove

on the wall. Chained below it was the twisted figure of what had once been a man. Tibb saw only the back of the poor creature's tormentor, but that was enough. Given his preference, he would rather not look the man in the face.

He had no choice. As Naph cleared his throat, Admon Faye turned to look at them. Even in the half-light, that horrid visage made Tibb's stomach churn. Nevertheless, he forced himself to smile. Admon Faye smiled back, and the cruelty and cunning Tibb saw there caused him a new struggle with his intestines.

Naph cleared his throat again. Obviously he had trouble facing the master himself. "This—ah—fellow says you'll know him," Naph managed finally to mumble.

"I know you?" Admon Faye asked. His voice was open and friendly, as if they stood together in a sun-drenched city square instead of a fetid, black dungeon.

"I fought with you beneath the castle in Chaomonous," Tibb said, struggling to keep every trace of bitterness out of the statement.

"Ah, yes." Admon Faye nodded, looking down. "It went poorly for us, didn't it?"

"Quite poorly." Tibb still wasn't sure he'd been remembered.

"Where's your friend?"

Now Tibb was sure. "Dead."

"Ah," Admon Faye said. "Pity." He even made it sound as if he meant it. "So," he went on brightly, "you've come to join us!"

"Everyone else is here."

"Seems that way, surely." Admon Faye chuckled. "But there's room for all. Our mysterious employer who lives upstairs has proved generous to us who've joined his service. I welcome you!" The hideous slaver grinned and offered Tibb the implement he'd been holding. Tibb saw now that it was a metal rod. Its tip still glowed. "Go ahead." Admon Faye nodded, gesturing to the gasping figure stretched upon the rock shelf.

Tibb realized that this was the real test. He passed it easily. The wizened body scarred with burns made no difference to him. His purpose had been to rejoin the band of Admon Faye and to take his revenge. If this was necessary, so be it. He plunged the hot poker down.

And the High Fortress of Ngandib, which was indeed both alive and malevolent, listened to the screams and cackled with sadistic glee.

The crisp wind cut through Dorlyth's tunic, chilling his upper arms. It ruffled his wiry, golden gray hair. He paid no heed to this breeze, nor to its promise of frost. He divided his attention between the small army that drilled in the glade below him and the blue of the Mari sky.

The glade of mod Carl was seventy miles west of Dorlyth's castle, well within the westernmost spur of the Great South Fir. It was a convenient place of meeting, on the border between the Downlands and the Furrowmar, but easily accessible to the men of the Westmouth region as well. He'd used it as a staging ground before, during previous wars of confederation. It had served especially well this time, since Dorlyth's major allies were from the furrows, Ngandib-Mar's highland farms. He'd had no trouble assembling this force—they'd been called to arms in midsummer, after the rows had already been planted. But harvest time had come and he was starting to lose them. It wasn't so much that they wished to be in the fields working—Mari men preferred fighting to farming, and they knew their women could get in the crop as well as they could, if not better. The problem was that they'd been together almost two months and were yet to fight a battle.

"He's not coming!" Belra spat, a phrase he'd repeated twenty times a day for the past two weeks. Belra sported a red handlebar mustache under his bulbous nose and had enormous green eyes that sparkled when he laughed and flashed when he grew angry. They were flashing now.

"He'll come," Dorlyth repeated absently, and Belra launched into yet another bad-tempered tirade. Dorlyth didn't bother to reply. He left that for his cousin.

"It's hard on my warriors too, mod Belra," Ferlyth said quietly. "A problem that worsens each day. But I'm with Dorlyth. I'll not take us out unprotected."

"But we don't even know where he is!" Belra pleaded, waving his huge hands for emphasis.

Dorlyth shrugged. "I *never* know where he is, but he always comes when I need him. And we most definitely need Pelmen before we take the field in *this* war."

"I'm not suggesting that we go into battle without some powershaper, but we all know that Joooms is available—"

"Mercenary sorcerers never give you their best," Ferlyth interrupted in the rich, clipped tones of an aristocrat.

"Besides," Dorlyth added, "with all due respect to the lizard, Joooms is no match for the Autumn Lady when she's angry. At her best, she can rout even Pelmen."

"You needn't remind me," Belra grumbled. "I fought at Mar-Yilot's side in the last conflict. The woman is awesome."

"And yet it seems even Mar-Yilot is checked by the power of this new Flayh," Ferlyth mused. "While we've lingered in this glade, we've missed very little action. The armies of those two have only skirmished."

"We'll not have the warriors even for skirmishing if we pause much longer!" Belra argued. "Naturally I'd prefer Pelmen Dragonsbane behind us. Who wouldn't? But he's not here!"

A rider clothed in the blue and white diagonals of Belra's house rode fiercely through the drilling company and up the grassy rise. "A warrior, Lord Belra!"

"Whose?" Belra barked.

"My lord, he's not of the Mar! He wears the gilded mail of the Golden Throng of Chaomonous—and he rides from the southeast!"

Belra snorted. "So you think that means he's come through the Fir?"

"Well, it *seems* so, my lord—"

"And that's just what our enemies would have us to believe! Ridiculous. None but thieves can pass through that tangle of weeds and brambles. This is a spy, sent behind us. Take him!"

Ferlyth glanced over at Dorlyth, surprised that the aging warrior hadn't intervened. "No protest?" he asked as the rider galloped back toward the forest.

"Why should I protest?" Dorlyth's lazy reply did not match the eager excitement in his old eyes.

"It's no secret, mod Karis, that your own Rosha has married the Golden Land's young queen. Could this be a messenger come from him?"

"No," Dorlyth grunted. "No messenger. He uses only blue flyers to contact me. And Belra's right. None but thieves can penetrate the Great Fir. Thieves—or heroes."

Ferlyth raised his eyebrows knowingly. "Perhaps."

"We should know in a moment," Dorlyth muttered, and all three lords watched the wall of giant trees on the far side of the clearing. Suddenly three riders broke from the thicket in rapid succession, each throwing anxious looks behind them. Then a powerful charger leaped a bush and raced to the center of the clearing. Astride its back sat a powerfully built man arrayed in the glistening gold armor of Chaomonous. Above his helmet he whirled a great sword almost four feet long. Dorlyth grinned proudly at the sight of that blade. It had once been his own.

"Why—it's your son!" Belra blurted in surprise.

"As I said," Dorlyth chuckled, "only thieves or heroes." He spurred his charger forward and raced down to meet Rosha mod Dorlyth.

Rosha jerked off his helmet and slung it from his saddle horn as his father reined in beside him. His black curls shone with sweat, and rivulets coursed down his handsome cheeks. "Hot in there," he muttered.

Dorlyth sat back in his saddle and beamed. He said nothing for a moment, just looking his son up and down. Then he growled "Hail, mod Dorlyth, of Chaomonous king!" He laughed as the blood rushed to his son's face.

"I'm no king," Rosha snarled, but a pleased grin found its way to his lips anyway.

"Apparently not," Dorlyth muttered, "or you wouldn't be traipsing around alone in the wilderness of a neighboring land. What are you doing here?" he demanded sternly.

"You know why I'm here," Rosha grunted, unconsciously imitating his father's gruff manner. No longer did the stutter of his youth plague him. He had the relaxed confidence of a natural victor.

"How did you guess the place?"

"I didn't *guess*! Since I was a boy, I've heard you bid goodbye to your warriors with 'See you next week at the glade of mod Carl.' You think I didn't learn anything in your keep?"

"I thought at least I taught you better treatment of women," Dorlyth snorted, and Rosha looked away in embarrassment. "Did you tell Bronwynn you were coming?"

Rosha scowled at his father. "Did you ever ask my mother's permission to ride to war?"

Now Dorlyth looked away. "Maybe once or twice."

Rosha was surprised. "Really? What'd she say?"

"She said 'no.'"

"What did you do?" Rosha frowned.

"I went anyway." Dorlyth shrugged, and Rosha laughed aloud. "But I didn't enjoy it!" Dorlyth added seriously, cutting short his son's mirth.

"Why, *I* didn't come for enjoyment," Rosha grumbled.

"Yes, you did. For enjoyment and excitement and to get away from the boredom of the castle. Did she send anybody after you?"

"I didn't look back."

Dorlyth nodded. "Knowing Bronwynn, she did. But they probably had the wisdom to turn around when they reached the Fir. Unlike my son," he added with a snort.

"You want me to go back?" Rosha snapped.

"Eventually, yes!" Dorlyth frowned. Then his bearded lips parted in a huge smile. "But not for a while." He could contain himself no longer and he reached out to grab his son by the shoulders. The small army had been watching all this quietly; now they cheered. Rosha was well known to all of them, and they valued the addition of his blade to their cause.

Dorlyth sat back again in his saddle, his eyes a bit moist with pleasure and pride. "We need you, son. We face a formidable foe with no assurance of victory, and that famous sword of yours will be welcome. But not just your sword. Bronwynn is sure to be alarmed by your absence. If there's any way she can contact Pelmen, she's sure to send him after you. I hope this doesn't offend, but we need him even more. Let's hope you attract him to us!" Dorlyth pointed across the clearing. "My tent is in the trees there on the north side. Unless things have changed drastically, you're hungry."

"I sure am!"

"Then let's go eat," Dorlyth muttered and he wheeled his horse around to lead the way. He was proud of himself. He'd resisted the urge to kiss his boy on the cheek in front of his warriors.

It started as a simple meal. It soon turned into a feast. Dorlyth had not hunted that day and had little to offer Rosha but a hunk of bread and some cheese. But then the friends began arriving, bringing with them dressed pheasant, fresh brook trout, a saddle of aged venison, some snails, eels, and vegetables, as well as flutes and stringed instruments, jokes and sly winks, and many good wishes for Rosha and his new bride. They fed the fire until all forty of them could feel it, and laughed and sang until the forest rang with their celebration. When the northwesterly winds kicked up, stirring the leaves around them, they huddled closer together and laughed even louder. Every jest, regardless how small, reaped a happy reward, and some ancient grudges were forgotten—for the night, at least. Rosha was compelled to recite the history of his courtship; this he did with relish, proudly demonstrating his newfound control over his tongue. He good-naturedly ignored the constant interruptions, patiently enduring one ribald comment after another as he told his story. He tailored his telling to suit his audience, and his father fingered his beard and nodded knowingly. He would get the full story when the revelers slept, and the logs on the fire had turned to glowing embers. Then he would learn Rosha's true feelings, when honesty could be valued over wit.

The story told, there were more songs and much more merry laughter. The ring of warriors struggled to hold that spirit of elation as long as possible, but it died as necessarily and naturally as the fire. Then the first man, feeling badly about it, slipped away, freeing others to follow. And at last the two men sat alone, gazing into the glowing embers, and spoke in voices made rough by the chill and an excess of talk.

"Are you happy?" Dorlyth asked. It wasn't the first time he'd asked the question tonight, but it was the first time Rosha really answered.

"I suppose so."

Dorlyth grunted. "Then you *are*. For what you suppose, that's what's so."

"And yet..."

"And yet you're here. So you can't be entirely satisfied."

"I'm satisfied," Rosha protested. "I just came because I was worried about you!"

"Come to protect your infirm old father?" The aged champion grinned, his eyes gleaming.

Rosha chuckled. "Come to protect your backside, anyway. Your reflexes aren't what they used to be!"

"How could *you* know that?"

Rosha never answered. His mouth sagged open and he stared. Dorlyth proved his reflexes were still excellent as he whirled around, slipping sword from scabbard in the same fluid motion. Then he stared, too.

The moon clung to the horizon, peeking down at them through the firs. It was orange, and huge. The cloudy figure that stood beside the fire pit seemed to glow with that same apricot radiance. She regarded them passively, almost shyly. But Dorlyth had faced those regal, golden eyes before. They betrayed no hint of fear. "Mar-Yilot," he whispered, and the wind stirred the fallen leaves and seemed to echo him.

She was not beautiful, nor even pretty in the ways that men normally evaluate women. Her auburn hair ringed a pale, thin face and hung limply to bony shoulders. She was slender, and her ochre gown draped upon her like curtains wrapped around a sapling. She still strongly resembled the wan, silent waif she once had been—vulnerable yet exceedingly wise.

But her carriage demanded respect. She was lordly. And Dorlyth knew her power and trembled before it.

"Where is he?" she asked at last.

Sparked to action, Rosha grabbed for his sword. "Stay it," Dorlyth muttered. "She's here, but her body's not. Your blade can't harm her."

Mar-Yilot raised her eyebrows a barely perceptible fraction. "Your son?"

"He's young yet."

"May he live to grow old as you," she said flatly. "Where's Pelmen?"

"Why do you seek him?"

"Don't toy with me, Dorlyth. That angers me. Tell me where he's hiding."

"I don't think he's hiding, really," Dorlyth murmured. "I don't know if he's even in the Mar—"

"There's shaping about that bears his stamp—or if not, at least the mark of his talent. Grave things are shifting, Dorlyth. Unless he'll talk to me, I mean to make war upon him." She spoke earnestly but dispassionately—a woman fully in control of herself, actively shaping her own destiny.

"How do you know it's him?"

"Who else could it be?" she snapped.

"This evil Flayh has—"

"Flayh!" Mar-Yilot spat in disgust. "Who is this Flayh? A cloth seller! A trader in tools and cooking pans! When the seven shapers wrestled together and Pelmen battled me toe to toe, where was this Flayh? In Lamath of the dragon lovers, counting his money! Don't speak nonsense, Dorlyth. Tell me where Pelmen is and let us reason or make war."

Dorlyth chose his words carefully. "Am *I* a sorcerer, my Lady? Can *I* divine your hiding places?"

Her amber eyes gazed at him balefully, a stern mother about to rebuke a lying child. She paused a moment, then said very deliberately, "The old one is dead in the last conflict, and Terril murdered his twin. That leaves five. The twin-killer has declared for the lazy king, Mast is idle in retirement, Joooms waits in Garnabel, unemployed. And that leaves Pelmen and myself. Would you have me believe you uncovered?"

Dorlyth's mouth was very dry. He said nothing.

"Very well." The Autumn Lady nodded. "I know your lair—this glade of mod Carl is hardly a secret, and no one has cloaked you here. When I return, I *will* see Pelmen. Unless you truly are uncovered, in which case . . ." Her voice faded away and she permitted herself the slightest of smiles. "In which case I'm hardly responsible," she finished. Then she disappeared with a flash of golden brilliance. The moon, too, had disappeared below the trees.

Dorlyth and Rosha stood in the darkness, stunned. Then the old warrior grunted. "I hope he decides to come find us. Otherwise, the next time she comes hunting him, she'll kill us all. She won't be trying to. She just *will*."

## CHAPTER THREE

# The Dogs and the Dragon

PELMEN COULDN'T sleep. Throughout the night he agonized over the same question that had plagued him for weeks: Where was Serphimera? At the first sign of dawn, he bounded from his bed and took to the streets of Lamath. He didn't expect to find her, but he needed to be doing something.

He left his blue gown in the room Erri had provided. He wanted to be able to move freely and talk to anyone. He went from the beautiful heart of the city quickly, intending to make a long sweep through the shanty townships that had mushroomed on its edge.

Barely a year before, a huge crowd had gathered in the city square to watch him being pulled apart by a pair of tugoliths. A few days later he had been publicly hailed as the Prophet of Lamath. Despite that, nobody recognized him now. Clothed in the simple garments of a Lamathian peasant, he walked briskly through crowded, dirty alleyways, visiting spots Serphimera had been known to frequent.

No one had seen the raven-haired priestess. Or if they had, they wouldn't admit it. Several volunteered that they *had* seen the dragon, however, and that thought chilled his heart. Signs of the resurgence of the Dragonfaith were everywhere. By midmorning he'd passed a score of newly painted shrines, each bearing the two-headed icon above its open doors. Like a dead fire catching new life from a tiny ember, the Dragonfaith had returned. With his imitation dragon wings, Flayh was fanning the growing flame. Pelmen sank into a meditative despair.

Had Serphimera been duped anew? Had Flayh contrived to use her somehow in his scheme to reenslave Lamath? Although Pelmen could prove no connection between Flayh and Serphimera's disappearance, the thought kept recurring, and he'd been unable to stifle it. His bitterness grew.

"Man?" someone called. Pelmen broke out of his deep reverie and looked around. Had this been addressed to him? "Man?" the voice called again, and Pelmen walked toward a tall, iron-spiked fence that lined one side of this broad avenue. He realized now where he was and who—or what—was speaking. He gazed down into the tugolith pit.

"Yes?" he replied to the gigantic animal that had summoned him.

"Dolna is gone and Thuganlitha is being mean." The beast reported this dutifully, assuming that Pelmen would understand simply because he was human. Tugoliths tended to appear simpleminded. They were, in fact, the brightest of beasts, for they alone had mastered human language. But people who talked with them frequently forgot that, since the huge creatures used their limited vocabulary mostly to bicker childishly with one another.

"I am not!" Thuganlitha snarled. It was evident that he was lying. Not only did his guilty tone of voice give him away, but Pelmen could see that he had another tugolith wedged against a wall and was pricking the screaming animal's hindquarters with his horn.

"Stop that!" Pelmen ordered.

Thuganlitha left off the pricking and looked up at Pelmen suddenly. "I'm not doing anything." He scowled.

"Oh yes, you are," chided Chimolitha, the tugolith who had called for Pelmen's intervention.

"Oh no, I'm not!"

"Oh yes, you are!"

"You told," Thuganlitha snorted, yielding the point but raising a new issue.

"You shouldn't do that," Chimolitha explained.

"Why not?"

"Because it makes Dolna angry."

"I don't care," Thuganlitha sneered. Apparently he didn't, for he went back to horning his unfortunate victim.

"I said stop!" Pelmen shouted, throwing up his hand. He did it out of reflex, responding to the injured tugolith's screams. Otherwise he would not have revealed his abilities in such a public place. The act left a number of tugoliths extremely confused. Thuganlitha ended up sprawled upon his back in a far corner of the pit, a perplexed expression on his enormous features.

Chimolitha, however, took this all in stride. Such acts of justice were only to be expected from their human masters. "Thank you," she said courteously.

Pelmen, a bit embarrassed by his incautious display, started slinking away toward the city square. Suddenly the scaly monster's expression changed. Pelmen had at last been recognized. "Man?" the tugolith called. "Aren't you that Pelmen person?"

"Ah, yes," Pelmen replied quietly as he hurried on down the street and beyond the end of the pit.

"I like you!" he heard the tugolith call as he rounded the corner. He raced along, not daring to look behind for fear he might find an admiring tugolith in pursuit. The beasts could easily push their way out of their enclosure if they chose to. Pelmen hoped no one would ever be fool enough to give them the idea. He found it ironic that only a beast had recognized him today, but that was easily explained. On that morning when he'd nearly been executed, no one had gotten a closer look at him than had Chimolitha. He was greatly relieved when he arrived back at the refectory of the skyfaither brotherhood.

On the site where once stood the old Temple of the Dragon, Erri had erected a huge, square meeting hall. It was sparsely furnished and utilitarian, suiting the personality of its builder. It was here that Erri held court and where he also fed as many of the city's beggars as could crowd inside, nor was it simple fare he placed before them. Although he ate nothing but a coarse bread pudding himself, Erri provided his guests with the best food Lamath had to offer. This practice had stirred great debate among the brothers. Some criticized the extravagance. Others heatedly argued that this would make the city's poor too dependent upon the faith. Erri squirmed a bit in discomfort as he listened to the arguments, for they all bore the seeds of truth. But he didn't change his policy. He continued feeding the masses, paying for it out of the riches that had accumulated over the centuries in the coffers of the Dragonfaith. The wealth was there. Why not use it to meet the needs of the hungry? And who could distinguish by sight who was deserving and who was not? There were certainly some professional beggars who availed themselves of a free meal each day.

There were others who had grown overdependent. But Erri could point to a growing number who had come originally to gorge themselves on hams and spice cakes, but who'd stayed to don blue garments. No one was compelled to do anything. Erri had resisted urgings to sermonize before serving the meal. Brothers and guests alike could eat their fill of whatever they liked. But Erri's unassuming example continued to have its impact on some. Many now took only bread pudding.

Pelmen was jostled and shoved at the doorway, but the crush of the crowd at last pushed him inside. Erri spotted him immediately and hailed him over to sit down. The saintly prophet lowered his voice—an unnecessary precaution amid the scraping of spoons and the rumble of conversation—and asked, "Any news of her?"

"None." Pelmen took a large roll and a slice of roast. Asceticism was fine for others. He'd never pretended to adopt it himself.

Erri nodded. "I didn't expect you to learn much. What will you do now?"

"You mentioned a monastery reopening in the Lakelands district. Perhaps I'll go search there—"

A commotion at the doorway caused him to break off, and both he and Erri stood up to see who had caused it. The man who stepped into the great hall contrasted sharply with the ragged beggars and the brothers in blue. He was heavily armored in plates of burnished bronze, trimmed with gold. His helmet was adorned with delicate arabesques of that costly metal, and plumed with golden feathers. A fish-satin robe of the same dazzling color draped from his shoulders to brush the flagstone floor. But if his costume seemed out of his place, the man's stern visage fitted with the rough faces around him. It was a soldier's face, sallow and harsh, lined by years of command. This was General Joss, until recently the Lord of Security for the land of Chaomonous and now Bronwynn's ambassador to Lamath. Erri waved him over. The general smiled sardonically and picked his way through the chomping host.

"Lord Ambassador, welcome. I never expected you here—"

"Nor did I," Joss said quickly. He stepped over the bench to seat himself between two of the brothers. "I didn't learn until this morning of the arrival of your elusive guest." The general's hard eyes locked with Pelmen's. "I came to greet him in the name of my queen."

Pelmen nodded. "Hello, General. I've never seen you looking so splendid."

Joss glanced down at his fancy trappings. "I personally find this outfit repugnant. However, it goes along with the office. I'm willing to make the sacrifice for Chaomonous." The general studied Pelmen's peasant garb and said, "I see you've kept your same tailor." Pelmen laughed at that, and the general permitted himself a brief smile. These two men had long been adversaries. Joss was working hard to establish cordial relations.

"I wonder, Lord Ambassador, how you learned that I was here?"

"He has his sources," Erri said as he took another spoonful of pudding.

"I find it expedient to keep informed. Pelmen, I have an urgent message for you from our queen."

"What is it?"

"You want me to tell you here?"

"Is it a state secret?"

Joss blinked. "Perhaps, perhaps not. I'm just unaccustomed to revealing private messages in a public place."

"This is where you found me. What is it?"

Joss frowned. Then he lowered his voice and spoke. "Young Rosha has left Chaomonous. The queen requests that you seek him out and return him to the court."

Pelmen raised his eyebrows. Rosha's action didn't surprise him, but Bronwynn's response to it did. "Return him? Didn't he tell her where he was going?"

"He left without a word."

"Sounds like his father."

"Do you know where he is?"

"Not exactly, but I can guess. He's gone to find Dorlyth. Surely Bronwynn knows that."

"The queen is concerned for his safety," the general said. "Shall I inform her that he is all right?" He smiled humorlessly.

"You know that I can't say that. Rosha's gone to war."

Joss leaned across the rough table and spoke with a quiet intensity. "Then I urge you to seek him out. The queen is distraught without him and naturally assumes the worst. If he's not located soon, she'll disregard all our advice and organize an army to go after him. I think you realize that Chaomonous can ill afford another war at this time." The general sat back then, his face assuming that expression of stony resolve used by leaders challenging their troops. "Consider this an act in defense of your country."

Erri smiled, though he didn't intend to. "You speak as if Pelmen is a Chaon."

"Isn't he?"

"I think we of Lamath might justifiably lay claim to him as well. Then again, so could the Maris, and if he goes to Ngandib-Mar, I'm sure they will. Pelmen? What will you do?"

Pelmen pondered this question, reviewing his options. He realized he didn't have that many. Serphimera wasn't here and evidently hadn't been here, so his search was at a standstill. Flayh's influence surrounded him. He could wait here and battle the sorcerer with Erri, or he could go to the Mar in search of Rosha and be sucked into the battle there. Somehow it made more sense to engage Flayh in the sinister shaper's own region. Who could know? Perhaps Serphimera was locked in Flayh's dungeon. His lady had a penchant for walking into trouble. Pelmen's eyes flicked up to meet the general's gaze. "I'll go find him."

Erri sighed. "And probably find a battle as well."

"I will if he's joined his father. Wars follow Dorlyth like clawsps chase sugar."

"More magic!" Erri grunted with disfavor.

"I know you don't approve."

"There's much more to it than my disapproval—"

Joss interrupted them. "Then I may relay the word that your search has begun?"

Pelmen nodded. "You may. I'll not have time to inform her myself. But you'd better tell her to be patient. If he's gone to fight a war, he's not likely to leave until it's over."

"If she knows you are with him, perhaps she'll feel comforted," Joss said as he stood to leave. Then he bowed slightly. "For the sake of both my queen and my country, I thank you." He bowed to Erri. "Good day, Prophet." Then he stepped over the bench again and left quickly.

"Is it necessary that you go?" Erri asked quietly. "Can't Rosha take care of himself?"

"Against any other warrior, yes. Against the powershapers of Ngandib-Mar, he hasn't a chance. Nor does Dorlyth. I've been delaying the inevitable, Erri. I've got to face Flayh."

"You'll be killed."

"That's always a possibility—"

"You've heard my warning," Erri said sternly. "Rather than rushing off to shape these other powers, I wish you'd wait here until the Power shapes you!"

"Perhaps the Power *is* shaping me, my friend," Pelmen said quietly.

Erri's eyes narrowed in surprise, then he looked away, studying the far wall of the room in puzzlement. Finally he shrugged, and nodded. "I'd offer you a horse, but I know you'd rather fly."

"I'd rather ride." Pelmen grinned. "It's getting on toward winter! It gets cold enough up on those wind currents to freeze your tail feathers!"

"I wouldn't know about that, never having had any tail feathers."

"But thank you for reminding me. I'll drop by the stables and greet my old friend Minaliss before I go."

"Your horse!" Erri said, his eyes widening in remembrance, then turning sad. "I neglected to tell you. He broke out of his stall about two weeks ago. I'm sorry, Pelmen. I sent a group of riders to retrieve the horse, but they simply couldn't catch him."

Pelmen's eyes dropped to the tabletop. "Well. I'm sorry too." He smiled wistfully. "Seems like all my friends are leaving me."

The prophet looked up sharply and frowned. "Oh, no. It's *you* who are leaving *me*."

"Yes. But I leave you in good hands," Pelmen said as he stood to go. Erri caught him by the sleeve and pulled him down to whisper:

"What about this pyramid our friend brought us?"

Pelmen frowned. "Hide it. Guard it carefully. If the Power chose to send it, it must have some importance."

Erri nodded, then said, "Do me a favor. Don't change into a bird until you're out of the city square. I spend enough of my time explaining you as it is."

Pelmen laughed. "It's a promise!" Then he stepped over the

bench and pushed through the crowd, leaving Erri to mutter about there never being enough time to get everything said.

Pelmen took no notice of the fat little man sitting by himself at the table nearest the door. Nor did the disguised merchant see him. In the presence of free food, Pezi heeded no man.

Lord Syth rode hard for the gates of Seriliath, his cape billowing back over the hindquarters of his war horse. In his train raced a dozen other riders, all cloaked in capes of the same blue and gray, wearing expressions identical to that of their master. A frown masked Syth's handsome features, and they all saw it frequently, for he tossed worried looks behind them with every passing mile. They were not being chased—at least, not that they knew. But all save Syth believed they'd made a terrible mistake in traveling the roads today. It was common knowledge among them that Mar-Yilot was in the Seriliath tower, casting spells in search of Pelmen. That meant they weren't being covered.

"Open it!" Syth bellowed as the small troop pounded down a ridge and back up toward the massive gates. His words could not have been heard over the clatter of steel-shod hooves on the granite highway, but the huge doors swung inward anyway. Syth did not slacken his pace. He shot through the gap like a missile from a catapult. He didn't pause to acknowledge the gatekeepers' cheers, nor even seem to hear them. But cheer they did, as their returned citylord drove his stallion up the steep, narrow street that led to the palace.

The noise of his arrival alerted the shopkeepers and tradesmen. These stood in their doorways and added their voices. Shutters flew open above them and still others joined in the tumultuous welcome. Syth mod Syth-el, Lord Seriliath and rightful Jorl of the Isles, had returned at last from his island home. He'd come to rejoin those rebel chieftains who had chosen him to lead them against the king. The people of Seriliath loved Syth, as their hearty welcome attested. But though they loved her less, they were far more fascinated by Mar-Yilot, his wife. They all craned their necks, searching for some sign of her. When she didn't appear, they all assumed that the rumors were true—that the Autumn Lady was already in the city, and waited with the others in the palace. Naturally, no one had seen her arrive. She traveled where she willed on butterfly wings. But it was always a thrill to learn that the auburn-haired shaper was among them again.

As he pounded through the final gate into the palace courtyard, Syth's anxious expression hardened into a proud, victorious smile. Behind his back his retainers exchanged smiles of mutual relief. For the first time this day, they could all breathe easy once again.

Syth cocked his head to look up at the battlements, but no noble flags fluttered there. He'd expected none. It wasn't wise to advertise one's location in a time of war. As he walked his horse into the stables, however, he saw the livery of the two waiting lords hanging from the rafters. His smile grew wider. He walked briskly through the main door, nodding at fawning servants and snapping off orders. In a half hour he had bathed and shaved. He was donning a fish-satin dressing gown in preparation for greeting his guests, when he was himself visited.

"You're here today?" Mar-Yilot asked quietly.

He wheeled around and saw her standing by the drapes. He reached out to touch her, then saw the aura of orange light surrounding her and stopped himself. "Why don't you come on down?"

"I'm busy."

"Still hunting Pelmen?"

"And not finding him."

"I don't think you're going to," Syth said as he tied the sash around his waist.

"I thought we agreed you would come tomorrow, when I could cover you." Her obvious aggravation didn't surprise him.

"I didn't agree to anything. It doesn't matter anyway, because I'm here."

"You could have been killed."

"But I wasn't. Which tells me a couple of things . . ."

"It tells you nothing," she snapped.

". . . about the road. First, it's free. I encountered no opposition, either from the king or Dorlyth's band of peculiar patriots, so—"

"Dorlyth and Ferlyth are in the glade of mod Carl."

Syth's eyes widened and he smiled appreciatively. "Good! Then we know we can travel south without fear of—"

"You know nothing!" she repeated, more forcefully this time. "You're guessing, and guessing is for fools!"

Syth deflected her scolding with a confident smile. She'd been chiding him since they were children, and he was used to it. "It is, at least, an educated guess, reinforced by my personal surveillance of the Nethermar Road."

"You were lucky."

"Aren't I always?" he asked, grinning at her. She didn't smile.

"As I said, while I did find Dorlyth, I did not locate Pelmen. He could have tracked you here!"

"Possible, but I don't think so. I don't think the falcon is anywhere near." He ignored her sigh of exasperation. "I attribute all this manipulation of the powers to Flayh, and not to—"

"Why! Why do you keep insisting on that!"

"Because I, my dear, listen to the rumors that are muttered in the alleyways. While you're fluttering around on your butterfly wings, I'm dodging the mud holes and talking to people!"

It was an old argument, one they reopened each time they faced a battle and disagreed on how to fight it. She shook her head. "I won't believe it until I see it."

"That's what I'm afraid of! You'll be so intent on finding Pelmen you won't see the new danger until it's too late!"

"The real danger *is* Pelmen," Mar-Yilot said with a deadly drone. "I nearly conquered him the last time we battled. This time I'll not fail."

"I don't know what excites you more—fighting Pelmen or loving me!" Syth said it half-jokingly. Mar-Yilot would not dignify the comment with a reply. "Listen," he pleaded, "none of these acts bear Pelmen's seal. All of you shapers have a certain style, and this talk of red-eyed demons and a resurrected Vicia-Heinox doesn't sound like Pelmen at all!"

"They sound like an upstart merchant?" she asked flatly.

"They do. Like *this* merchant. And what I think I learned on the road is significant . . ."

"What you guessed," the shimmery figure corrected.

"All right, what I guessed. And this is it: I think Flayh didn't attack me because he's as worried about Pelmen as you are and he's looking elsewhere!"

She refused to be moved by his dramatic pronouncement. "So?"

"So tomorrow I'm leading our army south. I want to do battle with King Pahd before Flayh realizes Pelmen's not a threat—and sends his black dogs after us."

Her golden eyes revealed no anger, no fear, nor in fact any emotion. She regarded him calmly, inscrutable as a cat. "And what do you expect of me?"

"You could cover us, maybe." He smiled sardonically. "That might be nice." She gazed at him, unblinking. "Or you could get ready to toss a gale at the foot of the Ngandib Plateau, mirror Flayh's terror spell back at him, or whatever else you choose. You're the shaper. I'll leave that up to you."

"Will you?" she said cuttingly. Then she began to fade away.

"Mar-Yilot, come on down now, will you?"

She stopped her disappearance long enough to answer, "Maybe later." Then she was gone—or rather, that projected part of herself had rejoined her body in the tower that soared above.

"Witch," Syth muttered. He said it with deep affection.

The dogs came in after dusk, their long red tongues lolling lazily over glistening fangs. They slunk through the alleyways of the city of Lamath, moving in slowly like a horrible black mist. Those who chanced to see them ran shrieking homeward, locking their doors behind them, for these were no ordinary dogs. Their black coats had no glossy sheen, but rather seemed to suck light in and swallow it. Nor did their eyes reflect that nearly human sensibility cherished by dog lovers. Instead they glowed with red-orange evil, as if these canine heads were merely skull masks with eye-slits, revealing fires burning within in the place of brains. Then the howling began.

If the look of these beast-clad demons was horrid, the empty sound of their baying was even more so. Lamathians all around the vast perimeter of the city reacted in panic, hiding in basements or under beds. Others left their houses, fleeing the deathly howls and racing away from the circling packs toward the center of the city. Flayh had made his move.

Pezi had been at the table since midday and had eaten all the way through the afternoon into suppertime. He had paused to look up only once, when a woman he thought he recognized had come into the hall and gone to the head table to talk with the little prophet fellow. She was a petite brunette, and Pezi thought she looked like one of the cute merchant wives from the castle of Uda in Ngandib-Mar. He'd decided it couldn't be, however. She was wearing one of the light blue robes that seemed to be the rage in this very religious land. He'd forgotten her completely when they brought out the evening mutton.

He was working on a steaming slab of it when the panic began. At first there was only an annoying baying and some distant screams. These puzzled him, but he didn't become alarmed until he heard the clatter of hoofbeats outside the meeting hall's doors. Suddenly the room filled with initiates from every sector of the city, all waving their arms and shouting wildly as they raced to Erri's table. Pezi watched as Erri calmed them and appointed one to tell the story. "Dogs!" the man shouted. "The city is ringed by slavering dogs with huge teeth and fires for eyes! Great mobs are pouring into the city square outside! Listen, Prophet!" The messenger hushed, and the horrified screams from outside were clearly audible throughout the room.

"It's Flayh, obviously," Erri said. "He and the royal family have chosen to make this the night. And if Pelmen had only . . ." The prophet trailed off.

Pezi wrinkled his nose in concern. Any mention of Pelmen made him feel very uncomfortable.

Erri was shouting. "Don't just stand there!" he said to his initiates. "Start bothering the Power with petitions!"

Eating interested Pezi. Praying didn't. And since he knew these dogs were indeed from Flayh, and that they were surely heading for this very hall, he did the only sensible thing—he kicked over his bench and dashed for the double doors.

The streets were filled with screaming people, and Pezi soon joined them, also screaming at the top of his lungs. A pack of the black hounds rounded the corner a hundred yards away, and he bolted for safety.

He ran shrieking down an alleyway, certain a dog would leap from every darkened corner to tear out his throat. None did. In fact, for all their howling, Pezi had yet to see one of the beasts actually spring at anyone. But he reasoned that if *he* were a hungry dog, he'd pick somebody fat and slow to pounce on. Since he fitted that description so perfectly, Pezi could not allow himself to rest. He waddled breathlessly onward.

Despite his panic, there was a pattern to his flight. He picked his alleys well, seeking those that would lead him closer to the prize that had lured him to Lamath in the first place. He made his way to the tugolith pits. He was planning to kidnap some monsters.

It was, on the face of it, a ludicrous idea. But given Pezi's present circumstances and the childlike nature of the beasts he planned to steal, it all made perverse sense. Pezi was out of favor with his uncle Flayh—a dangerous state to remain in for very long. He needed to pull off some coup to restore himself to Flayh's good graces, and the gift of a herd of gigantic beasties seemed to be just the thing.

The trouble was, Pezi knew nothing of his uncle's plans. He'd expected some activity in Lamath, but nothing on this scale! Flayh was going all out to topple the prophet, evidently planning to replace him with that dolt of a princeling from the royal family. The dogs were to panic the populace—a very effective ruse, Pezi noted with a shiver. He noticed fires had been started—by the royalist supporters, no doubt. But how was all of this to turn the tide against the prophet?

He happened to glance up in time to see his answer flash by overhead. He grunted involuntarily and froze against the wall. The shadow quickly passed, and he shuddered. He shook his head and chuckled in terrified amazement. Now he understood. A howl only thirty yards behind him made him jump, and sped him quickly on his way. In moments he reached the tugolith pit.

The giant beasts were restless. The chaotic night had affected them, too. Even monsters could get frightened, especially when they knew enough to recognize fear in people, but not enough to realize why the people were afraid. Thuganlitha was taking his anxiety out on an unfortunate peer when the fat little form above him caught his enormous eye.

"You here again?" he snarled. This was actually a major mental feat for Thug. He'd made the connection between this round little man and the one who'd been watching them for days.

Pezi summoned his courage. This particular tugolith could be nasty, and Pezi didn't relish the thought of traveling with him. But it was time to seize the beast by the horn—metaphorically, of course—and set his plan into action. With luck, Flayh's nighttime attack could provide just the cover needed to sneak a pack of six-ton beasts out of the city. Besides, Pezi doubted any dog could get at him if he rode astride one of Thuganlitha's more accommodating comrades. Pezi cleared his throat. "Indeed, I *am* here again, Thuganlitha. I'm pleased that you remember me."

"I remember something else," Thug rumbled menacingly.

"Oh?" Pezi chuckled nervously. "What's that?" He was afraid he knew.

"I said I would horn you."

Pezi remembered. "Ah, yes. Well, perhaps we can delay that until Dolna's instructions have been followed."

"Dolna?" a sleepy voice right below him asked. "Where's Dolna?"

Pezi was relieved to see the peaceable Chimolitha joining the conversation. *This* tugolith had sense.

"Dolna's been delayed—by the fires, you know. But he's sent me to gather you beasties together and lead you out—"

"He called me a beastie!" Thuganlitha trumpeted, enraged. He suddenly began making every effort to get out of the pit and at Pezi. Sudden terror gave the fat merchant's skin the color and texture of a toadstool.

"Man? You shouldn't call us that," Chimolitha complained.

"I—I'm—profoundly sorry! I apologize! I really do! Sincerely!"

"He apologizes, Thuganlitha," Chimolitha drawled.

". . . called me a beastie, called me a beastie . . ."

"Thuganlitha!" Chimolitha trumpeted into Thug's ear. "He apologized."

Thuganlitha stopped horning up the dirt and looked back at Chimolitha balefully. "Why do they always apologize?" he mourned.

Chim shrugged. "Because you scare them."

"Why can't they wait until *after* I've horned them?"

"Because they'd be dead!" Chimolitha sighed, exasperated.

"I know." Thuganlitha grinned wickedly and rolled his huge eyes back up to fix on Pezi.

"Ahem," the merchant went on, seeking to muddle through.

"The fact remains that Dolna has sent me to lead you out of the city to safety."

"Dolna?" said Chimolitha. "Where is Dolna?"

Smiling politely, Pezi patiently repeated himself. He figured he'd be doing a lot of that in the days to come.

Herded by the howling to the vast city square, the mob stood outside Erri's window and clamored for a miracle. At one point the prophet stepped out and watched as a line of blue-clad initiates struggled to hold the people back. Suddenly there was a shout, and the sea of faces turned skyward. Knowing what he would see, Erri turned his own unwilling gaze above, as someone shouted, "The dragon! Lord Dragon is upon us!"

Gliding across the city's center flew Vicia-Heinox, scaly wings flung wide and both throats screaming. Apparition or not, the dragon certainly looked real, its scales casting back a polished copper reflection of the thousand blazes that flamed throughout the city.

"Lord Dragon has reclaimed us!" someone in the crowd screeched. In moments it became a chant.

"All right," Erri said to himself and to the Power; he turned on his heel and went inside. Moments later when his grim-faced initiates burst into his cell to spirit him away, they found him already packed. The book was tucked under one arm; over the other shoulder he'd slung an ancient seabag, containing among other things the precious pyramid. He smiled sadly. "Shall we go?"

"Where, Prophet?" someone pleaded anxiously.

"Why, where else?" the old sailor barked. "To a ship, man! To a ship!"

## CHAPTER FOUR

# The Dread

PELMEN FELT the net the moment he crossed the last line of pines and soared out over Ngandib-Mar. There was that odd, prickly feeling he'd experienced so many times before, like cold fingers rubbing the down of his underbelly the wrong way, or spiderwebs breaking around his beak. Alert to the danger, he plummeted a thousand feet toward the grass of the parks and burrowed there among the bushes like a quail. The sensation passed. He'd escaped a magical net and he trembled with relief. Nevertheless, the shaper who had cast it was now warned. It would be woven again in moments, and Pelmen slapped the brush with his widespread wings and skimmed the grass tops in an evasive loop to the southeast.

He didn't think. He simply flew. After an hour of weaving through the crystal-berry bushes, he changed direction again and shot once more into the heavens. He was gambling that he had eluded the net and for the moment, at least, he was right.

He still had a long way to go across a large chunk of Ngandib-Mar. He had no doubt that Dorlyth had rallied his supporters in the glade of mod Carl. But where were they now? If they were covered—and surely they must be—they could be anywhere in the Mar and yet remain completely hidden. He might have flown over them already, or even among them, blinded by the covering spell into seeing men as crystal-berry shrubs. But he reasoned that the glade was a convenient location to wait until battle started, and it was obvious that the Mar was not yet fully mobilized. Dorlyth picked his battlefields carefully. Pelmen hoped his warrior friend had lingered.

Naturally, the covering shaper would have hidden the glade.

Although he'd been there many times and had often cloaked it himself, Pelmen knew he would have to study the surrounding forest carefully or he'd miss it. If he couldn't find it from the air, he'd be forced to take to the ground and his human form and waste time and energy in the magical activity termed "piercing the cloak." That would be dangerous as well as time-consuming, if this rival shaper was still trying to net him. Expecting the search to be arduous, he paused for a moment atop the Rock of Tombs and rested.

The Rock of Tombs was nearly cylindrical, looking from the distance like a blanched, broken bone pointing jagged splinters at the sky. It towered over a gentle wood that formed the deceptively innocent northern edge of the Great South Fir. The spire's sheer faces were scored with vertical crevices; at the bottom of nearly every crack was jammed the coffin of an ancient Mari great. As a tower of tombs it was old—older by far than the dragon. In those distant days, wedge-shaped sarcophagi of white marble had been hoisted to the heights. When all the words were spoken and the last song sung, each wedge had been loosed above a fissure. It had fallen, then, like a snowy-white axe head, to lodge thunderously in the mountain's cleft—and in the people's history. Pelmen had visited the place frequently, for there were powers on this Rock, and sometimes they'd proved helpful. Their presence here formed a kind of fog of force, and he hoped to hide himself within it. He needed some respite from the threat of that net.

Who had cast it? That was a senseless question and Pelmen knew it. Speculation was a waste of time, for he knew of several who could weave such, and there was always the possibility of a new shaper appearing on the scene—as Flayh had done. He disregarded the thought, turning all his attention to the important task at hand. It would take his total concentration to fly safely to the glade while so exposed. Once there, he could reassume his human shape and either cloak himself or come under the coverage of whatever shaper Dorlyth should have hired. But he couldn't fly and cloak both. Even a wizard of unlimited power couldn't do more than one thing at a time. At least, Pelmen hoped not. *He* surely couldn't.

The wind stirred his feathers. Pelmen rocked uneasily from one taloned foot to the other, then scratched his way higher onto the pinnacle of the Rock of Tombs. For all the protection it offered, there was danger here, too.

It wasn't ghosts he feared. Had that been so, this was a frightful place indeed, for if ghosts there were, the most powerful in the Mar surely prowled these desolate crevices. Ngandib-Mar had long been a magic land, and among its greats had been many shapers. Wedged into a crack somewhere below him was the body of Nobalog, the wizard who had given life to a castle. There, too, were some who'd helped in the making of the dragon. A wedge had also been cut and dropped in the memory of the shaper named Sheth, although that sorcerer's remains were not within it. Vicia-Heinox had consumed him. Still, if his spirit lived on, would it not be here as likely as in any other place? Here the mighty clustered together in sleep.

But Pelmen didn't fear dead sorcerers; he feared living ones. The powers upon this spire of stone could be used against him as easily as he could use them to his advantage. That was why he recoiled in shock as a pastel glow appeared on a crag above him and shaped itself into a female form.

It could only be Mar-Yilot. Pelmen changed shapes and turned to face her. Then he gasped in surprise. The woman blinked her eyes and struggled to focus them on him. "Pelmen?" she mumbled.

"Bronwynn!" he replied. "What are you doing here?"

"I . . . I guess . . . looking for you?" Her eyes sagged shut again and she reeled. He jumped up the rock and reached out to steady her. His hand passed through her arm. Then he understood.

"Bronwynn," he said quietly but with grave authority, "you must listen to me."

"I'm listening," she replied, a bit petulantly, like a pouting child.

"You must open your eyes."

She obeyed him, then seemed to catch interest and to waken. "Where am I?" she asked quickly.

"At home in your bed, I wager. You tell me, Lady Bronwynn."

"I . . . I'm sleeping. Aren't I? And all of this is a dream—" Suddenly she looked down and caught her breath at the sight of the forest so far below them.

"Don't be frightened, Bronwynn, and don't fall!" Pelmen snapped.

"What would happen if I did?" she asked anxiously.

"You'd wake up in the Imperial House of Chaomonous, and we'd have lost this opportunity. Look into my eyes!" Bronwynn obeyed. "Now tell me why you're here."

His eyes held hers, and she relaxed into them, forgetting the fearsome height completely. "I was longing to see you, to hear news of my Rosha. I stood on the rooftop, gazing northward for a sign. At last I saw on the horizon a tiny speck of blue—I was sure the flyer brought word from you, and I raced to Maliff's side to grab the message from his hand. It was from Lamath, true, but not from you. Nor did it bear any news I wished to hear. Ambassador Joss was reporting that the royal family had again seized control of Lamath and that the dragon was once more in the sky. I think I cried myself to sleep. I wish *that* were the dream instead of this!"

"What of Erri?" Pelmen asked stonily.

"Disappeared, and the core of his followers with him."

"And Joss?"

"He's still in Lamath, awaiting my instructions. I don't know what to do. I'd rather march to Ngandib-Mar!"

"No!" Pelmen commanded. He quickly added, "My dear Queen, I urge you not to. There's no need for you there, not as yet. And if Erri is fleeing, he may need your home as a haven."

"Why should that prevent me from marching?" Bronwynn snapped.

"Recall for a moment what happened the last time Chaomonous warred upon the Mar?"

"The Golden Throng was destroyed and the Dorlyth killed my father. But I'm not my father, and I—"

"Then don't be the fool he was! You've missed my point, Bronwynn. When he left for Dragonsgate, your father left his crown behind as well. Ligne usurped his throne before he was a day's march up the road."

"Ligne's dead—"

"You think there aren't scores of others like her? Many witnessed her rise to power and would like to model their own success after hers. You haven't held the crown even as long as she did! Be wise, Queen Bronwynn. Be wise and stay home."

"I want to see Rosha!" Bronwynn frowned.

"I'll find him for you, my Lady, and send you word as soon as I do."

"Can't I come with you?" she pleaded.

"You're not really here," Pelmen explained. He passed his hand through her head to demonstrate. "You see?"

"And yet I *am*! This isn't just a dream—is it? I don't understand."

"I told you long ago, my Lady, that you had the potential within you to shape. You're experiencing dream-search, a low-level cousin of a spell some—Mar-Yilot, for example—are very practiced at controlling. The difficulty will be in believing it really happened when you wake. But this is shaping, Bronwynn. The powers are unleashed. They're abroad now in every land, and dormant shapers will soon be waking to force those powers to their bidding. You're a budding wizard, Bronwynn. You must be careful, for there may be others in Chaomonous who are already blossoming. *That's* why you need to remain at home, if for no other reason that you know—"

"What?" Bronwynn interrupted, snapping her head to one side as if answering someone's call. In that instant she disappeared.

Mar-Yilot stood at her tower window and snarled in dismay. "Lost you!" she wailed. "Lost you again!" A wind swirled around the spire in response, the backwash of an enormous projection of her power.

"In my net," she murmured. "You were in my net and I could have reeled you here like a fish—like a fish, Pelmen! Oh, I'll have you yet. Where are you now? Hiding? Show yourself, Dragonsbane," she sneered, "or do you fear this frail girl who taunts you!"

No one stood in the tower beside her, nor were there any mirrors to reflect her image back at her. But in that moment Mar-Yilot looked anything but frail. The backwash wind whirled into the window, streaming her autumn hair back over her shoulders. Her eyebrows knitted above her grain-colored eyes as she peered defiantly into the distance—the far distance. She saw neither the walls of Seriliath nor the fields beyond them, but rather other fields and forests a hundred miles distant. She sought vainly to think like a falcon, diligently searching through the bushes and trees where Pelmen had first brushed her net. She cursed herself for not being ready for him. Her attention had wavered for just a moment and she'd lost him. It would not waver again!

In her fury, Syth was forgotten.

The army of the north galloped down the cobbled streets of Seriliath, and the townsfolk responded with delirious pride. As the gray and blue standard of Sythia Isle snapped fiercely above their heads, the citylord's followers shouted themselves hoarse.

That was for show. Once out of sight of the fortified walls, Syth slowed his riders to a sensible, cautious trot. "We need to move slowly so Mar-Yilot can track us," Bainer explained unnecessarily to Tuckad mod Pak. Bainer always talked when he was nervous and today he was frightened out of his wits. It promised, therefore, to be a tedious journey for his companions.

As usual, Tuckad ignored Bainer. "Why doesn't she ride *with* us?" he growled at Syth, who studied the road ahead calmly. Tuckad mod Pak was the Lord of Drabeld, the other major fortified city of the north. A quick-thinking man with a mercurial smile and the shoulders and strength of a woodsman, he was Syth's foremost ally in this conflict. He was tenacious and wouldn't be put off.

Syth didn't even try. "Frankly, she chose not to."

"Can't you control your woman?" Tuckad demanded, and Bainer gritted his teeth at the sudden hostility.

Syth diffused it with a low chuckle. "I can hardly control myself," he muttered and he winked at his comrades. Bainer cackled in relief. Tuckad smiled at the mane of his horse and waited for Syth to be serious. "She's Mar-Yilot," Syth said soberly. "She does as she chooses. And I . . . well, I do too." Syth shrugged and gazed down the road.

"And has she chosen to cloak us?" Tuckad asked, his eyes grim.

"Why, of course she has!" Bainer grunted. "You think Syth would lead us out if she hadn't?"

"Has she, Syth?" Tuckad continued.

"She's covering us," their leader told them confidently, and Tuckad sat back in his saddle, satisfied. Syth's eyes returned to the road, their studied calm hiding the uncertainty that still seethed inside him. He'd made a statement of faith, not of fact. He had no skill at shaping, to perceive whether that glowing aura of protection arched over them as he hoped. His faith was not groundless, however. Of one thing he could be forever certain: Mar-Yilot loved him. As long as he was with this army, so in spirit was she. She would never willingly expose him to any danger. But shapers were so easily distracted. . . .

He had tuned out Bainer's meaningless chatter. When Tuckad spoke again, he paid attention. "Where do the Hannis join us—Garnabel Bridge?"

Syth nodded. "Just north of the High Plateau. Kam joins us there too."

"Kam is a very small fish. I'm far more concerned about our merchant allies—and a bit distrustful as well. Merchants don't usually fight anybody but other merchants. What quarrel does the House of Hann have with our lazy King Pahd?"

"No quarrel with the king. Plenty with Flayh, however. For all the fact that this Flayh now shapes, remember, he was once the prince of the merchant house of Ognadzu. It's a recent grudge, I gather, but fiercely held. Hann is the second trading house in the Mar these days. With Flayh always at the king's ear, how can they hope for any better? As always, it's merchant *versus* merchant over markets."

"If that's the case, why haven't the other traders joined us? Blez—we pass through their lands this morning—and Uda, Wina and the others? They've not declared for any side that I've heard."

"Nor will they, until the first battle's won by someone. Then they'll make the most profitable commitment. They're traders, remember?"

Tuckad nodded. "Well. Cerdeb meets us at the bridge as well?"

"No, Cerdeb has circled south of the High City, not north. We'll meet him at Kam's castle. And much as you might think Kam an insignificant friend, you can't deny he's well located."

"Very well indeed!" Bainer cackled, finding a spot where he could break back into the conversation. "He sits on the very doorstep of Ngandib!" He proclaimed this as if it were a priceless pearl of new information, instead of a basic factor in all of their calculations. Bainer was a bore. He could fight, however, and that was why, despite being boring, he was a baron.

He wielded a wicked mace. Besides, on the battlefield, Bainer rarely said a word, and that was when his friends liked him most. For the moment they tolerated him, thinking their private thoughts as he rambled on.

They met no one. That was curious, for it was the harvest season, and they'd expected to encounter an occasional hay-wagon, at least. As the autumn sun passed its peak and started its descent, Tuckad voiced his reservations. "Something's wrong. There's no traffic."

"It's wartime, Tuckad. The peasants are keeping their heads down."

"No peasant I know cares a fig about war if his crop is in the field rotting. No. It's too unusual. Someone's stopping traffic up ahead of us. They're waiting to ambush us in the ravines." There was no alarm in the Lord of Drabeld's voice, but he did say it with conviction.

"How do you know?" Syth asked.

"I can smell it," Tuckad grunted. "And I smell the screaming pig behind it."

Tuckad's words drew unexpected laughter from the other two men. He'd once again revealed his obsession. "We're far from the lands of Chanos," Bainer scoffed.

"Not far enough for me," Tuckad snapped. "We can never be far enough for me."

"Bainer's right," Syth said. "The lands of the roaring boar are miles from the River Road. You've battled Chanos so long his stench is always in your nostrils."

This was true. Tuckad's lands abutted those of Chanos, and they had fought about that border since the day they met as boys. They'd warred over everything else as well, most especially family problems. The two clans were linked by a half dozen marital bonds, each relationship as stormy as the next. In times of peace, they hated one another cordially, trading insults across the banquet tables and storing up bile for the next conflict. When at last the standards were raised again, all the Mar could be certain that the green bow of Tuckad and Chanos's roaring boar's head would be on opposite sides of the field.

Tuckad was adamant. "You mock my intelligence, son of Syth. Would the city of Drabeld elect a fool? I smell the pig because he's *there*, because he's always there, wherever I am. I claim no shaper powers, nor does he, yet we can track one another as unerringly as any wizard. Mark me well. You say your lady's cloaking us, and I believe you or I'd not be here. But if for some reason she's not—if she's busy at her spell-book or battling some shaper elsewhere—they'll take us in the ravines."

"I hope they do await us in the ravines. I've told the Hannis if we don't meet them at the bridge to turn north and follow the road. We'll trap them between us in the very gorge they seek to use against us." Syth said this coolly, not daring to look at Tuckad. He feared his keen companion might penetrate his bravado.

"Nonetheless, may I suggest we send out a dozen riders to watch our eastern flank?"

"Always a good idea, my friend. Will you see to it?"

Tuckad and Syth exchanged a quick glance, Tuckad smiling appreciatively at this opportunity for a respite from Bainer's incessant prattle. Moments later, when they reached the beginning of the lengthy gorge called the ravines, a small troop of riders pounded up the gentle slope to their left. The main column kept to the road, which followed the riverline. In another hour, the slope had become a sheer cliff. With this wall to one side and the swift-moving river to the other, the small army was obviously vulnerable to attack. The ravines were famous for ambushes—although usually the attackers were slavers, descending on unsuspecting caravans carrying goods to the north or gemstones southward. Rarely had major battles been fought here. Mari chieftains preferred honorable combat in open spaces. Even so, no Mari lord would dare to travel the riverline without coverage. The danger was obvious, but no enemy could attack what couldn't be seen.

Syth was drowsing in his saddle when Bainer suddenly interrupted himself. "What's that?"

Syth's eyes fluttered open. "What?"

"There!" Bainer pointed. They spurred their mounts forward to examine the object that had just come bouncing off the cliff when another fell, striking the ground near enough to them to be instantly recognizable. It was a severed head.

"Whose—" Syth gasped, horrified, but words failed him. He knew the face. It belonged to one of Tuckad's foremost supporters. His head reeled. This was no Mari practice.

"Look," Tuckad grunted and he pointed.

Syth pulled his gaze from the grotesque vision and looked beyond it. Blocking the road were three armor-clad warriors, backed by a horde of grinning retainers. Three standards fluttered on the breeze, and Syth read their symbols at a glance. On one were the diagonal blue stripes of Belra, Citylord of Garnabel. The second flag held the spreading oak of Ferlyth mod Kerlyth, Lord Carlog and Jorl of the vast Furrowmar. And on the golden background of the third was the green cross of Dorlyth mod Karis, hero of Westmouth.

Syth's mouth gaped wide in shock. "Dorlyth? *Here?* How did he come to be here?"

"He's an enemy, isn't he?" Tuckad rasped, his face contorted with rage. "He's got a shaper to protect him, doesn't he?" The warrior glared at Syth; then his scream exploded and he gouged his mount's flanks with his spurs. As his greatsword flashed into view, a hail of arrows began dropping from the rocks above. The army of the north surged forward to follow Tuckad.

As warriors poured around him Syth shook his head, stunned by what had happened. "Then Pelmen has penetrated my lady's veil," he gasped, the sound of his words disappearing in the swelling thunder of roared war cries. "But why against us? Why not against the dog! And this," he added, pointing at the grisly object at his horse's feet. "When did Dorlyth stoop to severing heads?"

For the first time today, Bainer wasn't talking. He'd removed his right gauntlet and was meticulously untying the thong that bound his mace to his saddle horn.

The battle was going poorly, but it could not have gone otherwise. Their flanking scouts had been beheaded, so there was no horn of warning. Their magic cloak had been penetrated, and there was no shaper there to shield them. The enemy was above them, ahead of them, and behind them, and the river waited silently to their right, ready to swallow quietly any who fled its way. Tuckad had been right. They'd been ambushed in the ravines. There was no hope.

Still, the army of the north fought valiantly. Syth and Bainer joined the fray together, hard on the heels of their maddened comrade. Tuckad was driving wildly for the standard-bearers and cut one down before the ambushers closed around him. He was shrieking, "Show me the pig!" over and over, and Syth broke off and sought to fight through the crowd to succor him. Bainer stayed behind, wordlessly hammering helmets.

A swordstroke knocked the Lord of Drabeld from his mount just as Syth slashed down the last man between them. Syth engaged the attacker and beat him off, then wheeled his war horse and grabbed Tuckad's forearm. "Come up!" he shouted. The wounded warrior clenched Syth's wrist and swung up onto Syth's charger. Syth had spotted a peasant's hovel leaning against the base of the cliff and now he rode for it, trying to hold Tuckad on behind him with one hand as he guided his horse and parried swordstrokes with the other. At last they broke free of the mêlée and thundered toward the lean-to. Syth dropped from the saddle in time to catch his moaning friend as he fell and half-dragged, half-carried Tuckad into the dim interior. He noticed five pairs of eyes gazing at him from a corner of the room where the peasant and his family cowered in terror. He ignored them, ripping away Tuckad's armor and trying to stanch the flow of blood with his hand. The only light was that from the small doorway. Suddenly the room was filled with shadow, and Syth glanced up to see who blocked the door.

"I wanted to show him," the figure grunted, jerking off his brightly painted cuirass. "I wear Belra's armor by my king's command, but tell that snivelling cur it was the roaring boar who slew him!"

The bright sun behind Chanos's head kept Syth from making out the man's features, but Syth knew the voice well enough. He looked back at his dying friend, then sighed with grief. Tuckad was already dead. "He was right," Syth growled at the warrior who gloated over them. "You really are a screaming pig."

"And a fool," someone beyond the doorway snarled, and Syth heard a thud. Chanos grunted, and his head snapped back into the light so that Syth could see his grimace. Then Chanos tumbled forward, falling across the body of his boyhood foe.

Syth craned his neck to see through the doorway and immediately wished he hadn't. What he saw made him sick. The armor was Dorlyth's but the face came straight from his nightmares. He'd never met the man, but he recognized him instantly—by reputation. "Admon Faye?"

The slaver nodded curtly. "And you're Syth mod Syth-el, Lord of Seriliath."

"Why do you wear Dorlyth's armor?" Syth asked flatly.

"Isn't it obvious?" the hideous slaver replied.

Syth nodded solemnly. Then he glanced down at the dagger hilt protruding from the back of the slain Chanos. "I thought you were the king's man. Wasn't this pig the king's, too?"

"I'm Flayh's man, not Pahd's. If you want the truth, I'm no man's but my own. I just know how to cooperate. This fool apparently did not. I told him he must stifle his grudge and remain disguised for the sake of the grand design. He didn't. Now he's dead."

"Did you really think you had tricked us?" Syth asked bitterly. "Dorlyth doesn't sever heads! But that's only one of the many acts you're famous for!"

The slaver shrugged and smiled sarcastically. "Of course, we couldn't hope to deceive such a clever man as yourself, mod Syth-el," he goaded. "But then, you'll not be able to reveal us. As for this dead fool, we'll drag his body off and dump it in the river. Your hot-tempered lady will be left to figure it out by herself. I wonder, will she take the time to reason through the ruse?"

Syth watched Admon Faye's eyes. "She might," he said quietly, but Admon Faye knew he was lying and chuckled softly. Syth knew his woman well. Of course she would believe Pelmen and Dorlyth had done this. She wanted to believe such. He had to survive to get the truth back to Mar-Yilot! He was still on his knees and his sword was behind him, but it would be difficult for Admon Faye to get through that small door and to him before he could get the dagger out of Chanos's back. He waited for the slaver to charge.

Admon Faye chuckled again. "Planning your escape? Sorry, Syth. You must realize I can't allow that." He pulled the shield off his shoulder and tossed it through the doorway. Syth dodged it, then looked back at the slaver in surprise. "Dorlyth's, you know. We want to be sure your lady knows who's responsible. As for you, I didn't come to kill you. Lord Flayh just wanted me to deliver *this*." Admon Faye suddenly tossed the contents of a small bag into the hovel and wheeled outward to hide his eyes.

At the flash of green light, Syth screamed. Then he toppled onto his back, his body as rigid as that of a statue. His eyes, wide and staring, no longer saw this world. He wasn't dead, but he beheld the sights of hell all the same.

The family of peasants, already terrified, found their terror multiplied a thousandfold. Witnesses, too, of the green flash, they visited hell beside him. This was a common tool of the magic wars, generally termed "the dread." As far as anyone knew, the spell was irrevocable.

Cold blue moonlight reflected off Syth's armor as the column hurried northward through the night. Bainer rode beside the wagon that bore Syth's body, unaware that it bore another passenger as well; a butterfly rode astride the stricken man's helmet. Mar-Yilot had joined the retreat.

Too late! She'd seen the trick too late. Pelmen had toyed with her while Dorlyth sprang his trap, and now her lover was lost! Guilt feasted on her feelings, gorged itself upon her. She was only dimly aware when the column took the last fork for Seriliath.

The walls of the city looked silvery cold, like cliffs of ice standing silently against the stars. The pace picked up. Soon the lead riders were exchanging muted conversation with the gatekeepers, and the portals swung open to admit the weary warriors. As they climbed the winding cobblestones to the castle there were no cheers. The city slept on. It was four in the morning, and the turning wheels that bore their lord and his mourning lady made as little impression on the sleepers as the milk wagon. As dawn broke and the city came awake, the word would spread, and with disbelieving tears the people would fill the streets to mourn the fallen. For now they slept on, and Mar-Yilot envied their rest. She wondered if she would evèr sleep again.

As the wagon reached the palace, the butterfly left, soaring up through an open window high in the tower above. There Mar-Yilot took her human form and stepped to a mirror to check her appearance. She looked horrible. Her hair was in disarray and her cheeks were so pale they looked bleached. At least her face wasn't tear-streaked. One advantage of her altershape was that a butterfly couldn't weep. She pushed her hair into some semblance of order, then steeled herself to descend the stairs. This was for Bainer's sake. Bainer would need to see her strength.

The armor-clad body had been laid on a bier in the lord's chamber. Neither torches nor candles burned here, but the room was lined on both sides by tall windows, and Mar-Yilot had ordered that these be opened despite the cold. Moonlight fell across the body. The loyal Bainer crouched over it.

"Is he dead?" she asked tonelessly.

Bainer didn't seem startled. "Would that he were."

"Why!" Mar-Yilot snarled, her anger flaring.

"Because he lives, my Lady, only to gaze on hell! Look at him!" Bainer reached forward to raise Syth's visor, but Mar-Yilot stepped forward and caught his hand.

"No," she whispered. Her eyes forced him back away from the body. Then she turned away, and sighed deeply. "You saw his face yourself?"

"I closed his helmet."

"And you're familiar with the dread?"

"I'm no novice in magical wars. I've seen it before."

Her golden eyes flicked back to lock onto his. "Who's responsible?" she grunted.

"It was Dorlyth mod Karis. By my mace, I swear it. And Ferlyth and Belra with him."

Mar-Yilot trembled with rage. "And Pelmen?" she asked.

"I saw *no* shaper on the field today," Bainer said boldly. "Who it was is for you to say. I know only what I saw in Syth's eyes, and that's far more of magic than I ever cared to learn in a lifetime."

"I had him in my net!" Mar-Yilot wailed, and the tears welled up inside her.

Bainer stumbled backward, mumbling, "Should I go, my Lady?"

She fought the sorrow down, controlling it once more. Then she sought out his eyes in the dark. "You must do one more thing, Bainer, before I release you from this ill-favored alliance. Carry him home to Sythia Isle. Go now, before the light of day brings the mourners out to clog the streets. I'll cover your every step and cover the barge as well until you beach upon the island. Do that for Syth, Bainer, and for me. Then you're free to seek your best interests elsewhere."

"Free?" Bainer snorted. "For what? To join the king? To link myself with the traitor Dorlyth? Or would you have me blend back into the landscape like these other barons who are so afraid of losing they choose not to choose 'til the battle's lost? I'll bear Syth to the islands, my Lady, and return home. There I'll wait."

"For what?" Mar-Yilot asked bitterly.

"For your command. You'll think of something."

Mar-Yilot took a deep breath and gazed at this loyal friend. "Indeed, Bainer, perhaps I have done so already. Send the servants in to fetch him, and prepare to carry him home."

Bainer nodded and left. As he closed the door, the sorceress collapsed across her lover's body. She permitted herself very few tears, however. By the time the servants arrived, she was already back up in her tower. From that lofty perch she cloaked the last, long leg of Bainer's weary march, giving her full attention to getting her loved one home. Once the barge had beached on Sythia Isle she departed, unwilling to waste even a single moment. She threw herself over the balustrade and fluttered off toward the south—a very angry, very dangerous butterfly.

## CHAPTER FIVE

# Wings of Fire

PELMEN SAW the glade clearly from the sky. Obviously Dorlyth was no longer there, or it would have been cloaked. He was about to veer northeast to fly to Dorlyth Castle when he decided to check the glade anyway. Perhaps his friend had left him a message. He was shocked to drop through the trees and find a small army assembled on the grass.

"Pelmen!" Rosha shouted.

"He's come indeed!" Ferlyth added as Pelmen struck the ground as a falcon and immediately took his human form. Dorlyth said nothing, but stood struggling to stifle a self-satisfied smile. He wondered to himself how Pelmen always managed to time his entrances so precisely and put it down to the actor's instinct.

Pelmen had arrived at a critical moment. Dorlyth and Ferlyth faced a mutinous, foul-spirited band of men. Nor did Pelmen's abrupt appearance automatically end the confrontation. "What's happening?" he asked.

"It's a bit of a rebellion," Ferlyth answered.

Dorlyth shrugged. "Some of our warriors are angry with me. Probably with reason."

"Where's your coverage?" Pelmen frowned, and Dorlyth raised his bushy eyebrows.

"*That's* the reason."

"No one's cloaking you?" Pelmen gasped, astonished. "How long has this been going on?"

"Long enough for us all to have been fried by a fire circle, if any shaper had thought us worth the trouble. Fortunately, we've managed to wait here rather quietly without offending anyone."

"No one knows you're here?"

"Now I didn't say *that*." Those eyebrows, grayer now than Pelmen remembered, underscored Dorlyth's frown. "The Autumn Lady knows our whereabouts, and probably Flayh does too. I must say I've never longed to see anyone so much as I've wished that you would appear."

"Is this all of you?" Pelmen asked, turning to the band of fighters.

"Not all," a brave man finally answered, not troubling to hide the bitterness he felt. "We were never many, but we were enough. But Lord Belra's broken with these two lords and gone to Garnabel to hire Joooms."

Pelmen raised an eyebrow and looked back at Dorlyth. "Belra, Lord Garnabel? An ally?"

"Well he *was* . . ." Dorlyth sighed.

"I've always respected him as an enemy. He'd certainly make a worthy friend."

"Perhaps we can win him back, now that you're here."

Pelmen gazed at his old friend. "I really didn't come to fight," he said honestly.

"You never do." Dorlyth shrugged. "Yet you somehow manage to become involved. I know, I know. No promises. But while we stand here talking about it, would you mind putting a cloak up over us? We've been naked so long I've started to feel the chill."

Pelmen smiled. "It's been in place ever since I entered the clearing. I care about my security, unlike some foolhardy friends!"

Dorlyth nodded sardonically and turned to face his surly army. "There now," he said, gesturing. "Pelmen Dragonsbane. I said he would come and he's here. Would any man deny that we're now the best protected force in the land?" No one replied. They all knew Pelmen's reputation. "And with that protection, we now have some chance against these demons in dogflesh. Sharpen your swords. Now we're prepared to fight!" Dorlyth turned his back and started walking away, effectively dismissing the mutinous company. The warriors began slipping away to their own tents as Pelmen, Rosha, and Ferlyth fell in behind the striding leader.

Once inside the fish-satin tent. Dorlyth breathed a sigh of relief. "Dramatic timing, my friend, but you could have saved some wear and tear on my old heart by appearing sooner."

"I didn't even know I was coming! I got a message from Bronwynn requesting that I find her vanished husband, so naturally I expected to find him here. I had no idea you were so vulnerable!"

"Why don't you check on us from time to time?" Dorlyth scolded. "Mar-Yilot does."

"Has she been here?" Pelmen asked with alarm.

"Once," Rosha grunted.

"Which is often enough," Dorlyth added. "By that, I mean her form was here—like a wraith."

"There are several things that Mar-Yilot does that I can't. That's one of them."

"Not true," Dorlyth muttered. "I've seen you. Trouble is, you don't practice. If you would, maybe we could stay in closer touch with you."

"In any case, I'm here now. And since, as you say, I always get involved, regardless of how I might try to avoid it, you can be sure that I'll do what I can to aid you."

"Good. Rosha, send a flyer to Garnabel. Inform the impatient Belra that he can leave Joooms in peace and spare himself some treasure. And tell him to get his red mustache back down here—we need to plan."

Rosha nodded and started through the tent flap. "And while you're at it," Pelmen added, "why not send your wife word of where you are."

Dorlyth turned to frown at his son. "Haven't you done that yet? I thought you loved that girl!"

"I do," Rosha snapped. "It's just that, if I tell her where I am, she's apt to send an army to protect me! How would you like an army chasing you around?"

"Right now I wouldn't turn it down," Dorlyth joked, winking at Pelmen.

The wizard didn't smile. "The trouble is, she may send it anyway."

Dorlyth quickly grew serious. "That wouldn't do at all. We've enough factions within this nation. We certainly don't need our wealthy southern neighbor sticking her big nose in where it isn't needed. You realize that's just a figure of speech, son, not a comment on your lady's facial features."

"*Do* send the flyers," Pelmen urged, "but be careful how you word your message to her. What am I saying! She's your wife. You know how best to deal with her." Rosha nodded—a bit doubtfully, Pelmen thought—and left the tent.

Dorlyth stroked his beard reflectively. "She's thinking of invading?"

"I've done my best to dissuade her. Perhaps she'll listen."

"I hope for her sake she does. Ferlyth, tell him what you know."

Lord Ferlyth turned his icy blue gaze on Pelmen. "Terril the twin-killer has entered the service of Lord Flayh—whether willingly or unwillingly is not known. It *is* known that Flayh has sent him south—to the extreme south, across Arl Lake and the westernmost spur of the Great South Fir. His orders are to create havoc in that region."

"Which is southern Chaomonous."

"Exactly. It is also known that Terril has been promised the whole of Chaomonous as a fiefdom if he can succeed in taking it. I assume he'll use every resource at his disposal. You would know more about that than I. As you recall, Terril's altershape is a—"

"Yes," Pelmen said thoughtfully. "Terril the twin-killer is a sugar-clawsp."

"Of course, Terril's not much of a warrior," Dorlyth put

in, "But he certainly can cause problems if he's highly motivated."

"And nothing moves Terril like greed," Pelmen murmured. He was deep in thought, remembering the days long ago when he'd battled the clawsp and the other shapers to a standstill.

"I hate to interrupt your meditations," Dorlyth drawled, "but since you're here, there's another friend you might want to visit."

Pelmen glanced up, his brow wrinkling with curiosity and hope. "What friend?" he asked eagerly.

Dorlyth laughed. "You say that as if you're surprised you have any friends!"

"It's just that the ones I do have keep disappearing! What friend?"

Now Dorlyth frowned. "I'm sorry. I fear now my news will only disappoint you."

"Why? Who is it?" Pelmen demanded.

"It's just a horse—"

"A horse? Minaliss?" Pelmen grinned.

"If that's what you call that big roan stallion you stole from the merchant Pezi—"

"Where is he?" Pelmen whooped with delight, and he dashed out the tent flap without waiting for an answer.

Dorlyth turned to Ferlyth and slipped his tongue into his cheek. "It's so reassuring, isn't it, to have a shaper who always maintains his composure?"

Shivering at the cold, Pelmen walked the perimeter of the camp, checking the efficacy of his spell. Cloaking was a simple task once a shaper disciplined his mind to it. Pelmen could keep this magical baffle in place even in his sleep—provided his sleep was not disturbed by that other, far more potent Power. He remembered when he had lain down with confidence, certain no force on earth could penetrate his carefully woven barrier. He smiled ruefully at such memories now. He was no longer his own. The Power had placed a stamp upon him, and part of that mark was a humility born of uncertainty. He could never be sure, now, when he might be summoned. Often, in responding to that call, he'd witnessed his own careful plans evaporate in the shift of circumstance. Yet he wasn't unhappy in this. There burned within him a sense of personal purpose that had always been lacking when he'd called himself his own. And the world, with its entangling webs of sorcery and deceit, seemed to him an altogether less frightful place, for he knew that righting it did not depend on him alone. He took comfort in that—the uncertain comfort of faith.

"Pelmen!" Dorlyth barked from his tent. "Come in out of that wind, fool! You'll freeze your rump and won't be able to ride!"

Pelmen realized that his fingers and toes were indeed numb, and he headed toward the shelter. "I should think a numb bottom might be an advantage," he jested.

"If you want to experiment, you can stand here in the tent flap and stick it out, but I prefer your hands and eyes and brain to go unfrozen, since that's what's protecting us. There," he said, pointing across the tent with one hand as he closed the flap behind Pelmen with the other.

Pelmen's eyes widened and he smiled. "Bless you," he murmured. "But how did you manage—"

"I had to bring Minaliss in any case, didn't I? Might as well bring my bathtub along on his back."

"How did you get it on his back?" Pelmen exclaimed.

Dorlyth rolled his eyes. "It wasn't easy, I'll grant you. I had to lie." He leaned forward. "I told him it was for you."

"Why did you have to bring him in any case? How did you come to find him?"

"He found *me*, I didn't find him. As to why—I figured you'd come wheeling in here on the wing, instead of mounted like any sensible warrior on a war horse."

"But then what about your bathtub?" Pelmen asked, raising a mocking eyebrow. "won't you have to leave it behind when we ride?"

Dorlyth frowned. "I've been studying that. You wouldn't mind riding on top of it, would you?"

Pelmen laughed and stepped out of his sandals as he walked across the fish-satin floor. "When is this ride taking place? And where are we going?"

"Bathe first," Dorlyth said, pulling the curtain between himself and his guest. "We can discuss more minor matters later Ferlyth? Rosha? I'm for a game of Drax; what of you?"

The others responded from the far side of the tent as Pelmen peeled off his garments and stepped into the steaming water

At first, his toes protested the sharp contrast between this and the cold outside, but they quickly grew accustomed to it. Soon he was soaking in water up to his chin, letting the warmth soothe muscles weary beyond expression. He relaxed. His mind more weary even than his muscles, floated with the bobbing of his hair in the water. Ears immersed, he heard only enough of the raucous game being played beyond the curtain to be soothed by it. He was among friends—powerful friends, who could be trusted to bear their share of responsibilities in the coming conflict. Those reassuring voices, distorted by the water, lulled him. For the first time in what seemed like years, he rested.

The game ended with Ferlyth the victor, which wasn't unusual. Dorlyth was a wily soldier and an artful strategist, but for some reason was an awful Drax player. As Pelmen stepped from the bath, Dorlyth was heaping verbal abuse on his laughing son for not helping him win. Pelmen chuckled to himself, and Dorlyth shouted, "There's warm skins there," and went back to his recriminations.

Pelmen dried off, wrapped himself in the skins, and stepped out to join his companions. "Feel better?" Dorlyth asked.

"Much. I feel like I'm home. Why don't I spend more time here?"

"You never answer me when I ask *you* that," Dorlyth grumbled, "so why should I answer you? Sit down."

Pelmen sat on a mat and leaned back against a saddle. "When do you plan to ride?"

"Not before Belra returns, and that will take a couple of days. And not then without some purpose. We've been rather safe here, but we've also been blind. Unless Lord Garnabel brings some news with him, or you know something, I've no idea what our best move might be."

"What do you want to achieve?" Pelmen asked soberly.

"The overthrow of the present Pahd and the demise of this new shaper who controls him."

"You blame Pahd for this war?"

"I blame Pahd for not stopping it! Yes, I blame Pahd. Force of habit, I suppose—there's been a Pahd at the root of every war I've fought in."

"Except the war with Chaomonous. *I* was the cause of that, remember?" Pelmen leaned back against his saddle and laced his fingers behind his head. "And Pahd helped you end that one."

"You're defending the sloth?" Dorlyth asked sharply.

"Perhaps. But not his slothfulness. Pahd's been a poor king, but then he never should have been king. You should have." Ferlyth, who had been listening carefully to Pelmen, nodded in agreement.

"Let's not cover that ground again," Dorlyth grunted.

"Very well. I'm saying only that Pahd has always been weak and we've all known it. But that war with Chaomonous was precipitated by more than just my confusing of the dragon. It had been carefully plotted by the merchant council, led by the very man who now controls poor Pahd."

"Flayh," Dorlyth murmured, nodding. "Rosha's told me a bit about this new shaper. I remember well how he and Tohn mod Neelis took council together against me through their crystal pyramids. Rosha tells me one of those talking devices is now in Bronwynn's hands."

"It is, though I keep advising her to lock it away forever. Flayh attacked me magically through the pyramids. Except for good fortune—or some powerful intervention—I'd bear scars of that battle on my face."

"They say Flayh does," Rosha broke in excitedly. "They say his face and bald pate are a pale blue, but for a pair of pink handprints over his eyes!"

"Who says that?" Pelmen asked.

Dorlyth shrugged. "There were certain members of the court who occasionally passed along information to us. One happened to glimpse the shaper's face. I'm told he usually remains hidden."

"The same spy told you?"

Dorlyth shook his head. "Those who once helped us have now disappeared. Flayh is more secretive than Pahd. And he's hired a deadly enforcer to keep his secrets safe."

"Who's that?" Pelmen said flatly, certain that he already knew.

"Admon Faye," Rosha said under his breath.

Pelmen nodded. "That's bitter news, but I'm not surprised. The two men have worked together before. Indeed, they seem to fit one another. Especially now, since you tell me the face of one is as marred as that of the other." Pelmen subsided, absorbed in his own thoughts. They were bleak and heavy with despair, for he well knew that Admon Faye was first and foremost a slaver, and that his familiar haunts were in the Great South Fir. Often in these weeks since Serphimera's disappearance he'd imagined her kidnapped by the killer. This was the worst thought imaginable, more terrible than the possibility of her death. Admon Faye was a cruel man—Pelmen had experienced that cruelty firsthand—and Flayh was doubly so. While Pelmen's relationship with Serphimera had never been made public, it was surely no secret to those who made secrets their business. Pelmen had given both men plenty of cause to hate him. What might these two do to her, in order to get at him?

"Pelmen!" Dorlyth growled, and the shaper came to himself.

"Yes?"

"I thought you were about to disappear!"

Pelmen grunted. "Just thinking of Admon Faye."

"I try to do that as little as possible myself. Ruins the digestion."

"Rosha," Pelmen asked sharply, "have you heard any word about Serphimera?"

Rosha had been lost in thoughts of his own, revolving around those precious pyramids. Now he frowned. "I thought she was with you!"

"She was. She disappeared at the southern edge of the Great South Fir."

"You think the slaver's got her?" Rosha asked anxiously.

"I don't know. I don't know what to think."

"Who's Serphimera?" Dorlyth frowned.

"A woman," Pelmen said. "A priestess."

"A priestess!" Dorlyth snorted. "Of Lamath, then? I warned you to stay away from those Lamathian women! All they think about is religion!"

Pelmen nodded sadly. "That's certainly Serphimera. And that's another of my fears. Flayh has managed somehow to create an illusion of the dragon and has resuscitated the dead Dragonfaith."

Rosha gazed at him, dumbfounded. "The dragon flies again?"

"So your own lady tells me, as well as witnesses in Lamath. In fact, I've chanced to have conversation with the ghostly beast myself. I worry that perhaps Serphimera has reverted back to her old faith . . ."

"I don't follow any of this," Dorlyth grunted impatiently. "The dragon's alive again? And your woman is its priestess?"

"Let's just say that Flayh is far more powerful than I realized when I battled him through the crystals. And that power appears to be growing."

"So. He's a shaper, you're a shaper. Pahd's a swordsman, I'm a swordsman. Admon Faye's evil is well known to all of us, and so is his skill with weapons, but my son here bested him in a face-to-face struggle. Let's fight them."

"I wish it was all so simple, Dorlyth." Pelmen sighed.

"You mean it's not? Why not? What's different between this and any other war of confederation?"

"The level of powers in use. Flayh is more than just another shaper. He has powers beyond any I've seen, beyond any I knew existed! He controls King Pahd, and thereby this nation. He controls a vision of the dragon, and thus he enslaves Lamath. You tell me he controls Terril as well, who potentially could demoralize Chaomonous. He's brought the High Fortress to menacing, hostile life and a horde of scoundrels led by the prince of thieves! I can't best him alone—I doubt the Autumn Lady and I together could, despite the fact that she's at the height of her power during this season. And—a fact not to be forgotten—she opposes and threatens us. Your army—our army—is mutinous. Your allies, apart from Ferlyth, have departed. We're small in numbers, if not in courage. My friend—it's not so simple. Not simple at all."

Dorlyth snorted.

"You don't believe me?"

"*You* don't believe you. You've summed up the odds in such a way that anyone but a fool would surrender immediately. But I know you, Pelmen, and that's exactly what you are—a fool. A believing fool. Otherwise why would you be here? You know me, too, and I'm just as big a fool as you! We've a battle ahead, and by all reckoning we'll lose it. But we'll not quit it, will we?" Dorlyth paused, frowning with great ferocity. "Well, will we?"

Pelmen gazed at him. Then a smile spread across the wizard's face. "Dorlyth, for all your frequent protests, I sometimes think you have greater faith than I."

Dorlyth snorted again.

"No," Pelmen went on. "We'll not quit. But we'll not be fools either."

"As if we could help it," his grizzled companion muttered sourly.

"What?"

"Never mind. Let's plan how and where to hit them. What about assassination?"

"We'd be assassinating ourselves to attempt it. His castle's alive, I told you."

"Makes no sense," Dorlyth muttered, but he was a Mari, and Maris did not question magic. "What about some kind of alliance?"

"That's more practical. We have friends in Lamath—"

"I'm not talking about your silly little priests in their flapping robes! I'm talking about warriors! Other shapers! Mar-Yilot for example. We've done nothing to her—perhaps she'll join us."

"Convincing her may prove difficult." Pelmen smiled, remembering frequent encounters with the thin, waif-faced witch. "Don't disregard the bluefaithers. Your son was once one of them."

"Yes, but he carried a sword under his robe, too! Didn't you?" Dorlyth demanded of his son. "Well, didn't you?" he repeated.

Rosha hadn't been listening. "What? Oh, yes." He frowned and looked at Pelmen. "If we could only communicate quickly with the others! I wonder about those other pyramids. Flayh has one—where's the other?"

"Safely hidden away by Erri, I hope."

"By Erri!" Rosha shouted.

"That's right. It was entrusted to Erri by that unfortunate merchant who witnessed my battle with Flayh. I gave Erri the same advice I gave your wife: To hide it away from Flayh's grasping hands and to forget it. I suggest you do the same. Those shards of crystal were never intended as devices for communication. There is another possibility for contact, however. Bronwynn appears to be developing shaper powers. She sought me, today, in her dreams, and found me on the Rock of Tombs."

"Really?" Dorlyth asked enthusiastically. He pressed Pelmen for details. He saw every advantage to having a shaper in the family. But his son paid no attention. Although the news concerned his wife, Rosha never heard it. Despite Pelmen's injunction, he could not forget those crystalline objects that held such power. Bronwynn had one; now Erri had another. Rosha knew, now, why he'd come home.

"Not that way!" Pezi squealed, but he was too late. Riganlitha, a particularly clumsy tugolith, had walked through yet another farmer's garden wall.

Pezi urged Chimolitha to carry him up to the puzzled Riganlitha's side, then politely asked to be allowed down. He was standing between the two giant beasts with the rest of the herd clustered behind them when the irate farmer came boiling around the corner of his house. The man stopped short when he actually saw his uninvited guests. Riganlitha had a sheepish look of embarrassment on his huge face; but to the startled Lamathian, it looked like a monstrous snarl.

"We're sorry," Chimolitha announced solemnly, and the farmer's jaw dropped open.

"It... it talks..." he whispered to his wife, who stood behind him, prudently using his body as a shield.

"I can talk, too!" Thuganlitha said belligerently from the back of the herd, and the farmer and wife beat a hasty retreat into their cottage. The remainder of the conversation took place through the garden window.

"What are those things?" the wife called to Pezi.

"I'm not a thing!" Thuganlitha snorted before Pezi could reply. His bellicosity couldn't be mistaken. The wife disappeared from the window and was seen no more.

"These, ah, these are tugoliths," Pezi explained. He said it in a loud whisper, as if all of this were some grand secret.

"Tugoliths? Really?" the farmer said, his interest perking up. "I've heard of them all my life but I never thought I'd actually see one!"

"There are more of us than that," Chimolitha corrected.

"Than what?"

"Than one."

"Oh."

"Sorry about your wall," Pezi explained hastily, pulling his purse from his pocket as he walked toward the window. "We are, ah, trying to be inconspicuous, you see, so we're, ah, keeping to the back roads—"

"Where are you taking them?" the farmer asked suspiciously.

"Taking? Them? Oh, I'm not taking them anywhere. No, no. No, we're just out for a casual stroll—"

"Are they yours?"

"Well, actually—"

"We're Dolna's," Chimolitha said flatly.

Riganlitha asked, "Where is Dolna?"

Thuganlitha had shouldered up next to a part of the wall that was still standing and now asked Riganlitha, "Was it fun?"

"Was what fun?"

"To break the wall."

"I think we'd better run along now." Pezi smiled fearfully, and he counted gold coins into his hand. "Would three suffice?"

The farmer was no longer looking at him. He was watching with horror as Thuganlitha gleefully demolished that section of wall that had survived Riganlitha's clumsiness.

Pezi winced at the crash behind him, but he held his false smile in place as he said, "Perhaps six?"

A tool shed crumbled next. Rakes and pruning hooks flew into all corners of the garden.

"Why not twelve?" Pezi suggested.

"Can't you stop the thing?" the farmer croaked.

"Care to suggest how?" Pezi asked.

"Why not hit it?"

Thuganlitha stopped chortling and frowned.

"I think he heard you," Pezi said sorrowfully, just moments before the rampaging animal took off the end of the house. Pezi heard some terrified screams but he didn't wait to investigate them. He waddled quickly back to the relative safety of Chimolitha's side.

Ten minutes later, as Thuganlitha bragged to the others of the herd about how easily it all had fallen, Pezi stood in the rubble of the crumbled cottage counting gold coins into the hand of the dazed farmer: ". . . fifty-six, fifty-seven, fifty-eight. There now. That ought to be sufficient."

"My house . . ." the man murmured.

"Maybe you'd been thinking of remodeling it anyway?"

"My garden . . ."

"By the way, let's just keep this our little secret, shall we? My animals and I—we'd prefer not to be noticed." With that, Pezi climbed up behind Chimolitha's horn once again and told her to proceed. Soon the last pair of gigantic hindquarters had disappeared into the woods toward the south, but they could be heard for a half hour thereafter—uprooting every tree in their path.

Rosha guided his horse through the mists, moving cautiously but still maintaining a quick, steady pace. He was certain his father had discovered his absence by now, and just as certain that Dorlyth would follow him. Doubtless Pelmen would come as well; thus there was a good chance they would catch him. But he'd gambled that Dorlyth would think first of his responsibility to his other warriors and that that would delay them. That's what made his father a good leader—and kept him from being a hero.

Not that he hadn't been a hero in days gone by. Dorlyth's exploits had given content to more ballads than Rosha could count. His father dismissed them all as the imaginations of ignorant songsters, but Rosha had heard enough different versions of the old stories to piece together the actual events. By any analysis, they were impressive. Rosha idolized his father and had consciously modeled his life after Dorlyth's. He firmly believed that individual acts of courage could change the course of history, and he longed to find that crisis where he could play the pivotal role. He'd lost his chance to slay the dragon to the stumbling of his tongue. When Bronwynn had needed his strong arms to help her regain her throne, they'd been bound behind his back—due to his own dullness. Now he sensed a new opportunity, a chance to demonstrate his courage and his cunning once and for all to his father, his bride—and to himself. He would steal the third pyramid from Flayh's own tower.

He hadn't moved into this blindly. He had a plan for getting into the castle, a clever plan that had flashed upon him in a moment of insight and fanned a flame of excitement within him that he'd been hard pressed to conceal from the others. He'd studied it carefully, turning it over in his mind as he'd hunted, probing its weaknesses, contemplating its results. It would take skill and daring to carry it out, not to mention great stamina, courage, and some measure of simple luck. In short, it demanded a hero. That was exactly how Rosha saw himself.

He knew Dorlyth would view the attempt as foolhardy, and Pelmen would, as well. But they were leaders, both of them, with nothing to prove, plenty to lose, and countless people depending on them. No one depended on him, Rosha thought sullenly. Certainly not his tart-tongued, confident little queen. How could the ruler of the largest, most powerful empire among the three lands be dependent in any way upon him? What had she seen in him originally, if not his raw, unrealized potential to become a force among men? He was a hero. He could be nothing other. And he thought it fortunate that, for the moment at least, the ties that bound him could not overrule his sense of adventure, nor divert him from accepting this challenge. The evil Flayh possessed a magical artifact of immense power and antiquity, and Rosha would steal it or die. It was that simple.

His horse stepped into a clearing and he noticed suddenly that the fog had fled. A few yards away an elderly woman stooped to tie up a bundle of firewood. He would have ignored her, but suddenly she glanced up at him, and her eyes held his in their grip. They were a deep gold in color and unusually commanding, and he felt compelled to address her. "I'm going to the High City," he announced.

She looked at him, startled, he thought, then her eyes narrowed, as if to pierce him through.

"I'm Rosha mod Dorlyth," Rosha told her. He didn't know why he felt so talkative.

She raised her eyebrows as if she thought him strange, and he had to confess to himself that he did indeed feel strange. He said so aloud. "I feel a bit awkward, talking to you like this." He smiled.

The peasant woman curtsied and gave him a thin, knowing smile. "I'm certain you do, my Lord," she rasped.

"It's just that . . . I feel . . . my father and Pelmen are behind me. I must be going!" he finished with a shout, aware of how senseless and unnecessary that last statement had been, and totally confused as to why he'd said it. He drove his heels into the flanks of his horse and the animal bounded across the clearing and into the heavy brush on the far side.

Alone now, and pleased with the information she had garnered, Mar-Yilot untied the scarf that had disguised her and shook her auburn tresses free. Then, with a self-satisfied chuckle, she set about the business of starting her fire.

A touch on his shoulder and Pelmen was awake. His eyes blinked open and he peered up into Dorlyth's troubled face. "Rosha's gone," Dorlyth said, his normally rough voice made raspier by the morning cold.

Pelmen frowned, and made the sacrifice of rising from his warm bed onto his elbow. "Gone?"

Dorlyth gestured to an empty corner of the tent. "You see."

Pelmen swung his legs out of the warm furs and got to his feet, keeping the rugs wrapped around his shoulders. His toes curled at the cold of the tent's floor. "He'd make a skillful thief if he could creep out of here past both of us."

Dorlyth grunted in agreement and gazed impatiently at the floor as Pelmen wound strips of woolen cloth around his legs. Then he flipped the tent flap aside and stepped into the cold morning air. Pelmen followed him out.

"Perhaps he's hunting."

"He hunted yesterday," Dorlyth replied.

"Unsuccessfully—"

"Or so he said."

"You disbelieve your son?" Pelmen asked Dorlyth's back.

The warrior shrugged. "My son is an excellent hunter and these woods are full of game. He was quiet yesterday. Too quiet. You didn't notice?"

"I attributed it to poor shooting."

Dorlyth looked out toward the north, but there were no directions this morning. A thick mist clung to the bushes and huddled around the trunks of the trees. The air was damp, and the dead leaves on the forest floor clung quietly to their heels. "I can't remember the last time Rosha shot poorly." He swung his head around to gaze sadly at his companion. "It wouldn't surprise me if he spent yesterday bagging and cleaning his provisions in order to travel today. I taught him to do that." There was a trace of pride mixed into Dorlyth's anxious tone. "The question is—where? Back to his wife?"

"That might be the best thing he could do," Pelmen comforted, but he didn't believe for a moment that Rosha had returned to Bronwynn, and he knew Dorlyth didn't, either.

"Perhaps, but that's not where he went. Where, then? It had something to do with our conversation of the night before last—"

"How do you know?" Pelmen frowned.

"He got very quiet after that—evasive—smiling too broadly and all that. What was it? Bronwynn's appearance on the Rock of Tombs?"

"I doubt it. That tale barely held his attention," Pelmen said thoughtfully.

"The dragon then? Has he gone off to—"

"The pyramids," Pelmen interrupted. "That's it. He was concerned to find a way we could communicate quickly with Erri and his wife."

"But you told him plainly that wasn't what they were for!"

"I'm afraid he'd already made up his mind."

Dorlyth studied the wet ground. "And where is this third pyramid again?" He knew the answer. He was just double-checking facts.

"With Flayh."

Dorlyth raised his head to meet Pelmen's eyes, and said "You don't think he's fool enough to try to penetrate the High Fortress alone, do you?"

"He's your son," Pelmen said pointedly.

Dorlyth shook his head, then leaned back to gaze at the branches interlaced above them. "That's not very reassuring, you know."

"Shall we start tracking him?"

Dorlyth nodded curtly as Pelmen turned away. "Before you go sprouting wings on me, listen. Can you hunt from the sky and maintain the coverage of this glade?"

"You know I can't."

"Well, I didn't think you could, but you can never know anything about a shaper's powers that is certain. Suppose we search on horseback, like normal people? You can continue to cover the glade then?"

"If I work at it."

"Then let's go."

"Into the fog," Pelmen said glumly.

"As long as it's not so thick I can't see the ground, we'll do all right. Trust me, Pelmen," Dorlyth added with a trace of his old grin. "I'm a fair tracker myself, even if I can't fly."

Dorlyth woke Ferlyth and quickly explained the situation. "Do you need me to go with you?" his cousin asked.

"No, no. Just do your best to keep this crew together. Actually, I think you have the tougher job!" Dorlyth winked at Ferlyth, then beckoned to Pelmen. Moments later they were mounted and on the trail.

The two men shivered as they tracked. The mist crowded around them, robbing them of any sense of progress. Rosha's trail climbed out of the glade to the northeast, up a mild but steady slope. It was difficult to follow, but not impossible. It had been Dorlyth, after all, who had taught him how to hide his tracks, and no war horse could move through a freshly laid carpet of fallen leaves without disturbing it somewhat. Rosha was skillful, however, and both men were challenged. Dorlyth might even have enjoyed the morning had he been less concerned for his impulsive son's safety.

They talked a little at first. Dorlyth questioned Pelmen further about the nature of the pyramids, and the shaper related all he knew. Then Dorlyth asked about Rosha's chances of actually getting inside the High Fortress without being detected. Pelmen's answer dispelled any hopes.

"The castle's alive," he muttered. "Alive and malevolent."

"Then there's no way the boy could succeed?"

"None."

"Not even if the Power intended him to?" Dorlyth argued, raising a shaggy eyebrow.

Pelmen glanced over at him. "Perhaps there *is* a way, if that be the case." He looked askance at his friend, and asked, "You believe that's a possibility?"

Dorlyth snorted in response and urged his horse to move faster.

"I could fly," Pelmen suggested, but Dorlyth again refused the offer. Pelmen's cloak continued to cover the glade.

Neither man spoke for over an hour. Each was absorbed in private conversations with himself. This pursuit reminded Pelmen of his unsuccessful search for Serphimera. Despite his effort to blank them out, the anxieties flooded his consciousness again. All he could think about were his lady's beautiful emerald eyes.

Dorlyth thought only of his son. He imagined himself in Rosha's place, hungry for adventure, yet pursued by friends intent on preventing him. What would he do? Twice they lost the trail completely, only to pick it up again through Dorlyth's imaginative identification. "He's just like me, you know. I taught him all he knows."

Abruptly the trail grew clearer—entirely too clear, in Dorlyth's thinking. He looked across at Pelmen in dismay.

"He's decided he's lost us and picked up speed," the shaper suggested.

"It doesn't take that much longer to hide your tracks. And you can't make any speed through woods this dense anyway. It doesn't make sense."

"He's young. He's in a hurry. Come on." They spurred their mounts forward and raced along the clearly discernible trail, churning up an orange spume of leaf fragments behind them. The tiny pair of auburn and gold wings of a nearby butterfly went unnoticed in that splash of autumn color.

They broke from the woods together with a crash of brush. Pelmen screamed, "Stop!" and yanked back on his reins, but Dorlyth had seen it himself and already was reining in his mount. Piles of leaves skidded them forward, but both horses managed to stop just short of tumbling off the edge of the cliff.

They gazed over a precipice into a chasm two hundred feet deep. Across the yawning fissure they faced another cliff; on top of it, the forest continued on. "How could he jump that?" Dorlyth exclaimed.

"He didn't," Pelmen spat before his friend had finished. "We've been duped!" They wheeled their horses in alarm and would have plunged back into the forest. Instead they both gasped at the wall of fire that blocked their retreat. Violent spires of flame soared fifty feet into the air, stretching high above the bare upper branches of the oaks and walnuts.

"Mar-Yilot!" Pelmen barked. It was clearly the Autumn Lady's style.

"It took her a towering rage to build *this* blaze!" Dorlyth shouted, his face gone white with shock.

"She's an illusion mistress! Remember her ploy in the Downland's skirmish and ride!" They'd faced Mar-Yilot's fire ring together before and found that only part of the flames had been real. Finding the illusory blazes had taken skill and some risky gambles, but they'd succeeded in breaking out and leading their army to safety. Although he could smell smoke, Pelmen hadn't yet felt the heat. Perhaps this fire was all illusory, and the smoky scent a trick as well. Dorlyth had been right; Mar-Yilot couldn't generate a fire this big without feeling genuine wrath, and they had done nothing at all to harm her.

They angled for the outer edge of the flames, hoping to skirt them to freedom. But the fire sprinted before them, and now the furnacelike heat hit Pelmen in the face. They turned their mounts before it, racing the conflagration to the cliff. It beat them easily, and they turned their backs to it and rode wildly along the precipice, hoping to skirt the blaze at its other end. They failed. The arc closed, trapping them.

Dorlyth reined in, then leaned down to whisper soothingly to his terrified animal. Pelmen bolted on, unwilling to accept any fire as real until it scorched his face. Blistered, with Minaliss protesting vigorously, he turned away, and rode back to face his companion of so many victories.

Dorlyth's color had returned—or perhaps he'd just roasted his cheeks. He wore an enigmatic smile that Pelmen didn't like at all. The wizard refused to acknowledge it. "We've got to jump," Pelmen snapped, jerking his thumb toward the chasm.

"Not a chance. Our horses are weary from the morning's ride, and they're terrified. With reason," he added, glancing up at the roaring, red-orange wall.

"We've got to try! It's our only chance!"

"*My* only chance." Dorlyth smiled serenely. "You'll fly out."

"No!" Pelmen shouted. "We'll both go out on horseback! They can make it. I'll show you!" Pelmen hurriedly wrenched Minaliss around to face the fire, rode as close as the blaze would allow, then wheeled back toward the precipice and galloped for it. The horse responded eagerly, desperately fleeing the fire, but the brittle leaves provided little footing, and the animal jumped too soon. Pelmen left its back on the wing. Without the extra weight, Minaliss was able to get his forelegs onto the turf of that far cliff. Momentum carried the horse up onto the shelf, and it turned with a snort to look back across the chasm. Pelmen had swooped down to stand beside Dorlyth, a man once again. He struggled to look hopeful. "You see? You can make it!"

Dorlyth looked at the ground. "That Minaliss is a marvelous horse. Yet even *without* your weight, he barely made it. Mine never would—especially with me aboard its back. Although it may have to jump eventually. As I might." The old warrior eyed the edge.

"Don't talk like that! We'll get you out!"

"You'll keep trying as long as I let you," Dorlyth murmured. "But I won't let you try much longer. For me, the day is lost. It had to come. Inevitably it had to, though I'd never imagined this . . ."

"Stop it!" Pelmen said frantically. His face wore the panic of a healer who finds himself helpless.

"And don't feel guilty!" Dorlyth snarled. "My day would have come much sooner but for you! My only question is, why this? What's made the woman so angry?"

"You *know*, Dorlyth mod Karis," a soft yet savage woman's voice spat out. Dorlyth had his sword out, slicing toward the source of it, before she finished her sentence. The blade whistled through Mar-Yilot's wispy body, touching nothing but air.

"She's miles away," Pelmen muttered.

"One can always hope," Dorlyth answered.

"No. One *cannot* always hope, Dorlyth mod Karis. *You* cannot, any longer."

"Why him?" Pelmen raged. "Why not strike at me directly!"

"I'll get you eventually, Dragonsbane." She used his title mockingly. "*You've* robbed my Syth of hope."

"What?"

"But first I take your friend, for it was he who sprang the trap!"

"I don't know what you're talking about!" Pelmen roared.

"My lover stares at hell and you claim no knowledge?" Mar-Yilot screamed.

"None!"

"You lie! It was you who locked him in a spell of dread!"

"I've never laid a spell of dread!" Pelmen shouted.

"Pelmen, fly on," Dorlyth muttered earnestly.

"I'll *not* leave you! And I'll not let this witch go until—"

But Mar-Yilot was already gone. And the flames kept advancing, raising the temperature on the ledge to an intolerable level. "Fly on," Dorlyth urged. "Go now. Don't fret about why. I'm sure you'll unravel it eventually, and it's meaningless to me anymore. Forget the coverage of the glade—it's already broken, and that may be where she actually *is* at the moment.

Go find Rosha. Protect him, or help him, or whatever. Use your judgment. Don't stay and watch me die."

Pelmen fought to control both his rage at the woman and his terrible grief. "No!" he shouted. "I'm taking my altershape! Grab my legs!"

"A falcon can't lift a man," Dorlyth protested, but already the bird fluttered above him. He grabbed the yellow legs in resignation and waited as the falcon beat the air furiously. It was no good.

Pelmen stood beside him again, eyes wet. Dorlyth embraced him, pounded him on the back, and said, "Thanks for all the joys, old friend!" Then he hugged Pelmen again, fiercely, and growled in his ear, "Care for my boy." He released the wizard. "Now. Go on."

Pelmen's human eyes regarded Dorlyth quietly, still disbelieving that this could be happening, but forcing himself to face the truth of it. Then they were falcon eyes, wild and cold, and they were gone on a whisper of wind.

Dorlyth sighed and glanced around. He gazed challengingly at the advancing blaze, squared around to face it, and grasped his great sword firmly in both hands. "Come on then," he whispered.

The fire advanced toward him, blistering his face. He held a hand out before him, guarding his eyes as he peered through the flames. The ground beyond them was black and smoking, but was already free of fire. If he could only get through this blazing wall—

But it was no use. To run through it was suicide—and a painful suicide at that. Better to go over the edge. Abruptly it occurred to him that there was a chance . . . He rushed to the edge and peered over it.

The face of the cliff was as sheer as glass—or so it appeared at first glance. But Dorlyth was desperate now. The fire was already roasting his back, and he reasoned that the slightest handhold was preferable to burning or falling. Three feet below the lip of the edge he spied a small crevice. Enough to wedge his dagger into? Once in, would it hold his weight? He spent little time analyzing. He dropped to his knees, fetched out his dagger, and lay along the edge, reaching as far down as he could in hopes of planting the knife point. He nearly fell in the process, but managed to wedge it in. Would it hold him?

He heard an equine scream behind him as his horse, on fire now, plunged wildly over the cliff. There was no more time. He clung to the hilt of his dagger with one hand and lowered himself over the ledge with the other. Then he released the edge completely and clung with both hands to his dagger, bracing his feet and knees against the cliff as best he could.

Fire swept the cliff above him. He closed his eyes against it and bowed his head. His knuckles were scorched. His muscles knotted. It took forever for the leaves along the cliff to burn.

But at last the crackling above him stopped. Dorlyth tilted his head back to scan the edge and saw blackened weeds and curling smoke above him. He knew the ground would still be so hot it would burn his hand, but he could endure no longer. With the last of his strength he hauled himself back up onto the cliff, and collapsed there, rolling onto his back. Heat rose through his tunic, and he thought that all his efforts had been wasted. He was still going to die. Then his mind became as black as the scorched earth that surrounded him.

## CHAPTER SIX

# Climbing

BY EARLY afternoon Rosha had passed the last stand of bare, spindle-branched trees and was onto the plainlands of the Furrowmar. He had stopped looking over his shoulder, but his thoughts were still more behind him than before. The experience with the peasant woman plagued him. Why had he spoken so frankly to her? Why had he spoken at all? He never opened his thoughts to anyone! Even Bronwynn had to badger him for details about his feelings.

The certainty grew with every passing mile that magic had prompted that exchange, and the realization filled him with forboding. Of course, he *was* back in the Mar, and the woman could have been merely a local witcherwoman. But even that thought chilled him. If a miserable, hovel-dwelling herb gatherer could bend his will so effortlessly, what would he face within the fortress of the master shaper? "When you worry about the future," he quoted Dorlyth to himself, "you're prepared for neither it nor the present." He willed his doubts from his mind and concentrated on choosing the best route across the plain.

He was crossing the edge of his cousin Ferlyth's lands now, but would pass many miles east of his aristocratic relative's grand castle. Ferlyth's line of the family had been Jorls of the Furrowmar for centuries. As such, they owned vast holdings in this, the grain-growing heartland of the Mar. They had proved to be intelligent, benign rulers, and had built great loyalty among the peasants of the region. This had been a strong factor in keeping the jorldom in the family, for although the six jorldoms were theoretically hereditary, they were in fact subject largely to the results of war. In the aftermath of particularly bloody conflicts, vacant jorldoms had been distributed by the elected kings in the same capricious, politically motivated manner that the shurldoms were normally awarded. Dorlyth himself, for example, became Jorl of the Westmouth after his crucial victory over the invading Golden Throng. King Pahd had shown less wisdom in making his southern-dwelling cousin Janos the Jorl of the Nethermar region. The natural choice would have been the citylord of either of the two walled towns of the north. His flagrant nepotism had united those cities against him, and was one cause of this current conflict.

Janos had not helped the situation. He was an arrogant, free-spending Furrowman, who disdained everything about the lowlanders of the north—everything, that is, save their great wealth. His agents made sure he got the jorl's share out of every diamond mine in the region. Although he'd been only a lad when Janos was an aggressive teen, Rosha had known the Jorl of the Nethermar from childhood, and he'd learned early that Janos could not be trusted. The present king was older than his cousin, but even so, he'd allowed Janos to manipulate him. Rosha reflected that that wasn't a great surprise. Pahd had made a career of being manipulated by others.

"But by no one so much as by Flayh," Rosha muttered to himself, riding down a furrow between lines of dead stalks.

The corn had already been harvested. The brittle, yellow stalks leaned away from the westerly winds, waiting for either the sickle or the first snow to put them out of their misery. The chill in the air suggested it would probably be the snow.

Rosha felt no ill-will toward Pahd himself. In fact he rather liked the lazy, laughing king. But it was Pahd's laziness that had permitted Flayh to absorb so much political power. That, combined with Flayh's vile ambition and magical ability, made the powershaping merchant an awesome antagonist. Pahd had clearly failed his subjects. "Once Flayh has been defeated," Rosha muttered, "Pahd must be replaced."

But by whom? That was a matter Rosha had often considered. He would have scoffed at the suggestion if made by another, but in his secret fantasies it ever seemed the crown came finally to his own head. Were Rosha to be honest with himself, this whole adventure had been born out of those fond fantasies. They had begun to gnaw upon his mind as he sat in bored silence through interminable sessions in his wife's court. If he were but king of the Mar! *There* would be a match for his lovely little queen!

Whenever he caught himself in this line of thought he had to laugh at his own foolishness. True, he was a jorl's son, as well as a bear's-bane and an acknowledged hero. But he was hardly kingly material. Besides, there was still Flayh to contend with—and Pahd and Lord Janos, whose lands he would soon be entering. If he didn't start concentrating on the present instead of plotting his triumphant rise to the throne, he might never live to see the following dawn!

The lands of Janos bordered the family estates of the Pahd mod Pahd-el. Together they ringed the southern rim of the High Plateau of Ngandib. They were divided by the river, which ran past the western edge of the plateau on its way northward to the coast. Most visitors northbound for the High City would take the road around to the eastern face of the plateau and up the Down Road which climbed the sheer cliffs there. Rosha intended to cross the river at the Carlog Bridge, but then to leave the road and follow the riverline northward to the plateau's backside. He hoped his daring approach would serve him well. Surely the absentee Jorl of the Nethermar would not expect a solitary enemy to come riding through his property.

Besides, it would be nightfall before Rosha reached the bridge. The darkness would cover him.

He reached the bridge a few minutes after dusk. There was no traffic, but he waited until the sun was wholly gone, just in case. Then he rode quickly across it. Without hesitation, he turned his horse off the road and started up the Riverline. No one stopped him. He saw no villages, nor even a single dwelling standing alone. By midnight, he'd reached his destination. There he dismounted and bade good night to his weary horse. He ate a good meal, then wrapped himself in a layer of furs and lay down. Despite the long day's ride, it was difficult to sleep. Lying on his back, he gazed upward along the route he planned to take in the morning. Sleep took him at last, and he dreamed.

When he was seven, Rosha had been brought to a feast at what was now Janos Castle. The fortress backed up against the base of the High Plateau less than a mile from this spot. There was a vast green field before the castle's gates, a lovely place for the children to romp and play. Rosha remembered throwing himself down its gentle slopes, laughing gleefully as he rolled. At the end of one of his rolls, as he'd giggled in the grass, waiting for the dizziness to pass, he'd suddenly spied a huge snake climbing up the cliff face toward the plateau. Startled, he'd raced to find Dorlyth and reported it. It took a moment for Dorlyth to identify the object his son described, but he did at last and he named it. Rosha remembered grimly how the other warriors at that rough oaken table had laughed at him. But Dorlyth hadn't. Instead, he'd looked his young son in the eye and told him a tale of the ancients. Once, long before the huge reservoir was carved into the plateau above, the people living upon the high plain had been surrounded by enemies. They had at last run out of water—a desperate circumstance, and all the more frustrating because they could watch the mighty river flowing by the plateau's western base on its way to the Nethermar and the North Coast. They would have surrendered then, but for the urging of a local powershaper, who had enlisted the aid of every potter in Ngandib.

Rosha could still recall his father's words of long ago: "Together they made a tube of clay, full seven-hundred feet in length, and baked it in the burning summer sun. Then, by magic, that great pipe rose, then descended over the plateau's western edge, down, down, until its bottom touched the river and went into it. Then, as you sometimes suck fruit punch through a piece of straw, the shaper sucked up the water until it flowed into buckets on the top of the cliff, and the land and people were saved! That great, baked-clay straw—*that* is what you see climbing the cliff face. Of course, a later shaper carved the reservoir, and the springtime rains have long since come and filled it up so it's never wholly dry. Still, one can never tell, and so the clay pipe remains. When you're a warrior, son, remember. To kill a man you cut the jugular—to kill a castle, cut its water."

Rosha had left the table that day oblivious to the condescending smiles of the other adults and had returned to stand in the midst of the field. He no longer ran and rolled—instead he'd stood silently, regarding that distant pipeline with awe.

Morning came, and Rosha woke to survey the task before him. No direct sunlight reached this place, nor would any until the noontime sun peaked over the cliff high overhead. He was glad of that. By the time the sunlight bathed him, he hoped to be well on his way to his goal. It was a frosty morning, and the shadows made it colder. Nevertheless, he peeled off layers of clothing. His bare arms and shoulders quickly grew gooseflesh, and his teeth chattered together, but he ignored his discomfort. A hundred feet up, when he'd worked up a sweat, this chill would seem a pleasant memory.

He sorted out those things he needed to take from those he could leave behind. The necessities he settled upon were his great sword, tied into its scabbard and slung over his back, a flask of water, his lunch, a dagger, a few gold coins tied in a pouch and hung from his belt, his trousers, rolled and tied at the knee, and his mail shirt—a gift from his father when he'd first ridden off to war. The rest of his possessions he wrapped in a bundle and stuffed behind the bottommost joint of the pipe. He stripped his horse and set it free. There was good grazing round about and water nearby, so the beast would be cared for if he didn't return. Indeed, Rosha did not expect to be returning—not this way, at least. He wondered, sighting up the tube, if he really could make it to the top. He doubted he could come back down. But then, how *would* he get down? He shoved the thought out of his mind. One step at a time! He consumed a quick but heavy breakfast, and turned to his task.

It was clear now that Dorlyth's story had been embellished

by time. Rosha had been to the technologically advanced cities of Chaomonous and Lamath. He'd seen a pump before, though he really didn't know how one worked. There had obviously been a pump here once, although it was gone now. Rosha was a bit disappointed. The sucking ability of the ancient power-shaper had made a much more romantic story. He was also puzzled, and a little of his awe returned when he realized he'd never before heard of a pump that could raise water such an enormous height. But there was no more time for thinking. It was time to climb. The tube had been made of ceramic cylinders each two feet long, jointed with seals of baked clay. It looked as if it would be easy to climb the joints, and he wondered why no one had tried it before. He took a last glance around him, wrapped his arms around the pipe, and started shinnying up.

There was an island in the Border Straits that had long served as a haven for pirates. The pirates were gone now—perhaps because they'd followed the rest of the world's brigands to join Admon Faye in the High Fortress. For whatever reason, the island and its primitive dwellings were abandoned—or had been, until Erri arrived.

There was much confusion the first few days, as Erri's initiates struggled to accommodate themselves to their new environment. Few of those who'd followed him had ever developed survival skills. Fewer still knew anything about the sea. Yet events had cast them adrift upon an uncertain future, and they had to learn to fend for themselves. Many of them suffered severe depression. Just days before, they'd been the lords of Lamath. Some began to whisper that they wished they'd stayed behind. It was inevitable that the whisperings would turn into mutterings, then to open declarations of dissatisfaction. Those closest to Erri worried and wrung their hands. Yet the prophet himself didn't seem disturbed at all, not did he voice any personal bitterness at his abrupt fall from power. In fact, he appeared to be smiling more than usual. It was hard to gauge his mood. He said little to anyone besides the Power.

He spent his days standing upon a huge boulder that towered over the seething sea. Sometimes he looked down, watching the waves hit the rocks with a rhythmical roar. But most of the time he studied the southern horizon. At last he saw the sail he'd been expecting and, while it was still a half hour distant, he began to summon the brothers to gather.

When the new ship anchored in the small cove beside the two vessels that had brought the rest of them to this island, there was already a large crowd waiting on the beach. Erri stood barefooted in the surf, watching as the rowboats ploughed the waves toward him. He waded out to meet the first one and helped guide it up onto the sand. Several of its occupants leaped out to help him. The man in the bow did not. Instead he clutched the side of the boat with one hand and his stomach with the other. His gown was the sky blue color of that of all initiates, but his face was a sickly green. He rolled his eyes to gaze up into Erri's and murmured, "Prophet. This wasn't how I'd planned to greet you."

Erri laid a hand on the man's shoulder. "Come on, Naquin, stand up. You don't have any disease that can't be cured by solid ground."

The former High Priest of the Unified Dragonfaith stepped out of the boat with Erri's assistance and almost collapsed into the foam. The prophet caught him and led him up onto the dry sand. There he helped Naquin sit and sat beside him.

Naquin looked around unsteadily, then felt the land on either side of him and asked with pale, trembling lips, "Are we still moving?"

"Just relax a moment." Erri smiled. "You'll soon feel better."

"Nothing in the Temple of the Dragon ever prepared me for *that*," Naquin sighed.

"I daresay you've experienced quite a lot in the last few months that your father and his advisors never prepared you for."

"Oh, yes." Naquin nodded. Erri could tell the man was feeling better already by the hint of animation in his voice. "Quite a lot. On the other hand, I found politics in Queen Bronwynn's court not much different from those in Lamath."

"How was Bronwynn when you left her?" Erri asked with intense concern.

"Distracted," Naquin sighed. "Terribly distracted over Rosha's absence. And distracted, too, over some strange new experiences . . ."

"What kind of experiences?"

"Magical, I'm afraid." Naquin sniffed, evidencing his disapproval. Erri nodded knowingly. He seemed unsurprised. "Well, doesn't that bother you?" Naquin asked.

"Should it?"

"Well, I hardly believe the Power would use powershaping to accomplish Its purpose, do you?" Naquin had once been the premier priest of the Dragonfaith, despite being a nonbeliever. Erri had given him a faith to believe in and a responsibility for sharing it. As sometimes happened with new believers, the pupil was more dogmatic than his teacher.

"I don't know," Erri said flatly.

"You don't know!" Naquin was shocked.

That didn't appear to bother the Prophet. Not much did, these days. "No. I thought I knew, until very recently. But these past few days I've had the luxury of time for thinking and I've been using it. And I wonder. Just how much do I really *know* about this Power? It seems that every time I'm certain I know something, the ground shifts under my feet, and I discover something new that just raises more questions." Erri grinned brightly at his frowning follower. "Who knows *what* the Power might use to accomplish Its purposes? Or *whom*?"

Naquin didn't return the smile. He'd been in Chaomonous—and on his own—for some months, acting as the spiritual leader to those initiates Erri had sent with him. He'd buried a few of those charges, committing them into the Power's keeping. He'd led a number of Chaons to don the sky blue cassock, and some of those had accompanied him here. Naquin had a stake in this new belief men termed the skyfaith, and it made him uncomfortable to hear his leader talking this way—especially in front of the newer initiates. "If that were true," he asked quietly, "how could we be certain that the Power can be depended upon?"

"Oh, I never have any question about the Power's hold on me, or about the task I've been assigned. That much is clear and remains so. I'm just never certain who else is on the same side. But that doesn't matter, anyway. It doesn't keep me from doing what I must. I see your work goes well." Erri beamed at the new arrivals on the beach. The rowboats had already dropped off thirty and were headed back to the ship for more.

Naquin accepted this praise with a tight-lipped smile and a slight nod. Then his frown returned. "But what about Lamath?" he asked gravely. "Is all hope lost?"

"Lost?" Erri exclaimed. "Oh my, no. If anything, it's been found again."

"Then steps are being taken toward your resumption of governmental control?"

"No, no. At least I hope not. *I've* not taken any. No, nothing kills faith so effectively as making it part of politics. You ought to know that yourself, with your past experience."

"Well, I—"

"Governing Lamath distracted me from my real assignment. Personally, I wouldn't mind the royal family maintaining their dynasty for another hundred years, but for the fact that they've endorsed this renewed Dragonfaith business. And that wouldn't bother me so much if they were honest. But it's not a faith at all. It's politics and power. And it's all being done at the direction of this man Flayh. I may not always know who works beside me, or how the Power moves, but I *do* know this man Flayh is against all that we've tried to accomplish."

"Because he's a powershaper," Naquin snarled.

"No. Because he wants to be all-powerful."

Naquin nodded. "Then perhaps we should return to Chaomonous and join ourselves to the queen's army."

Erri looked away. He slid his hands backward through the sand and leaned back to gaze at the cloudy sky. He seemed to weigh his words carefully before he spoke. "I think not."

"But if this Flayh is our enemy—"

"He's the Power's enemy."

"Then we must work to defeat him!"

"By performing our appointed tasks." Erri looked back at Naquin, his face solemn. "Do you expect to destroy Flayh and his thugs and his dogs with an army of Chaons? The thugs, maybe. But not the shaper. And even if successful, how would the Golden Throng knit the three lands back together into one? By force of arms? No. Perhaps Bronwynn's army will be part of the Power's total plan. I don't know. I do know that if Bronwynn departs Chaomonous prematurely, she'll leave a vulnerable kingdom behind her. These magical powers she's experiencing are not without purpose. When you get back to Chaomonous, you must urge her to wait."

"Then we're going back?" Naquin frowned. "I had thought . . ."

"We would advance on Lamath like conquering heroes?"

Erri smiled. Then he stood up and turned to face the large gathering of blue-robed believers. Many conversations died as all eyes turned to look at him. He waited for the last of the rowboats to beach, then he began:

"Brothers. We've gathered here just to be together briefly and to talk and encourage one another, to draw strength from each other. Soon we'll go back to our appointed tasks. It won't be easy for any of us. But it *will* be good.

"Lamath is no longer under our rule. Now we can go out freely and mingle with the people, as we should have been doing all along. We're few, but we're enough. We've all been together in the capital. It's time we divided and went our own ways, to find those who need what we offer.

"Naquin, lead your people back to Chaomonous. But don't stay in the city. The queen doesn't need your guidance; she has her own. The people of Chaomonous are educated skeptics, but it's an age of uncertainty. Naquin, your strength is an unshakable certainty in your faith. That's a security the Chaons need.

"Then there's Ngandib-Mar. Tahli-Damen?" Erri called, and the blind man, trembling, stood up. "Turn around, my friend." The former merchant obeyed, and many of those seated on the beach behind him gasped at the sight of those empty, pale blue eyes. "This man lost his sight to powershaping. But he says he sees life more clearly now than he ever did before. He'll return to the land of magic, to the realm of this evil Flayh himself. Who will be his eyes? Who will walk beside him?" Erri paused then, searching the crowd. He saw a hand slip furtively into the air and smiled knowingly. "Good. That's settled then. As for the rest of us, it's time we returned to Lamath. Not as a group, however. Rather, we go in teams of two or three. Someone will need to go with me—"

"I'll go!" said an enthusiastic young man in the front of the crowd, bounding to his feet.

Erri's forehead wrinkled slightly. "Strahn? *You* want to travel with me?"

"I do indeed, sir." Strahn nodded, blushing now at his own forwardness.

"You think you can handle it?" Erri asked, and the young man nodded energetically. The real question, the prophet thought to himself, was whether he could handle traveling with Strahn.

He smiled warmly, however, and announced, "Very well then. Strahn it will be. As for the rest of you, find partners. Get well acquainted. Tomorrow morning we'll all be on our way." He was finished. He waved his hand in a gesture of dismissal.

"Tomorrow?" Naquin said a bit peevishly. "Some of us just got here!"

Erri smiled at the man and reached out to pat his shoulder apologetically. "I know. I wish there was more time. But there's not. You've got to get back to warn Bronwynn. Don't expect her to listen to you," Erri added, grinning brightly. "Bronwynn doesn't listen to anybody much. But you just be faithful to your task, and encourage her to pay heed to the problems in her own land before trying to solve problems elsewhere. The Power will use you."

Naquin looked mournfully out at his ship, anchored in the tiny harbor. "I don't relish getting back on that thing again."

"By all means, sleep on dry land tonight," Erri urged. "You look weak. Have you eaten lately?"

"Oh, I've *eaten* all right." Naquin nodded, rolling his eyes.

Erri understood. "Strahn?" he called.

"Right here, sir!" Strahn barked, causing the prophet to jump. Erri hadn't realized the young initiate was hovering right behind him.

"Ah, take Naquin and find him some food, then get him a good place to rest for the night."

"Yes, sir. Anything else?" Strahn was a handsome boy with very bright, even teeth. These gleamed as he beamed his smile at Erri, causing the prophet to sigh.

"Not at the moment," he mumbled, and Strahn marched Naquin off toward the makeshift kitchen.

Now Erri was able to turn to Tahli-Damen, who stood several feet away, waiting uncertainly. Ten feet beyond him stood the young merchant woman who had arrived in Lamath the night the dogs came in. Erri beckoned her over and asked, "Does he know you're here?"

Wayleeth shook her head.

"Do I know who's here?" Tahli-Damen asked suspiciously. He didn't look happy at all.

"I requested a volunteer to travel with you, Tahli-Damen. This is that volunteer." Erri looked at the woman. "Speak to him."

Wayleeth cleared her throat. "Hello."

"Wayleeth!" Tahli-Damen exploded, and several nearby conversations stopped as bluefaithers turned to watch. "Wayleeth, did you follow me here?"

"If she did," Erri interjected, "it's because the Power prompted her to come."

"No, it isn't!" Tahli-Damen roared. "It's because she feels sorry for me! She's afraid I'll get hurt! She can't let me out of her sight!"

"All of which seem good qualifications for the woman to serve as your eyes."

"She can't be my partner!" Tahli-Damen thundered. "She's my wife!"

"And just what do you think a wife is to be!" Erri thundered back. Then he glanced around at all the staring eyes and waved them away. Bluefaithers all around made a great show of returning to their conversations. "Now listen to me, Tahli-Damen. I've talked with Wayleeth myself at length. She is as committed to this task as you are. Will you deny her the opportunity to perform it simply because the two of you happen to be married?" The prophet glanced at the sky, then back at Tahli-Damen's scowling face. "It's dusk. The two of you need to talk. Go find a quiet spot and do that. The ship leaves for Lamath tomorrow morning, and Strahn and myself will walk with you to Dragonsgate. Go now."

Tahli-Damen waited until Wayleeth took his arm and led him away. Then Erri tilted his head back and spoke to the darkening sky: "Exactly what, in my twenty some years of life at sea, qualified me to be a marriage counselor?" Then he shook his head and walked away, muttering under his breath "Strahn . . ."

His arms no longer ached. They tingled now, as if asleep. Yet that was no relief, for along with the dulling of the pain came a heaviness that he was certain could not have been worse had boulders been manacled to his wrists. His mail shirt had become a portable oven as sweat coursed down his chest and back, drenching his belt. His feet, too, seemed weighted with lead. There were times when he could do nothing but cling to the topless pipeline and gasp for breath.

His emotional state ranged from elation to despair—sometimes swinging from one extreme to the other in a moment. Occasionally, as he looked downward to find footing on a ceramic joint, he would catch a glimpse of the land below. He no longer regarded it as just 'the ground.' He had climbed high enough to stretch the horizon out for miles. Sometimes he rejoiced because this was his land; he loved it and gloried in looking down on it from on high. Moments later he might look down in terror, certain he couldn't make it to the top, but just as certain that to try to climb down would prove suicidal. Those were the times when he gripped the round pipe and hugged it close, laying his cheek against its cool surface and fighting the childish urge to weep. He longed for the ordeal to be resolved some way, any way. His climb was one of those feats sometimes undertaken as a means to an end which come to demand such effort that the original purpose is eclipsed. After the second hour, Rosha thought little of Flayh anymore, of how he could enter the High Fortress, or of the pyramid he intended to steal. He thought instead of his life and wondered if this day would be his last. He thought, too, of his wife and sorrowed for her, imagining her mourning when she heard of his death. He thought of Pelmen and muttered a fervent prayer to the Power. He made his appeal in the form of a contract—if the Power would get him safely off this endless water pipe, he would once again don the sky blue robe and become a true initiate. He thought of a host of other things he'd not considered in years. That led him to reflect on things he'd always intended to do. He thought a lot about thinking itself. He wished he could block out all his thoughts and concentrate solely on climbing. But each time he tried, he became so aware of the heaviness in his arms and legs and the knotted muscles in the back of his neck that he welcomed back the distraction of his memories. And still the pipe went up.

There were several blessed interruptions. These helped him solve the riddle of how this ancient pipe had once lifted the water so high. There was not one pump, but several, and several pumping stations. These were located in small caverns chiseled out of the cliff face. The water was relayed upward from one cavern to the next—or had been. The pumps were decayed beyond all usefulness, and the small pools within the caverns were brackish. How long had it been since the water flowed through this system? Centuries, by the look of things. Did anyone alive even know these pumps existed? His father surely didn't. But they were here, and he was grateful. Each time he reached a cavern, he crawled inside its mouth and sat, dangling his legs over the edge, gazing out to the distant west while he rested his shoulders and arms.

How far up had he climbed? He wondered as he crawled into yet another pumping cavern. How much further to go? Surely it couldn't be much. But he'd thought *that* while sitting in the mouth of the last cavern, which seemed now to be miles below. It was midafternoon, and he longed for sleep, but this cave, like the rest, was full of water. There was no place to stretch out. He dared not nap on this narrow ledge. If he dropped off to sleep here, he could very well slip to his death. Yet even as he reminded himself of the danger, he was starting to doze. He woke with a jerk and immediately forced himself back out of the cavern and onto the pipe. He tried looking up to see the top, but the sun was now above him, and he couldn't stand the glare. "Doesn't matter anyway," he grunted. All that mattered was for him to keep on climbing until there was no more pipe to climb.

Suddenly that happened. But he felt no elation. Despair came instead. For he looked into yet another cavern—larger than the others, much larger—yet still a water-filled cavern. And the pipeline had ended. He craned his head, shielding his eyes against the sun with one hand as he gripped the pipe with the other. He couldn't be sure; it appeared that the top of the cliff was only another fifteen feet above his head. But he couldn't get to it!

He crawled into the mouth of this last cavern. Once again he sat dangling his feet, but this time he faced the water. What was he going to do? He tilted his head back and studied the cliff face above him once again. It was smooth. There wasn't a handhold in sight, even if he could have gotten up to it. He held off the panic as long as he could, but it finally broke through and he had to grip the ledge with both hands to keep from tumbling backward in shock. He was trapped!

The sun touched the western horizon before Rosha finally stopped despairing and started thinking. Once he did, it didn't take him long to reason out a solution to his dilemma.

There was no relay pump in this cavern. More important, there was no sign that there ever had been. That was curious.

Why would it have been removed? Why would another pump be needed this close to the top of the plateau? Another thing, the water here was relatively clear, not brackish like that in the dark pools he'd passed on his way up. Rainwater? Perhaps, but the overhang was too severe to allow any but the most slanting rains to penetrate the cavern. Besides, rain came mostly from the sea to the east, not from the west. It wasn't rain-water—at least not rain that had blown into the cavern. He was convinced, finally, that this pool was connected underwater to the main reservoir. He didn't need to climb any higher. He needed to swim down and under the wall instead.

Or so he hoped. It seemed logical enough. Certainly it was worth a try. But what would he find under this chilly water? A connecting tunnel too narrow for a man to pass through? Or perhaps an ancient grill put in place to prevent anyone from doing just what he was attempting? Rosha shrugged. He'd done far too much thinking for one day. Better just try it.

First he ate the rest of his food. He knew it wasn't wise to swim right after eating, but he was famished. He chewed well, concentrating on clearing his mind, then scooped up a handful of water to wash down his meal. Next he made a quick check to insure that everything he'd brought with him was securely tied to him. He took a deep breath and dove in.

He didn't fight his way down. He didn't need to—his mail shirt and heavy sword carried him toward the bottom. He kept his eyes open, struggling to see through the ink. He wished it was noon instead of dusk. The high sun shining down on the reservoir might have made the tunnel visible—if there *was* a tunnel. He had to go by feel.

His feet at last touched rock—a gently sloping wall—and he crouched against that slime-covered granite and pushed off toward the far side. His lungs began to burn. He swam with heightened urgency. He couldn't tell how far he'd gone. His chest pleaded for air, and he decided to go up for a breath and try again later. He didn't make it. His head bumped rock before it broke the surface. He was already in the channel, and he had no idea how long it was. A frantic desperation surpassing anything he'd felt on his long climb seized him as he propelled himself forward. He swam in terror, the great sword around his neck weighing upon him like an anchor, his mail shirt feeling like a full suit of armor. He swam as far as he could, closing his eyes against the sting in his lungs, fearing every moment that he'd crash against another wall and be lost. His reserves of strength had been depleted by the long day's climb. He could go no further. He fought his way up, lashing at the water, angry at it for obstructing him, angry at himself for his foolishness, angry at death for taking him so casually—

Then he was out. His head broke the surface of the reservoir, and he sucked in the twilight sky. His gasps for air substituted for a victory shout. He had made it to the top! He would not permit the great distance that still separated him from his goal to intrude into his wheezing of celebration. He was alive, and for the moment that was all that mattered.

He had to get out of the water—his shirt would pull him back under if he didn't. He glanced around. While moments before he had been wishing it was noontime, he was suddenly glad it was dusk. There were sentries positioned around the lake. At least, he thought they were sentries—obviously, they weren't taking their responsibilities seriously. Evidently they were set not to guard the lake but the plateau, for no head was turned toward the water. All eyes were fixed either on the purple sunset or on the faces of their lovers. Since there seemed little chance of invasion up the sheer walls of the cliff, sentry duty around the rim provided a wonderful opportunity for intimate trysts.

Rosha made his way toward the nearest shore, carefully keeping his head down. Soon his feet touched the bottom, and he rested for a moment, neck-deep in the water. He wondered why these guards had been posted at all—to watch the skies for flying powershapers? It didn't matter. What was important was for him to reach the fortress that loomed over the lake at least a mile away. It wouldn't do for him to clamber up out of the water behind some passionate couple. Rosha decided to make his way to the rear of the High Fortress through the water. He started walking.

The High Fortress was impregnable. He knew that. Every lad in the Mar knew that before the age of ten. Then again, every Mari boy also knew that there was no way onto the High Plateau save by the Down Road. Rosha had proved today that that was a myth. Could the castle's invincibility be a myth as well? The fortress stood atop a rock ridge that jutted six hundred feet above the level of the lake. From this angle, he thought he could make out ledges and projections that made scaling it a possibility. Perhaps he could climb to the top of the ridge, then scale the back wall. Obviously the guards did not fear an approach from the lake. Could it be that the rear of the castle was as poorly guarded? He calculated the possibilities as he slogged the last hundred feet. The closer he got, the more possible the task appeared.

It was night when he reached the rock wall. He was weary beyond all belief. But he couldn't rest here. He had to climb at least part of the way. He started up. Thirty feet above the level of the lake he found a crevice in the granite and beamed with excitement. It looked big enough—he shoved himself into it, and found to his great relief that it *was* large enough to hold him securely. In moments he was lost in delightful sleep, safe from prying eyes.

But it wasn't eyes that had been watching him, ever since his head broke the surface of the reservoir. The living fortress had noted his appearance, and had been reporting his progress to its master ever since.

—He is sleeping in a crevice at the base of this fortress, it told the powershaper.

Flayh chuckled and said, "Don't disturb him. I'm certain he needs his rest."

## CHAPTER SEVEN

# Silent Entry

A CHANGE had come. Pelmen slipped through the nearly deserted streets of Ngandib and considered it.

He had, at long last, wholly committed himself to the battle. Not that he'd shirked his responsibilities before—he had just been bound by his friendships to limited courses of action. But one by one, his friends had been separated from him. Serphimera was missing; Rosha was missing; Erri was in hiding; Bronwynn was under pressure from a rival sorcerer well out of his reach; and Dorlyth was lost to him forever. These things had created in Pelmen both a terrible loneliness and an exhilarating fury.

Pelmen did not anger easily; he was far too powerful to permit himself that luxury. But when his wrath was finally kindled, a new aspect of Pelmen's personality emerged. It was so fearsome even to himself that he'd spent a lifetime trying to bury it. When his rage came, it was not with heat and passion—and their consequent foolishness. Rather it was cold, critically calculating—cunning. Now Pelmen was enraged. And in Flayh he had finally found a foe who demanded he unleash his every resource.

How to get at the man! He gazed up at the bleak towers of the fortress, his eyes blazing. He glanced around at what had been a cheerful, bustling city and silently railed at Flayh for what he'd done to its people. That shaper's mean spirit dominated these Maris as totally as his frowning fortress dominated their plateau, and Pelmen was struck once again by how quickly people yielded control of their lives. His deepening bitterness reflected itself in his hard expression. Was the High Fortress watching him? He wasn't close enough yet to hear its conversation.

Was Rosha inside? Pelmen scolded himself for wasting a day searching the roads by air. If he'd gotten to the top of the Down Road in time he could have stopped the young warrior on his way up! When he'd finally had the good sense to fly here to the city, it was evidently too late. He'd watched the same sordid scene repeated again and again at the top of the road, as Admon Faye's so-called guards had seized and abused one upward-bound traveler after another. But Rosha had never appeared. Pelmen had been forced to conclude that Rosha had already been subdued and arrested by the time he'd arrived.

Was he wrong? Had Rosha never intended to penetrate this place and steal the third pyramid? Was he even now bound for some other place? Chaomonous, perhaps, to aid his bride against the sinister Terril? Pelmen fervently hoped that might be the case, but it didn't change his resolve. He was going to get inside this castle and he was going to do it without the aid of magic. He was going in the simplest, the most inobtrusive way, the way so many terrified Mari citizens had gone in before him. He was about to be arrested.

"Look, mates," a voice behind him said, slimy with cruelty and malice. "Someone's paid us a call." Rough hands seized him under the arms while others smacked the sides of his head, and his legs were booted out from under him. One thug held him up by grabbing a handful of his hair; as he struggled to regain his feet, fists pummelled his stomach and groin. Moments later he disappeared into the black maw of the High Fortress of Ngandib. It all went according to plan.

He'd gambled that Flayh took little interest in the private entertainments of his bodyguards. This policy of arrest and abuse of local citizens was certainly unrelated to any security need. Pelmen knew the High Fortress was alive. In the event of attack it would simply notify its master, and Flayh would deal with the problem magically. Pelmen really didn't know why Flayh kept this garrison of thugs and bullies around—unless it might be that he preferred having such a dangerous collection of men under his thumb rather than out in the woods, possibly conspiring against him. In any case, no one seemed to notice as the three cutthroats who had abducted Pelmen dragged him down into a dark corner of the fortress and prepared to beat him.

He used no magic, save that sleight-of-hand variety he'd learned in his years onstage. Powershaping would attract the attention of the castle, and that was the last thing he wanted. Even so, the three thugs thought themselves bewitched as this cowering peasant turned suddenly into a savage. Pelmen slipped a dagger out of one man's belt and back in between two of his ribs. There was a single grunt and gush of blood, but by the time the other two realized its source, their own throats had been slashed open. Pelmen left them behind, gasping and wrestling upon a suddenly sticky floor. Killing did not come easily for him, but he always did what was demanded. He doubted if the world would miss this trio.

He did not sneak through the hallways. Nothing would have attracted attention to him so quickly. Instead he shuffled along, looking like a bored slave. No one stopped him. He drew no stares. He didn't fear being identified by men.

But what about the fortress? Was it watching him? Despite the care he'd taken not to use his power, could the fortress somehow sense Pelmen's exceptional abilities? As he moved through the corridors, he turned his ears to hear the creaks and pops in the masonry and woodwork that formed the words of castle-speech. Occasionally he lightly touched the walls, checking for condensation that might indicate the High Fortress was engaged in some difficult act of shaping of its own. He strained to smell meaningful scents, monitored the temperature of the air on his cheeks, pressed all his senses to analyze his surroundings while maintaining an expression of careless incompetence. Still, the castle said nothing. That greatly disturbed him. He'd expected to hear a steady stream of invective from the fortress, since any act of shaping was excruciating to a living castle. He knew that made no difference to Flayh and was certain that the small sorcerer was up in his tower, just as busy as ever. Why wasn't the castle screaming?

Since he was already in the upper dungeon, he explored it quickly. It was empty. This did not surprise him, knowing the mentality of slavers. Why keep prisoners? It was too much bother to feed them and watch over them. It was much simpler either to enslave them or kill them. Of this Pelmen was certain—the slave pit of this castle would be filled to capacity.

Was that where Rosha was? No. A man like Rosha was far too dangerous to enslave. He would be killed outright. Pelmen gritted his teeth and pressed on, determined to tour the upper levels.

He found the stairway to the royal tower unguarded. Where were these slavers? He'd expected to encounter at least a few along the way! Of course, this lapse in security was understandable in one sense. Why should anyone want to assassinate a king who already slept like the dead? Pelmen shuffled to King Pahd's door, listened for a moment, then stepped inside. The room was empty, except for Pahd, and the king never saw him. As usual Pahd mod Pahd-el was fast asleep.

Sleep was Pahd's great passion. He preferred it to eating, to drinking, or to lovemaking. He could sleep in any position and through any event. He'd also developed the feigning of sleep into a high art, to discourage those fools who tried to pry him from his bed. Only one thing had consistently been able to lure him from the sack, and that was a promise of challenging swordplay. Pelmen wondered if even that could excite him now. The king slept in self-defense to avoid having to face the tragedy his laziness had brought upon his nation and his family. Oh, he would surely blame it on his mother—but it was Pahd's fault.

Pelmen had learned the story from Ferlyth. Pahd's mother, Chogi lan Pahd-el, had become infatuated with Flayh and had encouraged her son to invite him into the High Fortress. The lazy king had agreed—it was easier than arguing—but within days, they both had realized their mistake. Flayh had taken the castle over.

No one had protested this but Sarie, Pahd's wife. Pelmen remembered the woman as a slovenly, giggling party giver who had encouraged Pahd's laziness primarily just to frustrate her mother-in-law. It was hard to imagine her standing up to Flayh, but evidently she had done so—and immediately thereafter had contracted a violent illness. Apparently she'd been sick ever since. Ferlyth had heard it was Flayh's chief hold over Pahd; despite his laziness and self-indulgence, it was well known that Pahd worshipped his little wife.

So now he slept, Pelmen thought, to block out her illness and his own guilt. The king stirred, and Pelmen stepped back to the door. Pahd raised up on one arm, looked blearily at Pelmen and whispered, "Sarie?" Then the drug of sleep reclaimed him, and he settled back into his pillows, a satisfied smile curling across his lips.

Pelmen closed the door quietly, speculating sadly on what might have been if Dorlyth had consented to rule this nation.

Now where? he wondered to himself. He sought to stifle it, but it came anyway—a sudden pang of despair. Besides hunting for Rosha, he had entered this castle with the hope that it might lead him somehow to Serphimera. He was running out of places to look.

The same servants who had denied her entry only days before now welcomed her with smiles. Serphimera nodded and smiled back, a bit uncertain as to how she was to behave. Resentment, scorn, abuse—these responses she had great experience in handling. Warmth and friendliness were new to her.

It had been an arduous walk from the Great South Fir to this, the northern tip of Ngandib-Mar. It had taken weeks, for when she'd set out initially she'd had no idea of where she was bound. Harder to bear than the travel itself had been her guilt at abandoning Pelmen so abruptly. But how could she have done otherwise? The Power's requirements had been crystal clear, yet Pelmen had refused to heed them! She had been needed here, he had been needed elsewhere, but each time she'd tried to point that out, he'd rejected her words, protesting that above all else they needed to stay together. She had realized finally that he would never willingly yield to their separation and she'd departed, knowing only that she must travel northward. Had he searched for her? She'd seen no sign of it. She hoped he had, but realized he might have decided she was more trouble than she was worth. She couldn't help it. She'd had to come.

Of course, the people of Sythia Isle hadn't understood that when she'd arrived. She'd been stared at, laughed at, and insulted. She'd had to beg to be allowed to visit their stricken lord, and then was only permitted to do so under heavy guard. When she'd reached out to touch him, one warrior nearly beheaded her, but stopped in midstroke when Syth suddenly sat up in bed. It had been no surprise to Serphimera. That was the reason she'd come.

"Is he awake?" she asked the guard outside Syth's door.

"I am!" Lord Syth called from within the room, and Serphimera nodded at the warrior and stepped inside.

"You're looking well this morning," she murmured.

"I've never felt better!" Syth responded, and he bounded out of bed to prove it to her. "You see? No ill-effects! And all because of you!"

"Oh, no," Serphimera demurred, shaking her head. "I really had very little to do with it."

"Yes, yes, I know, it was all the Power, not you. I've heard the speech. But are you going to stand there and deny that you made any personal sacrifices to get in here to heal me? Please don't, Serphimera. I don't like to call my friends liars."

Serphimera glanced away in embarrassment and saw motion by the bed. When her eyes widened with surprise, Syth looked that way too. The filmy image of an auburn-haired woman had suddenly appeared there and was looking down at his empty pillow with a frown. "Mar-Yilot!" he shouted, and the vapory form swirled around to face them.

"Syth!" the woman began joyfully. Then she stopped short, her golden eyes fixed on Serphimera.

Syth ran to her, flinging his arms around her shimmery form in an attempted embrace. He grabbed nothing but air, but he didn't seem to mind. "Mar-Yilot! I'm healed!"

The Autumn Lady looked past him stonily, as if she were the solid one and he but a wispy vapor. Her eyes didn't leave Serphimera's. "Who are you?" she asked, her voice devoid of all expression. Serphimera recognized the look—undiluted jealousy. "Are you a shaper?" Mar-Yilot demanded flatly.

"I do not shape the powers," Serphimera answered evenly. "Rather, I am shaped—"

"I can see that already, despite that ugly sack you're wearing."

"Mar-Yilot!" Syth scolded.

Serphimera smiled graciously. "You misunderstand."

"I understand that you're in my bedroom with my husband, and that he's no longer under the dread. Am I wrong to assume you had some part in that?" Mar-Yilot did not mask her hostility. Syth looked at Serphimera and rolled his eyes in embarrassment.

"A part, perhaps, but not the major part. I am but a tool, a conduit of the Power—"

"Whose power? I know all the wizards. Are you afraid to name him?"

"I *did* name him. The Power."

"What are you talking about?" Mar-Yilot frowned, propping translucent hands on equally translucent hips. "Are you trying to provoke me?"

"I am not."

"Then speak sensibly and tell me whom you serve!" Mar-Yilot demanded. "You're robed like a stupid dragon lover," she added spitefully.

Serphimera smiled again. "That's because I once *was* a stupid dragon lover. I'm afraid this habit has become—a habit. I've already told you whom I serve. You may indeed know all the wizards, but it seems you've not yet met that One who is the source of all the powers."

"You say that as if I'm about to meet him."

"I hope so."

"He's the one who healed my husband?"

"It was the Power, yes."

"Then what exactly are *you* doing here?" Mar-Yilot spat.

"Mar-Yilot!" Syth barked. The crisp authority in his voice forced the sorceress to turn to him. "Rein in your temper and sheathe your claws! While it's obvious that this woman is beautiful, she's not attracted to me nor I to her. She has another. And I—" he tempered his shout with tenderness. "I have *you*."

Mar-Yilot gazed at him guardedly, her amber eyes very sad. "You mean you still want me?" she asked.

"Of course I want you."

"Even though I left you uncovered in the ravines?"

From the look on Syth's face, Serphimera could tell that this memory was painful. But Syth smiled through his hurt and said, "I'm sure you had a good reason."

"Not good enough," Mar-Yilot murmured, looking away. Then she brightened, and for the first time Serphimera saw her smile. "But you're healed! Oh, I wish I could touch you!"

"And I you!" Syth grinned, his eyes gleaming in a way that made Serphimera blush. "Where are you?"

"In a bush near the High City."

"Be careful!" Syth frowned in alarm. "I've tasted Flayh's treachery once already! I won't lose *you* to him!"

"Flayh's treachery?"

"Of course! It was Flayh who planned that ambush and trapped me into the spell of dread!"

"But I thought—Bainer told me it was Dorlyth!"

"A bogus Dorlyth, yes! Part of a plan to confuse and divide Flayh's opposition. It was Admon Faye in Dorlyth's armor!"

Mar-Yilot moaned and closed her eyes in dismay.

"What's wrong?" Syth demanded anxiously.

"I've killed the wrong man!"

Syth stared at her. "You've killed Dorlyth? In vengeance for me?"

Mar-Yilot nodded remorsefully. "I ringed him with fire and drove him off a cliff. But that's what Bainer *told* me!" she pleaded in self-defense.

Syth looked away, then shook his head and sighed. "Then Flayh's succeeded after all. Through this lady's help, I'm no longer among the fallen, but his ruse has felled another who was just as much of a threat."

Serphimera had been seized by grief. While she'd never

met Dorlyth, she felt she knew him, for Pelmen talked of him constantly. Where had Pelmen been during all this?

Mar-Yilot was watching her reactions. "Did you know Dorlyth mod Karis?" the sorceress asked.

She shook her head. "No. But he was a very dear friend of—a very dear friend."

Recognition swept across Mar-Yilot's face and her eyes widened in a stare. "You're Pelmen's woman!" she announced.

The words startled Serphimera, and she blushed, but only for a moment. Then she looked up and met the shaper's gaze. "Yes," Serphimera said. "Yes, I am."

Mar-Yilot looked at Syth. "I've got to go," she said with a smile and she disappeared.

It took a moment for the two of them to recover. Syth looked at Serphimera and shrugged. "She's like that," he explained apologetically. "She'll be back."

"I can hardly wait," Serphimera responded, and she permitted herself a grin.

When life within the High Fortress grew tedious, Tibb honed his dagger. He didn't speak to anyone. He just sat in a corner with a whetting stone and ground it against his blade. And he watched. He'd gathered quite a store of knowledge about the happenings within this keep just from observation. He shared it with no one. Although he knew many faces, he knew very few names. He made no effort to make friends. He'd had a friend, once upon a time, and he was loyal. Once he'd kept his vow of vengeance, perhaps he would make another.

At the moment, he sat at the foot of a rarely used staircase. It was rarely used because only those who had been summoned by Flayh ever ascended it, and the powershaper himself never came down. Admon Faye had set him to guard it while he went up to talk to the master. That wasn't necessary—everyone in the castle knew the shaper had some mysterious means of guarding himself. But the ugly slaver had positioned Tibb here just the same—rather like a man leaving his dog at the door.

Tibb sneered into the gloom that pervaded this corridor and reviewed his situation. For some reason, Admon Faye had made him a sidekick—literally so, for when the slaver needed someone to kick, that someone was always Tibb. If he needed a shirt to wipe his bloody hands on, that shirt would be Tibb's.

When he needed a butt for his joke, that butt was Tibb. Whenever the slaver's bitterness and bile and hatred of life welled up inside of him and spilled over in violence, Tibb was conveniently near. The little man always protected himself from the blows, but he never lost his temper. He absorbed the vilest curses without blinking. He never complained. At times, it almost seemed that Admon Faye actually liked him, for he had protected the little man on occasion from the bullying of other brigands. But Tibb rather suspected that this was really because the slaver considered him a kind of private stock. Tibb was his pet—a miniature terrier whose toughness amused him. No one could abuse Tibb but himself.

Tibb never argued with Admon Faye's commands. He just kept sharpening his dagger, waiting for the day . . .

A heavy boot rammed into his backside, lifting him from the bottom stair and landing him on the corridor floor. He didn't need to look to see who'd done it. To his knowledge, the powershaper didn't go around kicking people. Admon Faye *always* did.

"Some guard," the slaver snorted.

Tibb looked up at him blandly and said nothing. He stooped to pick up his dagger and his whetstone.

"Still working on that dagger, I see." Admon Faye chortled. "You're no warrior, little sneak. A warrior sharpens his great sword. Whose back do you plan to stick that into?"

"Yours," Tibb answered without hesitation.

Admon Faye threw back his head and laughed uproariously. When he finally managed to control himself he wiped his eyes and chuckled. "I'd thought it was something like that. Ah, little sneak, I am so grateful you're here. Life in this fortress would be unrelieved boredom without your clowning."

"I'm telling the truth," Tibb intoned.

"I know!" Admon Faye cackled. "That's what makes it such a scream! Vengeance, isn't it? Because your bungling friend managed to get himself killed in the battle under the Imperial House?"

"You abandoned us—"

"Ha!" Admon Faye hooted, genuinely amused. "You make it sound like I was your mother!"

"We thought you were our leader."

"So now you're going to knife me in the back."

"Not *now*," Tibb responded quietly, setting off another fit of giggles in the hideous slaver.

"Not *now*? Come now, Tibb! Not ever! I've given you one chance after another just to see if you had the courage to make such a move! Oh, that dagger's sharp all right, but it stays in your scabbard. And it *will* stay in your scabbard, until you've filed it down to a nub! You'll never kill me. Do you want to know why? Because hating me is all that gives your life meaning!" Admon Faye finished with a triumphant grin.

Tibb gazed up at him. "I will kill you. I'm just waiting for the proper time."

"The proper time!" Admon Faye snickered. "And when will that be?"

"When it costs you something important. I want it to really hurt."

Admon Faye's eyes lidded dangerously. "I'll bet you do." He looked away, as if bored with this threatening banter and remembering something that needed doing. "Come on. We've got to collect the rest of the lads and go wait down the hall."

"Wait for what?" Tibb asked.

"It seems Lord Flayh has allowed an intruder to penetrate this castle, and he wants us to get out of the way so the fellow can go right to his door."

"How does he know?" Tibb frowned.

Admon Faye shrugged expansively, then gave Tibb his brightest, most grotesque smile. "Come on, little sneak," he said, slipping his long arm affectionately around Tibb's shoulders. "Let's go play a game of darts. Maybe you'll get lucky and plant one between my eyes!" He hustled Tibb down the corridor, laughing all the way.

Tibb said nothing. A few minutes later they were indeed playing a game of darts. But he never did get a chance to aim one at Admon Faye. Just as he was about to take his turn, they heard a war cry from the tower above.

## CHAPTER EIGHT

# Fire Fall

HUNDREDS OF feet above the surface of the lake, Rosha found an open window. He slipped his fingers carefully over the sill and pulled his head up to peer inside it. He saw no one. He quietly drew himself up until his upper body was level with the sill, then threw his legs over it and stepped into the castle. His heart pounded. He expected a troop of warriors to pounce upon him. None did. After resting a few moments from his long climb up from the crevice, he felt an enormous flood of confidence washing through him, sending fresh energy to every muscle.

He had done the impossible. For this, his name would be sung in the taverns of the Mar long after his bones had rotted to dust. But there was a question in his mind. It all seemed too easy. Of course, no one would be expecting someone to try to enter the castle from the rear, so he did have the element of surprise. Even so, it seemed that if Flayh was half the shaper he was rumored to be, then penetrating his fortress would be unthinkable. Rosha wondered if the man had been overrated. True, Pelmen had spoken of his immense power, but Pelmen always gave his enemies more than their due. And no less a shaper than the Autumn Lady herself had dismissed Flayh as a money-counting cloth seller. Rosha's contempt for the man grew.

As he slipped into an empty corridor, he was jabbed again by a splinter of doubt. Was he forgetting something important? As he'd done several times in the past two days, he performed a mental exercise that alleviated his stress; he referred the question to the Power and forgot about it. He knew there was something false in this. After all, he wasn't even sure he believed in the Power. Certainly his father didn't, and Dorlyth was his model. Nevertheless, he'd heard Pelmen talk of faith and of yielding up one's failings. Rosha had come to view this Power as a safety net—there to catch you if you fell, but otherwise not worth worrying about. Religion was the concern of prophets and missionaries. Heroes had to concentrate on victory. Therefore he would devote his attention to disposing of this substandard power shaper. If he got into trouble somehow, it was the Power's responsibility to get him out of it.

As he passed near the barracks, he overheard loud, boisterous laughter. Slavers! Where were the proud, principled warriors who had once guarded this ancient keep? Gone, Rosha thought, abandoning the sloth king to join the armies that would overthrow him. Were these belligerent cutthroats the best Flayh could do for replacements? The man sank even lower in Rosha's estimation.

They weren't even guarding Flayh's own tower! The spiral staircase was open to him! Rosha danced upward, unseen, unheard, unchallenged. His sword was out, and he was ready. Here was Flayh's door. He crouched and listened at the keyhole. He heard shuffling footsteps and indistinct mutterings, and Rosha's lips curled in a disdainful smile. *This* was the new terror that had been loosed upon the land? This mumbling merchant hiding away in a tower like a royal madman? Some powershaper! Rosha thought. He threw his body toward the door and let out a piercing battle scream.

His shoulder never touched the wood. The door flew open before him, and he landed on the floor with a clatter. He bounded to his knees and looked up; his stomach plummeted as he suddenly recognized his own stupidity. Flayh sat quietly facing the door in an ornately carved chair. He was cackling with satisfaction.

After several tension-packed hours of listening, Pelmen clearly heard the High Fortress speak:

—The intruder you permitted to penetrate these walls is now among the towers.

He had been waiting for just such a word. All the same, it came as a shock, and he reeled back against a door jamb. He'd been discovered! The castle was finally revealing his presence!

—No, the High Fortress went on, obviously answering a question.

Flayh's question, no doubt. Pelmen wished he could hear the powershaper's end of the conversation.

—Evidently he still believes his success is due to his own stealth, the High Fortress snorted derisively.

Pelmen huddled against the door, certain that in the next moment either a squad of slavers would burst down the hallway to arrest him or a stone in the ceiling directly above him would dislodge and drop to crush him. He prepared to respond—but neither happened. Instead, the castle spoke once more.

—He's at the top of your stairs. Now he's at your door. He's drawn his great sword. Why did you not allow this fortress to dispose of the vermin while he climbed the outer wall?

Before the pops and breezes that formed these phrases faded away, Pelmen was pounding down the steps of the royal tower en route to the tower of Flayh. The castle hadn't noticed him at all, and the reason was now apparent. It had been busy tracking Rosha.

—Very well, master. Deal with the fool as you choose. He *is*, after all, your plaything.

Somewhere between the bottom step of the royal staircase and the corridor floor, Pelmen turned into a bird. He didn't realize he'd changed until he heard the fortress scream.

—There's a shaper! Another shaper is within this house! That was all it managed to explain before breaking off into an agonized grumbling of foundation stones.

Pelmen darted down a hallway and swooped around a corner. He suddenly found himself in a thicket of pike staves and greatswords. Slavers clogged the corridor, all facing toward Flayh's tower entrance. He flashed over them. "A falcon!" one of the slavers shouted.

Another voice grunted, "What? Where!"

Pelmen knew the voice well and had long loathed it. He and Admon Faye were lifelong enemies.

"That's no falcon, it's a powershaper! Strike it down!"

Pikes and swords chopped the air, and Pelmen lost a feather or two as he dodged and glided through this moving thicket of steel. Admon Faye himself stood on the first stair, fanning the air above him with his blade and shouting curses at his men. Pelmen ducked past the flashing sword, dipping his talons into the flesh of the slaver's face in passing. Then he was wheeling up the stairwell toward Flayh's door with powerful strokes of his wings. He was aware of Admon Faye's scream of pain as well as the sobs of the castle, but he was intent solely on getting through the door above him before it slammed shut.

"Close that door!" Flayh was shouting at the castle, but so great was its agony that it was a fraction late in complying.

Pelmen shot through it and swooped toward Flayh's face. He threw his talons out before him and screamed, and Flayh was forced to take his dog-shape in self-defense. Pelmen hit the floor beside Rosha as a man once again and jerked the bewildered youth to his feet. He stabbed his finger toward a heavily curtained window and commanded, "Jump through that!" Then he whirled to face Flayh, his arms up in the stance of a shaper ready for war. The dog metamorphized back into human form and took the same position.

They had battled each other through the pyramids, but this was the first time they had met face to face. Pelmen recoiled from the grotesque sight. Flayh's face had been tattooed a pale powder blue, the same shade as Tahli-Damen's eyes. In this darkened room that blue tint was more noticeable; like the pyramids themselves, Flayh's face glowed. His eyes had been protected from the magical blast by the quick reflexes of his hands, but the marks they had left behind added to the bizarre picture. It was as if two white starfish clung to Flayh's face, each outlining a beady, red-rimmed eye. Now Pelmen gazed into those eyes, and what he saw there chilled him further. Flayh looked like a cornered rat, frightened, insecure, savage. There was none of the quiet confidence and almost sporting rivalry he'd grown accustomed to seeing in the faces of the Mari shapers he had battled. But then, Flayh was not a Mari magician, bred to enjoy fighting for fighting's sake. He knew none of the unwritten rules of the game. His eyes tipped his hand; Pelmen knew what spell to expect and anticipated it. "Don't watch!" he shouted at Rosha. Out of the corner of his eye, he saw the young swordsman bury his head in his hands.

As Flayh threw his spell of dread, Pelmen fashioned a kind of magical mirror to reflect Flayh's terror back. The spells neutralized one another. The only effect of this enormous outpouring of shaper power was a heightened urgency in the castle's shrieks.

For Pelmen, however, this was a shocking setback. He'd outguessed his opponent! By all rights Flayh should now be helpless, suffering self-inflicted dread! This was yet another testimony to Flayh's enormous resources. It was as if the hosts of the powers had rallied to Flayh's standard. Pelmen was momentarily stunned. Fortunately Flayh was too. The thunder of iron-shod feet on the stairway and a heavy pounding on the door jolted them both back to action.

"The door!" Flayh shouted at the High Fortress. "Open the door!"

Despite its pain, the castle tried to do so.

Rosha came out of hiding and raced over to slam the bolt back in place. Pelmen saw him go and shouted, "Rosha! Get out!" Then he tossed a fireball at Flayh's head.

Rosha was within three steps of the tower's back window, but he still didn't move toward it. He'd seen that ancient object that had lured him to the castle sitting on a small table across the circular room. He'd come this far—he hated to leave without it. The slender, gracefully carved pyramid of diamond glowed with a ghostly blue radiance, calling to him. Despite the flaming missiles that whirled around his head, he lunged across the room and grabbed it. The table collapsed beneath him, and an explosion above his head seared his neck.

"Will you get out?" Pelmen bellowed, hurdling Rosha and blocking the next blaze away. This time the warrior obeyed. Clutching the crystal to his chest he scrambled to the window, then flung the heavy drapes aside and jumped up onto the sill. There he had to pause. While he could see the blue reservoir stretching out beneath him, he saw also the outer wall of the castle, which he would have to clear. It was a very long drop . . .

Another explosion rocked the room behind him, and he heard the door splinter. He needed no more convincing. He hugged the precious pyramid and jumped.

Pelmen backed toward the window, deflecting fireballs and trying to think. Even if Rosha survived the dive, he would need magical assistance to escape the slavers. He had to help. The trouble was, these fierce exchanges had depleted his energies, while Flayh's power seemed only to grow. He had to get away.

Admon Faye burst into the room roaring a curse as Pelmen jumped up onto the windowsill. The slaver launched a sword at his head and he was forced to dodge it before he could change forms. At the same moment, one of Flayh's fireballs struck him in the chest, blowing him out the window. He lost consciousness with the impact, as his robes ignited. He fell backward like a flaming star and was gone.

Flayh gave an exultant shout, and raced to the window to watch Pelmen's fall. The High Fortress, however, kept up its horrendous howling. "Silence!" Flayh commanded, but the High Fortress wouldn't be silent. "What's the matter with you!"

—Don't you know? the fortress wailed in unspeakable agony. There's still another shaper within these walls!

Throughout the tugoliths' long trek through the riverlands of Lamath, Pezi had looked behind him more than he'd looked ahead. It was never a pretty sight. Uprooted trees, demolished hedgerows, trampled vegetable gardens—oh, what a hideous picture *that* was!—and of course, the occasional demolished farmhouse. Their path resembled the wake of a particularly vindictive tornado. And he'd thought he could sneak these beasts out of the country! Why, even if he could train them to walk on their tiptoes, the sound of their passing would still wake the dead! The ground shook beneath their feet. His attempt to take the inconspicuous back roads had come to naught—all he'd managed to do was to clear a new southern highway. Surely the authorities would be catching up with them soon. What was the penalty for tugolith-napping? Considering Thuganlitha's rampages, could he be charged with contributing to the delinquency of a minor?

That's how he thought of them—as children. Huge, undisciplined children. He couldn't imagine how he could have managed this far without the help of Chimolitha. She was the only force that held Thug in check. Pezi called her a she. He didn't know why, it just seemed natural. He'd never asked the beast's sex, of course. They were children, after all, and such a topic would be blushingly inappropriate. But she acted like a girl, somehow—helpful, obedient, and bright.

And Thug acted like a rampaging little boy. Pezi had told himself that if they could just make it to the Tellera Desert everything would improve. Thug couldn't destroy anything there, for there was nothing to destroy. Or so Pezi had figured.

They'd reached the desert that morning. Already Pezi wished

they were back in the comparative safety of the rivers. There was truly nothing in this desert—most especially, no food. For a man who'd made the kitchens of the world his only temples, that was more than a little disconcerting. But Pezi could handle his personal privation. He was far more worried about the tugs. A hungry tugolith was a grouchy tugolith, and a grouchy tugolith could—well, Pezi didn't even want to think about it.

"I'm so hungry I could eat a human," Thuganlitha said menacingly. It wasn't the first time he'd said that. He'd said it this morning, and Pezi had been so shocked he'd rolled off Chim's back and bounced onto the roadway like a rubber ball. Chimolitha had wondered aloud why he'd done that, and it was only then that Pezi realized Thuganlitha didn't understand what the words meant at all. It was just a saying some misguided Lamathian had taught him because it sounded cute. "Cute!" Pezi grunted to himself. How could anything about such a horrendously huge animal be thought cute!

"I'm so hungry I could—"

"You don't know what that means," Chimolitha interrupted calmly.

"I do so!" Thuganlitha snarled.

"What, then?" Chim challenged.

Thuganlitha stamped the ground, leaving a huge pothole, and snorted. "It means I'm hungry!"

"But what's a human?" Chimolitha demanded.

"Yeah," Riganlitha chimed in haughtily. "What's a human?"

Thug wheeled with a snort of rage and drove his horn deep into Riganlitha's hindquarters. The wounded animal shrieked and fled, screaming for mercy. Pezi hardly blinked—this happened at least a dozen times a day. As usual, Riganlitha retired to the rear of the cavalcade and found a sympathetic forequarter to weep on. Another tug licked his pierced hide solicitously. They could all empathize, for all bore similar scars of Thug's quick temper. All, that is, except Chimolitha.

"You don't know," she said passively.

"Well, you don't either!" Thug snarled, dancing beside her in frustration.

"I can ask." She shrugged. Pezi always hated it when she shrugged. It meant he got bounced around more than usual.

"Who?" Thug demanded.

"The man." Chim shrugged again. That began a chorus of interested responses from the tugs that tagged behind.

"What man?"

"Dolna is our man."

"Is Dolna here?"

"Where's Dolna?"

"He's sick."

"Dolna, I'm hungry!"

"Don't talk!" Thug roared.

"Where's Dolna?"

"Don't talk!" Thug screamed again, and he whirled his massive bulk around to face the others, the tip of his enormous horn glinting wickedly with Riganlitha's fresh, wet blood. The herd got quiet.

"This man," Chimolitha said, rolling her eyes upward to indicate the rather ample figure she bore on her back.

"You mean the fat man?" Thug asked.

"Man?" Chimolitha called. "What's a human?"

Pezi faced a dilemma. Chimolitha was simpleminded, but she wasn't stupid. Twice already she'd caught him trying to mislead her with a lie, and each time she'd rolled those saucer-sized eyes up to look at him and said, "That isn't nice." He'd suffered the shakes for hours afterward. He didn't want to raise her ire again, so he couldn't tell her a complete fiction. On the other hand, to tell the truth could be disastrous! He'd already caught Thug looking at him hungrily and licking his enormous chops.

"That's . . . a very . . . interesting question," Pezi began cautiously. He still didn't quite know what to say. "Humans are—ah—a certain *type* of person."

"Oh." Chimolitha nodded. Then her face clouded. "What's person?"

"Person? A person? Why, persons are people. You know, like me."

"Oh." Chim nodded. Once again she looked puzzled. "You are a person?"

"Yes," Pezi nodded, plunging unaware into the very danger zone he'd sought to avoid.

"Then you are a human?" Chim asked quietly.

"Yes—no! No, ah, no, no. Not me. No. Not at all."

Chimolitha was greatly chagrined. "Then how do I know?"

"Know what?"

"What persons I can eat," she whined. She added apologetically, "I'm hungry too."

Sheer terror danced across Pezi's broad features. Pezi wasn't smart. He wasn't even clever. But Pezi was a survivor, and could be very creative under pressure. He suddenly had an idea, one that pleased him so much that he giggled aloud. "Their robes," he cackled gleefully. "You can tell by the color of their robes. They always wear blue!"

They trudged along in silence as Chimolitha gave this some thought. The other tugoliths had all already turned their small minds to other things. To them, this conversation might have been about higher math.

"Man," said Chim, "what's blue?"

Pezi thought quickly. "The sky. Blue's the color of the sky."

Chimolitha stopped moving, which brought the line behind her to a halt as well. She turned her huge head backward to look solemnly at the sky. Then she lowered it once more to gaze down at the road. "I'll remember." She nodded, then she plodded ahead once more.

"I'm still hungry," Thuganlitha groused, and Pezi's anxiety level soared once more. Suddenly he got a whiff of something that made him rejoice—for more reasons than one.

"Onions!" he shouted. "I'm saved! I mean, ah, we're saved. There's an onion patch nearby. I've just remembered it. Wonderful. We'll eat onions for lunch!" His excitement was contagious, and the tugoliths in the rear began to crowd up around Chimolitha's flanks. She, however, seemed lost in thought. "Is something troubling you?" Pezi asked her gently.

Chimolitha nodded. "Man?" she asked. "Are onions a type of persons?"

Pelmen came to his senses in a terrifying position. He was looking straight down a cliff, and someone was beating on his back.

"Are you all right?" a voice shouted in his ears. Pelmen was seized by the shoulders and jerked upright, and he yelped with pain, for his skin was blistered and raw.

Then he laughed aloud, and shouted. "Rosha!"

The young man released a long sigh and relaxed. "Good. I was afraid you were dead!"

"Why aren't I? And where are we?" Pelmen added quickly, glancing around at this water-filled cavern.

"We're still on top of the plateau," Rosha answered soberly. "This is a part of the lake connected to the rest by underwater channels. Flayh and his people don't seem to know it's here."

"How did *I* get here? The last thing I remember was a fireball that blew me out of the tower."

"You hit the water right after me. The lake doused your flames, and I pulled you through the tunnel into here."

Pelmen looked Rosha in the eye. "Then we're even," he said solemnly. "I saved your life, and you saved mine. We can talk later of the wisdom of this enterprise."

Rosha grunted and smiled sadly. "I'd not have saved yours if your cloaking hadn't been so effective. The slavers filled the lake with arrows. We'd both have been skewered if you hadn't covered us."

Pelmen's eyebrow drooped in a sharp frown. "*I* didn't cover us!"

"What? You must have! They sure couldn't see us!"

"But I didn't."

"Are you sure you didn't cast it while you were falling? Just before passing out? I know you can maintain a cloak in your sleep—"

"I tell you I didn't do it!" Pelmen snapped, and Rosha was surprised at his intensity. "But if indeed someone *did*—and that seems the only explanation for our survival—then who? And why?"

"*I* cloaked you, Dragonsbane," said the waif-faced woman who stood suddenly behind them.

"Mar-Yilot," Pelmen whispered as he splashed around to face her. Rosha grabbed for his sword. His scabbard was empty. It was Pelmen who'd had his robes burned off, but Rosha felt the more naked. Pelmen paid no heed to his lack of apparel. He faced the woman squarely. "How long have you been there?"

"I just flew in. That's the advantage of a butterfly-shape. People see you, but don't notice."

"Then you're no longer cloaking the reservoir."

"Should I be?" she asked pointedly. "The two of you are

safe here for the moment. I thought I'd better join you to plan our way down."

"Our way?" Pelmen asked suspiciously.

"Pelmen, dear, you need help. You've been badly blistered and half-drowned. That, on top of a ferocious shaper battle at very close quarters that I'd wager has rendered you all but powerless for days. Of course," she added with a sardonic smile, "your friend the Power could possibly make up for the damage and energy loss. But that really isn't necessary."

"Do you know the Power?" Pelmen asked. He still did not smile.

"Not personally," the Autumn Lady said coldly,"but if he happens along, why don't you introduce us."

"You've not yet answered my foremost question."

"Which was?"

"Why, Mar-Yilot? Why did you save us just now?"

The woman brushed her auburn hair out of her eyes and gazed out the cavern mouth toward the horizon. The Furrowmar was yellow and brown with dying plants and crumbling leaves. It seemed for just a moment her golden eyes misted over. Then they cleared. "For the present, let's say I owed it to you. Both of you. There won't be time for fuller explanations unless we get down off this rock."

Pelmen didn't speak. Rosha didn't either. His eyes were fixed on his mentor, awaiting the powershaper's next move. After a long pause, Pelmen finally whispered, "Why should we trust you?"

Mar-Yilot, who had been waiting for that, cocked her eyebrow and propped her hands on her slim hips. "Right. Why *should* you trust the witch who just saved your hide? What's left of it."

Reminded of his burns, Pelmen turned his head away from her and looked at his scalded shoulder.

"It's rather pink," Mar-Yilot went on. "In fact, *all* of you I can see is rather pink. And," she added with a droll smile, "I *can* see all of you."

"I'll need some clothes," Pelmen mumbled.

"You'd do well to have a good salve on that first. Now to business. How do we get down? *I* can fly, but I wouldn't trust your feathers if I were you. And Rosha—" Here she looked at the young warrior directly for the first time, and her mocking tone seemed distinctly softer when she went on. "That is right, isn't it? Rosha?" He nodded firmly, face grim. "Well. It's a long climb down that pipe. Too long." Her voice was almost motherly. It made Rosha feel very strange.

"What do you suggest?" Pelmen asked wearily. His body was feeling the shock now. Much as he hated the arrangement, he knew the woman was right. They would be obliged to depend upon her.

"When I left our friends out there, they were sending swimmers into the lake. Thanks to that noisy castle, Flayh knows there was another shaper inside, but he doesn't know who, and he doesn't know for certain that the lake was cloaked. They're going to hunt for bodies, and they'll find two—which I've conveniently placed there already. These slavers!" She sighed. "They don't know each other and they don't care. They don't even know how many there are of them. It's child's play confusing such a company of fools."

"What they lack in organization they make up for in cruelty. Go on," Pelmen urged, leaning back against a wall of the cave. He was feeling very dizzy.

"I'll go get some rope, tie it on the rocks above, and drop it down. Then I'll fly back inside. Rosha, you'll climb up—I'll cloak you, of course—then you'll drop the rope down and I'll tie it around Pelmen, and you'll haul him out. Drop it down again and pull me up. I'd fly up but I can't take my altershape and keep the cloaking spell in place. Then we walk around the lake and into the city. That may be tricky. Flayh's surely not going to leave the perimeter of his fortress unpenetrated, and if he should guess rightly, he could nullify my spell. Pelmen, husband your strength. As we walk around the lake, add whatever coverage you can provide to mine. With luck, he could penetrate mine and catch us. Depleted though you may be, I'll wager my life he can't penetrate us both."

Pelmen nodded weakly. "A good plan," he murmured.

"We'll go to a friend's house where we'll find some food and a place to rest for the journey."

"Flayh will be searching," Pelmen grunted. "He'll throw a net."

"Once we're inside the house, I'll not shape unless I have to. He may be able to tell when we've slipped by his castle, but once we're into the city and we stop all shaping, he'll have no way to net us. He'd have to search every house to find us, and Ngandib is a very big place. Even if he did that, he'd still not find us, for we can hide as long as he can hunt. When he's grown discouraged and turned his attention elsewhere, we'll slip away, down the Down Road and north."

"How long will that be? Can you guess?" Rosha asked her.

Mar-Yilot looked at him again—just looked, as if studying his face. Then, with remarkable gentleness, she answered, "Soon, I think. This Flayh is a power—and from what I've seen today, an awesome one. But even Flayh can only do one thing at a time." She turned her head away, and added, "I hope."

Rosha had felt much better before that final disclaimer. Mar-Yilot shrugged, and Rosha sighed.

"Don't worry," she soothed, reaching out to pat his curly black hair. "You'll do fine." Once again, Rosha felt strange.

"Bring the rope—" Pelmen gasped, and they both noticed that he was now slumping down toward the water.

"You're fading," Mar-Yilot said, and she started to alter her shape. Then she took a last look at Pelmen's body and added, "I'd better bring some salve and a robe as well. Not for your benefit, particularly, but for mine. Nobody else will see you, but *I* will, and I have too much respect for you to watch you walk naked through the streets of the capital." The woman was suddenly a butterfly fluttering out the mouth of the cavern.

Rosha sloshed to Pelmen and hoisted him back out of the water. He let the powershaper's head slump against his shoulder, then reached inside his mail shirt. It was still there, safely hidden away—the sharp-edged, glowing pyramid. He had it. It had cost dearly. Not only had he almost lost his own life, he'd nearly gotten Pelmen killed as well. He had been stupid, and his father would chew both of his ears off. But he had it. He had it!

"How is he?" Mar-Yilot whispered, and Rosha jumped, startled. He hadn't seen her enter the room. "Sorry," the sorceress said sincerely, kneeling and laying her hand on his arm.

Rosha relaxed, and settled back onto his stool. "I don't know." He shrugged. "I'm no herbalist. But he did drink the soup. And he doesn't seem to moan as much."

Mar-Yilot nodded and studied Pelmen's face. "The salve helped. And he's getting plenty of sleep. That's good. He'll need that."

"Is Flayh still searching?"

"Diligently. I've felt the brush of his net at least twice. It's a good thing he didn't start that immediately, or he might have caught us tiptoeing around the reservoir."

"What about Admon Faye?"

"Shh—" Mar-Yilot hissed, pointing to Pelmen. The sleeper was stirring. She got to her feet and beckoned Rosha to follow her out of the bedroom. Once in the hallway, they closed the door, and Mar-Yilot answered Rosha in her normal voice. "There are groups of slavers on all the main roads, stopping everyone who passes. It's just for show. Admon Faye knows that, if Flayh can't find us, *he* certainly won't, but he's demonstrating his diligence. Or perhaps he's trying to terrorize those who are hiding us into revealing our whereabouts."

"Is there any chance of that?" Rosha muttered anxiously, thinking of the old couple who waited uneasily in the main room of the cottage.

Mar-Yilot smiled, and Rosha shivered at the sight. "Knowing what you know, would *you* betray me to an enemy?" Rosha understood. He shook his head. "Apart from that, these are my friends," she went on. "And they're certainly no supporters of this treacherous Flayh. They've assured me we can stay here as long as necessary, but I think it's best if we don't linger. Flayh's determined to catch us—more so than I expected. The longer we wait, the more time he has to think of ways to entrap us. And who can know what else is in that marvelous spellbook of his?" She nodded toward Pelmen's door. "Think he can travel?"

"Now?" Rosha frowned. "The man's been burned! He's exhausted! In shock! You expect him just to get out of bed and—"

"Yes, she does," Pelmen mumbled weakly as he opened the door behind them.

Rosha jerked around to stare at him, then ordered, "Get back in that bed."

"I'd like to, certainly. I feel as weary as the king himself. But the woman is right. There's no safety for us here. The question is, where *can* we be safe?" Pelmen directed this to Mar-Yilot.

"The glade of mod Carl," Rosha said flatly. "We'll rejoin Lord Ferlyth and my father." Rosha missed the mute exchange between the two powershapers. They'd silently agreed to put explanations off until later.

"I think not," was all Pelmen said. "What do you suggest?" he asked Mar-Yilot.

"Let's try the Down Road now. Kam's lands are at the base of the plateau, and he's an ally of mine. He'll furnish us with horses, and we can start up the Riverline."

"To Sythia?" Pelmen asked.

"Why not? Flayh knows someone helped you, but I'd wager all the diamonds on the Isle that I'm the last person he'd expect."

Once again something unspoken passed between the shapers, and this time Rosha saw it. He didn't comprehend, though, and Pelmen's response revealed nothing. "I'm sure you're right. *I* certainly didn't expect it. But why Sythia, when that's sure to be another focus of Flayh's attention?"

"To get you some proper healing, primarily," the woman grunted. Then she smiled smugly. "There is a woman there with healing hands. Perhaps you know of her. Calls herself Serphimera?"

"Serphimera!" Pelmen blurted with renewed vitality. "Serphimera's there?"

Mar-Yilot turned to Rosha. "I think he'll be able to make the trip."

Indeed, Pelmen was already limping around the bedroom in his borrowed cloak, muttering, "Shoes, shoes—"

"There's a pair waiting by the door, and a heavy cloak as well. The clouds and the cold tell me snow's on the way. Let's go."

"But what about Flayh?" Rosha protested. "Won't he be certain to watch the Down Road?"

"He can't watch every place at once." Mar-Yilot shrugged. "Maybe we'll get lucky. And if not, well—I know a trick or two."

Moments later they'd bid good-bye to the much-relieved couple and pushed out into the cold night. "Pelmen," Mar-Yilot muttered, "I'll cover us if you can manage a light."

Without another word a small ball of purple flame appeared at eye level four feet before them, and they started off, their breath steaming in the chill. Rosha and the sorceress flanked Pelmen, propping his arms over their shoulders as they had done when carrying him around the lake. But he bore most of his weight on his own feet now. Mar-Yilot had said the one name that bewitched him, and it had summoned hidden reserves of energy from within him.

Mar-Yilot appeared to be listening for something. Then she smiled encouragingly. "We're in luck. If he's casting his net, he's looking elsewhere at the moment. Let's hurry."

Rosha stalked along briskly, aware of the cold but more aware of the eerie appearance of this odd threesome. It amazed him to think that neither they nor Pelmen's ball of flame could be seen, yet in just moments there was new evidence of that fact. They heard boisterous laughter around a corner as they approached one of Ngandib's larger cobbled avenues. They slowed their pace and continued walking quietly. A group of slavers had surrounded a pair of teenaged girls and were harassing them for being out on the streets at night. The concealed trio walked slowly past them without drawing a glance. Several guards held torches. In the light from them, Rosha caught sight of the terrified face of one of the girls. He almost turned back in fury. Mar-Yilot caught his eye. He saw a fierce rage etched in her face too, but she only mouthed, "Later," and nodded forward. They left the noise behind them as they turned another corner.

In minutes they'd reached the main thoroughfare of the city, the wide boulevard that ran from the top of the Down Road to the entrance of the High Fortress. Bonfires lighted up the night at every major intersection along it, and slavers were in evidence everywhere. The trio kept well to one side, hugging the shop fronts, warily watching the vigilant guards and paying particular attention to the closest alleyways, in case they needed to flee quickly. No one stopped them. No one seemed to notice them. But when at last they could make out the entry point onto the Down Road, they all slowed to a halt and looked at one another in frustration. Twelve slavers stood abreast of the road, shoulder to shoulder, facing back toward the city, their weapons drawn and gleaming in the torchlight. They all looked extremely edgy. Mar-Yilot jerked her head toward an alley, and the three ducked into it.

Pelmen leaned back against a wall and closed his eyes. The walk had drained him. Rosha searched Mar-Yilot's face for some suggestion. He waited for her to speak.

"Obviously, we can't get past them," she whispered fiercely. "They may not be able to see us but they can feel us. Flayh's positioned them as he has for just that purpose—to feel us if we try to slide past." She fumed for a few moments in silence. Pelmen had let the light fade away, so Rosha could no longer see her. He could hear her anger, though, in the way she breathed. He waited.

"It could work in our favor," she whispered after a moment. "Rosha, you have your sword?"

Rosha winced. "I lost it. In Flayh's tower."

Mar-Yilot grunted. "You need a sword. Wait here while I borrow one." She started to leave, then stepped back to whisper, "Stay in the shadows! While I'm gone you're not being concealed!" Then she walked quietly away.

Rosha leaned back beside Pelmen and listened to the pounding of his own heart. Rarely had he ever felt so helpless. No longer did he feel the cocky confidence of a young warrior. He felt himself the plaything of wizards, an errand boy for the truly powerful. He fought to relax, earnestly hoping that no slaver would choose to wander down this alley.

Something touched his hand and he jerked in shock. For the second time tonight the sorceress apologized for startling him. Then she shoved a sword hilt into his hand, and his fingers closed on it gratefully. "Where'd you get it?" he whispered as his other hand felt for the blade.

"From a slaver who doesn't need it any longer," she answered. Rosha now felt the slick coating of wetness on the metal and understood. "Pelmen," Mar-Yilot whispered, "can you go on?"

"Yes," Pelmen muttered, but his voice was heavy with exhaustion. Rosha waited on Mar-Yilot's decision.

"We can't turn back now. I didn't hide that slaver's body, and they'll find it soon enough. We go on. The two of you wait here, ready to move quickly. I'm going to go up the street and cause a distraction. Maybe we can pull a few of those slavers out of line, but that doesn't matter much, if we can get the rest of their friends looking in the other direction. When I've drawn a crowd I'll quickly join you here, and cover us as we dash for that line of slavers. I'll help Pelmen, Rosha. You concentrate on cutting down those twelve men. They'll not see us coming, and they'll never know what killed them. And Rosha," she added cannily, "if it somehow doesn't seem sporting—remember that group of bullies around the two girls."

Rosha didn't answer. He clenched his jaw and gripped the haft of the great sword with both hands.

"One other thing, Rosha. Make sure you get them *all*."

He didn't hear her go, so Rosha knew she'd left them in her altershape. At the moment, they were uncovered again, but he felt much better this time. A weapon made the difference. "Are you sure you can make it?" he whispered to Pelmen.

"Not sure I can make it, no," Pelmen responded quietly, "but sure that I want to try."

Rosha nodded and took a deep breath. Then they waited. A few moments later they heard a commotion in the street. They heard laughter coming from some distance away, then running. Soon the slavers nearest them became interested, and several abandoned the warmth of their bonfire to run toward the site of the disturbance. Rosha chanced a peek around the corner. The human barrier still blocked their escape, but the slavers who had been keeping the line of men company had all disappeared toward the center of town. "Get ready," Rosha murmured, and Pelmen straightened up and took a deep breath.

Two feet suddenly hit the pavement beside Rosha. "Let's go," Mar-Yilot muttered.

"What did you do down there?"

The woman glared at him. "I stripped," she snapped. "Now move!"

The trio dashed out of the alleyway, all crouching in subconscious self-preservation. It was unnecessary. The slavers who blocked them never looked in their direction, so intently were they peering up the street. As he approached them, running lightly on his toes, Rosha lifted the sword above his head. Then he was upon them, like a vengeful, invisible demon. He started at one end of the line and hacked down two before the others realized they were under attack. He pierced a third through the heart and wounded a fourth, and by that time there was enough room for Mar-Yilot and Pelmen to hurry past. The other slavers were shouting in panic, aware that something terrible was taking place but not knowing how to prevent it. Their swords were out and they were slashing wildly at the air. In the confusion, two more slavers were killed by their own men. Rosha had circled behind now, and skewered three more slavers from that direction. Then he stepped back to catch his breath and decide how best to dispatch the last three. They were cursing one another and the darkness and flailing their swords before them, but they'd had the good sense to put their backs together.

"Come on!" Mar-Yilot called urgently, and Rosha nodded. Then he noticed that the three of them were standing very near the precipice. He sheathed his bloody greatsword, ducked under a swiping blade, and shoved the closest slaver backward. He threw his arms wide, carrying the other two backward with him. When Rosha stepped forward and shoved again, all three went over the cliff. Their screams faded away as Rosha raced down to join his friends, and the trio of the warrior, the witch, and the wounded disappeared down the road into the night.

## CHAPTER NINE

# Purple Cloud on the Golden Throne

A CHILL breeze swirled around the battlements of the Imperial House of Chaomonous, tousling Bronwynn's curls. The young woman shoved her hair back out of her face, adding to its unkempt appearance. It didn't matter how she looked. She was a queen. She didn't have to impress anyone, and the only one she wanted to impress apparently didn't care. Bronwynn scowled northward. Her thoughts vacillated between fantasies of tenderly embracing Rosha and of roasting him over a fire.

Try as she might she'd been unable to repeat the experience of dream-search. Had it really even happened that once? She couldn't prove it had, certainly. Nevertheless, in all her life she'd had no dream so conscious or so real. She was convinced she had actually talked with Pelmen atop the Rock of Tombs.

If only her fool Prime Minister had let her sleep! Just as she'd been about to ask Pelmen for the key to repeating the spell, Kherda had wakened her! She'd railed at the man for hours after that. Indeed, she still hadn't forgiven him, although she knew she should. He'd only been alerting her to a growing national crisis, related to the activities of sugar-clawsps, of all things. Bronwynn frowned to herself and scratched her head. "Sometimes this queen business is nothing but a bother," she grumbled aloud.

On the other hand, there were compensations. She glanced down at the vast plain north of the city and noted with satisfaction the growing number of pavilions that were springing up around its edge. Despite his misgivings, Kherda had followed her orders and summoned the Golden Throng. Her army swelled in size daily. Now if only Joss would hurry and get back to take charge of it . . .

Bronwynn stepped down off the wall and strolled across the huge roof of her castle. Her hands clasped behind her, her head down, she was only vaguely aware that Maliff, her falconer, was diligently exercising one of his feathered charges. For his part, Maliff was not aware of Bronwynn at all. The actions of his birds totally absorbed the man's attentions. People—even queens—were merely distractions.

In the midst of the roof there was a cavernous hole where her father's aviary had once stood. A broad ramp spiraled down its edge toward the palace garden. As Bronwynn set foot on this, she heard animated voices from below. Kherda was bringing a group of some sort up the ramp, obviously in search of her. She sighed. Too late to turn back. She might as well meet this delegation and get it over with.

"Your Highness?" someone called up.

Bronwynn recognized the mellow voice immediately and clapped her hands with genuine affection. "Gerrig?" she called. "Is that you?"

"Your Highness!" the burly actor called again as they came in sight of one another around a turn. "What a pleasure to see your beautiful face! For a day or two, I worried we might never see it again!"

Bronwynn warmly greeted the others in Gerrig's company—Danyilyn, a petite actress with radiant eyes and a lovely smile, and Yona Parmi, the one man in Chaomonous who knew Pelmen best of all. These were Pelmen's closest friends in all the Golden Realm, for this was the core of his acting troupe. Bronwynn made a point of ignoring Prime Minister Kherda as she hooked her arm in Gerrig's and asked, "Exactly what do you mean?"

Gerrig frowned and turned to look at Kherda. "The Prime Minister says he's told you about the clawsps . . ."

Bronwynn moaned. "Indeed. I've heard enough about sugar-clawsps to last a lifetime. How they eat, how they breed—"

"How they kill?" Gerrig rumbled deep in his chest, and the queen stopped walking and looked at him intently.

"How they what?"

"They kill, your Highness," Gerrig intoned, and Danyilyn and Yona Parmi nodded in agreement.

"Explain," Bronwynn commanded, looking at the actress.

"As you know, we've been performing in Pleclypsa," Danyilyn responded. "All went well until a week ago, when we began noticing swarms of sugar-clawsps buzzing around the city—"

"Clawsps don't swarm," Bronwynn interrupted matter-of-factly. She felt certain of this. In the last week Kherda had read her every book in the library concerning the subject, and not one had mentioned swarming.

"That's true, they don't," Yona Parmi agreed, leaning toward her. "Yet they're swarming in Pleclypsa. Three nights ago, they swarmed a member of our audience during a performance. You can imagine the screams. Fortunately, the poor man died quickly."

"And he wasn't the only one!" Gerrig burst in. "There were others that night, all leading citizens! It's as if they'd each been chosen for assassination! By the next morning, we were on our way here!"

Utterly perplexed, Bronwynn looked at her Prime Minister inquiringly.

"It would appear," Kherda began with his usual unnecessary formality, "that at present the southerly regions of the nation are the only areas infected. But as I warned you some days ago, my Queen, this malady among our insect population appears to be moving northward toward this city."

Bronwynn shook her head in disbelief. "Then they really *do* swarm." She missed seeing the Prime Minister's smug nod as she turned again to the actors. "Does anyone have an explanation?"

Danyilyn shook her head, while Gerrig gave the queen an elaborate shrug. Yona Parmi, however, tapped his chin sagely and squinted his tiny eyes. "You know, of course, that Pelmen and I spent a lot of time talking. If my memory serves me, he once mentioned some Mari powershaper who could transform himself into a sugar-clawsp. I wonder. Could this all be related?"

Kherda chuckled involuntarily, then stifled it. Bronwynn looked at him in annoyance, and the Prime Minister felt obliged to explain. "Well I hardly think . . . I mean, a powershaper here? To what purpose? And if this *should* be some Mari attack, would it not start in the north?"

Bronwynn scowled at the man and looked back at the players. "Obviously our Prime Minister knows very little about shapers." She glanced back at Kherda and went on. "Although he'd like us to believe he knows everything about everything." She looked at Yona Parmi. "Thank you, Yona, for your suggestion. I'll consider it—but I certainly hope you're wrong. I have an invasion to mount and an army to lead. I haven't time to worry about the odd activities of a horde of insects."

"An invasion?" Gerrig asked, raising his bushy eyebrows.

"My husband has run off to his homeland to find a war to fight in. I'm going to get him back."

"So you've summoned the Golden Throng?" the huge actor asked enthusiastically, missing the exchange of rolled eyes between Danyilyn and Yona Parmi. "That explains all the warriors on the road!"

"It should." Bronwynn nodded curtly. "But tell me, Gerrig—why do your eyes look glazed?"

"Your Highness," Gerrig mumbled, "you know I've had far more experience in acting the warrior than in being one. Nevertheless, it's always been my private dream to march with the Golden Throng . . ."

Danyilyn winced in obvious pain, and Yona Parmi massaged his temples. Bronwynn ignored them. "You're welcome to join my army any time you choose, Gerrig. But perhaps that's a decision that should wait until you've rested?"

"Indeed, we're all *very* tired," Danyilyn agreed as she placed her tiny hands in the middle of Gerrig's huge back and struggled to shove him toward their apartments.

"A rest will help us *all* think more clearly," Yona Parmi nodded. "We thank you, your Highness," he added, bowing deeply. Then he and Danyilyn ushered the big actor off the ramp and down one of the castle's long, well-lighted corridors.

"I felt you should hear this news quickly—" Kherda began, but Bronwynn cut him off.

"It doesn't change a thing. I'm still marching northward as soon as Joss returns from Lamath."

The Prime Minister heaved a despairing sigh. "I feared as much. My Queen, Joss arrived this morning and went immediately to the parade grounds. He sends his apologies, but explains that, given your commands, he felt he should make as much use of the daylight as possible. He'll come to the palace this evening to give his report."

"Ah, Joss!" Bronwynn said enthusiastically. "It's good to have at least one advisor with a warlike spirit!"

Kherda seemed ready to comment, then checked himself. "What about the sugar-clawsps?" he asked tentatively.

Bronwynn shrugged. "Have you ever thought of poisoning all the sugar in the city?" She didn't wait to see Kherda's expression but turned to climb the ramp toward her own royal suite. "I'm going to pack. Inform Joss that I expect a drill parade tomorrow. And Kherda," she added, stopping to look back, "send the heralds to proclaim it throughout the city. I want there to be a *crowd*."

Terril rode northward from Pleclypsa on a stolen pony, reflecting on the chaos he'd left behind him. The city was in turmoil. Most of its leading citizens were dead, assassinated by huge swarms of sugar-clawsps. The little creatures had done this eagerly, fanatically. They couldn't help themselves. They were acting upon the commands of their god.

Clawsps were small insects with shiny, purple bodies with a singleminded obsession for sugar. They took it wherever they could find it, from ripening fruits to the tables of kings. With it they built the sparkling castles of crystallized sugar that decorated the eaves of most human dwellings. Clawsps were docile creatures as a rule. Whenever they became alarmed, however, their violet armor exuded a stinking chemical that produced very nasty burns. Most mothers tolerated clawsps; while they could empty a sugar dish in a week, they never took it further than the roof outside the door. Once the dish was empty it was easy enough to put on a pair of gloves and break off a tower of the constantly growing clawsp castle to grind back again into granules. Meanwhile, the little buzzing guards kept childish fingers out of the sweets. The relationship had always proved of mutual benefit to human and clawsp alike. It meant, however, that Terril the twin-killer had a standing garrison in every house in the land. His only difficulty lay in mobilizing this vast army. The process was loathsome.

Each castle was an autonomous unit. Clawsps did not speak, but they did communicate through the sense of smell. That chemical that proved so painful to human fingers had a pungent odor that transmitted the concept of war. There was a variety of other scents as well, each with its own meaning. As a sugar-clawsp grew older, the odor it exuded became more powerful, until by shifts of scent it could dominate the younger clawsps round it. Clawsp castles were therefore ruled by elders. All an older clawsp needed to do to create a stir or arouse controversy was to make a stink.

No mere clawsp, however, could make a stink like Terril. Each time he buzzed into the clear hallways of a new crystal castle, he projected a scent more powerful than that of all the elders put together. In moments, he could raise the band to frenzy, for his odor communicated far more than simply war. In the small nerve centers of the buzzing bugs, it birthed the concept of godhood. Inflamed and inspired, the insects would swarm from the castle like miniature maenads, searching for a victim on which to vent their rage. A single clawsp was merely a nuisance. However, a thousand sugar-clawsps clustered upon every exposed part of a human body brought about a hideously painful death. Terril needed only to guide his mindless devotees to his intended target and make a single angry pass. Then he could glide to the side and watch as his victim went down beneath a glistening purple wave.

It was a most effective power—by far the most useful his peculiar altershape had gifted him with. But he loathed it. His stomach soured every time he had to enter a new castle. While his body glistened with the same purple oiliness as the shells of these insects, he saw them still with human eyes. The scent that summoned them to war choked his human sensibilities. The cacophonous buzzing of wings in motion assaulted his mind. But worst of all was the suffocation of their adulation, as slimy, stinking insects struggled to rub their armor-plated bodies across his.

Just thinking about it made Terril retch. It took powerful motivation to force him down those crystalline hallways. But Terril was powerfully motivated. Although he was not the kind of man who could admit such to himself, Flayh terrified him.

Terril had simply ignored the first invitation to the High Fortress. Flayh had then summoned him to court, the summons bearing the king's own seal. Terril had dismissed it with a characteristically haughty reply. Then one day, while in his altershape, he felt the net close around him—invisible, yes, but far more effective than a web of woven steel. It had irresistibly drawn him to Ngandib, to the High Fortress, up a narrow, fetid spiral staircase into a darkened chamber. There it held him fast as Flayh lectured him intermittently on manners. Between lectures, Terril had experienced physical and psychical miseries unparalleled in his existence. He was known throughout the Mar as an evil man for the cold-hearted murder of his identical twin. But when at last Flayh freed him from that tower, Terril had a new appreciation of just what evil *was*. Flayh was intensely evil. And the threat of one day finding himself locked in that tower again was motivation enough to drive him into a thousand clawsp castles and more.

He was driven by more than just fear. Greed was an old comrade that had traveled with him ever since he found his altershape and left the cow pens of Carlog behind him. Gerril had left with him, though at that time Terril's brother had yet to discover his powers. They'd set out to make their fortune from Terril's shaping and had tried to build a monopoly on sugar. Then Gerril had found his own altershape—as well as his conscience. For the first time, Terril saw something other than a mirror image when he looked at his brother, and the sight humiliated him. While Terril was a stinking, stinging insect, Gerril was a seven-point stag.

War had come—that uneven war when Pelmen stood alone

against six other wizards and prevailed. He would not have done so, perhaps, had the stalwart stag not aided him, and Pelmen's victory had cost Terril a treasure. He'd plotted his brother's death from that day. One winter he'd tricked his brother into the forest and into his altershape. A lonely hunter had sent the shaft through Gerril's neck, but it was Terril who'd guided the huntsman to the quarry. As Gerril had collapsed upon the snow, changing shape a final time as he drew his dying breath, his treacherous twin had taken to the wing, bearing with him a new nickname: the twin-killer. The moniker was a gift from Terril's comrade, greed. Greed drove him. And laced among the threats, Flayh had spun marvelous pictures of Terril seated upon the golden throne of Chaomonous.

But it was more than just fear and greed that drove him northward toward Bronwynn's capital. Deep in his soul, he nurtured a quiet longing for a new vengeance. The death of his brother in that frozen forest had freed him, at last, from a lifelong shackle. He prized that freedom. He would not submit easily to the yoke of Flayh. He would sit on the golden throne, yes, but not at the behest of any upstart merchant, regardless of how powerful. When the time was ripe, he would act. There were, after all, clawsps in the High Fortress as well.

Until that time came, however, it made sense for Terril to impress Flayh with his loyalty. This could be easily done. Flayh had given him explicit instructions regarding a merchant he wanted murdered, and Terril would happily oblige. As he crossed the bridge into the city of Chaomonous, he spied a petty peddler moving slowly through the streets.

"My friend!" Terril called. "Can you direct me to the castle of Uda in your fair city?"

The man turned to regard Terril with undisguised contempt. "You sound foreign. You're a merchant, aren't you?"

"Not I." Terril chuckled. "But I do have some business with one. Do you know the way?"

The man raised an eyebrow in disdain, then pointed forward. "You're going straight toward it. The large building on the right, just before you cross the bridge to the palace isle. It's no castle, though."

"Thank you, friend." Terril waved as he rode on. "You've been a great help." He heard the city dweller snort as he rode past and smiled maliciously. There would be time, he thought to himself.

Terril could hardly miss the house. It was draped with red and purple bunting, the colors of Uda, and was easily the grandest dwelling on this very grand avenue. Terril urged his horse into an alley, then changed his form. A moment later he buzzed into one of the open windows of Uda's townhouse in Chaomonous.

It took only a few moments of observation to identify the man named Jagd. From a corner of the ceiling, Terril watched as the little merchant moved around the main office, snapping orders, signing documents, and browbeating underlings. Terril suddenly realized that this Jagd was very much like Flayh. Both men were small in stature. Both were iron-willed, tight-fisted merchant lords, using and discarding people without a thought. Terril decided he could take pleasure in settling this score. While his minions burned this Jagd into senselessness, he would imagine they were burning Flayh. Terril whizzed unnoticed out of Jagd's open window and found a clawsp castle hanging from the eaves directly above it.

He didn't hesitate. He plunged into the inverted palace of crystallized sugar, his shell oiling odiferously. Moments later he led two thousand swarming clawsps into the house of Jagd of Uda. The man heard them coming and just had time to turn his head to look. No one kept better informed of current events than merchants. In that split second Jagd knew exactly what was happening, and his mouth gaped open in self-pity. Then he was screaming in horrified agony. Terril buzzed aside to watch, wanting to insure that the job was well done. When Flayh heard this news, Terril wanted there to be no mistaking that it had been carried out to the letter. Naturally the little powershaper would know who was responsible. Who but Terril could do murder by insects?

By the time Jagd stopped screaming and pitched over onto the floor, a crowd of his kinsmen and servants had rushed into the office. Terril waited until the resident herbalist announced that Jagd was dead before leading his purple army out the window. He was amused at the expressions he left behind him. Jagd's death had summoned almost as many shocked smiles from the terrified Udans as it had tears.

He wasn't quite finished. A disdainful peddler somewhere

along this road had raised his ire, and Terril was nothing if not vengeful. He found the man in moments and left him squirming in the streets, crying out for someone to take a knife and end his unspeakable misery. A very satisfactory conclusion, Terril thought to himself as he left his army clustered upon the peddler and soared off toward the heart of the city. That should be sufficient to panic the local residents. From this height he could look down on the Imperial House itself. Should he rouse the rest of the clawsps in the city and make his move immediately upon the palace? He could, he supposed. What recourse would its residents have against him?

Something caught his eye that made him pause. Far across the spires and roofs of the city he saw a vast field that rippled with wave after wave of color. A wall of people reared up into the sky over the plain, and now he began to hear their roar. He angled toward this deafening crowd noise, and was quickly able to make out the outlines of a wooden grandstand. The closer he came the more impressed he was with the size of this land's population. Never had he seen a crowd so huge in Ngandib-Mar. When he saw why they were cheering, his heart quailed.

There was an army spread out below him. Terril had seen many armies in his life and had even led a few. But at a glance he realized that the Mari definition of army had little in common with that of the Golden Throng. His tiny body shuddered. He'd expected to conquer a land this size with just a swarm of insects?

He circled down toward the foot of the grandstand, his mind working furiously. He needed to get control of himself. He was Terril the twin-killer, master magician, not some impressionable peasant. He had powers these Chaons could not imagine. He needed only to stop and take stock of them and to plan carefully his next step. First, however, he needed information.

He flew under the grandstand in search of a private place and finally found one. There he took his human form again and walked out to take a human measure of this throng he expected soon to rule.

It still took his breath away, but Terril's cunning was beginning to reassert itself. He glanced around and saw a group of adolescent girls in giddy, giggling conversation. "Pardon me," he said in as suave a tone as he could manage, and the conversation broke off into shocked stares. Terril chuckled self-deprecatingly and said, "I realize this may seem very odd to you, but can you tell me why this crowd has gathered?"

"You don't know?" One girl frowned archly.

Terril's eyebrows drooped menacingly, and the child's frown turned fearful. "Would I ask if I did?" he asked.

"The Golden Throng," another of the girls said quickly.

"Yes," the first said. "We've come to watch the Golden Throng!"

"I see. And where is the Golden Throng going?"

"North!" one said. Then she looked at her friends and added with a slight giggle, "I guess." It really didn't matter to them. When the girls quit giggling and looked back at the curious stranger, they experienced a terrible shock. He had disappeared.

"Just look at that," Bronwynn murmured, enthralled by the Golden Throng as it paraded before her. The cheers of the crowd below engulfed her. "Just look!" she cried above them.

Kherda obeyed. He gazed at the gilded column and nodded appreciatively. He was remembering the last time he'd stood upon this reviewing stand, on the day Bronwynn's father led the Throng away to war. He hoped Bronwynn wasn't thinking about that. He'd been up to his neck in treachery at the time. This present army seemed rather pitiful by comparison to Talith's throng, and the thought dismayed him. If that army had been so savagely destroyed by their Mari enemies, what could be expected from this military venture? Not even Joss had been able to dissuade her, although they'd argued far into the night. The girl was every bit as hardheaded as her father.

"Here comes Joss," Bronwynn shouted, pointing downward, and Kherda leaned over the railing to look. As they watched the solitary figure wrapped in a heavy cloak make his careful way up the steps of the platform to join them, they missed seeing the tiny purple insect swoop over their heads and down between them to alight on the underside of the rail. When Joss finally reached them he was wheezing, and Bronwynn patted him on the shoulder. "It's a long climb," she said in his ear.

General Joss noded grimly, and surveyed the force below them with a dour frown.

"It's a splendid army." Bronwynn smiled.

"It is a skeleton, my Lady." Joss did not mince words on matters affecting national security.

"But you've done wonders with it," she replied evenly, not looking at him.

"Drills and discipline are valuable, my Lady, but they hardly make up for a lack of warriors and weapons."

"I take it you still disapprove of my military adventure."

"My objections are a matter of record, your Highness, based entirely on objective analysis."

"My lady," Kherda began meekly, "what he means is—"

"I need no one else to interpret my words to the Queen," Joss snapped.

"Nor do *I* need any further discussion on the matter," Bronwynn announced. "It's heartening to know that the two of you can agree on something, at least. But my mind is made up." She glanced first at Kherda, then at Joss. "It's doubtful you'll change it."

"We are unprepared, my Lady," Joss grunted insistently, reopening the door Bronwynn had so emphatically shut.

Kherda summoned new courage and followed him through it. "We just hate to see your father's folly repeated—"

"You've compared me to my father quite enough, Kherda," Bronwynn snarled, cowing her Prime Minister.

"Obviously not quite enough," Joss said between clenched teeth, "or you would take it more seriously. Your father led the Golden Throng in search of *you*, my Queen, and lost it on a foreign field to a much inferior force. Had he not lost his army there, he might well have lost it here instead, fighting to regain the very throne he'd left behind."

"You supported the usurper!" Bronwynn flared. "And *you*, Kherda—you planned her triumph!"

Kherda cringed, and his eyes pleaded with the general to let the matter drop. But Joss had built a career upon faithfully pointing out realities, and would not be silenced. "Yes we did, my Queen. Reprehensible behavior, perhaps, but your father's foolishness was largely to blame. He left the state in chaos."

"And will you abandon me now to my foolishness?" Bronwynn spat, her eyes flashing.

Joss stiffened. "Your Highness, you know the truth. I never abandoned your father. Nor will I ever abandon you. But I cannot vouch for the loyalty of any other of your ministers, and there are many would-be rulers among the courtlings of the Imperial House. Your personal love for the Mari warrior is understandable, and your wish to aid him is, in some aspects, even justifiable. But this is not a reasonable decision. It is based on emotions alone."

Bronwynn sighed and gripped the railing. "Are you going to give me the whole lecture?"

"Your husband has not summoned you—"

"Maybe he can't!"

"But maybe he chooses not to!"

"He may be in trouble."

"But your arrival may bring him more! So the Maris are fighting among themselves. This is no new thing. It is, in fact, the norm for those barbarians. But if you believe our arrival at Westmouth with twenty thousand swords will bring cheer to the faction Lord Rosha backs, then you've sorely mistaken the Mari mind! The Golden Throng will put an end to their warring on one another. Instead, they'll unite to drive us out!"

"But you'll be our general this time—not my father," Bronwynn said with mocking sweetness.

Joss ignored her sarcasm and plunged on. "Then there's the other adversary—Lamath."

"You told me yourself that Lamath is in chaos!"

"Yet they remain our primary foe—our hereditary foe. And by calling me home you've broken any diplomatic relationship we might have had with them."

"I'll not have dealings with the men who overthrew Erri," Bronwynn grumbled.

"Then you'll likely face them in battle, for what will unite Lamathians more quickly than the threat of a Chaon invasion? Bronwynn—" Joss caught himself, shocked and embarrassed at this breach of royal etiquette.

Bronwynn turned to regard him with a cool smile. "Yes?"

"Please forgive me, your Highness." He emphasized the title.

"Oh, I think I've already done that," she said brightly, and she leaned over the wooden railing in a studied show of interest in the parade. Kherda hoped Joss would have the sense to abandon the battle and resign himself to doing their sovereign's bidding. He glanced at the old soldier behind the queen's back, and raised his eyebrows. Joss nodded, and the old warrior's shoulders seemed to slump. Bronwynn spoke again, and the Prime Minister leaned forward to listen. "I really don't care whom we battle, or where. It's just that I've waited inside that castle for too long. My mind's made up. It's time to *act*. Joss, take your finest regiment and return to the palace to make final preparations. We'll march this afternoon. Kherda, you—" She broke off, and pointed. "What's that?"

Kherda glanced over to see that his pasty-faced assistant was holding a message out toward him. The Prime Minister reached out and took it. In reading it, his own face drained of all color.

"Well?" Bronwynn snapped impatiently. "What is it?"

Kherda cleared his throat and blinked twice. "It's—Jagd of Uda, my Queen."

"Yes, yes," Bronwynn snarled. "And what does the chief of merchants want now?"

"Ah . . . nothing, my Queen. That is, he's unable to—I mean, he's dead!"

"Dead? How did he die?"

Kherda drew himself up to his full height and invested his reply with drama befitting its importance. "An assassination my Lady. He was swarmed to death by sugar-clawsps."

Bronwynn blinked. "Clawsps again."

"Yes, my Lady," Kherda said meaningfully.

Queen Bronwynn heard something in his tone of voice that made her spear him with an angry glare. "And you're thinking that I need to wait, that we have no business marching off to war while swarms of crazed insects ravage our citizenry?"

Kherda backed away from her as far as he dared, feeling behind him for the platform's rear rail. "Ahem," he said, clearing his throat. "I . . . the thought had occurred to me—"

"Exactly *what* do you think my presence here could add to the struggle against the tiny creatures?"

"Ahem," Kherda said again, still backing. "A . . . demonstration of . . . solidarity, perhaps . . ."

"I suppose I could tour the devastated area?" Bronwynn smiled sourly.

Kherda choked out, "That might be an appropriate gesture—"

Bronwynn suddenly looked downward. As her attention left him, Kherda felt like a fish who had suddenly managed to slip free of a hook. He sighed and sagged against the wooden railing in relief. "Who's that?" Bronwynn was asking, pointing at a cluster of figures moving through the crowd far below.

Joss looked where she pointed and sighed wearily. "It appears the missionaries are among us again." He didn't hide his contempt.

"They may have news of Erri," Bronwynn muttered. She quickly crossed the wooden platform and started down the stairs. Joss pursued her, but Kherda chose to cling to the railing, waiting for the rickety structure to stop shaking before descending. He was the only one to see the purple insect dart from its place and disappear quickly in the direction of the Imperial House. At first he was terrified. Then he laughed at himself. "A coincidence," he muttered. "What could one tiny insect do to me?" The platform had stopped rocking. Carefully, cautiously, Kherda started the long climb down.

"Naquin!" Bronwynn cried as she reached the bottom of the treacherous stairway. "How very nice to see you!" She smiled brightly, but it was as fake a smile as any she'd given to Joss or Kherda on the platform above. Bronwynn had always treated Naquin with courtesy, but she'd never found any common ground for a relationship with the man. That she kept trying was evidence of her great love for Erri. Privately, she wondered what the prophet saw in this rigid, blue-gowned ex-priest.

Naquin bowed elaborately, but failed to hold out a hand to help her the rest of the way down. Naquin had been raised as one of the pampered, not a pamperer. He still hadn't mastered all the niceties of being of lower station. "My dear Queen Bronwynn. You look much happier than you did several days ago. In fact, you appear quite radiant."

"Excitement, Naquin," the queen said briskly. "I'm about to take some action instead of waiting around the palace. Come. I'm about to return to the Imperial House. I assume you have news of Erri?" Bronwynn was striding toward her horse, looking backward in the obvious expectation that Naquin would follow. The man did, but some uneasiness registered on his face. Bronwynn wondered at its cause, even as she directed her Lord of the Livery to find Naquin a mount. Joss had joined them and was barking crisp orders that had servants scurrying in all directions. By the time Bronwynn and Naquin were mounted, a crack regiment had fallen in behind them to escort them back to the palace.

The skyfaither's uneasiness continued to show itself as he offered her Erri's greetings and told her the circumstances of his meeting with the prophet. It put her on guard. Her smile never wavered, but Bronwynn prepared herself for unpleasant news.

It wasn't until they'd entered the Imperial House and climbed the spiral staircase to the throne room that she finally understood. Bronwynn had smiled enough for today. Now she unleashed her fury. "Erri said I should *what*!" she bellowed, loudly enough to echo down the halls.

Naquin shifted position and repeated, "The prophet suggests you should wait. Naturally, you'll give the highest attention to his instructions."

"His instructions!" Bronwynn gasped, eyes wide.

"Why, certainly his instructions. He is, after all, your spiritual father, and when he—"

"I met Erri when he was a foul-mouthed sailor who still stank of fish! I'll not follow his instructions nor anyone else's! Get out!"

Naquin gulped, his eyes wide. "Get out?" he said and she shouted:

"You heard me! Get out!"

The skyfaither stiffened his already stiff back and pursed his lips reprovingly. "You're making a grievous error—" he began, but, when Bronwynn spun around and shouted for the guards, he turned his back on her in turn and marched self-righteously out of the castle. He'd performed his task. He couldn't be held accountable.

Bronwynn looked over her shoulder and watched him go. She chanced to catch sight of herself in one of the mirrors Ligne had placed in the throne room and was startled by the savagery of her sneer. She softened it, but didn't soften her voice as she shoved a guard aside and stalked toward her royal apartments. She was angry, and the thing that bothered her most was that she was fearing Naquin might be right.

No one saw this her way! Not one of her trusted advisors had tried to see it from her perspective. And from each one she received the same reproachful look, that expression adults reserve for impetuous teens who won't listen and who are going to be sorry they didn't.

As she burst into her room, a flock of maids ran to greet her, but she waved them all off. "I don't need you!" She sent them bustling out the doors. Her armor had been laid out for her on the bed. She strode toward it, grabbed it up, and began buckling on her glistening breastplate. She was suddenly conscious of the roaring crowd outside her window, and realized that the news had been published that she marched today. She walked to a mirror, scooped up a hairbrush, and told her reflection, "I can't back out now."

—Why not? the mirror answered back.

The hairbrush clattered to the marble floor. Bronwynn stared at the mirror in shock. "What did you say?"

—Why can't you wait? Are you not the queen?

Bronwynn stepped away from the mirror, and slowly looked up at the tapestry-draped walls. She thought she knew who it was—or rather, *what* it was—that was addressing her. This knowledge did not allay her amazement, not did it still the pounding of her heart. "House?" she said. "Are you talking to me?"

—Is that so difficult to imagine?

"But—I thought—Pelmen said you had retired from dealings with mankind! He said you wouldn't talk again!"

—Unless the Power directed.

Bronwynn looked from one wall to the next, making a slow circle in the center of her gigantic bedroom. She had difficulty breathing. "Then—you—the Power is—"

—It would be helpful if you could complete your sentences, the Imperial House harrumphed. This House cannot read minds.

"The—the Power commanded that you talk to me?" she asked, a tremor in her voice.

—It seems you wouldn't listen to anyone else.

"But—how is it that I understand you?"

—Why shouldn't you understand this House? the castle lectured sternly. You're of royal blood, are you not? And have you not demonstrated some talent at shaping?

"Am I—truly a powershaper then?" Bronwynn whispered, awed by the possibility and longing for confirmation of it.

—Who can say? the House grumbled. No one is a shaper

who has not found his altershape. This House has been—elsewhere. Has such a thing occurred?

"No," Bronwynn admitted.

—Then think no more about it. If it happens, it happens. At present, there are more pressing matters to attend to.

"The Power doesn't want me to go to Ngandib-Mar," Bronwynn said thoughtfully.

—Perhaps that's so, perhaps it is not. The only clear directive is simply to wait.

"To wait," Bronwynn mused. "That's all?"

—That's all.

The queen studied this for a moment in silence. Then she frowned. "But why?"

The shutters of her windows flew open with a bang. Anyone else would have interpreted this as a gust of wind, but Bronwynn now recognized it as an exasperated sigh.

—This House cannot foretell the future! the Imperial House of Chaomonous thundered, and Bronwynn thought seriously about getting under the bed.

"Sorry," she mumbled. "I just don't know what to do."

—Wait! The Imperial House roared. Does it have to be written upon the wall?

"I'll wait, I'll wait!" Bronwynn snapped, annoyed now. "I *meant*, what do I do about the march?"

—Send someone in your place! Is that so difficult to reason out?

"Someone else? But who could—" Just then, everything seemed to come into focus for Browynn lan Rosha. She summoned a messenger.

"Yes, your Highness?"

"Send me General Joss. Then go to the areas frequented by the players and tell Lady Danyilyn that I'd like to see her." As the messenger saluted and scooted off to obey, Bronwynn smiled. Who better to take her place than a professional actress?

Terril the twin-killer hung in the air sixty feet above the entrance to the Imperial House. Despite having to wear his odious body, elation surged through him. He was about to conquer Chaomonous.

The minute the queen left the reviewing stand he'd flown here, to the roof of her castle. He'd taken his human form then and dispatched a pair of the queen's blue flyers with messages to Flayh and to the new king of Lamath. Terril enjoyed the irony of this—launching the seeds of the queen's destruction from the roof of her palace. The messages warned Flayh and his Lamathian allies to prepare an ambush for the Golden Throng in Dragonsgate. Now he waited for her to march. Once she was gone, he would unleash his swarms upon the depleted staff of her castle, and the Imperial House would be his.

It was all so easy! Nothing at all like battling a rival shaper. War in the Mar was a guessing game where the whims of the powers always made the outcome unpredictable. This victory was so certain it was almost boring! Almost—but not quite. Tonight he would take his human form again to sleep in the bed of a king! He could hardly wait.

Suddenly the gates flew open, and the huge throng that had made its way here from the parade ground began cheering lustily. A double column of warriors marched out first and stepped smartly down the incline toward the market. As they approached the crowds that clogged the street, the column formed a wedge and began shoving onlookers back out of the way.

There was a rumbling from within the castle, then the first of the huge wagons issued from the portal. There were two dozen of these, each drawn by teams of eight heavy draft horses, and each flanked by golden-mailed warriors. The riders came next, encased in burnished plates of glistening gold, astride proudly prancing mounts draped in brocade of the same rich hue. Terril was impressed only with the wealth this all demonstrated. He scoffed at the thought of a warrior dressing like the belle of a royal ball. His multifaceted eyes searched the riders earnestly. There was still no sign of the queen.

With a sudden fanfare, the last column of riders divided, turning their mounts to face inward toward the open pathway they'd created. Out rode the queen in full armor, astride a grandly caparisoned stallion of jet black. Her visor was shut, but it was clear from the womanly shape of the armor that this was she. Her golden cape was trimmed with bright blue, a symbolic reference to the skyfaith. This was the only intrusion of any other color in the whole of the gilded parade, and it drew all eyes to her. She drew her sword and held it above her, then spurred her steed forward and rode to the head of the line.

Now it was time, Terril thought to himself, sickened by the thought. The stench of a thousand clawsp castles—the prospect made him want to retch. But as he soared upward to survey the world's most beautiful city, he decided it was worth it. Already he could smell the battle scent of his own purple shell. He plummeted toward the first large concentration of clawsp castles, even as the army wound their way across the bridge and onto the northern road.

Once started, he worked quickly, circling the outer edge of the city first, then spiraling toward its center. The insect army mustered—and it was terrible to behold.

They numbered in the millions, and the sinister drone of their wings drew Chaon eyes to the sky in terror. They moved in a single, gigantic mass, their shining shells glistening in the sunlight as if a storm cloud had donned a garment bespangled with violet sequins. The swarm's shadow raced across the map of the city of Chaomonous, blotting out the sun. It held the shape of an enormous spear point, aimed at the city's heart.

It was Maliff, the falconer, who first spotted the attacking horde. He knew immediately what it was. Maliff was bored by people and he had a speech problem, but he did stay in touch with current events. "Crawsps!" he screamed in horror. "There's sugar-crawsps upon us!" The young falcon he'd been carrying suddenly found itself clutched to Maliff's protective bosom, as the falconer dove through the door of the mews and slammed it shut behind him. He was too late. Already the clawsps were streaming in the windows.

They poured down the central spiral stairway of the castle like purple wine whirling down a funnel. They gushed out and down every branching hallway, filling the roomy palace completely in a matter of moments. Slammed doors slowed them momentarily, but couldn't stop them. They wiggled through keyholes and cracks under the doors, and raced fanatically onward. They searched for bodies to swarm. They found many huddled together in a corner of the servants quarters. Quickly they applied themselves to coating the outer layer of people with their flesh-eating chemical wastes. It was slow going, however, for the bodies of those on the outside protected those huddled deeper in the pile. It was small comfort, perhaps, to smother to death, rather than to burn, but there was a chance a few might survive.

Those caught in the hallways stood little chance at all. A few, however, made a valiant effort. One of these was the short, portly figure of Yona Parmi. He was on his way up the great spiral to the upper levels when the assault began. He threw his head back and stared upward as the huge hole in the palace roof closed with a rush of wings. Instinctively he ducked his head and ran, but not toward his own rooms. He ran instead toward the royal suite—and Danyilyn.

They had been unable to dissuade Gerrig from donning the golden armor—although the huge actor had found it difficult to find any that would fit him. They were bidding him good-bye when the strange summons had come for Danyilyn to report to the queen. Things had moved quickly after that—the army had nearly marched without Gerrig, but he had caught up. Yona had watched the queen depart, but Danyilyn had not yet returned. Now he raced to her side. He had no illusions about the next few minutes. Danyilyn was all the family he had. He would face death beside her.

He got to the door, but not inside it. They were around him, a stinking, burning tide. Parmi fought back. He batted the air and stomped his feet, and screamed more in rage than in pain. He saw a hundred tiny insects struggling to squirm under the door, and made the last decision of his life. He dropped to the floor on top of them, crushing these and preventing others from reaching the crack. Then with his last effort he raised his clawsp-coated right hand and plugged the keyhole with his little finger. It was a victory, of sorts. Yona Parmi died a victor.

Bronwynn was in conference with Kherda and the House when it started. She was the first to know, for the Imperial House was in the midst of a sentence when it broke off in a horrible scream.

"What *is* it?" Bronwynn demanded, and Kherda, who couldn't understand a thing the castle said, nevertheless turned white at the look on her face.

—Magic attack! the Imperial House wailed. Must go! Must return to the Power! Use your gift!

After a long shuddery wail, the castle was quiet once more. Only then could they hear the human screams and the droning that had been growing insidiously louder. There was much shouting and thumping outside the door, and through all this the queen and her Prime Minister gazed at one another in shock. Then a half dozen clawsps not wholly crushed by Yona's self-sacrifice wiggled under the door and shot up toward them.

Everything came together in an instant—the clawsps, the killing of Jagd, the warnings, and the castle's last speech. She remembered a quiet campfire in the Great North Fir with Rosha and Pelmen. The two men had traded stories about people she'd thought then were mythical, but knew, now, were real. This was Terril the twin-killer—the clawsp. Yona Parmi had been right.

"No!" she shouted at the incoming clawsps and she threw up her hand to stop them. From her palm issued a golden globe of flame.

Kherda fainted. The clawsps fried. And Bronwynn knew, now, she was a shaper. Any minute she expected to discover her altershape and she looked forward to that revelation with a fierce excitement. That didn't deflect her from her task, however. She raced to the door, threw it open—and burned a hundred-thousand insects from the hallway. The second ball of flame was much larger than the first.

Terril felt it. Although he wasn't in the hallway, nor even in that section of the castle, he felt it—another shaper. The moment he did, he fled for the hole in the roof and just missed being cremated by the third ball of fire, which was the largest of all. This exploded in the midst of the castle's garden, scorching every leaf and withering each blade of grass. But it also crushed the clawsp attack. A million burned insects covered the garden floor like violet snow. The rest were gone.

## CHAPTER TEN

# Sythia Isle

"WE'D BETTER go," Mar-Yilot interrupted, more harshly than necessary.

Kam and Rosha stopped laughing and looked at the woman in surprise. Then Kam gave his young friend a wry smile and shrugged. "She's right, of course." He twisted around to face the sorceress in order to explain, "It's just that I've not seen the lad since this time last year, and we still have some catching up to do. Ah, Rosha. There's never enough time."

"There's a remedy for that," Mar-Yilot snorted. "And you know what it is."

Kam grinned, and ran his fingers through his tight yellow curls. "Can't do it, dear lady. Much as I'd like to visit that fabled island of yours and pocket a few diamonds for myself, I need to stay here." He shoved an empty breakfast platter away and called toward the kitchen for someone to come and get it.

Mar-Yilot frowned. "It's only a matter of time before Flayh sends his thugs down the road to crush you—"

"Crush me!" Kam barked. "Mar-Yilot, you are a dear friend and a marvelous shaper, but you certainly do exaggerate. The House of Kam has sat here at the foot of the High Plateau for centuries and witnessed a score of armies descending the cliff to make war against it. Why, to ease their boredom in times of peace, the kings of Ngandib used to lay siege to this castle just for practice! But never has it fallen. Not once have they even breached a single wall! No, my Lady, you hurry on, if you feel you must. But don't fret about us. Kam can care for itself."

Rosha appreciated Kam's bravado, but he was watching the man's eyes and saw something false there. Mar-Yilot must have seen it too, but she didn't comment. That puzzled Rosha. He'd always heard that Mar-Yilot spoke before she thought. Since he'd been around her, however, he'd had the sensation that she was hiding something.

"So, Rosha," Kam said grandly, "we'll have to finish this up the next time you stop by."

"We'd like that." Rosha nodded.

"We?" Kam muttered.

"My father and I," Rosha explained. Kam's embarrassed response confused him.

"What—Oh yes! Right. Ah . . . listen, Mar-Yilot, I've got my best horses waiting for you. You really think Pelmen's well enough to ride?"

Frowning, Rosha flicked his gaze to Mar-Yilot just in time to catch her eyes studying him worriedly. She immediately looked at Kam, and answered with too much intensity, "I feel certain that he is."

"Good." Kam nodded. When there was an awkward pause, the blond warrior got to his feet. "Ah—just let me check to see if the horses are ready." He quickly left the hall. Mar-Yilot shifted in her seat and found a bite of biscuit to nibble.

"What's going on?" Rosha asked suspiciously.

"What?" the sorceress snapped, looking annoyed. "Nothing's going on, but we certainly need to be, so grab that precious bundle and let's move, shall we?"

Rosha persisted. "You're hiding something. What is it?"

"I'm hiding nothing!" Mar-Yilot snarled. "I'm just tired, that's all, and I'm not looking forward to a day of playing magical tag."

"Why haven't you told me what happened to your husband?" Rosha demanded, his face expressionless.

Mar-Yilot feigned surprise. "My husband? What about my husband?"

Rosha stared at her, his eyes hard. "You're not going to tell me, are you?"

The powershaper met his gaze. "I don't know what you're talking about."

Kam stepped back into the hall and said, "Everything's ready. Pelmen's already mounted and is waiting for you. Seems he's in a hurry."

"Very good." Mar-Yilot nodded and picked up the heavy

cloak Kam had provided for her, wrapping it around her shoulders. "Coming?" she asked Rosha cuttingly.

The warrior's only reply was to stand slowly and stalk out of the hall. He fetched his own cloak and the bundled-up pyramid and went to join Pelmen in the stable. His friend greeted him, but Rosha said nothing.

Kam bade them all good-bye with a cheerful smile, but his eyes were filled with worry. His cockiness fooled no one. His danger was real. And if there was any true hope for the survival of his house, it rested upon the alliance of these two powershapers. "Be careful," he warned them.

Mar-Yilot fixed him with a sobering look. "You could have your people ready to ride by midmorning. I could cover all of us, and you'd be out from under Flayh's shadow."

Kam hesitated a moment, then shook his head. "Not now. The dog is chasing you, not me. We'd slow you down too much, perhaps even cause your capture. What safety is there for my household in that? No," he added, glancing around at the stable walls, "I'll stay here. And if that dog of a shaper should happen by, perhaps Kam can be a thorn in his paw." He smiled again, waved, and the three riders galloped out of his gates.

They rode northward three abreast; Pelmen was in the middle, Rosha and Mar-Yilot flanking him should he fall. There seemed little danger of that at the moment. He seemed fit, and sat well in the saddle. The only evidence of his weariness was his detachment from them. He obviously thought of other things. Still, he concentrated enough to add his own coverage to the magic cloak Mar-Yilot wrapped around them. That protection enabled them to avoid a half dozen earnest patrols of slavers.

Mar-Yilot and Pelmen talked a bit at first, but Rosha said nothing. He'd not opened his mouth since he'd left the breakfast table. It was his manner of showing rage—an old habit, born in his stuttering childhood—and he felt certain Pelmen, at least, sensed his anger. The other two let their conversation die. When they avoided asking him what the problem was, he knew for certain they'd conspired against him. He savored his fury in silence.

After several hours they rounded the northern face of the plateau and hit the straight stretch of road that led westward to the Garnabel Bridge. Suddenly his rage spilled over; with volcanic violence, the words spewed from his lips. "Foul friends, the both of you! I'll travel no farther, not a pace, until you tell me what you've hidden!" He reined his horse about and jerked it to a stop, staring at his companions with glittering eyes.

His outburst startled them both, but Mar-Yilot quickly recovered. "I'm trying to cloak us!" she shot back at Rosha. "Just what are *you* trying to do?"

Rosha ignored her words, turning his hot gaze on Pelmen. "What are you not telling me?" he asked, half in demand, half in plea. It was the pleading that broke the powershaper, and Pelmen's posture, which had been so erect since their departure, wilted into a slump. He sagged in his saddle, and his eyes dropped from the road ahead to the tangles in his horse's mane.

When he finally spoke it was to the woman, and his voice was as thin and weak as Rosha had ever heard it. "Who should tell him?"

Mar-Yilot's lips—already pencil thin—seemed to disappear altogether into a tight line. Rosha twisted in his saddle so that his shoulders faced her squarely and scowled expectantly.

Mar-Yilot squinted toward the sun, then turned her gaze toward him. Rosha saw only a sliver of her golden eyes, as those auburn eyebrows pinced together in a frown. "I killed your father," she announced. Then she looked back at the road.

Pelmen's strength returned, and he sat back up straight. "Tell him why," Pelmen ordered, and Mar-Yilot turned back to look at him, a bit surprised by the authority in his voice. Her eyes flicked back to Rosha's, who was clenching his teeth and fighting the urge to cry out.

"I was blind. I was fooled. Flayh tricked me into believing that Dorlyth had ambushed my husband and that Pelmen had bound him with dread. I wanted vengeance, so I trapped your father and Pelmen in a ring of fire. I knew Pelmen could escape, of course. But I also knew he couldn't save your father."

"And that was your vengeance on *me*," Pelmen whispered hoarsely.

"In part." The woman shrugged. "I did intend to kill you, too, eventually, but I recognized that would take much more planning. Still, I knew you would suffer, as I had, the futility of having power and not being able to use it." Mar-Yilot spoke frankly, in all honesty, without rancour or bitterness.

To Rosha it sounded almost casual, as if she recited the

details of her breakfast instead of his father's murder. For a moment, as the blood rushed into his head and his tongue thickened beyond all possibility of usefulness, he calculated the time it would take to unsheath his borrowed blade, leap over Pelmen, and halve the woman in her saddle.

"Don't, Rosha," Pelmen murmured, and the quiet wisdom in his statement stilled the warrior's hand.

"Oh, go ahead," Mar-Yilot growled, and for the first time her voice betrayed the depth of her remorse. Rosha looked at her sharply and saw a tear glisten on her wan cheek before the woman could brush it away in irritation. "You have the right." Staring at her, Rosha was surprised at how very frail she looked.

"He had as much right to kill you as you did his father," Pelmen said evenly. Then he looked at her. "That is, none at all."

Mar-Yilot snorted a mirthless laugh. "If he doesn't, then no one has the right to kill anyone."

"Correct," Pelmen agreed, his eyes carefully watching the road. They were in danger. Mar-Yilot's confession had made her inattentive. He wordlessly took up her task until she could return to it.

The sorceress laughed, this time derisively. "I had heard you'd become a holy man, Pelmen, but this I find difficult to believe. By your logic, we've no right to kill Flayh!"

Pelmen nodded. "I don't think killing is ever a right. Unfortunately, it appears sometimes to be a responsibility."

"Responsibility to whom?" the Autumn Lady challenged. "If he's responsible at all to his father's ghost, he'll gut me here and now!"

"Did you see him die?" Rosha asked. The two shapers both turned to look at him, startled by his calm. "Did either of you see him die?" he repeated.

Pelmen and Mar-Yilot exchanged glances. "I didn't," Mar-Yilot muttered.

"Nor did I." Pelmen sighed. "He told me he preferred that I didn't watch."

"Where did this take place?"

"On the edge of a precipice not far from the glade of mod Carl. We were searching for you."

Rosha nodded thoughtfully. "There was a weird woman in

the forest that morning, to whom I confided all of my thoughts . . ." He looked inquiringly at Mar-Yilot.

"That was me," she admitted.

Rosha shifted position in his saddle. "Then if anyone is to blame, it must be me. For had I not been fool enough to attack Flayh's castle on my own, my father would never have fallen into your trap. And if I hadn't warned you he was coming, there'd have been no trap in the first place."

Mar-Yilot gazed at the warrior, her golden eyes softening with a new respect. "It's a rare young man who can accept his father's death with such equanimity."

"I wouldn't, if I really thought he was dead," Rosha said bluntly, and he hurried on to explain. "I think I would know if something like that were true. I'd feel it, somehow. I just can't believe he'd die like that."

The two shapers were stunned. Mar-Yilot withdrew from the conversation. She was no physician of minds, but she knew enough about denial to let the boy alone. Pelmen did not feel that freedom.

"I'm afraid you'll have to eventually—" he began.

Rosha cut him off. "Did you see the body?"

"No, but the fire—"

"Show me the body. Then I'll believe it." Rosha set his jaw, and turned his eyes to stare fiercely down the road. There was no more discussion. They rode steadily to the northwest—and every hoofbeat brought them closer to Flayh's net.

The two powershapers and the warrior were not the only travelers on the road that day. It so happened that on this same afternoon, Pezi and his tugoliths reached Dragonsgate.

They had survived the Tellera Desert. Of course, they'd demolished a caravan of foodstuffs that had been intended for the new king's coronation banquet, but that hadn't been Pezi's fault. And he'd offered the trading captain good money for the wagon Thuganlitha had sat on. Could he help it if the terrified merchant had already sprinted out of earshot by then? What had irritated him most about that particular adventure was that he'd gotten almost nothing out of it. By the time the hungry tugs finished gorging themselves, all he could salvage were a couple of squashed oranges and a clump of grapes. His belly had been vocally expressing its frustration ever since. Pezi would have loved to stop at the family castle at the foot of the pass to stock up on provisions, but he didn't dare. He was already on the bad side of most of his cousins. He wasn't about to destroy what was left of his reputation by taking Thuganlitha home with him.

Thuganlitha! That creature had become the bane of his existence. Pezi hated Thug, and Thug, of course, was only too willing to return the sentiment. It all could have been so easy without Thuganlitha along! To entertain himself as they'd traveled, Pezi had thought up a hundred ways of disposing of the beast. The trouble was, he lacked the nerve to put any of his plans into action. He kept hoping one of the other tugs would do it for him. None obliged. All except Chimolitha were as terrified of Thug as he was. And Chimolitha wouldn't because she was too fair-minded. She wouldn't harm anything unless she was convinced that it was right and necessary to do so. Thus far, Thug just hadn't quite stepped over her line. It made for a most unmanageable situation. Occasionally Pezi remembered that he'd intended to turn this herd into a fearsome battle unit. He usually tried to put that back out of his mind as quickly as he thought of it. The idea now gave him gas.

Pezi always got gas when he was nervous and he felt particularly gaseous today. He clung to his perch behind Chimolitha's horn and gazed upward with bulging eyes, waiting for some sight of the dragon. He'd seen the twi-beast in the sky three times since they'd left the capital, and that had given him heart. He'd hoped that perhaps they could go through the pass while the dragon was off terrorizing Lamathian villages. But that dream was dying. He'd last sighted the dragon the day before, and it was then returning to its ancient lair. He greatly feared they were about to find Vicia-Heinox home. And what would a dragon do with a line of tugoliths and one corpulent merchant? He hoped the rejuvenated beast had eaten recently.

Pezi had traveled this road a hundred times and he knew every turn. When they got within a few hundred feet of the last bend into the pass, he whispered to Chimolitha to stop. She did, and there followed a series of thuds that issued in a chorus of angry comments, as inattentive tugoliths rammed into the hindquarters of those in front of them. "Would you tell them all to shut up!" Pezi whispered in Chimolitha's funnel-shaped ear, and she obligingly bellowed, "Shut up!" at the bickering herd behind her.

"Not so loud!" Pezi groaned, holding his throbbing forehead.

Chimolitha rolled her eyes up to regard him a bit resentfully. "Man, why are you never pleased?"

"What?" Pezi blurted, startled. "Why, but—but I am pleased, I'm often pleased! Ah, ah, yes, very often!"

The animal swung her head sadly from side to side—a gesture that nearly dislodged Pezi completely. "You don't say so," she murmured.

The fat merchant clamped his legs and arms around the huge horn and hung on for his life. "But I do! I mean, I just did!"

The huge beast continued to shake her head in denial. "You yell a lot," she said mournfully.

"I don't either yell!" Pezi yelled. "I mean, I don't do it very often . . ."

"Dolna doesn't yell." Chimolitha sighed.

Pezi didn't like the direction this conversation was taking. He was also distracted by the din he heard going on behind him. When he craned his head around to listen more closely, he found to his chagrin that the other tugoliths were now arguing about what the words "shut up" meant. "Please don't talk!" he shouted, and the herd hushed. Evidently he'd picked words they could understand, and he sighed with relief. For the twentieth time he reminded himself to keep it simple.

"You yell a lot," Chimolitha repeated stolidly.

"Listen, Chimolitha, could we talk about this at a later time?"

She nodded. "Yes."

"Fine. What we need to do now is—"

"What later time?"

"I don't know!" Pezi exploded without intending to. Immediately he wished he hadn't and he hurriedly explained, "I'm just very busy right now, you understand? I'm under an enormous amount of pressure! I'm hungry, I'm—I'm tired, my nerves are in terrible shape! I mean, just look at me!"

Chimolitha rolled her huge eyes back and stared at him obediently.

"Not like that," Pezi quickly corrected, and he gestured down at the road. "Ah, look down there somewhere."

Chimolitha sighed and looked at the road.

"I'm sorry, Chimolitha, but I'm—I'm very nervous right now! Do you have any idea what's around that corner?"

The tugolith frowned in concentration, but she wasn't good at guessing games. Soon she gave up. "No," she admitted.

"There's a dragon!" Pezi announced.

The tugolith thought about that for a minute, then she nodded. "Oh," she said.

"And we've got to get passed it!" The beast filtered that through her brain, nodded, and then started moving again. "What are you doing?" Pezi demanded.

"Getting passed the dragon," she answered.

"But—!" There was no time for any protest, for Chimolitha was huge, and it didn't take her many steps to carry the horrified merchant around the last bend.

Peżi gasped as the enormous, scale-plated body of the twi-beast slipped into view. He clutched Chim's horn in utter panic. Then he glimpsed the two monstrous heads, and what he saw made him crow with glee. "Asleep!" he whispered excitedly. "The dragon is asleep! Chimolitha, you know what this means?"

She blinked. "The dragon is tired."

"Yes, right, that's right," Pezi whispered. "But it also means we can get past without disturbing it! We've got to move quietly. Let me down." Chimolitha lowered her huge chin into the dust and Pezi swung down, balancing a moment on her lower lip before dropping to the ground. Here the pass widened out so the animals behind Chimolitha were able to step around her. Pezi suddenly realized they were spilling out of the Northmouth and that some were approaching the dragon. He began jumping up and down and waving his arms furiously to get them to stop. The tugoliths did stop, mostly to get a better look at Pezi's strange antics. Although Pezi was mouthing the same angry commands he'd been shouting at them for days, no sounds came from his lips.

Riganlitha was puzzled. "I can't hear," he complained, and some of the other tugs said they couldn't, either.

"You *must* be *quiet*!" Pezi whispered with great intensity. "We must go past this dragon without waking it!"

"Why is the dragon sleeping?" Riganlitha asked.

"Because he's tired," Pezi snapped, unconsciously mimicking Chimolitha. "Now get in line and walk softly!"

"Walk softly?" Rig puzzled.

"Tiptoe! Like this," Pezi said, and he demonstrated.

His multiton charges obediently tried to imitate. Or rather, most of them did. Unfortunately, Thuganlitha had by now pushed his way out into the center of the pass and he was spoiling for a fight. He'd been outmaneuvered that morning by Pezi and had found himself at the end of the line going up the narrow defile, with no way of getting around the others. The unlucky tug that had climbed the hill ahead of him bore a dozen new scars on its backside and had been more than happy to let Thug by. The bellicose beast now danced arrogantly toward the center of Dragonsgate and regarded the sleeping dragon disdainfully. "What's that?" he bellowed.

"It's a dragon!" Pezi called back threateningly. "And if you wake it up, it will roast your hide!"

That startled Thug a bit, but he remained full of bravado. "He'd better not! I'll horn him!"

"Thuganlitha, please," Pezi wheedled, taking another approach. "Get in line and be quiet!" Then he added a fatal phrase: "It's for your own good!"

Thuganlitha never did anything for his own good. He turned his head and looked at the dragon, snorted, and muttered, "*I'll* wake him up." Then he charged.

"No!" Pezi screeched, running toward Thuganlitha to block his path. The inevitable outcome of such a senseless act suddenly occurred to Pezi; with a shout of, "What am I *doing*!" he turned and fled in the opposite direction.

"I find that a very good question," said a voice that seemed extremely close to him. In fact, it came from right above his head. Pezi stopped in his tracks and gazed fearfully upward at one of the heads of the new Vicia-Heinox. The thundering of enormous feet behind him abruptly halted. Then it started up again, moving now more quickly than before. Only now, the sound receded. Pezi looked around in time to see Thuganlitha wedging himself obediently back into line. The tugolith's eyes were wide with apprehension.

So were Pezi's as he turned to look back up at the glistening teeth and slavering jaws that hovered above him. "Greetings, your Dragonship," Pezi said. He gulped. Then he added, "Please don't eat me."

"Why ever not?" asked the dragon's other head, which Pezi noticed now had settled into the dust five feet to his left.

Pezi cleared his throat. "Well," he began lamely, "I could cite a long personal relationship between us that spans some years—" Pezi faltered and stopped when he realized both heads were chortling. "Or—or I could mention the centuries of commerce, from which both yourself and my family gained mutual benefit . . ." The heads were cackling now and winking at one another. "Or I could point out that while I might appear relatively large by human standards, I'd be no more than a mouthful compared to eating one of those!" Pezi earnestly pointed at the tugoliths.

"Yes," one head said thoughtfully. "What *are* those things?"

"They look as if they'd be tough to chew," the other head observed.

"They're tugoliths," Pezi explained. "They come from the far north of Lamath."

"Ah, Lamath!" the head above him said. "The land that loves me!" Pezi knew then that this head was Vicia.

"The land of dolts," Heinox snorted from his resting place in the dust. "But tell me, Pezi, what are these things *for*?"

"Why, well, they're—" Pezi looked around at his line of anxious behemoths, then leaned forward to whisper, "I'm taking them to my Uncle Flayh. I'm planning to make war beasts out of them."

At the mention of Flayh, both eyes in both of the heads narrowed. "And what do you think of Flayh now?" asked Vicia with a sinister sneer.

"Oh Flayh? Why, I think he's the most powerful man in the world, of course! And I need to get back on his good side!"

The heads both regarded him thoughtfully for a minute. Then Heinox raised out of the dust and said, "Come here, Pezi."

Pezi looked around, decided he was close enough, and anxiously murmured, "I *am* here!"

"Come closer," Heinox said, moving closer to Pezi himself.

"Are you going to eat me? Because if you are, I'd really rather not!"

"Pezi," Heinox growled, "stop acting like an idiot and come here!"

Pezi stared. While it had been the Heinox head who said

this, the voice was unmistakably that of his uncle. "You're—"

"Of course," the voice snapped. "Now come here!" Pezi huddled together with the head and listened closely. The watching tugoliths regarded this with awe. Their man conversed privately with dragons. Their opinion of him markedly improved. "I couldn't eat you even if I wanted to. This body isn't palpable. Your hand would pass right through it. It's an illusion I generate to support the revival of the Dragonfaith in Lamath. It also keeps traffic through the pass to a minimum. Most of the time I maintain the form of the dragon here without animating it, but when someone passes through, I'm forced to give my attention here. You, nephew, have bungled in at a most inopportune time!"

"Uncle!" Pezi pleaded. "Uncle, I'm—I'm sorry! I just thought—"

"No, you didn't, Pezi," Flayh snarled, still in a whisper. "You never had a real thought in your life. I've known about these beasts of yours for days! My new allies in Lamath had to arrest their keeper to prevent him from coming after you. However," he went on, softening, "now that I see them, perhaps there will be some use for them, after all. But get them out of this pass immediately!" Flayh ordered, stridency returning to his voice. "The army of Lamath is this moment on its way to Dragonsgate to ambush the Golden Throng in the pass. I'm in the process of tracking a pair of magical thieves. I haven't time for your lumbering beasts at the moment, so get them out of my sight!" At that, both heads lifted up and away from Pezi, then curled back against their body to return to sleep. The discussion was closed. Flayh had returned to casting his net.

"Well," Pezi told himself, "It's good to see where I stand." Then he straightened up to his full height for the benefit of his tugoliths and waddled back to the head of the line.

Chimolitha looked at him stoicly. "What did you say?" she asked.

Pezi puffed out his chest. "I told him to mind his own business and go back to sleep. Let me up."

Chimolitha nodded and lowered her head so he could climb back up behind her horn. Then she started forward, moving toward the Westmouth and Ngandib-Mar. The pack fell in behind. Even Thuganlitha seemed docile.

"Man?" Chimolitha said after a moment.

"Yes?" Pezi asked, feeling rather regal.

"It's a later time."

"What? What of it?" Pezi frowned.

"You yell a lot," the tugolith intoned, and Pezi groaned inwardly. He now remembered their earlier conversation. Chimolitha never forgot anything.

Pezi and his giant beasts distracted Flayh only momentarily. The sorcerer immediately returned his attention to creating that wall of magic netting that stretched across the Riverline to the north. He felt certain that the magical thieves who had robbed his castle would be riding into it any minute.

It wasn't that the crystal object was so precious. With the loss or theft of the other two, the pyramids themselves had become useless to him. Indeed, he was glad to be rid of them, in a way. They held a terrible fascination for the demonic dogs he had enfleshed to invade Lamath, and the presence of the dogs made him uncomfortable. Nevertheless, he was enraged to think something had been stolen from his own fortress and he'd been powerless to stop it.

Flayh had always been a merchant. While he'd spent decades wrestling with governments and dueling other merchant houses, those things had always been just business. But to a merchant, no enemy could be more hateful than a thief. Flayh felt violated. The sanctity of his impregnable tower had been defiled. And what infuriated him most was that he'd helped the rodents succeed! His living castle, his hired killers—even his own magical abilities, had failed him in his moment of triumph. It would not happen again. Wrapped in the darkness of his black-draped chamber, he held his net in place and meditated upon the alliance that had been made against him.

Mar-Yilot had linked with Pelmen. There could be no other explanation. Terril he already controlled. Joooms had trembled before him and had sworn not to interfere; like a cunning banker, Flayh had extracted certain securities Joooms could never disregard. Mast had been so frightened he'd taken his altershape and fled. The frog was now hibernating under a layer of ice at the bottom of a North Fir pond. Of the great shapers of legend, only Pelmen and Mar-Yilot remained untamed. If the Autumn Lady had at last learned the truth, then she indeed had cause to hate him. Mar-Yilot was no fool.

Despite her obsessive mistrust of Pelmen, she would reason her way to the truth eventually.

Flayh assumed she already had done so. That explained how Pelmen and the troublesome young son of Dorlyth had escaped the plateau. But if so, then he knew where they were headed. The woman was devoted to her lover and would not stay away from his sickbed for long. Were she and Pelmen traveling alone, they would doubtless fly, but they had this Rosha along. He'd been trouble for Flayh—now he would be trouble for his powerful benefactors, for they would be forced to ride northward under the cover of a magical cloak. That's why he'd woven his net carefully across the Riverline. Let that spell of invisibility touch it, and they were trapped.

As the day wore on, however, Flayh began to doubt. Not a tremor of shaping stirred his trap. Was it possible? Had they slipped through when he'd been busy with Pezi? He began to curse his nephew under his breath. Within moments his curses were full-throated cries of rage.

He felt enormous frustration at his own inexperience. He was far more powerful than the two shapers who fled his plateau, but they had been at this business for years. Like aged foxes pursued by an excellent but untried hunting hound, their seasoned guile compensated for their overmatched abilities. It galled him bitterly, but Flayh conceded at last that they had outsmarted him. He'd been too obvious in his thinking. They'd be fools to return immediately to their armies. Surely they realized that Flayh's spies had already spotted the uncloaked troop concentrations on Sythia Isle and in the glade of mod Carl. Should a cloak suddenly close again around one of those forces, they would be announcing their whereabouts as clearly as if they shouted it. No. They were in hiding. They could be anywhere!

With a vengeful bellow, Flayh jerked in his net and cast it randomly across the breadth of the Mar. The net was a type of penetration spell. It yielded to Flayh no visual image of the places it touched, nor was his image seen there, as with Mar-Yilot's dream-search. Its chief value was that it detected magic. It could pinpoint any act of shaping in the wide area it touched; should it brush some rival wizard in altershape, it would close as relentlessly as any net of cord upon a fish. The spellcaster could then draw the captured shaper to himself. With the desperation of a luckless fisherman, Flayh cast his invisible snare—and caught something.

He couldn't tell who it was, but he began working feverishly to pull the trapped shaper toward him. The afternoon disappeared into night, but Flayh took no notice. The tray of food that was brought to his door was later removed untouched. He concentrated on reeling in the trapped wizard, and as the time passed his spirits soared, for he could tell by the direction and speed of his prisoner's approach that this shaper could only be traveling through the air. Morning dawned as he pulled his captive the last few yards toward the tower. Triumphantly, he flung aside a drape to see which one he'd caught.

Flayh blinked, then stared, then swore in disgust. He'd expended all that effort to capture Terril, the purple bug! With a wave of his hand he jerked the unfortunate insect inside and closed the curtain. "Well, Terril, what a surprise," he snarled acidly. "Want to take your human form? Not a chance!" The vindictive shaper left Terril bound in the magical net as he walked to the door and threw it open. "Slave! Bring me a bottle!" Then he walked back to his helplessly hovering captive.

Flayh smiled perversely. "Now, why are you here? So proud of your victory you came to report it in person? But wait—if you had a victory to report, you'd do it from the throne of Chaomonous. What am I to gather, then? That you have—shall we say—miscalculated? That you've failed? But why else would you be buzzing around Ngandib-Mar in your silly little violet armor? Never mind, Terril, I'll hear the story soon enough, I'm sure. Slave! Where is that bottle?" A young boy raced into the room, holding a bottle before him. Flayh took it, turned it over in his hands, and muttered, "This will do." The slave disappeared in great haste. Flayh held up the bottle so that Terril could see it.

"I'm going to put you inside this, Terril. Oh, you could change shapes and break the bottle, of course, but I think perhaps I'll lock the bottle inside a metal strong box. Would that discourage you, do you think, from trying to shift forms? Why, if you tried, I do believe you'd suffocate. But that's up to you. My only concern is that you suffer." Flayh uncorked the bottle. "Get inside it."

Terril had no choice. Soon the bug was corked up and locked away, and Flayh returned his attention to searching for the two thieves. "Too late now," he muttered. "They're safely hidden. Where? Sythia Isle? Carlog? Mod Carl's glade?" Flayh sat down in a chair and opened his mind to the search. "They'll make a mistake," he murmured. "And I'll be waiting."

Fifteen minutes after Flayh jerked in his net in frustration, the three riders reached the spot where it had been. A kind of residue of shaping hung in the air, noticeable to both Pelmen and Mar-Yilot. They exchanged anxious glances.

"Flayh?" Pelmen frowned.

"Probably," Mar-Yilot answered gruffly. "But he's not looking here now. All the more reason to race on to the North Coast!" They spurred their steeds forward with new resolve.

They rode the rest of the day and through half the night, arriving finally at the cottage of Syth's bargeman. They had to pound on the door to wake him, but once he was up, he welcomed them warmly, rousing the rest of the family to prepare the hungry riders some food. Barleb talked to them nonstop through their dinner, but he didn't seem bothered by their lack of response. Their weariness was obvious. The moment they'd finished eating, he bundled them off to their beds. All three went instantly to sleep.

Pelmen awoke to the sound of a slight pattering on the roof. His weary body begged him to stay put beneath the warm counterpane, but his mind, now fully alert, could no longer pretend to rest. He forced himself out of bed and felt the shock of the icy floor beneath his feet. He scrambled for his stockings; in the process, he identified the noise coming from outside. He wasn't pleased. He jerked the cover off his bed and wrapped it around him, then shuffled down the stairs to the main room of the cottage. Someone was already up. He could smell the fire.

While they called it a cottage, this dwelling was really more of a mansion. It belonged to Lord Syth and served as a guest house for islanders trapped by nightfall on the mainland. Nevertheless, it felt like home to Barleb, for his forerunners had lived in it almost as long as Syth's ancestors had ruled the great castle across the water. The bargeman was relaxing before the fireplace in a large stuffed chair. When he saw Pelmen, however, he bounded out of it and gestured for his guest to sit down.

"I'll not take your chair," Pelmen rumbled, his voice crusty with sleep. He looked toward the ceiling. "Ice?" he asked.

Barleb frowned. "Yes, my Lord, I'm afraid it is. You'd best go back and take your rest. We'll not get across today."

"Not even if I order it?" Mar-Yilot called wearily from one of the rooms up the stairs.

Barleb's concerned frown deepened. "My Lady," he responded loudly. "Are you awake, too?"

"I was never asleep," the woman growled, and the two men heard the rustling of her climbing out of bed. She padded out onto the landing that ringed the main chamber and looked down, her hair a rat's nest of auburn tangles and deep dark circles gouged under her eyes. "Why are you looking at me like that?" she demanded, and both men suddenly took an interest in the fire. "I guess I look a mess," she mumbled, her speech slurred by sleeplessness. Only the most vacant-headed of fools would have dared any kind of reply. "What time is it?" She yawned.

"Early, my Lady," Barleb answered. "Perhaps if you lay back down—"

"I'm tired of lying down," Mar-Yilot snarled. It was one of the prerogatives of power that one never needed to hide one's grumpiness. Mar-Yilot certainly never did.

"Is Lord Syth expecting us?" Pelmen's question was a diplomatic way of inquiring if the sorceress had visited her husband's dreams.

"No." She sighed as she drifted down the stairs. "I didn't want to disturb his sleep. Besides," she added, "that would only heighten my frustration at not being there physically."

"I can certainly understand that," Pelmen murmured, his eyes studying the flames.

"What is this Serphimera woman to you?" Mar-Yilot demanded, and Pelmen had to smile at the challenge in her voice. They had been adversaries for many years. While Mar-Yilot had had only one love from childhood, she sounded almost jealous of Serphimera's impact on him.

"Why do you ask?"

"Just curious." The slender woman shrugged. "You just never seemed like the marrying type."

Pelmen looked at her with a mock frown. "You think you do?"

The woman looked at him, chuckled, and said, "You're right. Sorry. Didn't mean to pry."

"That's exactly what you meant to do," Pelmen snorted. It was a contest, as were all his encounters with Mar-Yilot, and he found he enjoyed it. In fact, he'd discovered he genuinely liked this thin, wry-faced woman. Then thoughts of Dorlyth surfaced again, and all playfulness left him.

It appeared that Mar-Yilot read his mind. She sighed and glanced around the room. "Things may have been very different, Pelmen, if we'd banded together sooner."

"I'm certain of it." Pelmen nodded. Then he smiled rather sadly. "But we've no way of knowing if they would have been any better. We have the opportunity now, at least, for which I'm grateful." He looked at the door, which had been firmly barred against the cold. "I just wish we could continue this conversation on the other side."

"There's little chance of that today, I fear," Barleb said earnestly.

"No chance at all, Barleb?" Mar-Yilot asked.

The bargeman sighed. "I learned long ago never to say never to you, my Lady. And if your guest is indeed Pelmen the Powershaper—well then, what value is there in a bargeman's opinion?"

"It's of great value to me," Pelmen murmured. "If you say we should wait, then we'll wait."

"Why?" Mar-Yilot demanded. "What good is power if you limit it with overcaution?"

"No shaper can control the winds, Mar-Yilot."

"Oh?" the woman said, arching her eyebrows. "That's not what I've heard. The rumor is that Pelmen Dragonsbane can shape the winds and bend them to his bidding."

"It's not I who shaped the winds, my Lady," Pelmen said quietly. "It's the Power who shapes them and shapes me with them."

"What's the difference?"

Pelmen raised his eyebrows and smiled. "Control. Initiative."

"You can't make it happen at will," she said, and he nodded. "But the Power can?" Pelmen nodded again. "Then ask it."

"Ask it?" Pelmen frowned.

"Ask the Power to clear off this ice storm and give us a

good breeze home. Then it can dump a blizzard on us for all I care." Pelmen stared at her as if she were mad. "What's the matter with that? It's a simple enough request, isn't it?"

Pelmen raised his brows again, this time in consternation. "I guess I'd just never thought of injecting my personal convenience into dealings of such importance."

"Why not?" Mar-Yilot demanded.

Pelmen thought for a moment, looking reflectively into the fire. "I suppose because it sounds like shaping, of a sort."

Mar-Yilot measured her words for a moment. When she spoke, it was with a gentleness and grace Pelmen had rarely known from her. "Is a child shaping her father when she makes a request? Do her smiles and pleadings force him to yield? Or is it his own nature that causes him to respond as he does? This Power of yours—you relate to it, and it to you, with a seeming mutual respect. Why shouldn't it respond to your request, if it values you?"

Pelmen pondered that as the woman circled around the chairs to a shuttered window. "I . . . don't know."

"If, as it seems, you're this Power's agent here, isn't your safety of some importance?" Abruptly Mar-Yilot wheeled back to face him, her lips parted in a brightly cynical smile. "Or is it that you fear to ask, because you're not quite sure if your mighty Power is able to deliver?"

Pelmen met her gaze evenly. "It isn't that, Mar-Yilot. It isn't that at all."

"Why then?" she demanded.

"Is it time to get up?" a sleepy voice asked from the stairway.

"Might as well, lad," Barleb called out, his eyes shifting warily from Pelmen to Mar-Yilot. "Who could sleep with two shapers a'bickering?" Evidently the bargeman expected the discussion to erupt into magical fireworks at any moment.

Rosha paid them no heed. He dressed himself quickly, stomped noisily down the staircase, and pushed between the two debaters on his way to the door. He had it unbarred before Barleb realized what he was doing. It was already open when the bargeman shouted, "Don't do it lad! The storm!"

Rosha looked out at the ice-covered ground, then glanced curiously up at the sky. It was clear. The sun was just now climbing up over the skyline of the city of Drabeld to the east of them. "What storm?" he asked.

Barleb frowned, and walked over to the doorway to look out. Then he scratched his head and looked back over his shoulder at his mistress. "Get your things, my Lady. We can go."

Mar-Yilot's eyebrows arched in surprise. Then she shot Pelmen a chagrined smile. "Your Power?" she mocked lightly.

"I have no idea." Pelmen sighed wearily. "I only know that now I can see Serphimera!"

There was a bit of wind blowing very conveniently out of the south. It carried them quickly and uneventfully across the ten-mile channel. Soon after they left the shore, Mar-Yilot lay down to sleep. Pelmen knew why. She was going by dream-search across the channel, to tell Syth they were on their way. Pelmen sat in one of the cushioned chairs, wrapped his cloak around him, and enjoyed the ride.

The Isle of Sythia had once been only a barren outcropping in the northern sea. In those ancient days it had no freshwater, no plant life, and only a single resource. That resource, however, happened to be diamonds. One day a poverty-stricken sailor named Syth, who operated a ferry between the larger islands and the North Coast, had the good fortune to be blown onto its rocky shores. As soon as the storm abated, he made his way to the court of the Jorl of the Isles, and claimed the barren rock as his own. Everyone in court laughed that day—but none more heartily than he. The ill wind that had blown him ashore had insured that his progeny would never lack for anything.

The first Syth made a fortune. Soon, however, his island was being pillaged, and he decided he had to move onto it to defend his jewels. He began to spend his wealth on improvements. Wells were dug. Bargeloads of top soil were imported. Trees, shrubs, and grasses were all brought out to the island to take root in the Sythian ground. Whole herds of wild beasts were transported over from the mainland. Naturally, along with all this, came people. The early Syths chose their tenants well; over the centuries, three pleasant little villages had matured in the island's natural coves. There were fishermen and weavers, cheesemakers and cobblers, farmers and blacksmiths, and every other useful trade. But the island's economy remained dependent upon the sparkling stones that lay scattered over the ground. Fortunately, there seemed to be an almost endless supply of gems. As a result, the Syths had built a dreamland, and had always managed it superbly. At the base of the two hills that humped up in the island's center, a magnificent mansion blossomed.

Pelmen could see it clearly, sparkling in the morning sun like the diamonds that had built it. Soon he could see something else. On the beach there waited a crowd, and it was growing.

They arrived to the sound of trumpets and cheers, and Pelmen wondered if the resulting goose bumps would stay upon his back forever. He shielded his eyes, rocking from side to side as he searched the crowd for his lady—and there she was! He beamed at her and waved. Serphimera returned his smile shyly and chewed her lower lip.

Once the barge touched the ground, he was off of it and running toward her. There was one long, searching kiss—then he held her at arm's length and scowled. "Why?" he demanded.

"I'll tell you after the feast." She said it firmly, but with a smile. Pelmen didn't argue. He knew there was no use in that.

The banquet was as sumptuous as any that might be thrown together at a moment's notice on the very threshold of winter. There was little fruit, and the vegetables were not all that fresh; Syth spent the whole meal apologizing. He needn't have, for Pelmen wasn't tasting what he ate. Nor did he really hear Syth's disclaimers. His eyes were engrossed in those of his lady, who seemed happy enough to return his gaze. Midway through dessert, Syth turned to his wife and announced, "I have entertainment planned, of course."

"What for?" Mar-Yilot groused. Then she smiled at her husband sweetly and murmured, "I don't care what it is, I can think of something far more entertaining."

Syth mod Syth-el cleared his throat and looked at his guests. "Ah—if you're finished, perhaps you'd like to see your rooms?"

The mansion's rooms were large but well heated, with glazed windows running from the ceilings to the floors. The walls were painted in cheerful colors that matched the thick-piled carpets, and all the settees were stuffed full of down for maximum comfort. Into one of these Pelmen and Serphimera sank, once Syth and Mar-Yilot had disappeared, giggling, into the castle's tower. Rosha tactfully retreated into his own assigned apartment. The moment he was gone, Pelmen grabbed Serphimera and kissed her. Then he sat back and said, "Now. Where did you go?"

There was honest, understandable hurt in his voice, and Serphimera shifted position and looked away before answering. "I came here."

"Directly? It took you that long?"

"Not directly, no. I really didn't know where this was, so I didn't know how to get here."

"But why did you come?"

Serphimera sighed, but not in exasperation. It was a sigh of embarrassment mingled with pleasure—she liked being cared for this deeply. "I told you, Pelmen, months ago, that neither of us were finished. I'd seen this place in a vision and myself here, doing . . . what I do. It was time to come, so I came."

"Without a word?" he demanded.

"What word could I give? I'd seen your travels too, my love—" She paused briefly, to let the term of endearment have its impact. "And I knew I would only impede you. It wasn't by my choice that I left you. It was the Power's."

Pelmen gazed at her, and the anger he'd built up over the months of separation dissipated in a moment. He kissed her dark hair. "So that's why I couldn't find you."

"Did you look?" she asked with a mocking frown.

"Of course!"

"Good," she muttered. "I was afraid you wouldn't."

Pelmen started to argue, then saw the dance in her emerald eyes and realized she was teasing. "And you had nothing to do with the rebirth of the Dragonfaith."

Her frown turned serious. "Nothing at all. Only great sadness that it's come so quickly."

He frowned. "You knew?"

"I knew," she said quietly.

For a long time Pelmen just looked at her. Then his eyes watered over, and he looked out the window at one of the twin hills that stood in the middle of the island.

"What's the matter?" she asked, but she already knew the answer.

"I'm wondering how much else you know, my Lady, about you, about me, about this coming war that you won't—or cannot—tell."

Serphimera breathed an unhappy sigh and thought a moment. Then she said, "I don't know everything, you realize. And I don't always interpret correctly what I see."

Pelmen remained uncomforted. "Only one thing I ask you to tell me, Serphimera, and all the rest can remain secret until it's fulfilled. Warn me of when I can expect you to disappear again." His jaw clenched and his eyes hardened as he waited for her response.

The priestess didn't flinch nor did she hesitate. She leaned toward him and said, "I will never again leave you, Pelmen Dragonsbane. Except, perhaps, through death."

Her answer made him want to shout, but his jubilation was tempered by that last condition. "Do you . . . know something . . . about that?" he asked tentatively.

Serphimera's beautiful face took on a severe aspect, and her voice had a sepulchral edge she used only for intoning prophecy. "I see us together to the mountain, Pelmen Dragonsbane. And then I see no more." The expression remained fixed for a moment—the face one might expect to find carved on a sculpture of a goddess. Then abruptly it crumpled, and she bowed her head, leaned against Pelmen's chest, and wept. He held onto her, wisely saying nothing. Finally she choked out, "That's all. And I don't know what it means."

Pelmen clung to her and let her sob, casting about for some appropriate reply. He never found it. Suddenly his mind filled with a completely different conversation, one she could not be a party to. His eyes slammed shut in pain and concentration, and once more, as had happened so many times before, the normally dark field behind his eyelids burned a hot, bright blue. *Rosha!* he wanted to shout, *don't do it!* But his own words were crowded out by the words of others. The link had again been made. The three pyramids were in contact.

## CHAPTER ELEVEN

# A Brilliant, Burning Blue

SAVAGE WAVES batted the rowboat toward the shore, drenching the sky blue garments of its seven occupants. Erri wrestled with an oar while shouting instructions to the other oarsman. The poor man struggled to hear, but the hammering sea drowned the prophet's words. Moments later their keel scraped the sand, and several initiates hopped out into the surf to drag the boat onto the beach. Erri hung over the side gasping for breath, then gestured for the three men who were to return to the ship to lean toward him.

"Row into the swells!" he shouted. "Don't let the craft turn edge-on into the waves or you'll be swamped! Ship oars as the peaks roll under you, then row for all you're worth into the troughs! Oh, what am I saying," he broke off, grumbling to himself. "You can't hear me anyway."

One initiate leaned toward his master's face, cupping a hand around his ear. "What?" he shouted.

"I said let the Power guide you!" Erri bellowed back. Then he shook his head in frustration, shrugged, and smiled brightly. When he jumped out of the boat they were all smiling back. He helped them push back out, then waved and turned for the shore. Suddenly strong young arms closed around his chest and picked him up. "Strahn!" he barked. "Set me down! I assure you I can walk!" The initiate doubtfully released him, and Erri ploughed through the foam as it first rushed up the shore past him, then sucked backward into the sea. He didn't stop until his squishing sandals were grabbed and slowed by the dry sand high on the beach. Wayleeth and Tahli-Damen waited for him here; she had her arm wrapped protectively around her husband's waist, and he was scowling sightlessly toward the ocean. The blind man had been scowling for the past two days.

"Look!" Strahn shouted enthusiastically as he joined them. "You see that huge boulder over there? I used to play by that boulder!" No one looked but Strahn. Indeed, the other three really didn't hear him. Already they were learning to screen out most of his irritating enthusiasm.

"Tahli-Damen, stop your frowning," Erri ordered. "You can't see it but the rest of us can, and it will only make this trip that much more unpleasant."

"You know why I'm scowling," the blind man grunted. "The choice was yours."

Erri winked at Wayleeth and smiled warmly at her. "Actually, the choice was *yours* some time ago. And a fine choice it was, too. Wayleeth, please excuse him."

"Oh, don't worry about me, Prophet. I'm used to him." The young woman's bright eyes returned to her husband's face, and the devotion Erri saw in them confirmed again this pairing. Some matches were certainly made by the Power himself.

"I used to pick up seashells near here! And down there at those rocks?" Strahn danced as he pointed. "We used to sit on those rocks until the tide came in and rose up around our necks! We made a game of seeing who could last the longest!"

Some matches, Erri complained to himself meditatively, seem to be made by mischievous powers intent on taxing patience to the limit. Strahn, Erri grieved silently to himself—how had he inherited Strahn?

"I told you I used to live near here, didn't I? Goats. My father herded goats right over there, at the foot of the Spinal Range!" The young man was grinning and pointing again, and Erri felt obliged to look.

"Yes," he murmured wearily, "I believe you *have* mentioned that. Eight or nine times, I would guess." It was his own fault, Erri reasoned. Begin anything new and exciting while opening yourself to receive any who might follow, and you're bound to wind up with some of the Strahns of the world. "Shall we go? It's a long walk to Dragonsgate."

"It's not *that* far," Strahn corrected eagerly as he fell into step with the prophet. "Why, my father and I—"

"What's that?" Wayleeth gasped, stopping as she said it and pointing. Tahli-Damen banged into her shoulder and his scowl deepened. He quickly forgot his irritation, however, when Erri grunted back:

"Dogs."

They had reached the top of the sandy strand and were about to descend into a small gully. On the far side, silhouetted against the red sky of the setting autumn sun, a line of hounds waited. They weren't normal dogs. These had been a part of that vast canine army that had ringed the city of Lamath the night Erri fell from power. They were Flayh's dogs, and Erri's mouth suddenly felt cottony with fear.

Strahn's stricken expression announced his terror to the world, but he still managed to stammer, "Wh-wh-what do we do?"

Erri swallowed. "What do we do? What we came here to do. We walk to Dragonsgate." Erri plunged down the hill, churning a plume of sand before him. He didn't look back to see if his small band followed, nor did he hesitate when he reached the bottom of the dune. He started up the other side, gazing into the fiery orange eyes of the hound directly above him. As if on cue, the dog slipped to one side and let Erri stalk on through the line.

Now Wayleeth and Strahn hurried to catch up, and Tahli-Damen did his best to keep his feet in all the sliding and tugging. "What kind of dogs?" the blind man demanded of his wife and guide. "Describe them to me!"

"They're . . . dogs. Black. But their eyes are . . . they're like flames—"

"Are these the dogs that attacked Lamath?" Tahli-Damen quizzed her, and Wayleeth nodded in assent. "Well, answer me!" he demanded.

"Yes!" she whispered vehemently.

"I see." Tahli-Damen nodded, unaware of the irony in his words. "They're the demon dogs then, aren't they, Prophet?"

"If you choose to term them such," Erri called back, continuing rapidly on. As he did, he noticed the line of hounds turning to trot along beside him. He stopped. They stopped. He waited until his band caught up, then started walking westward again. The dogs trotted forward, matching their pace to his. "It appears they plan to escort us."

"Why?" Wayleeth flared, hooking one arm through her husband's and turning her head to frown at the hounds. "What do they want from us?"

"I don't know," Erri replied offhandedly. He glanced at Tahli-Damen as he said it and took note of the blind man's grim expression. A bag holding that object that Tahli-Damen had borne to Lamath now dangled from Erri's neck, hidden by the fullness of his robe. Had these dogs come for the pyramid?

"I've never seen anything like them," Strahn whispered. "Where do they come from?"

"From Flayh," said Erri.

"But how?" the young man asked. "Did Flayh make them?" Strahn's voice quavered with horror at the very thought.

"He enfleshed them," the prophet grunted. "They're powers in canine form. Demon dogs, as Tahli-Damen said."

"And Flayh controls them," the blind man breathed ominously.

"Does he?" Erri asked, and Tahli-Damen, surprised, tried to look at him. "I mean, I don't know," the prophet went on. "I'm just wondering. Perhaps no one controls them. Perhaps they control themselves. Keep close, they're encircling us."

Dogs from either flank bounded out before them, and others dropped off to close the gap behind. The black hounds now ringed them, tongues lolling over gleaming teeth, glowing eyes gazing forward. They made no aggressive moves toward the bluefaithers, yet the potential for attack made all four humans terribly tense. Conversation died. After an hour of silent walking, Strahn could take no more. He stooped quickly to grab up a rock.

"No!" Erri commanded, and the young man dropped his stone instead of throwing it as he'd planned. "They've done nothing to us. We'll not bother them."

Strahn looked as if he wanted to argue, but he didn't. They kept walking.

Night came. The moon was not yet up, but the stars were bright. By this light the initiates kept watch on their four-legged companions. Eventually sleep became a necessity. "Let's stop here," Erri suggested.

"What about the dogs?" Strahn asked.

"They don't seem inclined to attack us," the prophet muttered. "We'll divide the night into three watches. I'll take the first one."

"Divide it into four," Tahli Damen said. "I'll do my share."

Wayleeth was startled. "But darling, you're—"

"Do they know that?" her husband snarled quietly. Wayleeth did not reply.

They built a fire and lay down to sleep, and the circle of dogs settled down, too, to wait for them. There were four watches. The three who'd actually been able to see all reported the same thing in the morning: The flaming eyes of the dogs had never closed.

As they ate their meager breakfast, Erri tried an experiment. He walked a few paces westward, and the dogs on that side of the ring parted to let him pass. Then he turned and walked back to the fire. He saw Wayleeth eyeing him curiously, but he made no comment to her. A few minutes later he walked a few paces eastward, back in the direction of the sea. The dogs on this side of the circle rose slowly to their feet, but did not part. When he came within six feet of them they bared their fangs. One more pace and they growled menacingly. Erri didn't chance another step. He propped his hands on his hips and said, "That's it then. You're herding us westward, aren't you?" The dogs stared back at him, but none made any reply. "Fortunately, that's the very direction we'd planned to go. Come my friends—let's be moving."

Two days after landing on the beach, the odd troop made its way up the pass into Dragonsgate. The dogs had not obstructed them in any way, but neither had the skyfaithers departed a step from their westward route. While the presence of the dogs had naturally heightened the tension of the journey, Erri could count at least two advantages in having this escort. Tahli-Damen and Wayleeth had laid their marital differences aside in order to deal with the crisis, and were now functioning quite smoothly as a team. She had learned to anticipate his needs before he spoke them, and was making a conscious effort not to smother him. And Strahn had been so cowed by the hounds' appearance that he'd stopped speaking entirely for a day and a half. Unfortunately, this effect had finally worn off; throughout the climb, the young man's tongue was in constant motion. Erri finally had to put a hand over the lad's mouth to shut him up. When Strahn fell silent, the prophet looked him in the eye and said, "Remember. Somewhere above us is a dragon." The sentence had its desired effect. Strahn's eyes widened, and when Erri pulled his hand away, he saw that fear had again sealed Strahn's lips. The prophet sighed with relief.

Then he looked at Wayleeth and her husband. "What are your plans?" he asked gently.

"Are you talking to me or to him?" the young wife asked.

"To both of you. I don't suppose you have two plans . . ."

"I really don't know," Wayleeth shrugged. "I'm with him. Where he tells me to go, I'll lead him."

Erri nodded. "And you, Tahli-Damen? Where will you direct her?"

The blind man walked on several paces before replying. "If we get past the dragon—"

"Oh, we'll get past the dragon," Erri interrupted. "Have no fear about that. The dragon's an illusion, albeit a convincing one. Just don't you be convinced."

"An illusion, yes," Tahli-Damen nodded, "but there's enormous force behind it. I've seen Flayh's power before. I know what we're walking into."

"Yet you're content to go on?"

"I wouldn't have it any other way," the blind man said with confidence.

"Don't worry," Wayleeth put in. "I'll steer him out of trouble."

"Ah, Wayleeth," Erri countered. "But what if the Power steers trouble to *you*?"

The young woman looked confused. "Would the Power do that?"

"Regularly," the prophet muttered; then he held his hand out to silence her and informed Tahli-Damen, "We're about to step into Dragonsgate."

They rounded a rock, first Erri, then Wayleeth and Tahli-Damen. Strahn didn't go around it immediately. Erri popped his head back around the corner to look at Strahn and announced, "You can come on. The dragon appears to be gone at the moment."

"Gone? That's wonderful! That's what I've been hoping for, all the way up this pass, that it would be out—"

"Strahn?" Erri interrupted. "I'd like to send these two on their way. After all, the twi-beast could return any minute." Erri turned his gaze upward slowly, directing Strahn's eyes skyward. Then the prophet returned to the couple.

"I'm satisfied in the knowledge that you're both listening to the Power. Go where guided. Do what you must. I rather hope things will wind up rapidly, but I have no idea what to expect, so if I don't see you again, know that you carry my love with you. If I do, it will be at a grand celebration." Erri embraced them both then and sent them on their way.

The dogs had watched all of this from some distance. Now as the little band parted, they seemed hesitant as to what do do. Erri glanced over at a couple of the hounds and saw that they appeared to be talking. He wasn't at all surprised. He'd long ago abandoned the notion that these were mere animals. After a moment, a decision was made. Half of the dogs, eighteen or twenty, accompanied Wayleeth and her husband down the Westmouth toward Ngandib-Mar. The other half remained behind with Erri and Strahn.

"Now what?" the young man asked worriedly. He didn't expect the pack to let them back down into Lamath.

Erri glanced around at the canyon walls. To his right was the sheer northern face of the pass. Forty feet up he could see the shelf where Vicia-Heinox had sunned itself, and behind it the yawning mouth of the dragon's cave. "Too steep," he mumbled. "Besides, the apparition might be using it." He looked to his left at the southern face. "That doesn't look any better." He turned around and craned his neck to look up the eastern face of the pass. It looked almost climbable. "Think we could get up that?" he asked Strahn.

"Why?" the young man asked.

"If I've understood the Power a'right, we've got to meet someone here. But I don't relish having to wait in full sight of that dragon, illusory or not."

His words had a powerful impact on young Strahn. "Of course we can make it!" he said enthusiastically and he turned around and tackled the hill.

Erri followed more slowly, conscious that the dogs were accompanying him to the base of the cliff. "You're welcome to climb with us, if you want," he offered. Then he cocked his ear—had one of the hounds whined, slightly? He looked at the circle of eyes, but heard nothing more. He took a deep breath and started up the mountain. "I'm an experienced old climber," he said to himself with a slight grin. "Let's see if I can beat this boy to the top."

Three hours later Erri clutched an icy boulder and gasped for air. The temperature was dropping rapidly—his breath whooshed out in great gusts of steam. He had to have some rest. It annoyed him to note that Strahn had already been to the top once and had come back down to fetch him up. He realized now that while he'd shinned up many a mast, the good salt air had never thinned away to nothing as did this mountain variety.

"Just a little bit higher," Strahn encouraged apologetically. "We're almost there."

"You said that same thing two hours ago, Strahn, when we were right down there!" Erri pointed to a cluster of rocks several hundred feet below them.

"I . . . I know, it's just that . . . well, look how much closer you are!"

Erri looked up at Strahn with a frown, then leaned his head back to try to see the summit. "Looks just the way it did when we were back down there! I can't tell that we've made any progress at all!"

"But we have, we have," Strahn said almost pleadingly. "Come on, Prophet, you can make it! There's a small cave at the top . . ." Strahn added this as he shot a doubtful look at the clouds.

"I know, I know," Erri grumbled. "I can see it too. Snow's coming."

"Perhaps if you could hurry—"

"I'm coming as fast as I can!" Erri shouted, sorry immediately for the outburst. As if his shout had shaken it loose from the clouds, the snow began to fall—and Erri took a deep breath and started climbing in earnest.

It was another hour before they made it to the summit. By that time they were both covered with frosty white flakes, and shivering helplessly. But, as Strahn had promised, there was a small cave, and they plunged into the back of it and clung together to hold some warmth between them. Suddenly Erri sat back, a puzzled expression barely visible on his face in the dim light.

"What is it," Strahn asked worriedly. Erri clutched for his chest, and Strahn shouted, "Prophet! Is it your heart?"

Erri glanced up at him. "My heart? No. It's this thing." He pulled the bag from under his vestments and held it up. "It's glowing hot all of a sudden." The prophet opened the velvet sack, and both of them were dazzled immediately by the pyramid's brilliant glow. Strahn whirled away from it, covering his eyes, but Erri sat forward and peered into its radiance. For there, visible within it, were the faces of two of his finest friends.

When the last sack of insects had been purged from the palace, Bronwynn sent word for Naquin to meet her. She greeted him with an apology and nothing more. Further words were unnecessary. The whole city had seen the attack begin, and few inhabitants were untouched by it. Word had spread quickly of Queen Bronwynn's incredible delivery of the castle, so the national mourning was tinged with euphoric patriotism. Chaomonous, already mobilized for war, now had the will to fight it. Everyone praised Bronwynn's wisdom in remaining behind, and the story of Danyilyn's impersonation drew laughs in every tavern as an excellent joke on the enemy. Nor was there any longer any question of who the enemy was. There had been magic involved in that massing of clawsps. Those Mari savages wanted another war. The previous humiliation of the Golden Throng still rankled most Chaons, and the queen's stunning victory had restored their national confidence. Important matters needed to be attended to. A state funeral for those killed was the first priority. But there was no question in anyone's mind that Bronwynn would then swiftly rejoin her army and lead it to triumph in the north.

No one questioned it except Bronwynn. She tried in vain to reopen the conversation with the Imperial House. The castle was silent. It was dead—so stone cold as to make her wonder if she'd imagined its speaking to her. There was no counsel there. Nor could Naquin offer any advice. These startling events had taken their toll on his own understanding of the faith, for he couldn't deny that the Power had issued the warning, nor could he ignore that magic had effected the victory. He was beginning, however, to rationalize things together in his mind. Since he'd first met Bronwynn, he'd regarded her as somewhat tainted by her connection with Pelmen. Now he viewed her with a newfound respect. He still couldn't quite tolerate the concept of magic, but miracles were certainly permissible. "Did you feel any . . . any sense of being . . . *controlled* from outside when you destroyed these vermin?" he asked the queen quietly as they waited for the funeral procession to begin.

"No," Bronwynn grunted, rather impatiently since she knew why he was asking. "Just a terrible rage. Which I still feel now," she added bitterly, as she cast her eyes back over the long line of coffins. They were draped in sky blue, by her order. Naquin had considered protesting, but thought better of it. After all, he had no way of judging the spiritual condition of the dead. "You have no further word from the Power?" Bronwynn snapped sharply, and Naquin jumped, startled.

"No, my Lady. Unless, perhaps, the command to wait is still in effect."

Bronwynn gazed away, over the heads of her grim-faced bodyguard. "I don't think so," she said quietly. Then she looked back at Naquin. "And when there's no other word, what more do you have to go on?"

It seemed to Naquin that she was much older than the young queen he'd argued with two days before. Then he thought no more about it. The procession had begun, and he stepped into his priestly role.

After the ceremony, Bronwynn returned to her apartments to pack. She did so haphazardly, packing a trivial item, then discarding an essential, her mind wandering constantly to other things. Rosha seemed very far away, like a pleasant dream that had never really come true. Everything she picked up held memories, and she finally had to sit on her bed and weep for a while before she could finish the job. It was foolish, she realized, to pack everything herself. A single summons and a dozen maids would rush to do it for her. But at the moment, she felt very private—she didn't need a lot of chattering women around her, trying to cheer her up.

Once packed, she called her guard to bear it all away and changed into comfortable riding clothes. She started out her door, but something stopped her. Curious, she thought. That would be a senseless, even dangerous act. Nevertheless, she walked back through her chambers to a small vault hidden in her bedroom and took out an object stored there. It was the pyramid that had belonged to Jagd, bagged in a sack of blue velvet. "Stupid," she told herself as she looked at it. Even so, she slipped the bag's drawstring around her neck. After donning a heavy cape, she went down to meet her personal brigade in the stable.

"Bad day to travel, your Highness," one of her guards commented, but there was no suggestion there that they wait. He, like the rest of her force, was ready to fight. They were all in a hurry to rejoin the Golden Throng. However, when it started to snow on them twenty miles north of the capital, her captain urged her to turn aside and lodge at a fortified manor near the campsite. She finally agreed.

Her hosts were a middle-aged pair who had maintained their elevated position in Chaon society through a policy of conscienceless pragmatism. While Talith was king, they had served him loyally. When Ligne overthrew him, they gave her a party to celebrate her victory. Now they swore absolute fealty to Bronwynn. Since they had plenty to feel guilty about, they were rather alarmed by her sudden arrival.

Bronwynn was aware of both their discomfort and the reasons underlying it. She didn't care. She had far too much on her mind these days to concern herself with the petty hypocrisy of the wealthy. As soon as the snow permitted, she rode briskly into her camp, ignoring the cheers of her soldiers. News of her victory had preceded her, enhancing the already considerable loyalty of her troops. Her warriors even revelled in her indifferent expression; as she galloped past, her eyes unflinchingly forward, she looked every inch the confident conquering heroine.

In fact, that cool expression masked a girlish crisis. Her mind was still enmeshed in her grief at the loss of so many faithful retainers. She also felt overwhelmed by the responsibility she now bore. It was one thing to take one's hereditary place as sovereign. It was quite another to be suddenly hailed as the national savior. The weight of the two together threatened to crush her unless she could talk about it to someone. That urgent need set her priorities for the morning.

By the time she reached the large circular pavilion in the midst of the camp, General Joss had already learned of her arrival and was waiting. "Greetings, your Majesty," he called as one guard grabbed the reins of her mount and another took hold of her stirrup and her hand. "And hail," he added as she dropped lightly to the powdery snow.

"You've heard," she said, jerking a rolled bundle down from her saddle before allowing them to lead her horse away.

"All Chaomonous has heard, my Lady. And well they should have. May the Mari savages hear soon, and tremble!"

"You sound pleased," she muttered, knocking a drape aside and ducking into her tent.

"Shouldn't I be?" he asked, following her. "In a single act, you've established a right to the throne more legitimate than any claim of your father, provided a rallying point for the entire nation, and increased by at least a third the size of your army. Does that not make you happy?"

Bronwynn had arrived at the center of the huge tent, beside a small, portable throne. She'd reached her destination, and that troubled her somehow, for she realized that the journey here had provided her with a purpose that had diverted her attention from other matters. Now she had to think about them again. "I'm not happy, no," she said brusquely. "Too many people died in that battle to feel any happiness about it."

Joss had no reputation for sensitivity. He did, however, maintain a close watch on the feelings and needs of his monarch. He therefore passed up the opportunity to point out that far more would die in the planned invasion of Ngandib-Mar than had been lost in the skirmish with the insects. While it was true, such an assertion would serve no purpose now. The girl was obviously depressed, and such words could only depress her further. Better to let her relax and review the events of the past few days from this new distance. Joss realized that Chaomonous suddenly possessed a splendid military opportunity. He was resolved not to squander it. His response to her was extremely uncharacteristic. With the voice of the most humble of slaves, in a tone more gentle than Kherda's, he asked, "Can I get you anything, my Lady?"

Bronwynn jerked around and frowned at him. "What?" she asked.

"Something to relax you? I have some good books in my quarters—"

The queen regarded him with a puzzled expression, then sighed and looked away. She hadn't the energy to figure Joss out this morning; instead she took his offer at face value. "Yes," she said as she walked to the bed. "Find the two actors, Danyilyn and Gerrig, and send them to me."

"As you wish, my Lady," the general said as he bowed his way backwards out of the tent. Bronwynn thought no more about his unlikely behavior. She was preparing herself to give bad news.

Gerrig and Danyilyn came grim-faced through the curtains. The news of Bronwynn's triumph had carried with it the threat of personal tragedy. The rumor was that many had died. No word had yet come as to who those were. Both pairs of eyes sought out Bronwynn's face immediately, hoping for a smile of encouragement. There was none there.

"Yes?" Danyilyn asked. It was a rather impudent greeting for one's queen, but Bronwynn seemed not to notice.

"Come in and sit down," she said gently. If any hope had survived in their minds it disappeared in the face of that somber invitation. They sat obediently, and looked at her. "You've heard by now of the clawsp attack on the Imperial House. I'm sorry, but Yona Parmi was among those killed. He died outside my door, apparently trying to protect my apartments from the insects. I thought you ought to know."

Gerrig wept brokenly, then began to mumble curses which built in volume and intensity to a profane tirade against the instigators of the attack. Danyilyn just gazed at the fish-satin walls of the tent, her face a study in bitterness. After a moment she looked back at the queen and saw that Bronwynn, too, was weeping. That surprised her momentarily, for while Bronwynn had become acquainted with Yona Parmi and had seemed to enjoy his company, she'd not known him well. Then Danyilyn put herself in Bronwynn's place and thought she understood. "My Lady," she said tentatively, "we appreciate your sharing our tragedy with us. Indeed, it's unusual for a queen to involve herself so personally. It makes me wonder. Is there something we can do for you?"

Bronwynn looked up and met Danyilyn's knowing gaze, and her relief at being understood unleashed a flood of new tears that interrupted Gerrig's diatribe. He watched as the actress moved over to kneel beside the queen and slipped her arm around Bronwynn's waist. He suddenly felt very much out of place. The back of his throat ached. He fought his way out through the veils of the tent and sought his solace in the solitude of the snow.

Bronwynn poured out her anxiety and frustration while Danyilyn nodded and occasionally hummed in agreement. It didn't take long for the young queen to move on from her current concerns to long concealed confidences. The actress responded in kind. Soon they were chattering like schoolgirls, losing themselves and their griefs in the warm bath of conversation. The snow swirled down outside, covering a swiftly swelling army poised on the edge of conquest. The two women were oblivious to it. For the moment, the bliss of newly discovered friendship held them in its protective trance. Eventually, of course, the conversation had to work its way back to Yona Parmi, but now they were better able to bear the sorrow of it together. They each felt sad for Gerrig, realizing that the explosion of their friendship had essentially locked him out. That led them quickly to thoughts of others, and Danyilyn voiced a realization that occurred to both of them in the same instant. "We need to get word to Pelmen."

"How?" Bronwynn asked. "We don't even know where he is."

"Which is normal," Danyilyn mumbled sourly. Then she jumped as Bronwynn danced lightly to her feet and across the carpeted floor to the bundle on her bed. "What's that?" she asked.

Bronwynn unrolled the cloth and pulled out the velvet bag. She gnawed at the knotted drawstring to get it untied, then jerked it open and produced from inside it an object of incredible radiance and beauty. "This," she said.

Danyilyn regarded the pyramid suspiciously. She knew immediately what it was. She also knew of its danger. "You won't be able to contact Pelmen with that! Instead you're liable to get his archenemy!"

"True enough," Bronwynn grunted, "but at this point I'm willing to talk to *anybody* who knows anything! Besides," she added haughtily, "I'm a shaper now, too!"

"My Lady, be careful!" Danyilyn warned, but she was too late. Already the crystal object's inner radiance was flaring into a brilliant, beautiful blue.

Bronwynn stared into the pyramid, as did Erri and did Rosha. The link was made.

"Bronwynn?" Rosha cried.

"Rosha?" his astonished queen replied.

"By the Power!" Erri muttered incredulously.

"Is that really you?" Bronwynn squealed, and Rosha eagerly assured her that it was. "Where are you?" she demanded.

"I'm in the Mar."

"Well, I'd guessed that," she snapped. "Where in the Mar?"

The magical pyramids did not transmit the user's voice alone. If Rosha peered into one facet of the three-sided object, he could see the faces of the other two speakers looking up at him from the other two facets. He could clearly see the scolding arch of Bronwynn's eyebrows, and it irritated him. His answer sounded gruffer than he'd intended. "I'm safe."

"Are you with your father?" she probed. She was shocked by the expression of grief that seized her husband's features. "What's wrong?" she asked, her voice suddenly tender and solicitous.

"By all accounts, my father is dead."

"But how—"

"It's a long story, not yet fit for the telling," he said brusquely. His own attitude surprised him. A few moments before he'd been sitting joylessly in his opulent guest room, longing for contact with this very woman. Now, he suddenly didn't feel much like talking. "Erri, is that really you?" he asked, trying to deflect attention from himself.

"Yes, it is," Erri said soberly. He seemed unwilling to go on.

"Are you safe?" Bronwynn asked doubtfully, her eyes still watching Rosha's.

"I think so."

"Where are *you*?" she asked, now turning her full attention to the prophet.

Erri hesitated. "I . . . don't think I can really say. In fact, I'm positive that I don't rightly *know* where I am. But I think that may be just as well. Does Pelmen know of this conversation?"

"He should," Bronwynn reasoned, "if he's anywhere near one of us. Do either of you know his whereabouts? I have a message for him."

"What is it?" Rosha asked.

"It's bad news . . ." Bronwynn hesitated, reflecting a moment, then chose to go ahead. "Made worse, I fear, by your word about your father. If you see him, tell him Yona Parmi is dead."

"Yona?" Rosha frowned. "How?" His grim expression grew more so as Bronwynn recounted the events of the clawsp attack. Erri listened to this news with evident interest—and appeared somewhat relieved at its outcome. Rosha grunted as she finished her story: "Terril. Did he escape?"

"I don't know," Bronwynn said. "We swept millions of insects from the Imperial House—"

"But no strange bodies were found?"

"If so, I wasn't told."

"Then he escaped. When a shaper dies in altershape he reverts to his human form. So. Terril is against us." Rosha pursed his lips in concentration.

"You're forgetting something," Bronwynn snapped, and he looked up at her inquiringly. "*I* am with you."

Rosha could usually absorb Bronwynn's inherited haughtiness without giving it any thought. For some reason, however, today it made him want to snap at her. "What do you mean by that? You think just because you killed some clawsps you're ready to match powers with Mar-Yilot?"

Bronwynn was stung by his sharp reply. Hurt, she fired back an unthinking retort. "I'm ready to match powers *and* armies with anyone!"

"What does that mean?" Rosha goaded.

"It means, Rosha, that I'm sitting on your border with forty thousand troops, ready to invade and offer aid wherever you need it! Now if you'll just tell me where you—"

"Did I *ask* you to do that?" Rosha shouted. "Did I ask for you to come in here and rescue me?"

"Well—no, but it just makes good sense, if you're in trouble—"

"I'm not in trouble!" Rosha barked. "I'm safe, I'm with friends, and we can handle our own problems without the Golden Throng interfering!"

"All right then, tell me, if you're so safe and secure, why you've not contacted me until now?" He'd asked for it, Bronwynn decided. She had a lot of anger inside her just waiting for release. Now she let it spew. "You left me in Chaomonous without a word! Not a word! What am I supposed to do, sit at home knitting until you decide to return? I had to send word to Pelmen to track you down, and I wouldn't have known *anything* if my own magical ability hadn't surfaced in a dream and allowed me to meet him on your precious Mari rock of dead people!"

"That's the Rock of Tombs," Rosha said icily.

"Whatever. I finally figured it out for myself that you'd gone off looking for glory! Talk about *me* sounding bold! What were *you* trying to do? Take on Flayh single-handedly?"

Rosha's jaws clenched, primarily because her barbs were striking so close to a target made tender by guilt. He struck back. "How do you think I'm able to talk to you? I took this mystical device from Flayh's tower with my own hands! I'm currently in league with the two most potent shapers in Mari history, and together—"

"No!" The word was thunderous. It came from none of the three, but it echoed in Erri's cave and vibrated the walls of Bronwynn's tent. The three sat in stunned silence. Then they heard something else—something chillingly dark and evil, emanating from some distance away.

"That was Pelmen," Bronwynn whispered.

"The 'no' was," Erri said calmly. "The laughter was someone else. My children—I think I can call you that by this time, since you've certainly treated one another as such—these devices were never intended for this purpose. I understand from our mutual mentor that any conversation through them ends in bickering. Now I've seen evidence of it, and that's confirmed by my own feelings. I'd like to grab you both by the ears and shake you! Now let us put these things away as we've been instructed and keep them safe! The Power has some purpose for them or we would not possess them now. But this is most certainly not that purpose!" With a head-splitting snap, Erri broke the link.

Rosha sat on his bed, awaiting the knock on his door. At last it came. "Come in," he mumbled.

Pelmen stepped in, as he'd expected; but he hadn't expected Serphimera to follow, or Mar-Yilot, or Syth. He hung his head in humiliation. No one said anything until he broke the silence. "The laughter," he said. "Flayh's?"

Pelmen nodded. "It was Flayh."

"Then he heard everything."

"Didn't you know he would?" Mar-Yilot flared, and it crossed Rosha's mind that he ought to feel fright. Suddenly, he realized that he did. Not only was he frightened of the Autumn Lady's wrath. He felt the backlog of days of terrifying circumstances suddenly catching up with him. In that moment it was as if

Rosha awoke at last to the mighty forces at work around him—forces he had not a breath of control over, forces he was't even aware of. He realized, vaguely, that Pelmen had come to his defense.

"No, he didn't know. That's my fault. I'd thought the object lost at the bottom of the reservoir. It never occurred to me that he'd managed to hang onto it, so I felt no urge to explain its full properties to him."

"Did *you* hear it all, too?" Serphimera asked Mar-Yilot, and the sorceress nodded in disgust. Serphimera's eyes met Syth's, and they sympathized with one another silently. Like Rosha, they were often in the dark. Neither of them had heard a thing.

"Now he must know we're together!" Mar-Yilot fumed.

"Probably." Pelmen nodded. "But he'd surely guessed that anyway. Maybe knowing it for certain will frighten him, somehow." Mar-Yilot shot him another look of disgust. Pelmen met her gaze. "It could have been much worse. Our position wasn't revealed. Nor was Erri's—"

"Who is this Erri, anyway?" the woman asked. "He sounded thoroughly sensible."

Pelmen gave her a slight smile. "That's one of the best descriptions of Erri I've ever heard. I hope you'll meet him one day."

Mar-Yilot snorted. "If I survive!" She shot another foul look at Rosha, then stormed out of the room. After a moment Syth followed her—but not before laying a comforting hand on Rosha's shoulder.

Rosha wouldn't look up. Pelmen nodded at Serphimera, and she, too, disappeared. Then the shaper sat on the bed beside his young friend. Rosha had put the pyramid back in its wrappings—the burned remnant of Pelmen's old cloak. He handed it to Pelmen, his eyes still on the floor. "You want this?" he asked dully.

Pelmen sighed. "Not really," he said, but he took it anyway and sat it, bundled up, on his lap.

"I'm sorry," Rosha growled.

"I'm sorry too. For you. It sounded like a most unsatisfying reunion."

"It was."

"Can I do anything?"

Rosha looked up at him finally. "You can take that thing

out of here and let me go to bed." Pelmen nodded, patted Rosha's back, and started for the door. "Pelmen," Rosha called, and the powershaper turned to look back at him. "I'm sorry about Yona Parmi."

Pelmen lowered his head, and nodded. Then he looked squarely at Rosha. "I keep losing my friends. Don't let your guilt cost me you, too." He left the room, closing the door behind him.

## CHAPTER TWELVE

# Frolic in the Snow

THERE WERE many handsome rooms in Syth's palace, but the grandest of all was the long hallway that spanned the length of the northern face of the house. A series of columns ran along the wall, interspersed with full-length windows. Some of these were of stained glass. One, the most prominent, pictured a butterfly in shades of auburn, amber and apricot. Most, however, were clear, providing a vista of the two peaks in the middle of the island.

It was a beautiful room throughout the day. It made a good spot for an early breakfast, as dawn painted the twin hills a pleasant pink. In the afternoon, the columns formed dramatic silhouettes, and the room had the somber mood of a brooding library. By nightfall the personality of the hallway changed completely. Except for the rare occasions when its chandeliers were lighted for a grand ball, its only light came from two giant fireplaces at either end—or from the moon through the windows.

Pelmen and Serphimera stood gazing out at the hills. With their coats of fresh snow, those peaks seemed to glow, reflecting back the moon's pale light. The view gave rise to thoughts of warmth and rest and security. It certainly was no invitation to travel. Yet that's what they discussed. Pelmen sighed and turned away from her. "Why, Serphimera?" he asked. "It's hopeless, don't you see?"

At that moment Mar-Yilot walked into the hall and smiled her most cheerful, cynical smile. "May I share your despair?" she asked. Her spirits seemed improved over the afternoon, but it was well that Rosha wasn't present. She didn't forgive easily—and certainly not this quickly. "What's hopeless?" she asked.

Pelmen was not inclined to respond, so Serphimera did. "I have had a vision, my Lady, of Pelmen and myself going to the mountain. We're trying to interpret our purpose and whether these crystal pyramids play a part."

"What mountain?" Mar-Yilot asked, wrinkling her nose.

"I don't know," Serphimera said with a slight smile. "Pelmen thinks he does."

When Mar-Yilot turned an inquiring look on him, Pelmen explained, "It's a mountain in the North Fir—a mountain where . . . the Power is." He appeared unwilling to say the words, conveying by his manner that it was a long story and he'd rather not go on.

Mar-Yilot raised an eyebrow. "The Power. Is it always there?"

"Each time I've passed it." Pelmen nodded, looking out the window.

"And what do you think you'll be doing there?" Mar-Yilot asked.

Pelmen shrugged and explained, "It was there Sheth met with the men of faith and refused their contribution to the crystal weapon."

Mar-Yilot frowned, as he'd known she would, and said, "This is a story I don't know."

"I didn't know it either—or rather, only a part—until I had a conversation with the Imperial House of Chaomonous."

Intrigued, Mar-Yilot gestured for them to sit in the comfortable chairs before one of the large fireplaces; she settled back in one herself to listen. Syth stepped in a few minutes later and joined them, but he didn't interrupt, for Pelmen had already begun the tale.

"This all happened centuries ago. At that time there was only one land, spreading from the sea on the east to the high plains of Ngandib, and from the cold wastes of northern Lamath to the spice islands south of Chaomonous. A mighty land, obviously, but perhaps a bit too big, for it began to crumble from within. There were those who shaped the powers, then as now. Others were in contact with the one who made all things, the One we call the Power. Still others scoffed at the thought of any powers beyond those of man, and set about to study the world in order to prove such. I suppose there had always been these groups, but they'd all been able to live together before. Gradually, however, that became impossible. They warred on one another, and the land was split into fragments.

"Certain leaders devised a plan they hoped would unite the One Land again. They thought that if there was only some overpowering threat which would demand the cooperation of all men, the race would be knit together once more. At least, that's the reason they gave for the making of Vicia-Heinox."

"Vicia-Heinox?" Mar-Yilot interrupted. "They *made* the dragon?"

"They did—and loosed it upon the world. Fields and villages were burned—whole nations, in fact, were destroyed, with names that would surprise you—"

"Surprise me!" Mar-Yilot pleaded, clapping her hands in fascination.

"Yes." Syth smiled. "What names?"

Pelmen looked into the crackling fire. "Ever heard of the nation of Arl?"

"Arl? You mean there was once a country down around Arl Lake?" asked the sorceress.

"It was the grandest of the remnants of the One Land, and it stretched from north of the High Plateau to the borders of what is now Chaomonous."

"But the great South Fir—" Syth began.

"It wasn't there," Pelmen said. "All that region was occupied. The dragon burned Arl away—the forest grew in its place." He paused for a moment before going on. Mar-Yilot sat entranced, delighted by the story. "The lands did not unite. But certain individuals did. A weapon was devised, fashioned of six diamonds, each shaped into three-sided pyramids and filled with magical power. The shaper named Sheth was appointed to meld them together and pass them on to the men of faith, but he changed his mind. He tried to attack Vicia-Heinox by himself."

"What happened?" Mar-Yilot asked breathlessly.

"Well, we know he lost." Syth shrugged, but his wife hushed him.

"Indeed he lost," said Pelmen. "The weapon was shattered again into the six diamond pyramids. The One Land has never been united. And the dragon has been with us ever since—or at least, until very recently."

Mar-Yilot looked thoughtfully at him. "Then these things your foolish friends were talking through are really parts of an ancient weapon—and you're contemplating remaking it and turning it on Flayh."

Pelmen nodded. "But it's hopeless. We could gather these pyramids, but that would leave three parts of the weapon still missing. What possible good would that do?"

"You say these crystals are cut from diamonds?" Syth asked. When Pelmen nodded, he said, "In my vaults are diamonds beyond your imagination. Huge stones, many of them still uncut. We can cut you some more pyramids, Pelmen. How would that do?"

"Thank you, Syth, for your offer—and who knows? Perhaps these that exist came from such an offer from your ancestors. But it's not much help, I fear. There's magic in these three pyramids—shaping beyond my imagination—plus contributions of skill in calibrating the exact cuts that would tax the most gifted of your jewelers. No, I'm afraid it's hopeless."

"Then why do we have these three?" Serphimera asked simply.

"*We* don't," Pelmen grunted. "We have one. Erri has the second, and I don't know where he is. I know where Bronwynn is, but the Golden Queen is headstrong in the best of times, and these are, for her, the worst. There's no assurance she'd surrender the pyramid she possesses."

"But there's a chance," Serphimera said quietly.

Pelmen looked at her, frowning. "Do you *want* us to go up that mountain? Thinking as you do?"

"Oh, Pelmen," Serphimera said, and there was more passion in her voice than Mar-Yilot or Syth had yet heard from her. "What does it matter what I want? And if I've seen it, and it's to be, how shall we set about preventing it? There is a chance,

Pelmen. Perhaps it only appears such to us—perhaps the task *is* hopeless. But this is the pathway that lies open. This is the light we have."

Pelmen leaned back in his chair and gazed again out the window. "That path looks far from open to me."

"What do you need, Pelmen?" Syth asked. "What can I help you with?"

The weary powershaper turned his eyes to meet the gaze of this new friend, and said quietly, "Horses. And a map."

"A map!" Mar-Yilot snorted. "What do you need with a map of the Mar! You know these lands like a—"

"He means a political map, darling," Syth interrupted. "The fastest, safest route to Dragonsgate. Am I right?"

Pelmen nodded.

"How did you know what he meant?" Mar-Yilot demanded.

Syth ignored her and went on, "My best horses are in Seriliath, but I have steeds here good enough to get you there in a day. There you'll pick up my fastest mounts—I'll send you with letters, but my stable master will know them already. And these will be strong enough to make Dragonsgate in four. What are you thinking?"

Pelmen had gone glassy-eyed. Syth's question startled him back into the present. "I was just remembering a horse I used to ride. Minaliss, I called him, because he had shoulders of steel. I wish I had him here."

Syth shrugged. "Perhaps in four days you'll feel the same about mine."

Pelmen grinned. "Maybe I will, at that."

"As to route—first to Seriliath, of course. Then to Tuckad's castle just inside the western edge of the parks region. Tuckad's dead, but his family is for us. You can carry a message to them from me." Pelmen nodded. "As to the third night—well, we've no allies in the Westmouth region. At least, none that far north. If you want to go south to the Hanni house on the plain—"

"Too far south, and I make it a practice to stay out of debt to merchants."

Syth nodded. "As I thought. One night of camping then, and the next day you should reach Dragonsgate."

Pelmen got to his feet. "It's late," he announced. "And tomorrow we'll be leaving early."

Mar-Yilot frowned. "We just got here! Do you think you're well enough to travel again so quickly?"

Pelmen looked at Serphimera. "I feel better now than I have in months."

"Ah." Mar-Yilot nodded. "I'd forgotten your wife was a healer."

Syth stood up and offered his hand. "Pelmen, you've long been an adversary. I like you better as a friend." They gripped hands, then Syth stepped aside and looked at Mar-Yilot, who'd gotten up to stand behind him.

At that moment the sorceress looked like a timid teenager—very thin, very awkward. Without looking at Serphimera, she suddenly stepped up and slipped her arms around her old enemy's neck. "I don't know anything about this Power business or what it is you're actually doing," she whispered. "But be careful! This dog is dangerous!" Then she pecked Pelmen on the cheek and quickly left the room.

Stunned, Pelmen looked at Serphimera, who raised an eyebrow. "Perhaps *I'd* better be careful too," she said frowning mockingly. Then she smiled.

Pelmen was entranced again by her beauty. "I don't think you have anything to worry about—wife."

She lowered her eyes. "I'd like to be that."

He nodded curtly. "All the more reason to get to Erri as quickly as possible." He embraced her and kissed her hair, then said, "Go on and get your rest. It will be a hard ride tomorrow."

He was right. It was. But by evening of that next day they were resting comfortably in Seriliath. There were some harrowing escapes. There were times of icy silence, for they both still held dark secrets from one another—trying to save each other from the coming grief. Yet the hours passed swiftly; regardless of what they faced, they were at last together.

The tugoliths enjoyed the snow. They were northern animals from wintry climes, and the deep drifts prompted them to dance and frolic. Even the disciplined Chimolitha couldn't resist an occasionally spontaneous romp off of the roadway. At those times she seemed totally oblivious to Pezi's strangled screams.

Pezi had taken it all rather badly. He'd always judged snow to be a good thing to be out of and a bad thing to be out in.

When the white flakes began drifting out of the sky, he'd eyed them suspiciously and had politely requested that they go fall on someone else. When they grew in size and began dropping in eager clumps, Pezi had started cursing them. Not long thereafter, he'd begun to feel that peculiar tickling in the back of the throat that heralded the onset of a cold. His curses had turned to pitiful moans; as the afternoon plodded on, and he'd started to sneeze. He began to picture himself as chief among the wretched of the earth. Soon he was weeping and gnashing his teeth. That first night, as the herd had grouped together to sleep under a stand of leafless trees, he'd huddled in his fish-satin tent and shivered in misery. When they'd started out again the following morning, Pezi began enumerating his troubles to his stolid, sensible steed. He'd been at it ever since.

Chimolitha ignored him. She viewed Pezi as she might a sore in an unreachable spot. He was a nuisance, an irritation, but she was sure she'd be healed of him eventually. Until then, she pressed on through the snow, enjoying the way it crunched between her massive toes.

Four days after leaving Dragonsgate, the column of saucer-eyed monsters came within sight of the High Plateau. Pezi exhorted them to move faster, but Chim refused to be hurried. She held to that same steady pace she'd maintained throughout the journey, and they came inexorably to the foot of the Down Road. There the gigantic beast stopped.

Pezi brushed the icicles from his runny nose and gazed upward in dismay. "Oh, no!" he moaned, distraught. "It's blocked!" For days he'd been able to maintain his hold on Chim's horn only by imagining his triumphal entry into the High City. The acclaim! The honors! The food! Now his dream was shattered—delayed, anyway—and Pezi was heartbroken. This was the last straw, the final indignity, a gratuitous kick in the groin from the same sadistic powers of nature that had dogged his steps for the last two years. It was just too much. Pezi clung tightly to Chim's horn, and sobbed.

Chimolitha rolled her giant eyes back to look up at Pezi curiously. She didn't like this fat fellow, but she did understand tears. And Chimolitha, for all her tough old hide, was the most soft-hearted of tugoliths. "Don't cry, Man," she said quietly. "I'll go up." She lowered her head and wedged her long snout into the snow that had drifted against the cliff face. Then she started forward, and upward. She pushed a mound of snow before her, and the higher she climbed the larger it got. Soon a part of it began dropping down off the road. Chimolitha was using her body as a plough.

If she expected any thanks, she didn't get it. Not that Pezi wouldn't have felt grateful if the circumstances had been a bit different. But since he sat astride her horn, and her horn was just above her nose, and it was her nose the tug was using as the point of her wedge, Pezi suddenly found himself buried under a suffocating blanket of snow. "Wait!" "Stop!" "Help!" he cried whenever he could spare enough breath to do so. That was infrequently, however, and it was many minutes before he could get the well-meaning beast's attention long enough to get her to stop.

Chimolitha rolled her eyes up to look at him again and petulantly explained, "I'm going up."

"But I'm going under! Can't you let another tug go around us and—" Pezi's words froze on his lips as he caught a glimpse of the valley below. There was no need for the tug to answer his question. She clearly took up all the road between the mountain and the dropoff.

"I can't go back," she explained unnecessarily.

"No! Don't try!" Pezi said quickly as he sat licking his lips and reviewing his options. Then he had it. "Why don't I just climb over your back and get onto the tug behind you?" he asked.

The question startled Chim, and her eyes grew wide. Was she supposed to know the answer? "I don't know," she said anxiously. By that time Pezi was already clambering over her back—by no means an easy task for a man of his ample girth.

Then he stopped. He'd suddenly found a very good reason why he ought to stay put right where he was. Thuganlitha smiled up at him wickedly and said, "Ride *my* horn!"

It was a cold, breathless ride to the top of the Down Road, but Pezi clung tight to Chimolitha's tusk and he made it. Suddenly they burst through a drift into a cleared area, scattering a half dozen shovel-wielding slavers in the process. Two men were so shocked by the abrupt appearance of the beasts that they cast themselves off the precipice and were never seen again. The rest had plenty to talk about at supper.

Pezi and his column garnered few cheers but plenty of awed

stares as they moved up the main street toward the High Fortress. At least part of Pezi's dream came true, however. Once inside, he quickly found his way to a table, and a platter of hot, steaming meat was set before him.

The only trouble was, he couldn't taste it. His nose was stopped up. He wrestled with severe depression over that, but did manage in spite of his despair to clean the plate, refill it, and clean it again. It had been a *very* long time since he'd had a decent meal, and he wasn't about to let a head cold interfere any more than was necessary.

When he rose, he still wasn't quite satisfied. However, there were matters of great importance that he needed to tend to. Besides, suppertime was not that far off.

He waddled importantly along the corridor leading toward Flayh's tower and started up the steps past the guard.

The little man leaped nimbly to his feet and blocked the stairs. "Are you crazy? You can't go up there."

Pezi stepped back, propped his hands on his fat hips, and snarled, "And just what is going to stop me?"

"This might," Tibb grunted, and Pezi noticed that there was a dagger blade scarcely an inch from his navel.

"Oh," he said. He took a generous step backward.

"The question is, why would you want to?" Tibb asked as he sheathed his knife and sat back down on the step. "Do you have any idea what he's like?" Tibb jerked his head meaningfully up the ascending spiral.

"Why, indeed I do! He's my uncle!"

"Oh," Tibb said. It was his turn to be surprised.

Thinking that had settled the matter, Pezi again started up the steps past Tibb, and once again stopped abruptly. The dagger was out and aimed a little lower this time. Pezi stepped backward—quite quickly for such a tubby man. "You're very quick with that thing," he harrumphed.

"I practice a lot."

"Why can't I see my uncle?"

"Flayh's orders. Nephew or not, no one goes up those stairs until Flayh's summoned him."

"How can he summon me if he doesn't even know I'm here?" Pezi thundered.

A chill ran up his back as a steel-cold voice behind him answered, "He knows."

Pezi choked and turned around very slowly. One glimpse was plenty to assure him of the speaker's identity, and he gulped and quickly looked away.

"Are those your beasts in the stable?" Admon Faye asked flatly, and Pezi nodded. "Then get down there. One of them's out of control."

"Thug!" Pezi yelped and he started rumbling down the dark hallway. Admon Faye met Tibb's eyes and smiled disdainfully. Then he turned and followed Pezi toward the stables. When the slaver reached the wooden landing above the cavern, Pezi was already halfway down the stairway. Pezi stopped there, and looked tentatively downward, ready to climb back up at the slightest hint that Thuganlitha might charge him. "Chimolitha!" he squawked. "Can't you do something?"

Chimolitha watched as Thug demolished a third stall in search of something to eat. She thought a moment, then answered, "Yes."

There was a loud crash as Thuganlitha splintered the timbers of a fourth stall with his horn. Pezi stared, dumfounded. Then he shouted, "Well then, *do* it!"

Chimolitha looked mournfully up at Pezi and asked, "What thing shall I do?"

"Stop him!" Pezi screeched. "Stop him from destroying this castle!"

"Oh," Chim said, understanding at last, and she looked sternly at Thuganlitha. "Stop it," she ordered.

Thug paused in the destruction of a nearby hay wagon, and looked at her. "Why?" he growled.

Chimolitha rolled her eyes back up at Pezi and repeated the question. "Why?"

"Because it isn't nice!" Pezi trumpeted and he stamped his foot. That wasn't smart: The stairway was unstable, and he was inordinately heavy. Thirty feet below him an enormous horned monster scowled up at him in frustration. The stairway shook, and Pezi quickly grabbed the railing to steady himself.

"Why are you angry?" Admon Faye asked calmly, looking directly into Thuganlitha's eyes.

The tugolith was surprised, and the reaction showed on his massive features. He thought for a minute, then rumbled, "I'm hungry!"

Admon Faye nodded and said, "Fine. What would you like to eat?"

Thuganlitha filtered the question through his tiny brain, then a wicked gleam came into his eyes and he turned his gaze on Pezi. He grinned. "Him."

Admon Faye leaned his head back and laughed, long and loud. Then he turned to smirk at Pezi.

Pezi gasped and shouted, "You wouldn't dare!"

"I wouldn't?" Admon Faye asked coldly, and Pezi trembled at his poor choice of words. Everyone knew Admon Faye would dare anything. The slaver turned and looked back down at the curious, upturned faces of the tugoliths. "It's tempting, Pezi, but I'll wait. You want meat, my friend? I'll send you some meat." He walked away to give the order.

The slave pit was overcrowded anyway.

Frost formed high on the windows. It was cold outside, but the air was clear, and the sunlight bouncing off the snow-clad hills made them far too bright for the eyes. Rosha drank from a steaming cup and gazed beyond them at the rich blue of the sky. Syth sat beside him, his feet propped on a short table, a heavy book in his hands. There was no sound in the room save the crackling logs in the fireplace and the occasional whisper of the turning of a page.

"Where are they, do you think?" Rosha murmured.

Syth looked up from his reading, did some silent calculations, and said, "North of Wina's eastern castle. I hope." His eyes dropped back to the page.

"I should have gone with them."

Syth glanced back up at Rosha's face, then closed his volume and laid it on the table beside his feet. "Why?" he challenged.

"You know why."

"No, I don't. It made absolute sense for you to remain, none at all for you to go with them. You were exhausted—"

"So was Pelmen."

"—and in need of a healing Serphimera's hands couldn't provide." Syth raised his eyebrows. "Pelmen's wounds were physical, yours of a different variety."

"What wounds?" Rosha grunted.

Syth gazed off at the distance himself and folded his hands

across his stomach. "It's no shame for a warrior to admit pain. Especially not psychic pain. You've lost your father. You're estranged from your lover. And, unless I miss my guess, you fear you've lost your nerve."

"What do you mean!" Rosha growled, almost coming out of his seat.

"What I said." Syth met Rosha's eyes with a frank stare. Embarrassed, the young man looked away. Then he seemed to melt backward into his chair, as if all the stiffness had suddenly gone out of his bones.

"How did you know?" he murmured.

"Given your recent experiences, how could you feel otherwise?" Syth asked. "All you've attempted since leaving Chaomonous has gone badly—or so you believe. You count yourself responsible for your father's death and for the near death of your mentor. You found yourself lured into a magic trap and experienced the humiliation of discovering your own naïveté. And then you were rescued by a woman." Syth smiled, more to himself than at Rosha, as if he found his recitation of Rosha's difficulties privately amusing. In fact, he smiled at how nearly the young man's circumstances matched his own. "Now I think I might have an insight some others may not have—perhaps not even your friend Pelmen. Then again, he may, knowing Serphimera. For you see, on more than one occasion, I've been rescued by a woman—a woman more powerful than myself. And such exploits just don't sound manly when recounted around a campfire." Syth now let his smile surface, and its warmth broke through the barrier of Rosha's distrustful frown. "You left your woman to prove yourself a man in the Mar. Now she's chasing you here, commanding a force the likes of which you could never muster. And you've found in addition to all of that that she can shape the powers." Syth grinned. "That can't help but make a man feel a bit inadequate. Believe me, I know."

Rosha nodded and half-smiled. Then he grimly studied his hands. Syth had touched a part of his trouble, but not all.

Now Syth leaned back in his chair and laced his hands behind his head, gazing at the dark wooden beams that supported the ceiling. "But what's really bothering you is the reality of failure." Rosha made no response, so he continued, "We build such high opinions of ourselves. We believe we're capable of anything. Who knows, maybe we are. But then the doubt sets in—and after that the dread." Syth turned his head and stared at Rosha until the young man was forced to look at him. "I know a great deal about dread as well."

"That was a spell!" Rosha protested.

"And yours isn't?"

"If it is, no one's cast it upon me but me."

"Perhaps." Syth nodded. "Then again, I can't be sure anyone cast mine upon me but me, either."

"Don't tell me that," Rosha grumbled. "You had a dread spell cast upon you by Flayh himself. And it didn't hit just you—it froze a peasant family too!"

"You heard about that? By the way, they're all right now. Serphimera apparently visited them too." Rosha nodded, barely interested. "But that still doesn't explain why the spell worked. What gave it its force?"

Rosha frowned. "I don't know. Magic."

Syth nodded. "Powers. Shaped powers. And what could end it?" Rosha shrugged. "This one your friends call the Power. And me."

"You?"

"Surely. I played a part in my own healing. I had to will myself to see past my own failure, past the loss in battle of so many men who'd trusted me, past the real possibility of Flayh's ultimate victory in this struggle, and past the inevitability of death itself, which seems like some kind of personal failure to so many of us. I can fail, Rosha. So can you. Why should we live in fear of proving what we already know?"

Rosha frowned out the window. "Isn't that admitting weakness?"

"Certainly." Syth shrugged. "But it's also an admission of fact. Our wives know it already. So do our friends. Nor does such an admission mean we have no strengths." Syth turned his gaze on this island that was so precious to him, and his teeth clenched together. His eyes smoldered with a resolve that reminded Rosha of Dorlyth as he said, "Just because we're outnumbered, outflanked, and probably outguessed as well, doesn't mean we can't give the dog a fight. And we will. We'll find all the allies we can—Belra's army, the Golden Throng, Pelmen's blue-clad initiates—and somehow we'll get into—"

He stopped suddenly, eyes on the window, a frown of concern on his face.

"What?" Rosha said, equally concerned, and he leaped up to gaze out the window himself.

"Not there," Syth grunted. "There!" He wheeled around and pointed up toward one of the beams. He'd caught a reflection in the glass of the purple shell of a sugar-clawsp. "Mar-Yilot!" he shouted as he grabbed up his book and launched it at the insect. "Mar-Yilot, come *now*!"

The sorceress sprinted into the hall. Her golden eyes were wide as she shouted, "What is it!"

"There's a clawsp in here!"

"Terril!" Mar-Yilot yelled without hesitation, and she hurled a ball of flame in the direction Syth pointed. The clawsp was in the air by now, buzzing wildly around the room as the three of them pursued it. "Take your proper shape and do battle!" Mar-Yilot screamed, but the insect ignored her as it swooped from one side of the hall to the other. Syth had retrieved his book and now he threw it again. He'd aimed poorly, however. It missed the clawsp and shattered a window. Immediately the insect doubled back and out the broken pane. An instant later the butterfly sailed out behind it, and both were lost to the sight of the two earthbound warriors. They pressed their noses to the glass anyway. They saw nothing.

Several minutes later Mar-Yilot darted back in the broken window. She dropped to the carpet in her human shape, and Syth and Rosha waited as she caught her breath. She shook her head and frowned; words were unnecessary.

"So the dog has his spies amongst us." Syth frowned. "We gave nothing through *that* conversation, since as yet we've no plans to reveal. But we must watch ourselves in the days to come. We need to be careful of lizards, too," he added, and Mar-Yilot nodded curtly.

Rosha glanced around the floor, alerted now for anything. He was still but a hapless warrior among the wizards, and the prospects chilled him. Even so, the freedom to admit his fear somehow loosed him from feeling it so strongly. He wanted to talk with this Syth further. Perhaps the man could help him find Rosha again.

* * *

Tibb marched down the Down Road behind the horse of Admon Faye. It had amused the slaver to position him here; as they descended from the High Plateau, Admon Faye called back mocking encouragements. Tibb expressed no resentment. He pretended not to notice that he was the only slaver who wasn't mounted. The insult rankled, but he saw advantages in being a walker rather than a rider. He cared nothing about the outcome of the coming battle. Since it would be the riders who would attack Belra's force while the foot soldiers blockaded the foot of the road, there appeared to be little chance he would be drawn into action. It wasn't that he was cowardly. His personal vengeance was simply more important to him than a victory for his employers. He intended to survive. He had every reason to expect that he would.

Poor Pezi had no such guarantee. Admon Faye had forced him to mount Chimolitha and lead the march down to the plain. The fat man had at first refused, but when the slaver had threatened to let Thuganlitha have him, Pezi had quickly climbed astride Chim's horn. He'd evidently not resigned himself to his fate, however. Tibb could hear Pezi's anguished pleadings from way back here.

Occasionally, Tibb glanced over the dropoff at the wide expanse of empty, white landscape. Quite suddenly, however, it was no longer empty. Out of nowhere, an army suddenly appeared. "Look!" he grasped, pointing down in excitement. Admon Faye casually turned his head and looked downward.

"What about it?" the slaver called back scornfully.

"It's an army!"

"Of course it's an army. Did you think we were out marching just for exercise?"

"But it just appeared!"

"That's right," Admon Faye responded calmly. "Which simply means Joooms has done his job."

"Joooms?" Tibb said, and Admon Faye craned his neck around to regard Tibb with disdain. Then he seemed to remember something and nodded.

"That's right. I'd forgotten you were Lamathian born. Never been in a war with shapers, little sneak?"

"Never," Tibb grunted.

"Mercenary cutthroats, most of them," Admon Faye sneered. He took pleasure in regarding others as poorly as he did himself.

"Look at those fools with him down there, believing themselves to be invisible, watching us descend and expecting to surprise us. They don't even realize they're uncovered."

"I don't understand. Why is their shaper betraying them?"

"Because we have his family."

"Where are . . . oh." Tibb nodded. The slave pit truly was filled to overflowing.

"Joooms should be grateful." Admon Faye shrugged. "Belra's paid him a fortune and won't live to collect a refund. Pezi, stop shouting! We're almost to the bottom of the hill."

Indeed, Chimolitha was shuffling down the last of the incline. The slaver had already explained very carefully to the beasts that they were to do exactly as Pezi commanded, or he would punish them. For some reason, Admon Faye had been able to communicate that order in a way that had gotten their undivided attention. When Pezi leaned down to Chim's huge left ear and said, "Turn toward this side," she moved left without hesitating. The other tugoliths followed her, maintaining a neat, orderly line. As soon as the last of the tugs was off the road and the riders began to form their ranks on the right flank, Pezi leaned back toward Chim's right ear and said, "Now turn this way." She turned to face the army of Belra, and the others followed her example. By then the cavalry was in place. Tibb stood beside Admon Faye's stirrup, listening to his ugly master berate the enemy:

"Look at Belra there—see him? Red mustache, blue and white armor? Sitting there in his saddle, so arrogant! He hasn't even deployed his force, you see? He thinks he's still invisible. He expects us to march right past him, then in turn he will march up the road and take the city without a fight." Admon Faye grinned, and looked down at Tibb. "He's a fool to side against *me*, Tibb. Any man who sides against me is a fool."

Tibb wondered if that was aimed specifically at him, but Admon Faye interrupted his thoughts. "Look there, next to Belra—You see the dark man? That's Joooms. Watch him!" Admon Faye's fist suddenly shot into the air. Tibb jumped, for Joooms had suddenly disappeared. At that moment it appeared that Belra suddenly realized he'd been betrayed, for Tibb heard him bellow with rage. "Now!" Admon Faye commanded, and the riders charged.

"Kill those men!" Tibb heard Pezi shouting at the tugoliths.

Like children released from school, the beasts cried aloud in glee, and barrelled forward. Not, however, before Pezi threw himself backward off Chimolitha's horn, begging the powers to let him land in a snowbank instead of under Chim's trampling feet. He got his wish. Throughout the course of the battle, Tibb could hear Pezi giggling joyfully.

A dreadful slaughter ensued. It became apparent immediately that the tugoliths would beat the riders to Belra, and Admon Faye wisely turned his cavalry aside and drew them up to watch. The tugs danced and gamboled gleefully across the snow, then plowed into their horrified enemies with the crunch of breaking metal. A few of Belra's followers had the good sense to wheel their horses right then and take flight. Those who didn't, out of loyalty, bravery, or simple indecision, were spitted on the tips of tugolith horns. Thuganlitha had thoroughly enjoyed his feast of slave flesh. As a result, many of his victims were quickly consumed. Chimolitha tossed Joooms's mount casually aside, charging onward through the ranks. Riganlitha trampled Belra, leaving the shreds of his broken body in the snow. He had been a noble warrior and a decent citylord and had always expected to die in battle, but not like this, certainly. Never like this.

Tibb watched it all, astonished. He was admittedly a rogue, a brigand. Even so, the savagery of this attack appalled him. Moments later, as the mounted slavers returned to the base of the road and started back up to safety, Admon Faye reined in beside Tibb and booted him lightly in the back. As Tibb tumbled into the snow, the ugly slaver cackled and asked, "What do you think of your master now, little sneak?"

"You know what I think of you," Tibb muttered as he got to his feet, brushing the white powder from his cloak. "Not that it matters." He pointed out at the tugoliths and asked, "What are you going to do about them?"

The encounter had been brief—evidently too brief, in the estimation of the tugoliths. Several of them still frisked around playfully among the carnage, but once all the horses and men were down, the game lost much of its appeal. Admon Faye took all of this in and murmured, "They're in a dangerous state, aren't they. Any suggestions?"

"None that would please you," Tibb grunted, and Admon Faye laughed again.

"Better get up the road, little sneak," he suggested. "Unless you wish to be squished." Then he spurred his horse forward. The animal was most unwilling; but, after it felt the spurs again, it trotted toward the vast patch of red-stained snow. Admon Faye smiled broadly and looked directly at Thuganlitha. "Did you enjoy that?" he called brightly.

"Yes!" Thug answered enthusiastically, and all the others agreed that they had enjoyed it, too.

"You want to do it some more?" he asked, his tone that of a teacher inviting her tots to learn a new game.

"Yes!" they said, almost in chorus.

"Very good! About a mile over that way is a castle. Kam lives there. We don't like Kam," he said with a scowl, and he got some sympathetic scowls back. "Let's go knock down Kam's castle and eat him!"

"Hurray!" The tugoliths all cheered and they frolicked away in the direction of Kam's castle.

Tibb watched them go and shook his head. He didn't know Kam, but he pitied him. Then he started up the Down Road, making a point of avoiding Pezi, who also climbed it on foot. He wanted a chance to think through what he had seen.

A few hours later, the House of Kam no longer existed. The tugoliths thought it was all great fun.

## CHAPTER THIRTEEN

# The Battle of Dragonsgate

MIDMORNING ON the fifth day after leaving Sythia Isle, Pelmen and Serphimera rode up into Westmouth. They were both exhausted. So were their horses. But anticipation of this moment had enlivened their senses. Both were excited and mentally prepared for anything. They expected an encounter first with the false Vicia-Heinox.

They galloped unhindered to the center of the pass, their horses kicking up the powdery snow behind them. There they slowed to a silent stop and looked about. The pass was empty. There was no sign of the dragon.

"He's gone," Serphimera said.

"Maybe Flayh's finally overextended himself," Pelmen responded enthusiastically. "Maybe he can't maintain the illusion any longer."

"Or maybe he's just off terrorizing our homeland," she muttered.

Pelmen looked over at her and smiled. "I thought *you* were supposed to be the hopeful one."

Serphimera shrugged. "You seem to be in such a positive mood today, I thought it might be a good chance to let my own fears out."

Pelmen nodded, his smile dying. Then he dismounted. "We need to give these animals a rest and decide which way we're going." He looked up and noticed she was studying him. "What is it?"

"Is Lamath your homeland? You never say."

Pelmen shrugged. "What makes a homeland? The place your mother chose to be when you were born or your own choosing when you're grown?" He helped Serphimera dismount as he went on, "If I must choose, I choose to be a citizen of the old One Land. That makes Lamath my homeland—and the other realms as well."

"Look there," she said suddenly, pointing, and he spun around. A young man robed in the gown of a skyfaither approached them timidly.

Strahn eyed them with uncertainly. He was unnerved by the dark blue color of Serphimera's habit. Although he'd never seen either Pelmen or Serphimera, he knew them both by reputation and stood in awe of them. But it didn't make sense that the prophet would send him in search of someone who was still loyal to the dragon. "Are you . . . Pelmen and Serphimera?" he asked hesitantly.

"We are. Who are you?"

"The Prophet of Lamath sent me here to meet you."

"How did he know we were coming?" Pelmen inquired with a curious smile.

"I don't know." The lad shrugged. "I was going to ask you the same question. But come, we've got to hurry!"

"Our horses are weary. They'll carry us no further without rest."

"Oh, you can't take your horses where we're going," Strahn said quickly. He glanced around the pass, looking for someplace to leave them.

"Where *are* we going?" Pelmen asked.

"Up there." The initiate pointed up the eastern cliff face. He didn't notice Pelmen's gape of surprise. "I don't know where to tell you to leave your horses." He frowned. "I don't think anyplace will be safe."

"From the dragon?"

"From the battle. You can't see the armies from here, but you can from above. The army of Chaomonous is just entering the Southmouth. The Lamathian army marched into the valley north of us just yesterday—they've been trying to beat the Golden Throng here. Anyway, they should clash this afternoon—right about where we're standing."

The need for haste was evident. Pelmen led the horses to one side of the pass and hurried back, his feet ploughing a trough through the snow. "Lead on, my friend," he shouted, and the three started their ascent of the cliff. What looked impossible proved to be merely difficult, once their guide showed them the path. They climbed quickly, speaking rarely. It was nearly noon and they were almost to the summit when sunlight glinting off of metal caught Pelmen's eye. He turned around and surveyed the panorama below. The view took his breath away—and also broke his heart. To his left, the glistening column of Chaomonous wound proudly upward through the mountains. To his right, well hidden in the rocks of the Northmouth, a contingent of blue-clad Lamathians waited. Expecting the Golden Throng to turn westward toward the Mar, the Dragonfaithers were poised for a quick, vicious thrust into the Chaon flank. They would be trying to divide Bronwynn's army, cutting off the retreat of the front half and bottling the back of the column in the steep defile. Pelmen frowned in dismay. This would be yet another senseless conflict.

"Pelmen," Serphimera called softly. "We're almost to the top."

The shaper dragged himself away from the sad spectacle

and bent his energies to finishing the climb. They found Erri waiting for them on the summit, and the prophet and Pelmen embraced like brothers. "You did find me, didn't you?" Erri smiled.

"I think you found us instead."

"And none too soon, by the look of things," the prophet murmured, stepping toward the edge to survey the impending conflict. Then he looked back at Pelmen and raised his eyebrows. "Do you think we'll win?"

"That all depends." Pelmen sighed. "Whom do you mean by 'we'?"

"It's strange," Erri said with a nod, "to find one's loyalties so thoroughly skewed by events. I spent a good many years in the Lamathian navy, and we fought many a skirmish with golden-sailed boats. I may know a few of those golden warriors down there, but those tiny figures in blue are my friends, my kin, and—before the Power—my ultimate responsibility. It's not an easy thing to wish defeat on one's own countrymen. I do understand the necessity of it, however, if Bronwynn's shining soldiers are to win through to battle Flayh." He glanced back at Pelmen, eyeing him keenly. "But perhaps you've come to tell me her army really isn't needed . . ."

"How would I know such a thing?"

"You've come for the pyramid, haven't you?"

"Yes . . ."

"You must have some purpose for it."

"Perhaps we would, if we could find the others that go with it. There were six pyramids originally, and three have been lost for a millennium. Thus far we only have one."

"Now you have two," Erri said purposefully as he reached within the folds of his robe and pulled out the velvet sack. "I'm happy to be rid of it." Pelmen passed the bag to Serphimera, who wordlessly hung it around her neck, concealing it within her voluminous habit.

"Thank you for keeping it safe, my friend. I only wish I could be more hopeful about its value."

"If it's in the Power's purpose, you'll find the others." Erri shrugged, and Serphimera nodded in agreement. "Until that happens, however, I suppose we must rely on more conventional means of resistance. It appears Queen Bronwynn must have this victory."

"So it does." Pelmen grunted, gazing down at the pass. The Golden Throng had reached the center of it now and was making the expected turn toward the west.

"I only hope it may be cheaply won. Today!" Erri announced. "I pray that every Lamathian might prove a coward—and thus survive!"

At that moment the warriors of Lamath launched their attack on the unsuspecting Chaon flank. As their blue capes furled brilliantly behind them, they looked anything but cowardly.

General Joss was no novice. He had not expected an attack from the Northmouth, but he wasn't entirely unprepared for it. That was, after all, the way to Lamath, and he'd given most of his adult life to battling blue-clad warriors. Had the blue riders kept silent as they started their charge, they would have met less resistance; for, while the snow slowed their mounts, it muffled the sound of their hoofbeats as well. The Dragon-faithers, however, roared out their battle cry. It warned Joss in time to turn his flank to meet them.

Without hesitating, he launched a counterattack. He sent his vanguard of riders directly into the Lamathians, breaking their charge and providing time to form the infantry into phalanxes. At the moment he had far more warriors in the pass than did his opposition. If he could succeed in walling off the remainder of the blue army, he might quickly rout them. The irony of this encounter flicked through his mind; at long last he was meeting his ancestral enemy with a fully outfitted army, yet the tight squeeze of Dragonsgate would permit less than a tenth of his force to participate. He'd made his reputation fighting border skirmishes and longing for a pitched battle on an open field. By the choice of the enemy commander, this was yet another border skirmish, and no one had more experience at such than Joss.

With his phalanxes formed, he sent one rushing forward to plug the gap, then closed the others behind it. Only then did he wheel his horse to check the location of his queen.

Half of Joss's riders always led the march. It was this vanguard that now mêléed the attacking Lamathians. The other half always brought up the rear, protecting against surprise attacks from behind. He'd positioned Bronwynn in this rear guard. He could see now that, just as he'd expected, she was struggling to get around the foot-soldiers and ride to the center of the action. He quickly formed another phalanx to block the Southmouth off from the rest of the pass and commanded the remainder of the column to remain stationary. Then he withdrew behind the line and waited for the queen to reach him.

"Who is it? What's happening?" Bronwynn shouted angrily as she galloped up beside him. The line of warriors closed tightly before them and drew taut across the Southmouth. Though they faced the battlefield, the general's primary purpose for them at the moment was to keep the Queen from racing into the fray. Joss had no doubt she'd do it if she could get through.

"We've been attacked by Lamath, my Lady," Joss responded calmly. "As yet there's no cause for alarm. We're better deployed than they. I think they expected to surprise us, but they mistimed their charge. They've lost that advantage now." Joss understated the case. In fact, the Lamathian assault had already been repulsed. The clash of armies and the screams of the dying distracted Bronwynn. She clapped her hands over her ears. Joss had long ago learned to block out those chaotic noises and he gazed unflinchingly at the section of heaviest fighting. The blue line was bending backward. Then it broke with surprising speed as three of Lamath's most stalwart attackers were abruptly cut from their saddles. Joss said nothing, but he did permit himself a smile. That clinched it. He was certain the battle was won.

And it would have been, except for the dragon. From high in the sky there came a shriek that iced the blood. Thousands of heads jerked upward to watch the twi-beast come plummeting downward, and the battle, clearly won a moment before, was suddenly clearly lost. A thunderous roar rose up through the canyon, the battlecry of the host of Lamath, still hidden beyond the cliffs. The wall of blue riders reformed, then redoubled its attack, and terrorized Chaons fled before it.

"My Lady, ride to the rear," Joss told Bronwynn firmly. He now unsheathed his own sword, prepared to die defending her escape.

"Command your army, Joss!" Bronwynn spat. "Don't try commanding me!" The young woman rose up out of her saddle, standing in her stirrups as she faced her panicked host. "It's a lie!" she screamed. "The dragon is dead! This is the trick of a shaper!"

The noise in the pass was incredible. Few, if any, of her warriors could actually make out her words. But the sight of their golden-mailed queen shaking her sword at the dragon shamed her men into turning around. Once again, that small part of the Golden Throng who were actually engaged in combat faced the enemy.

Bronwynn had rallied them; now Joss sought to direct them. That was no easy task. Ranks were broken. The footing, already treacherous due to the snow, was growing more so with the bodies of the fallen. He did what he could, but not without an added touch of personal bitterness. They might win yet, he thought to himself, but now it would not be his victory.

Bronwynn cheered with pride at the effects of her words. She shouted encouragement at the top of her lungs. But then she began to notice various golden warriors turning back to look at her expectantly. The awesome weight of her new reputation dropped upon her once again. Of course! They expected *her* to win the battle for them!

The dragon had not ceased its horrid screeching. It had passed down the long incline, petrifying Bronwynn's rear guard. Now it swooped back up the same route, flying low, causing rank after rank of golden warriors to collapse on their faces in fear. Bronwynn wheeled her horse around to meet it, her face a mask of rage that hid the uncertainty of her heart. It wasn't that she feared this on-rushing illusion. She feared instead trying to shape—and finding that she lacked the power.

Her hesitancy sealed her failure. The twi-beast shrieked up into her face, and she threw herself backward off her horse. She fell in the snow uninjured, but to her watching host it appeared she'd been knocked from her saddle. The results were calamitous. The tide of battle turned again.

From their vantage point high above the action, Erri, Pelmen, and Serphimera watched the lines surging from one side of the pass to the other. Erri soon shouted himself hoarse and was reduced to whispering anxious comments. They had all been cheered by the Golden Throng's initial resistance, but no one was surprised by the dragon's appearance nor its predictable consequences. While it was hard to make out individuals from this distance, Erri thought he could pinpoint Bronwynn, and had cackled when the tiny figure's challenging gestures had rallied her forces together. His eyes were still on her when the dragon-shape flashed back over her head. Like most of her army, he thought it had knocked her sprawling. "It knocked her off!" he rasped in shock. "The beast is substantial after all; it knocked her off her horse! Pelmen you must . . . Pelmen?" Erri looked around in vain, but the shaper was gone. He followed Serphimera's pointing finger and saw a falcon diving into the fray.

Pelmen didn't fly directly for the dragon. That would come later, when he had the attention of the combatants. It was necessary first to grab their attention, and he did so by flying to Bronwynn. The warriors who clustered around their dazed queen jumped back in amazement when a man dropped suddenly from the sky and kneeled beside her. Pelmen ignored them. "Are you all right?" he asked her quickly.

Bronwynn's eyes widened. "Pelmen? You're here?"

"Answer me," he demanded curtly.

"I'm fine!" she blurted out.

"Then get back on your feet immediately." He didn't wait to see if she obeyed. He shot into the sky again and circled the center of the pass three times, screeching loudly. Then he dropped to the canyon floor in the midst of the battle—and disappeared. So did the rest of the Golden Throng.

Erri grunted and looked at Serphimera. She was smiling serenely back at him. "He is rather impressive, isn't he?" the old sailor rasped.

Serphimera raised her eyebrows. "Rather." Then she bent over to look back at the pass.

As quickly as it had vanished, the Golden Throng reappeared. During that moment of cloaking Bronwynn's army was unaware of what was happening, but it faced a newly stunned enemy. The blue-robed warriors were backing away in confusion. Pelmen took advantage of the relative hush by making an announcement. In a voice rich with the polished tones of the theater, he shouted: "Men of Lamath! Your dragon is dead! If any man asks you who told you so, tell them I! Pelmen Dragonsbane!"

As if on cue, Flayh's illusion came whistling down out of the heavens. Its double-throated roar of rage was real. It echoed Flayh's own thunderous bellow in a castle tower more than a hundred miles away. That was quite all right with Pelmen. He now had everyone's attention and was ready to give his demonstration. He shot skyward in his falcon form. This time he flew straight for the dragon.

The struggle for Dragonsgate had become a shaper battle. Yet it really wasn't a contest. Flayh was too far away. With all his art and power, he couldn't outmaneuver an experienced wizard who was there on the scene. All he could do was roar in frustration as the falcon flew through his illusion and emerged above it. The spectators below stared upward in rapt silence as the falcon banked to one side and swooped around to pierce through the dragon again. It did so a third time before another voice, if anything richer and more mellow than even Pelmen's, thundered, "You've heard the Dragonsbane, cowards of Lamath! Men of Chaomonous, at them again!"

No one asked who'd spoken those words. The armies simply responded to them. The Golden Throng charged forward with a shout. The men of Lamath raced desperately for the Northmouth and the road home. And Gerrig, who had shouted, leaned against the eastern cliff face, cackling with glee, and congratulated himself on another fine performance.

The Golden Throng camped in Dragonsgate. The ensuing celebration made the walls of the canyon ring. It had been a long time since Chaomonous had enjoyed such a victory—certainly not in the lifetime of any of these warriors. The fact that it had been won for them by magic stole nothing from their triumph. Instead, it enhanced their images of themselves as an army. The men of Chaomonous considered the Golden Throng to be charmed. Their very location exhilarated them. They would sleep this night in the ancient lair of the dragon, in the pass that had born the name of the twi-beast for centuries! What other army in history could make such a boast?

While the warriors whooped in delight, their leaders renewed an old quarrel. Bronwynn's pavilion had been erected in the center of the pass. Within its fish-satin walls she and Joss engaged in a heated debate.

"We must go *northward*, my Lady! Any other move is suicidal! We have routed them today! One day's pursuit and we could utterly destroy them!"

"I don't want to destroy them," Bronwynn said firmly. "I want to turn westward and march on Flayh's fortress."

"Your friend Pelmen has told you of its impregnability!" Joss pleaded. "How can you turn away from a clear-cut victory and certain conquest and march through the snow to an unavoidable defeat?"

"I've made up my mind—"

"If we move west, the Lamathian army will march back into the pass and cut off our retreat. The Golden Throng will be trapped on the Westmouth Plain. Again."

"I said I've made up my mind!"

"My Lady, consider this. Divide the force. Give me a part of it to pursue these dragon worshippers—"

"You've *never* suggested dividing our army! You've always said there could be no quicker path to ruin!"

"Yes, my Lady, but you've shown me there is indeed a quicker path—marching westward without utterly destroying Lamath!"

"I will not destroy Lamath! That's final!" Bronwynn shouted.

Both she and the general were terribly shocked when a voice from just inside the doorway said, "I can't tell you how much that relieves me."

"Who's there?" Bronwynn demanded imperiously.

"Can't you see me?" Erri asked.

Pelmen answered, "I'm afraid she can't." Then the shaper removed the cloaking spell.

General Joss already had his sword out. Now he pointed it at the four intruders and demanded, "How did you get inside?"

"I think that's obvious," Pelmen said quietly.

"There was no need," Bronwynn snapped. "I would have let you in."

"I was certain of that. A few of your warriors, however, took offense at the garments of my friends. This seemed the simplest solution." Pelmen spread his arms. "Bronwynn?" he asked.

Had they been alone—were she not the queen—had she not experienced shaper power that somehow demanded she maintain her independence—she would have run into his embrace. Instead, she walked deliberately across the tent and reached out her hands to take his. "Welcome, Pelmen."

"Am I?" he asked. "I fear we've intruded . . ."

"You're *all* welcome. Erri?" She reached out with one arm and hugged the prophet warmly. "I'm glad you're alive."

"And I'm glad so many of my people still are, despite your victory. General Joss, I hope you'll accept her decision."

"I always accept my monarch's decisions. I don't always agree."

"Perhaps you'll eventually come to agree with her."

"Or perhaps we'll all die in the snows of the Mar," Joss replied coldly.

"If so, it won't be due to the army of Lamath," said Erri.

"You're certain of that?"

"So I believe."

Joss snorted. Beliefs were meaningless to him. Still, he held his tongue. Decorum demanded it.

Bronwynn turned to Serphimera. "He found you again, I see." She smiled. Then she looked at Pelmen. "And you found my Rosha." Pelmen nodded. "Is he safe?"

"He was when we left."

"Then he still doesn't need my aid?" Bronwynn asked archly, her nose angled upward. She was prepared for an unpleasant reply.

"My Lady, at this point we all need one another's aid. Whether he realizes that yet or not, he will."

"If he doesn't kill himself playing the hero," Bronwynn snorted.

"He's not playing the hero. He is a hero." These words were the first Serphimera spoke. They got immediate attention.

"What does that mean?" Bronwynn asked after a brief pause.

"Only that Rosha is being the one he must be—as you are, as Erri is, and as am I. The Power inspires us all, yet each of us takes his own approach. We must. We're different people."

Bronwynn looked at the priestess a moment, and her expression began to soften. "Then do you think this . . . this grand march of mine . . . my army . . . do you think the Power might have inspired it?"

"I don't think such," Serphimera said briskly. "I *know* it."

Bronwynn peered at her, then looked back and forth from Serphimera's face to Pelmen's. "Really?" she asked, her eagerness growing.

"When she says she knows," Pelmen murmured, "you can believe her."

"That's such a relief!" The queen sighed. "You don't know how I've battled with the fear that it's all been a monumental blunder! And today, just before you came, when I saw that it all would be lost—" She interrupted herself, fixing her eyes on Pelmen. "Thank you for being here," she said earnestly. "Although I still don't know why you've come."

"I've come to reclaim the pyramid I entrusted into your care. I think you know the one?"

"Oh, the pyramid . . ." Bronwynn said, as if hesitant about surrendering it. Her hesitation lasted only a moment. "I'll get it." She walked to her bed, dropped to her knees and plunged her hand underneath it. Her servants had found the object there when they'd broken camp that morning. They'd dutifully returned it to the same spot when the tent was erected that afternoon. "Here it is," she grumbled, pulling the blue velvet bag out and holding it up. "What do you want it for, anyway?"

Pelmen looked at Serphimera. "That's an excellent question. I only wish we knew the answer."

## CHAPTER FOURTEEN

# Blind Mission

"TAHLI-DAMEN?" Wayleeth asked tentatively.

"Yes, my dear," her husband answered, with a distant formality that made her heart hurt.

"Why are we doing this?" She asked it simply. She did not imply that they had made a mistake, that he was a fool, nor even that she was unhappy—although she was. She tried to keep all those feelings out of her voice as she asked, wishing in all sincerity for an answer that really made sense.

"Because the Power says we must."

There it was again—a reply she'd heard before—a reply without substance. For although Wayleeth tried daily, she heard no such thing from any such Power. Or, if she *was* hearing the Power's voice, she certainly didn't recognize it. Her spirits sank a bit deeper. Her gaze dropped to the snow-covered ground around them. Her eyes teared.

They rode through the Mar on horses provided by the House of Uda. Tahli-Damen had suggested it, but only upon Wayleeth's request had the cousins now in control of the family fortune surrendered the animals. They considered Tahli-Damen a crazy man. Wayleeth, on the other hand, had good sense. If she felt this was the only way to care for their mentally diseased kinsmen, they would indulge her.

The horses had sped them across the countryside, but not enabled them to shake their implacable escort. A ring of dogs still accompanied them, but they no longer took much notice. Tahli-Damen, of course, couldn't see their black companions. Wayleeth was busy, spending the quiet hours of the ride thinking about past choices.

She was a dutiful wife. That's what she'd been trained to be, and she did it well. Her task had been easy when they rode her husband's talent to prominence within the Merchant League. She'd been a gracious, lovely hostess, always doing the proper things at the proper time. Now she traveled toward the High Fortress at the direction of a blind fanatic who once had been her husband, but seemed no longer to consider himself so. It made no sense—and yet she did it. The question that bothered her most was not why they rode to Flayh's castle. That she could logically attribute to Tahli-Damen's mental condition. What she couldn't understand was why she didn't protest.

She glanced up and gasped in disgust and horror. She stopped her horse and Tahli-Damen's as well, and sat gaping soundlessly at the field before them.

"What is it?" he asked. When she wouldn't speak, he demanded, "Tell me what you see!"

Wayleeth swallowed with difficulty, battling nausea. It wasn't a sight she could readily describe, but she tried. "The snow . . . is churned up. It's . . . slushy, as if trodden underfoot by enormous horses. And it's . . . it's stained. Bright, bloody red. There are—" She gulped for breath. "—bodies, frozen bodies in the snow. Some are . . ." But she couldn't bring herself to tell him of the half-eaten human and equine remains scattered before them. She struggled, but could not stop the coming of her silent sobs.

"A battlefield then," Tahli-Damen grunted, believing he understood. He couldn't understand. He couldn't comprehend this at all. Wayleeth counted it yet another blessing of his blindness. No wonder he could be so optimistic—and so holy. "Enormous horses, you say?" he mused. "I wonder what that could be?"

Wayleeth offered no suggestions. She just covered her mouth and tried to stop trembling.

"How close are we to the plateau?" Tahli-Damen asked her.

Wayleeth took two deep breaths, bit her lips, then replied with perfect composure, "We're at its base."

"Good," her husband muttered. He dismounted clumsily.

She frowned. "What are you doing?"

"We'll walk the rest of the way."

"But—"

"Our cousins told us the city is full of thieves and blackguards. Horses would make us too conspicuous."

Wayleeth gazed down at him bitterly, wanting to shout at him, wanting to scream. How inconspicuous did he think he could be, wearing a sky blue robe with eyeballs to match? But she didn't. Instead she climbed down off of her horse. "It's a long way up," she muttered.

"It's early yet. We'll make it before nightfall."

"There are slavers up there."

"They'll not bother themselves with a pair of foolish fanatics," he told her with smiling confidence.

But Tahli-Damen was wrong.

After the escape of the magical thieves, Admon Faye had publically beheaded every slaver assigned to the Down Road on the night when Rosha had eliminated twelve and escaped with Pelmen and Mar-Yilot. Now the rogues atop the Down Road watched it with a vengeful care born of fear. It was tense, yet boring work, and they laughed with glee at the diversion of two blue-clad initiates from Lamath.

"What have we here?" One slaver chuckled as he seized Wayleeth by the collar and jerked her around to look him in the face. "Why, it's a girl!" he whooped. "Mates, we got us a religious girl!"

"Really? Let's check!" another man cackled as he stooped to grab the hem of Wayleeth's robe and jerked it upward.

"Stop!" she cried, struggling to hold the garment down over her.

Another group held the struggling Tahli-Damen. "This one's blind," one of them shouted.

"Let's toss him off and go play with the woman," another suggested.

They would have done so, had it not been for the dogs. They heard the snarls as the hounds bounded up the road into their midst.

"Dogs!" one slaver shouted and he fled up the street toward the castle.

"Get away!" another rogue cried to his fellows, but his words were unnecessary. The group was already scattered. The slavers had seen these devilish creatures before and wanted no part of them.

"Come on!" Wayleeth shouted as she grabbed Tahli-Damen by the hand. "Run, will you?" she screamed, dragging him. They ran up the street as far as the first alley, then ducked down it, Tahli-Damen banging against the wall of a shop in the process. She dragged him on until they came to a door, then she dropped his hand and pounded on it with both fists. "Please!" she cried desperately. "Somebody let us in!"

"Who is it?" a voice from within growled.

"We're—strangers. Friends!" Wayleeth amended quickly. "We're trying to escape some slavers! Help us, please!"

There was a brief pause, then the voice grunted, "Go away!"

Wayleeth stepped back. "Go away?" she said to the bolted door in disbelief.

"Go away!" the voice yelled again, and the heavy wood did not muffle its angry, insistent tone. The resident of the Mari capital didn't wish to tangle with slavers.

Wayleeth's face crumpled, and she began to sob. She leaned against the door and cried, and Tahli-Damen stretched his hand toward the sound to pat her comfortingly. She knocked his arm away and scowled at him, an expression totally wasted. "Leave me alone!" she snarled.

"Wayleeth," he murmured tenderly and he tried reaching out to her again. "That was horrible, my love, horrible. But you mustn't miss the most important thing."

"And what's that?" she snapped.

"The Power *did* take care of us."

She wished he could see her face, for her look expressed far more than words ever could. But he couldn't. He gazed sightlessly toward her with a smile she was sure he meant to be encouraging, but which struck her as merely idiotic. She leaned back against the bolted door, and thought once again about her choices. It would all be bearable, she told herself, if once—just once—the Power would address itself to *her*.

"Mother, can't you—" Pahd mod Pahd-el began, but his mother didn't let him finish.

"I've done what I could," Chogi lan Pahd-el answered her son brusquely.

"But she's dying!"

"That's not my fault. She ought to stop speaking against him." The heavyset woman stood by the door, her lips pursed, her hands folded primly before her.

Pahd paced back to the bed, but not to lie upon it. He couldn't sleep, and for Pahd there was no greater torment. His wife's condition worsened by the hour. He knelt beside Sarie and peered again into her waxy face. Then he seized her hand and called over his shoulder, "Mother! What can I do?"

Chogi snorted. "You know what you çan do. You've known all along. You've just been too lazy—"

"I've not been lazy!" Pahd flared. "I've not yielded to the man because it wouldn't be right!"

Chogi arched a weary eyebrow. "Integrity, suddenly. You'll forgive me, perhaps, if I seem a bit dubious, but I am your mother, and I know you rather well."

"He wants me to kill Maris!" Pahd pleaded.

"What of that? We've always killed Maris! It's been the family business for years!"

"Not when I rode with Dorlyth," Pahd murmured, his body stiffening with deserved pride. "That day we killed Chaons and drove them, screaming, from our realm!"

"Dorlyth is dead." Chogi grunted. "And your wife will be soon, unless you quit spouting inanities and face facts. Why can't you trust him, Pahd? He wants to make you the ruler of the world!"

Pahd looked at his mother with disgust, then pointed down at Sarie's unconscious form. "You can look at that and ask me to trust this wizard?"

Chogi's eyes half closed, and her lips formed a thin, rigid line. "Trust him or don't, you either serve him or she dies. It's your choice. She's your wife." Chogi leaned back against the door and folded her arms across her chest. She did not fear the look of rage that turned his face scarlet. She'd seen it all his life and knew it was meaningless.

Pahd whirled away from her, stalked to the wall, and jerked a scabbarded greatsword down off its hanger. He buckled it on as he strode toward the door, and his mother stepped calmly out of the way. So rarely did Pahd leave his own chambers that Chogi's guards in the outer hall almost fell over with surprise. He ignored them, walking briskly down the steps of his tower and turning toward the tower of Flayh.

The husky slaver on guard at the foot of Flayh's stairs insolently pulled out his sword. "You can't pass," the man drawled.

Pahd whipped out his blade, brought it slashing around to clash against the slaver's, and sent the man's weapon bouncing crazily down the hall. The slaver's insolence evaporated as Pahd's sword tip danced within an inch of his nose. "I *will* be king in my own house!" Pahd roared. Then he sheathed his weapon and stomped up the spiral, leaving the guard to melt in relief against the wall.

When he reached the top of the stairs, he found that the door was already open, and Flayh was seated in a chair, waiting for him.

"Come in! Come in!" the wizard called with a false friendliness. Pahd stepped into the room and slumped into the chair Flayh offered. "You're very welcome, King Pahd. I had hoped you might come to see me."

"What do I have to do?" Pahd growled.

"Have to do?" Flayh asked. "You're the king, my Lord. You can do as you wish."

"What do I have to do to get you to release Sarie from this fever!"

Flayh frowned. "Sarie. Yes. A difficult case. I've tried to help, you know. She resists."

"Just tell me," Pahd said wearily. He slipped his greatsword from its scabbard and dropped it, clattering, onto the flagstones. Pointing his finger toward it, Pahd muttered, "It's yours."

Flayh gazed into Pahd's face and said, "I recognize that's no mean offer."

"It's yours. All I ask is that you spare Sarie."

"I accept your offer, Pahd," Flayh said quietly. "For you see, I need you."

Pahd snorted. "Why? When you've got monsters that squish your enemies between their toes? When you've got slavers to slit their throats? What need do you have of me?"

"Legitimacy." Flayh shrugged. "Oh, I must admit, the tugoliths are rather amazing. And cute, too, don't you think? Remarkable! Did you know that was my nephew Pezi's idea? Really amazing. These slavers, though. Rude lot, aren't they! Terrorizing people—they're necessary for security, of course, but worthless against major armies like the one that is marching to us."

"What army?" Pahd grunted. "You've smashed the last of the resistance."

"Most of it, yes. But not all. Syth still lives, as does his aggravating woman. And this nuisance son of Dorlyth. But they're a paltry threat compared to the army that marched through Dragonsgate today." Flayh's visage had grown stony with bitterness. "I understand you object to killing Maris. You surely could feel no shame at the slaughter of Chaons?"

Pahd frowned. "Chaomonous? Through Dragonsgate?"

"I tried to stop them. Even sent the army of Lamath to ambush them. All to no avail—because of Pelmen." As he said the name, Flayh's face lost all expression. His eyes, however, were icy.

"A shaper battle?" Pahd asked uneasily. He loved a good fight, but shapers had a way of confusing the conduct of battle that made him anxious.

"Of a sort." Flayh shrugged. "You don't worry about him. Concern yourself instead with the Golden Throng—and triumph."

Pahd nodded. He stooped down to pick up his sword and sheathed it as he walked toward the door.

"And Pahd . . ." Flayh added, stopping him. "As to Sarie—well, I'll do what I can. But she must do something as well."

"What's that?" Pahd asked flatly. He was beaten. He hadn't the energy to bridle anymore.

"Tell her to stop resisting."

Pahd hung his head. Then he sighed and left the room. Pahd knew well his limitations in the matter. He could control his wife about as well as he could control his mother—that was, not at all. Defeated, he made his way slowly back to his royal chambers. No one took much notice when he passed.

"We must go on," Tahli-Damen said firmly.

Wayleeth shook her head, and looked around at the circle of dogs. They sat in the frozen mud of an alley on the eastern side of Ngandib. The gray afternoon slipped toward night, but Wayleeth would go no further without some sign.

"Tell the Power I've got to know that too, before I'll move," she mumbled.

"I thought you *did* know that," Tahli-Damen answered. "Isn't that why you followed me to Lamath?"

The hint of mockery in his tone enraged her, but she wouldn't say what she felt. She couldn't—not without denying the things she'd avowed to Erri—that she had heard the Power, that this was her purpose as well as her husband's, and that she believed. Wayleeth sighed. Then she answered honestly, "I thought I did too."

"What changed?" asked Tahli-Damen.

"Can't you see?" Wayleeth pleaded. Then she buried her head in her hands, silently abusing herself for her terrible choice of words. It took several minutes for Tahli-Damen to respond.

"Of course I can't see. I'm blind, Wayleeth, and I can't appreciate any of the horrors you've described to me over the past week. I can't see anything except a shapeless blue haze that lingers always before my eyes. Wayleeth—my dearest—is it meaningless? Is all this that I've tried to do, this faith, my pilgrimage to Erri, my mission—is it all, to you, what it is to our kinsmen, the nonsensical ravings of a lunatic? Because if it is . . . my darling, if it is . . . I'd rather die. If there is no purpose in my blindness, then I see nothing but despair, and I'd rather die." Tahli-Damen chuckled then, and Wayleeth heard a bitter edge to the sound that had not been there since the first days of his magical affliction.

"I don't hear daily instruction from the Power," he told her. "Most days . . ." He hesitated, as if unwilling to reveal this, but then continued. "Most days I hear nothing at all. But I go on. Wayleeth, by faith I go on, because not to go on, not to believe, is to admit I'm nothing but a stupid fool, who..." Here he had to stop to control his own emotions. "Who, without wishing to, has led the love of his life into the darkest possible circumstances."

Wayleeth stared at him, aware of what he was saying and wanting to reply in the most helpful manner possible. Although he'd clung to her hand for many miles and relied upon her eyes for direction, he'd not revealed any real need for her until that moment. Now that she understood it, she responded in the only way a devoted wife could. She took him by the hand and pulled him to his feet, murmuring, "All right. I have my sign."

They walked to the High Fortress in the company of their canine comrades, who seemed to grow more excited with every step. No one stopped them, but Wayleeth didn't view that as good fortune. She fully expected to die within the next few moments. She thought she might prefer ending things out here in the open rather than within that looming tower. It was not to be, however. They walked straight to the open gate of the cavernous stable and up inside. No one guarded it, which puzzled Wayleeth only for a moment.

When she saw the tugolith, she realized human guards were totally unnecessary. She also understood the enormous hoofprints in the snow and the mangled corpses. She remembered tugoliths now; although she'd never seen one, the merchant academies were all excellent.

The beast that walked menacingly toward them wore an extremely nasty expression. She didn't scream—she couldn't say anything at all. Instead she clutched Tahli-Damen's arm and pointed fruitlessly. Her husband frowned and cocked his head.

"I'm hungry!" Thuganlitha announced. Since no alarm had been given, he assumed these new arrivals belonged here in the castle. The woman's trembling did not surprise him, since he'd grown accustomed to humans trembling in his presence. He addressed his complaint to them, making it clear that he wanted action immediately. It really wasn't a threat.

Wayleeth didn't know that and she shrank back in horror. Tahli-Damen, however, smiled a kindly smile and modeled his reply after Erri. "My child, if I had anything to eat I'd give it to you. In fact, I have nothing. I'm hungry, too."

The beast peered at Tahli-Damen as if he were crazy, then bellowed again, "I'm hungry!"

Tahli-Damen no longer smiled. "And as I said, I am hungry also. But I have a mission to perform in this place, and it cannot be put off while I obtain food for you. You will excuse us."

Thuganlitha's enormous eyes grew bigger in surprise. Then the color of Tahli-Damen's robe suddenly registered in his simple brain and he remembered a certain conversation with the despised Pezi on the road. "I can eat *you*!" he roared in delight.

"Eat me?" Tahli-Damen snapped. "How ridiculous! That sounds like the dragon talking! Wayleeth, is the illusion of the dragon standing before me?"

Wayleeth stammered, "N-n-no . . ." But she couldn't manage to be any more specific.

"Humph," Tahli-Damen grunted, puzzled. "Well, you are obviously someone with a tasteless sense of humor, and I haven't time for jokes. Stand aside, please. We have business within this fortress."

Thuganlitha didn't understand all of what Tahli-Damen said, but he'd gathered he'd been insulted. It shocked him. No one spoke to him like that! "I'll horn you!" he roared, and his words thundered off the stable's rock walls.

"That isn't amusing," Tahli-Damen scolded. "Wayleeth, lead me on into this castle."

Perplexed at having his threat so carelessly disregarded, Thuganlitha watched dumfounded as Wayleeth hurried forward, hustling Tahli-Damen toward the stairway. Before the tugolith could respond, the pair was up the stairs and out of his reach. Then his rage spilled over, and he vented it by charging the wall. This was solid stone, chiselled from the knoll upon which the fortress rested. He could do it no harm. Yet his impact was so great that those watching from above half expected the wall to collapse before him.

"I'll horn you!" the incensed tugolith trumpeted. Then he took up a vigil at the bottom of the stairs. His brain was small, but some things he knew, among them that this was the only way into or out of the castle. He'd missed horning this insulting man on the way in. He would not miss another opportunity!

Any confrontation with the tugoliths quickly drew a crowd upon the landing above the stable, and this group murmured with astonishment. But what startled the onlookers most was not Tahli-Damen's demeanor nor the gall of the woman who led the blind man up the staircase without permission. Rather, it was the pack of fiery-eyed dogs that surged up the stairs behind them. Someone raced away to inform the sorcerer.

Flayh already knew. His ever vigilant fortress had seen the dogs approaching and reported it immediately. Flayh met the scurrying messenger in the hallway and brushed impatiently by him. "Where are they?" he snapped, and the would-be messenger shouted some reply at his back. The wizard never heard it. He was talking to the High Fortress.

—They have followed the blind religionist toward the apartments of the king, the fortress wheezed in pain.

"Why are they here?" Flayh snarled. "Why?"

The High Fortress had no answer and dared not make any reply. Flayh hurried up the wide spiral toward the lavish bedroom of Pahd mod Pahd-el, muttering anxious curses to the walls. He stopped at the top of the stairs. The dogs stood in the hallway outside Pahd's door, gazing at Flayh as if they'd been waiting for him. Instantly he was a dog himself, and the ensuing conversation was carried on in the yaps and growls of the canine tongue.

"Why are you here?" Flayh barked.

"We follow this one."

"But why?"

"Because he once carried a piece of the gate. He may again."

"That wasn't in the agreement!" Flayh howled. "You swore you would remain in Lamath and would never return to this place!"

"We swore," one of the pack snarled, "but you swore an oath as well, and you've not kept it."

"I've not had time!"

"You've not made time! You were to gather the pieces and remake the gate! What steps have you taken toward that?"

"I know where all of them are," Flayh said, guarding his thoughts very carefully. He was frightened, and he didn't like the feeling. His fears were well founded. The powers he'd enfleshed as dogs could kill him if they chose. It wouldn't do to let them know he'd lost the only pyramid he'd actually possessed.

"Where?" demanded one of the powers, thrusting his muzzle into Flayh's face.

"I know," Flayh repeated, maintaining his composure. "If I tell you where, you must swear you will leave!"

"Where!" barked a half dozen dogs at once.

"Swear!" Flayh snarled with authority.

Several dogs answered, "It's sworn."

"One of the objects you seek was in Dragonsgate yesterday morning, possessed by Queen Bronwynn of Chaomonous. Another is in Lamath, in the hands of that peoples' prophet. Now go as you've sworn!"

With a full-throated bay of the chase, the pack left the hallway as quickly as they'd come. Flayh waited for a moment, then took his human shape once again. "Are they out?" he asked the walls.

—They have left this fortress and are racing swiftly toward the Down Road, the castle said with relief. The agony of so many powers present within its walls had been unbearable. It enjoyed the respite, but realized it would be brief. Soon Flayh would be back in his tower, and the cancer of magical pain would grow again.

The sorcerer swept toward the double doors of the king's apartments and slammed them open. He pointed his hands at the two blue-robed figures and shouted, "What are you doing in my fortress?"

Terrified, Wayleeth cowered against the far wall. Tahli-Damen, however, simply turned his head in the direction of Flayh's voice. He'd recognized it immediately, for he'd heard it often at general meetings of the Merchant League. He'd found cause to tremble at it recently, for Flayh's ball of flame had been the last thing he'd seen. He did not tremble now. He smiled with the grace of a man of faith, and said, "We've come on an errand of mercy, Lord Flayh. And it appears we've arrived in time." He turned his head toward Sarie, directing Flayh's eyes there. The wizard looked, then cursed in frustration. For the first time in weeks, Sarie was sitting up in bed.

"So," Flayh said, controlling himself enough to smile. "You're feeling better, Sarie lan Pahd?"

Sarie stared at him woozily, trying to make out who he was. When she did, she threw her arms over her head and screamed.

King Pahd jumped to her side, putting his body between her and Flayh.

"Come no closer," Pahd growled.

Flayh frowned. "What did you say?"

"I said come no closer! Harm her again and I'll lead no army in your defense!"

"I thought we'd settled that," Flayh murmured quietly. He turned his head and called over his shoulder to a guard. "Fetch Admon Faye to me." Then he looked back at Pahd, whose blazing eyes bulged from their sockets in agitation. Flayh spoke softly, almost tenderly. "You *will* lead the combined armies of the Mar, Pahd, or I'll kill your wife outright. But you'll not lead them in my defense. I guess I overstated your importance to me, trying to make you feel you had some worth. But listen, Pahd—I have no need of your protection. I wish your presence at the head of my army only for the sake of convenience. If the legitimacy of your royal claim ceases to be an asset to me, if you become more trouble than you are worth, I'll simply replace you. Then you can spend all your time here, watching your dear wife suffer. And she will, Pahd, I assure you she will. I thought we'd understood each other," Flayh finished sadly. "Do we understand one another now?"

Pahd gazed at the wizard as long as he dared, but at last he had to look away. He sought support in the eyes of his mother. She only frowned and raised her chin in contempt. He turned to Wayleeth, but saw only terror in those eyes. There was no comfort in the face of Tahli-Damen either—just a sightless smile, as if the man gazed permanently upon heavenly fields. Someone came through the door and he sought encouragement there. He met instead the ugliest sneer in the world, and looked away quickly lest he retch on the bed, conscious of Admon Faye's chortle. Pahd knelt beside his wife and put his arms around her. This allowed him to hide his face in one of her pillows. There he would wait until the powershaper left.

"Slaver?" Flayh asked. "Are your war-beasts hungry? Feed them these Lamathian fanatics. Perhaps they'll welcome a taste of home." Then he whipped around and left the room. The appearance of the dogs had startled him and demanded immediate response from him. But he had important matters to tend to—a search to conduct and a new spell to perfect. He had no more time to waste upon such a trivial matter as Pahd mod Pahd-el.

Tibb had not seen Tahli-Damen enter the High Fortress, but he'd heard about it. Everyone inside the castle had heard about it within ten minutes of its occurrence. The rampaging tugolith in the stables made certain of that. When Tibb heard that the sorcerer had summoned Admon Faye to the chambers of the king, he hustled toward Pahd's tower himself. Tibb never wanted to be very far from his hideous master.

He got to the spiral steps in time to break the fall of one of the blue-clad intruders. The man came hurtling down the stairway just as Tibb rounded the corner, and the two hit the stone floor together with a noisy crash.

"Tibb!" cried the slaver in his most mockingly genteel tones. "You always arrive just in time! I fear that poor fellow tripped upon the staircase. Do help him up, won't you?"

Tibb growled and hobbled to his feet, then grabbed the fallen figure by his torn collar and roughly hoisted him up. He suddenly saw Tahli-Damen's eyes and he stared.

"Recognize him?" Admon Faye called, coming on down the stairs and pushing Wayleeth before him. When Tibb shook his head, the slaver chuckled. "No, I guess you wouldn't. You didn't join us until after our dealings with this merchant of Uda." Admon Faye smiled at Tahli-Damen's uncertain frown. "Flayh—pardon me, *Lord* Flayh—didn't recognize you in there. But I did. I have a good memory for faces." It was true. His own face was so memorable that everyone recognized him. In self-defense, he'd trained himself to memorize the faces of others. "You used to be the ruling elder of Uda in the Mar, didn't you?"

"Briefly," Tahli-Damen admitted.

"Until Flayh and Pelmen burned your eyeballs blue!" the slaver crowed. He made the words obscene. Tahli-Damen didn't reply. When his mirth subsided, the slaver went on, "You caused my employer a great deal of grief when the last Council of Merchant Elders met."

"You were there?" Tahli-Damen asked.

"Don't you recognize me?" Admon Faye asked in surprise.

"I cannot place your voice." The initiate shrugged, reminding Admon Faye of his blindness.

"Of course! You can't see me!" the slaver chortled. "You don't know who I am, do you?"

"I think I do," Tahli-Damen murmured.

"What? Speak up!"

"Could you be Admon Faye?"

The hideous brigand smiled. "I could. I surely could."

The bellowing of Thuganlitha, although several floors below, could now be heard clearly. The tugolith had overheard a comment made by someone on the landing above him about blue fools, and had taken the phrase as his own. It had become a rhythmical chant, punctuated by the stamping of his giant feet. "Feed me blue fools! Feed me blue fools!" he shouted, over and over again. It was becoming a great annoyance.

Admon Faye shoved Wayleeth down to land beside Tahli-Damen on the floor. "It seems you're being invited to dinner." The slaver smiled politely. "Actually, I believe it will be a rather swift passage for the both of you, which seems somewhat unlike our Lord Flayh. He appears to have a great many things on his mind; otherwise he'd want your killing to take more time. But since he was so explicit in his sentence and since we *do* need to quiet down that racket, I'll bid you good-bye. Tibb? Do you think you can manage to feed these two to our enormous pets?"

Tibb nodded and pulled Wayleeth to her feet. "That way," he grunted, thrusting the two initiates before him.

There were probably many reasons for what Tibb did next, some of which he was unaware of himself. He hated Admon Faye, of course. He was a Lamathian and had in years past spent time on his knees before a dragon statue—a different branch of the faith from that of these light-robed fanatics, true, but in Tibb's mind religion was all the same. He'd met and been impressed by the young woman who was now queen of Chaomonous, and she had thought highly of people who wore these light blue robes, although Tibb couldn't guess why. And, while some of the slavers had been amused by the antics of the tugoliths, Tibb couldn't shake the image of that blood-stained snow from his mind. For these and other reasons, Tibb propelled his two prisoners past the hallway that branched toward the stables, heading instead for the slave pit.

"Be brave, Wayleeth," Tahli-Damen advised with that constrained elation of would-be martyrs everywhere. "The Power has some purpose in this." Wayleeth didn't reply, nor really even hear her husband's platitude. She'd realized that they'd missed the turn, and was anxiously watching new developments.

A moment later the corridor came to a dead end at a heavy wooden door. There was a key in the lock, and Tibb turned it. When he opened the door, the stench sent the two initiates reeling backward. Tibb reached in, grabbed two hapless figures out, then slammed the door shut and relocked it. He turned to Tahli-Damen, seized the hem of the blind man's robe and jerked it up and off. Tahli-Damen didn't protest; instead he murmured encouragingly, "We came naked into this world, Wayleeth. We'll go naked out of it." Once again, Wayleeth did not reply. She'd nearly been stripped once already today, but she had the impression that this little man had quite a different purpose.

Tibb threw the robe to one of the starving slaves he'd pulled out of the pit. "Put that on," he growled, and the slave quickly obeyed.

Now it was clear to Wayleeth what was taking place, but she didn't explain to her husband. She feared that if he knew, Tahli-Damen would not permit this exchange to be made. Silently she shucked off her own garment and passed it to the other slave as Tibb nodded approvingly. Then the slaver unlocked the door again, pulled it open, and started to shove the two naked initiates into the anonymous hellhole. Wayleeth stopped him first with a question: "Why are you doing this?"

Tibb's snarling expression didn't change. "Dragon knows." He shrugged. Then he pushed Wayleeth backward into the fetid swamp of the slave pit and slammed and locked the door.

Wayleeth sat in the black silence, listening. A few moments later the horrendous thumping and bellowing from the stables finally ceased.

It was a horrible place to be, but they were alive. And Tahli-Damen, who by now had pieced it all together, said, "No, the dragon doesn't. But the Power does."

## CHAPTER FIFTEEN

# Dragon Dung

PELMEN AND his companions spent the night in Bronwynn's gilded pavilion. They got little sleep—the celebration outside continued until daybreak. Then too, they each wrestled through the hours of darkness with burdensome personal concerns—all, that is, save Erri's youthful companion. Strahn's merry snoring insured that no one else would sleep.

Despite the restless night and despite the bleary eyes that greeted her when she stepped outside to meet her warriors the next morning, Bronwynn gave the order to break camp and march toward the Mar. General Joss stood stiffly at her side, an expression of confident obedience to his queen fixed upon his face. Only the general himself could know if his stomach still churned with frustration. Joss would certainly tell no one.

As the servants and soldiers dismantled their tents, Erri and Strahn made preparations to slip quietly away. Just as they were leaving, however, Pelmen stopped them. He had Serphimera by the hand. "Prophet, could we hold you here another moment?" Pelmen asked. Then he explained what he wanted Erri to do.

"You mean you're not already?" Erri growled, a frown wrinkling his face. "I thought surely you'd already taken care of that."

"We've not had the opportunity," Pelmen murmured, and his arm tightened around Serphimera's shoulder as he added, "We might not get another chance."

Erri nodded and turned to his companion. "Strahn, go fetch the queen. I think she'll want to witness this." The young man raced off, returning quickly with Bronwynn in tow. She did, indeed, wish to take part.

So it was, in a ceremony as simple as it was ancient, that Pelmen and Serphimera were married. In the heart of Dragonsgate, at the center of the three lands, on the spot where the bloodthirsty beast that had brought them unwillingly together had died, they were wed. And when it was over, the prophet who had linked them shuffled off to the north, and the queen who'd been their witness marched westward with her army, leaving them alone in the pass. Pelmen and Serphimera did not feel slighted. There were important tasks to be accomplished—none, perhaps, more so than their own quest. They had taken advantage of an opportunity. Now they bent their attention once again to the pyramids.

They sat on a flat rock that had been cleared of snow, near the northern cliff and the dragon's cave. Pelmen had pulled the three crystals from their wrappings and set them before him. "Where are they?" he murmured aloud, and all three objects seemed to glow a little brighter at his words.

"Is that wise?" Serphimera asked. "Could Flayh not be listening?"

"Perhaps," Pelmen granted. "I brought them out in the hope that they might inspire us. Where can the other three be?"

Serphimera glanced around the pass. "Hidden here, somewhere?"

"In Dragonsgate?"

"Isn't this where the weapon was destroyed?"

Pelmen nodded. "But I hardly think something so large and sparkling could escape the dragon's attention throughout a millennium. He liked sparkling things anyway. That was how the merchant houses gained his favor. They brought him diamonds."

Serphimera nodded. While she'd worshipped this dragon throughout her whole life, she'd loved an idealized vision of the beast. She knew little about the real Vicia-Heinox. "What did he do with them?"

Pelmen chuckled. "He liked to toss them in the air. One head would toss a diamond up, and the other would catch it. The trouble was, the two heads kept swallowing diamonds, which is why the beast needed—" Pelmen stopped himself, his expression that of a man who's just heard a thunderclap.

Serphimera had heard it also. Without a word, they bagged up the three pyramids. Then Pelmen stepped back away from the cliff face, and pointed out a cave mouth some forty feet above their heads. "There," he said, and Serphimera nodded and hoisted up her skirts to tie them out of the way.

It was a difficult climb, but they had the eagerness of inspiration to drive them upward. Soon they were onto the shelf. The smell within the dragon's old lair was loathsome; as they crawled inside and stood up, Pelmen and Serphimera exchanged looks of mutual sympathy. "How can we bear it?" she gasped.

"We'll manage," Pelmen said and he pointed to several signs of human habitation. "Someone else did." A year before, this cave had been the dwelling place of Tibb and his unlucky companion Pinter. The remains of their fire was visible beside the mouth of the cave.

"Are you *sure* they did?" Serphimera questioned. "They're not here now, are they?" She said it with a slight smile that assured him she was teasing. She had no intention of turning back.

They both turned to face the wall of dragon dung which was the source of the horrible stench. "They must be in there somewhere," Pelmen muttered.

"Shall we start?" Serphimera asked and they each picked up a flat stone and began to dig. The outer layer had solidified and was hard to break through. The deeper they dug, however, the softer the substance became. With blessed adaptability their noses became inured to the smell. Before long they had shed every trace of fastidiousness and dug with their hands. The task was far from pleasant, yet they were together, and there was a certain joy in that. They were soon befouled from head to foot, but since both were in that state they were careful not to judge. And their purpose was clear. They worked with the certainty of inspiration and the faith that they must find what they sought.

They uncovered mounds of gemstones—huge rocks of crystal that, once cleaned, would sparkle like the stars. They also found weapons, chains, helmets, and breastplates—the undigested accessories of all those the dragon had consumed. But so far they had found nothing that even resembled the objects they needed. "It was centuries ago that he swallowed them—*if* he swallowed them," Pelmen said. "We have to expect they would be in the earliest layers."

Serphimera grunted agreement, preferring not to open her mouth to comment. Suddenly, however, the wall she was working at so diligently collapsed before her, and she couldn't help screaming "Pelmen! Come here and look at this!"

"What is it?" Pelmen shouted, nearly sliding down as he scrambled over piles of dung to get to Serphimera's side. "Have you found another one?"

"Just look!" the priestess said again, her face radiant with discovery.

The light was poor. Quickly Pelmen summoned a ball of orange flame and waved it through the hole created by Serphimera's digging.

They both gasped. Then they plunged forward together, squirming and shoving until both wiggled through the hole. They clasped hands, and turned around slowly, surveying the room. It, too, had been fouled by the dragon, but that could not hide its splendor. The floor was paved with delicately painted ceramic tiles. The walls were lined with thick, polished slabs of gorgeous marble, which reflected back the fireballs' illumination brilliantly. The ceiling rose far above their heads and was curved like the underside of a dome. The room was huge—two hundred feet from one wall to the other, Pelmen estimated—and was circular. From where he stood, Pelmen could make out three sizable corridors angling off from it in different directions, all running deeper into the mountain. But the room's dominating feature stood in its center. A circular dais rose on concentric marble rings to a height of thirty feet; on top of it sat a jewel-encrusted throne. The platform wasn't fully visible. Piles of dung and hoarded treasure hid a large part of it. But Pelmen could make out its form and knew immediately what it was. He stood in awestruck silence, gawking upward.

"Where are we?" Serphimera asked, her reverent whisper preserving the wonder of the moment.

"We're in the throne room, my love."

"Of what?"

"That's the throne of the ancient One Land."

Like excited children, they explored it. In the world outside, the sun went down, but they paid no heed to the time. They investigated every part of the huge throne room, Pelmen stopping every few minutes to read and interpret another inscription he found carved in the marble. He did so effortlessly. They were inscribed in those same strange rune-shapes he'd learned first from the ancient book. Once they completed the circuit, they left the throne room, intent on exploring the corridors. They soon realized this could be an endless task. The hallways went on and on, expanding outward into still more hallways, and those into others. Pelmen understood, now, why the capital city of the One Land had never been found. It was a city under the earth.

They tired, eventually. Without a word to one another, they returned to one of the first rooms they'd explored together. It was a bedroom; by the richness of the canopied trappings and the size of the canopied bed, they'd judged it to have been the sleeping chamber of the kings. Serphimera had found a marble tub in a small adjoining room. After experimenting with a pair of handles, she found that she could fill the tub with water. They stripped off their stinking garments and climbed in, washing the dung from their bodies. Then they made their way to the bed. Here at long last their love was consummated. It was, after all, their wedding night. They slept.

Tomorrow there would be more work. Somewhere near the bottom of that dung pile that obscured the throne, they expected to find the missing pyramids. But for the moment Pelmen and his bride dreamed in one another's arms, in a sunless realm untouched by trouble for a thousand years.

Erri hurried down the road into Lamath as fast as his legs would move him. Strahn, however, was not so eager. That quickly became obvious. When he got ten yards ahead, Erri turned and scowled at the lad. "What's the matter now?" he barked.

Strahn didn't look at the prophet, but rather past his head. For an answer, he pointed and grunted, "Them."

Erri turned around and looked, and the sight startled him enough to make him jump. A line of the black dogs stood across the base of the road, blocking them.

"I see," Erri muttered. "Well, we've been among them often enough. They ought to seem old friends by now. Come on." Once again the short prophet barrelled forward down the hill, and the younger brother hurried to catch up. As they approached the fearful line, Erri expected the dogs to part and make a path for them, as they had previously done. When it became clear that this time the hounds weren't moving, Erri slowed his pace. When they still didn't budge, he stopped. Then something happened that he had never expected. One of the black dogs spoke.

"Where?" it rasped, its teeth gleaming.

Erri's mouth fell open in surprise, but he quickly regained his composure. These beasts had revealed their intelligence often enough. He should hardly be astonished that they talked. "I'm going after the army of Lamath—"

"Where?" growled another dog.

"Why, I assume they're less than a day's march up the road—"

"No!" barked still another.

"Where?" growled the first dog menacingly.

"Show!" howled the hound that stood beside it.

Erri didn't understand. "I don't know what you're asking—"

"Show!" the dog howled again and leaped forward. Erri was knocked onto his back and was set upon immediately by a dozen dogs who snuffled down his collar and up the skirt of his robes.

"Where?" some dog demanded again, and another said, "No!" to his fellows. At last Erri began to understand.

"If you're looking for that magical object, I no longer carry it with me!" he shouted, and the dog atop his chest pressed its muzzle down into his face, driving Erri's head back into the snow. Fear seized the prophet then. It wasn't the proximity of those glistening fangs, nor the shock of the beast's cold nose on his skin. It was the bottomless fires that stood in place of the dog's eyes and which testified that this hound was not of the natural world.

"Where?" the slavering beast snarled.

"Halfway to the Mar, where it belongs!" Erri shouted, not really even sure what he was saying.

"Mount!" one beast barked joyously to the others. Then, with the hideous baying of a pack that has scented its quarry, the dogs were off at a run. But they didn't dash up the road to Dragonsgate as the prophet had expected. Instead, they took off across the frozen ground toward the northwest, loping easily along a direct line toward the Great North Fir. Moments later Strahn was beside him, lifting Erri to his feet.

"Thank you for your marvelous moral support!" Erri grumbled as he straightened his garments and brushed off the snow. If Strahn was offended, the lad didn't show it. Erri sighed and once again took off down the road.

"Where are we going?" Strahn asked, walking beside Erri now.

"We're trying to catch up with the army," the prophet grunted.

Strahn hesitated. "The army! Why?"

"Because they're our people and they need our help. Are you coming or not?"

"I'm coming." Strahn nodded, but he made it clear by his pace that he wasn't coming very fast. Erri ignored him, racing onward. Strahn was amazed how quickly the little man could move.

By afternoon, Erri caught up with the tail of the column. Without introducing himself, he made the acquaintance of Agarnalath, a Lamathian warrior who was as honest as he was gruff. He was bitter and didn't mind sharing his bitterness with this strange little man who'd suddenly joined himself to their shambling retreat. "You call this a retreat? It's flight! A rout. We've been routed! When I rode with Asher, we were never even defeated, and now *this*! A rout. A humiliation!"

"I knew Asher," Erri observed casually. "He was a good man."

"Good! He was great!" Agarnalath snarled. "A great man! And we lost him to this slimy lizard. A waste! An utter waste! Great men come along once in a generation, and to lose a man like that—Bah! Who's going to lead Lamath now?"

"That's a very good question." Erri nodded. "We've certainly had pitiful leadership since the dragon was killed."

"Prophets," the warrior said, shrugging elaborately. "What do they know about running a country?"

"Nothing." Erri grunted emphatically.

"Oh, they were well-meaning enough," Agarnalath said in deference to Erri's robe, "but they were innocents! The world is full of hard men, my friend, and do you think a handful of prophets can turn aside all those swords just by wearing light blue robes? Not a chance. I should know."

"And I should have known, too," Erri muttered.

"What?"

"What was their biggest mistake, do you think?" Erri asked.

"The biggest?" The man scratched his beard, glanced back toward the south again, then yawned before he answered. "I don't know. Well, yes I do. Not planning for a strong defense. You've gotta have a strong defense or the brigands of this world will slit your throat!"

Erri pondered that. "And yet, this army was collected in a period of days . . ."

"Of course! We were all sitting around the bars of Lamath, waiting for some action!"

"Then it seems, had the nation been threatened, the prophet could have collected you together as quickly as this young king did."

"Then why didn't he?" the warrior grunted. "Lamath *was* threatened, but no one called on us to help. A waste. Because that boy is even less a king than his crazy father was!"

Erri squinted his eyes thoughtfully. "So what we need is a truly great king—a man like Asher."

"That's it. That's what we need. Send this boy back to his fancy estate."

"And yet you followed him," Erri said. He let just a hint of accusation creep into his voice, and it made Agarnalath squirm with embarrassment.

"Yes," he sighed, "I did. But you have to realize, that dragon's reappearance carried a lot of weight. Sham or no sham, it was impressive."

"I saw it," Erri grunted, and the warrior looked at him questioningly. Fearing he might be recognized, Erri deflected the man's attention back toward the dragon. "But why did everyone believe in him so quickly? Everyone knew the beast was killed!"

"Well," the veteran sighed, "old beliefs die hard. And slowly, too. I should know! I was a fervent believer in Ultimate Devotion!"

"Serphimera's group?"

"What a lady." The man smiled, his eyes glazing over as if he saw a vision of her on the horizon. "Now, *she* was great."

"She is indeed."

"Is?" Agarnalath cried. "She's alive?"

"She's alive." Erri nodded. "In fact, we watched the battle together yesterday."

The warrior winced at the mention of the battle and shook his head. "Serphimera alive. I thought she'd been eaten by the old beast!"

"So you were ready to follow the dragon again, because of that?"

"I guess so. And you know, when I started hunting around for a place to worship the Lord Dragon, all the old shrines were gone! Your skyfaither friends had destroyed every last one of them!"

Erri frowned, then nodded. "That was a mistake."

The old warrior looked at him, puzzled. "A mistake? But you were right! It's ridiculous to worship a dead dragon!"

"So it appears to me. But nothing confirms a man in his faith so quickly as trying to force him to abandon it. Religious persecution stiffens resistance." Erri shot Agarnalath a twinkling smile and added, "I should know!"

"But it makes good sense to close the chapels!" the veteran grumbled. "Keep a lot of fools like myself from folly!"

Erri gazed up at the man until he caught the warrior's eyes. Then he grunted. "It *didn't*, did it?"

The prophet was a small man. Although wiry and quick, this burly warrior could have felled him with a blow. Another man might have died for such a pointed insult. But Agarnalath just looked at Erri, pondering the words. Then he shrugged. "You're right."

Erri glanced away, out at the numbing sameness of the white snow, and clasped his hands behind him. "No, this mixing of faith and government is bad business. You're absolutely right. What we need now is a great king. Someone like Asher."

"Asher," the warrior groaned. "Where will we find another Asher?"

"Who knows? Maybe there's one in the making right now." Erri thought of Rosha.

Throughout this conversation, young Strahn had walked thirty yards behind them. Just as the warrior would occasionally check to see if Chaomonous was coming, Erri would turn and wave at his young companion, urging him to catch up. Strahn had not refused; he'd simply failed to comply. Now Erri bid Agarnalath a good journey and waited for Strahn to catch up.

"Why have you been walking back there?" Erri asked peevishly.

The lad shrugged. Erri waited, and Strahn finally offered a meek explanation. "He's wearing dark blue."

"Yes?" Erri waited again.

"And carrying a sword!"

"That's true." They walked on a few more paces in silence.

"I'm afraid," Strahn finally confessed.

"What are you afraid of? The man's first and foremost a Lamathian! He's . . ." Erri suddenly caught sight of his young companion's face. Strahn had set his jaw and hunched his shoulders, prepared to absorb another lecture. That vision drove Erri's rebuke right out of his head. He saw, instead, a young man of whom he'd demanded much—but *to* whom he'd failed to give himself. It was a startling discovery. The problem was clear: Erri's favorites, his brightest initiates, were elsewhere. Naquin was on his own somewhere in Chaomonous. Tahli-Damen had marched unflinchingly into the jaws of Flayh. The others—those who had been closest to him during his brief period of rule—were scattered now across the country, each trying in his own quiet way to affect a deep, meaningful change in this society. Strahn was a more recent addition, a new boy. But now, as Erri looked at him, the prophet allowed himself to see potential he'd never noticed before. The Naquins and the Tahli-Damens were on their own now. But it was a world of young Strahns who would reshape the One Land and direct the attention of its citizens to the Power. And it was with the Strahns of the world that Erri needed to concern himself. Erri pondered a moment in silence. Then he said, "You know, I'm afraid too."

Strahn looked at him sharply, more worried now than ever. "Really?"

"Sometimes." Erri smiled at his companion. "But then it passes." He waved his hand at the line that stretched out before them. "These are our people and they're frightened too. Let's go see if we can encourage them some. Maybe then we'll all feel better."

Strahn stared at Erri, his expression still one of puzzlement. But this time when the prophet picked up speed to rejoin the tail of the retreating column, the young man went with him.

Erri smiled inwardly and told himself that one day Strahn could even be a great man.

Pelmen woke with a start, and sat up in bed. He was surrounded by total darkness. One moment later, a ball of flame bobbed above the bed, and he had to lower it a little to keep from singeing the canopy. He remembered now where he was, and who lay beside him.

Serphimera slept on her side, her long hair spilling across the pillow she clutched so closely. He sat for a time watching her, admiring the shape of her lips and the curve of her thighs. He briefly considered remaining here. Flayh knew nothing of this place. They could be safe here, turning their backs on the troubled world and living peacefully within this endless artifact. Then he smiled at his folly and woke her.

She was alert immediately. "Is it time?" she asked.

"I have no idea what time it is. It could be morning or midnight and we wouldn't know." He noticed Serphimera shielding her face from the glare of his light. He waved his hand and it moved over a bit, out of her eyes. "Yet we're both awake. And there's little enough time left to those who struggle outside. Let's get on with it."

They rose and dressed, leaving the glorious bedchamber with a shared lingering sense of sadness. Once in the hallway, Serphimera turned the wrong way. "Where are you going?" Pelmen asked.

"Isn't that the way out?"

"Maybe there is an exit in that direction, but we'd probably emerge someplace in the Great North Fir and be hopelessly lost. I don't think we have the time to go looking for it."

"You mean the throne room is that way?" Serphimera asked, pointing behind her, and Pelmen nodded. The priestess smiled brightly and shrugged. She'd never had much of a sense of direction.

A few moments later they stood once again in that circular chamber that had once bound the three lands into one. "Where do we start?" Serphimera asked.

"At the bottom of that pile," Pelmen answered, pointing.

"How do you start at the bottom?"

"You just wade in," Pelmen murmured, and he did just that. She sighed and followed after him. They dug an hour before they found the fourth pyramid. They found the fifth only moments later, and with shouts of jubilation they threw themselves into their digging with a new excitement. Oblivious to the substance they tunnelled through, they dug with the keen exhilaration of anticipated victory.

Three hours later, they admitted to each other their growing frustration. "I must rest," Serphimera wheezed, and she waded toward the steps of the dais and sat down. Pelmen squatted where he was, and heaved a disheartened sigh. It seemed Serphimera's eyes widened suddenly, then closed again. "We know it's here," she encouraged him.

He nodded. "That seems reasonable. But what if it's not? What if we can't find it?"

"Then you won't have to remake the weapon. And you won't be obliged to use it."

Pelmen turned his head and met her most penetrating stare. "You know the price of using it?" he asked.

"I've always known the price. Long before you told me of its making—perhaps before we even met—I knew that cost. I just didn't know the circumstances until now."

"And how do you know now?" he asked. "Another vision last night?"

She looked away, unable to meet his eyes any longer. Then she nodded—a brief, quick jerk of her head.

"And you know we'll find the sixth pyramid?"

"We already have," Serphimera murmured, and she pointed toward his foot. "You kicked it up just now when you squatted down."

Pelmen slowly looked downward and saw the pointed tip of the sixth crystal pyramid. He reached down and reverently picked it up. The set was complete. "There remains only the task of putting it together," he said, and Serphimera nodded.

"Where do we do that?" she asked briskly.

Pelmen shook his head, shocked that they actually possessed all the parts of the ancient magical object. "I know where Sheth was to have taken it, once he'd made his contribution."

"They're alive with magic," Serphimera said quietly, "so obviously his contribution was made. Who else was to participate in the project?"

"The men of faith, who resided on the mountain in the Great North Fir. That's the mountain of your visions."

Serphimera nodded again, her expression a mingling of tragedy and resolve. "We'll go up that mountain, Pelmen. We'll not come down it."

He frowned. "Are you sure? I mean, before you said you just couldn't see beyond—"

"I'm sure," Serphimera interrupted. There was no point in discussing it further. They sat there for several minutes, each lost in private thoughts. Finally, Serphimera got to her feet. "I guess we'd better get started."

"It's a long way to the mountain," Pelmen said after a moment. "Maybe we ought to rest again before we go?"

She caught his meaning instantly and responded with a shy smile. They returned first to the marble bath, then to the giant bed. It was a long time, however, before they slept.

Pelmen and Serphimera stepped out of the lair into brilliant afternoon sunlight. The early thaw had come, melting the last of the muddy snow from the pass below them and leaving a swamp of thick brown muck in its place. They quickly climbed down, found their mounts where they'd left them, and loaded their precious treasures into the saddlebags. Only then did they notice they had company.

A huge pack of dogs encircled them, pinning them to the canyon wall. Serphimera gasped. "Dogs!"

Pelmen gazed around at the circle. "They're not dogs at all."

"But how do you—"

"Look at their eyes," he told her, and Serphimera did. She shivered, and Pelmen put a protective arm around her shoulders. "What are they?" she whispered.

"Powers. They've been given that form by Flayh."

"They're not illusions?"

"No, these are not like the false dragon. They're real—real enough that those teeth could tear us open and those jaws snap our bones." He murmured this in such a cold, flat manner that Serphimera looked away from the dogs and at him. His eyes remained fixed on their adversaries. It was evident his mind was hard at work.

"You can escape, at least," she whispered, and that drew his attention back to her.

"And leave you?" His mind flashed immediately to Dorlyth.

"There's too much at stake for us to—"

"What's wrong with you?" he snapped. "You saw us *both* going up that mountain, didn't you?"

"Yes," she answered softly.

"Then we know we'll not die here. Come on." He lightly touched the flanks of his horse with his heels, and it took a few tentative steps forward. Serphimera's horse quickly followed, wanting to stay close to its companion. They moved slowly toward the line of dogs, horses and riders alike closely watching these unnatural beasts for some movement signaling attack.

No attack came. As had happened with Erri and his followers, the line turned westward and trotted before them, while those behind closed ranks around them and matched their pace. "It's as if they're escorting us," Serphimera murmured.

"Into the Mar, yes. The question is, will they permit us to go our own way once we're there?"

"What was that you just said about the mountain?" Serphimera asked, her eyes straight ahead but a sly smile playing on her lips.

Pelmen permitted himself a rueful chuckle. After a moment, he said, "There are *some* advantages to knowing *some* of the future."

The seriousness of their circumstance settled slowly in on both of them. "Do we dare talk?" Serphimera whispered. "Is there some way Flayh could be hearing all our conversations through these?"

Pelmen studied each of their entourage in turn, twisting in his saddle as he did so. he didn't know the answer to her question. In fact there was really no way of knowing if Flayh himself might not be one of their traveling companions. Pelmen shrugged at her. "I guess we could talk of other things. If he's listening, it would at least waste his time while wasting none of our own. Why don't you tell me everything that happened from the moment you left me at the edge of the Great South Fir?"

"I already did!"

"Then tell me again," Pelmen urged her, his eyes upon one of the dogs. Serphimera proceeded to do that, Pelmen interrupting her frequently with questions. They came down out of the pass, making good time. Without saying so, Pelmen began angling northward. The dogs did not interfere, although he'd expected them to. In fact, it almost seemed that those ahead of them had anticipated his change of direction. The pack stayed right with them, moving soundlessly through the melting snow. And when Pelmen dared to spur his horse into a gallop, Serphimera trailing him closely, the pack silently matched the pace. There was no outrunning them and no eluding them, but neither did the hounds make any hostile advances nor attempt to turn Pelmen and Serphimera from their course. Within a few hours, they'd reached the edge of the Great North Fir and turned to ride parallel to it toward the northeast. Pelmen reflected that they surely made an unusual sight—a mounted man and woman, surrounded by a sprinting pack of bizarre hounds. It didn't matter. Their horses were rested and willing to run, and every purposeful stride took them nearer to their destiny on the mountain of the Power.

Serphimera noticed it first. "It's getting bigger."

"What?" Pelmen asked her.

"Our escort. It's getting bigger. Haven't you noticed?"

"No, I haven't." Pelmen frowned.

"Watch the forest," his bride said, pointing, and soon he began to see them—new dogs, just as black as those who'd led them from the pass, slipping out to join the others. It continued throughout the day and into the night. The pack that had numbered in the dozens threatened to swell into the thousands and moved like a black flood across the white landscape. They raced just inside the Great North Fir under a canopy of widely spaced evergreens, across ground still covered with pristine snow. In their wake they left a muddy swathe of dog prints a quarter of a mile across.

The riders didn't slacken their pace, and the dogs did not complain. When their horses began to give out, however, Pelmen and Serphimera stopped and camped. It was only then that their normally silent companions began to whine, growl, and finally to bark impatiently.

"It's as if they can't wait," Serphimera observed, and Pelmen nodded.

"Yes—but what is it they can't wait *for*?" Night had fallen and firelike eyes ringed their campfire like row upon row of orderly fireflies. Pelmen didn't cloak the camp. He saw no sense in it.

The next morning they rode on, upon mounts barely rested from the days of exhausting travel and still skittish of the unnatural beasts surrounding them.

"Have you noticed we no longer need to guide our horses?" Pelmen asked his wife.

She nodded. "I wonder what would happen if we tried to turn south?" Several nearby dogs turned their heads and looked up at her. "Not that we will," she explained to them, and they all looked back at the trail. She shot Pelmen a wide-eyed, silent exclamation, and they both laughed. It was hearty laughter. They had covenanted to enjoy their last few days.

Midway through the third day of their journey, Pelmen's horse drew up lame. They could travel no further. The two riders dismounted, and talked over what to do next.

If the dogs seemed restless at night, they seemed frantic now. One beast tried to shove his muzzle between Serphimera's legs, and she shouted in surprise and stomped on his head. The dogs persisted, surrounding them so tightly that the two humans had no place to step. Pelmen finally understood what they were yapping. "You want us to try to ride *you*?" A chorus of excited howls greeted his question, and two dogs turned their noses toward the mountain and waited patiently for the people to sit astride them. "We'll break your backs!" The shaper protested.

"Sit!" growled one hound menacingly, and Pelmen shrugged at Serphimera. They relieved their horses of the provisions they'd been carrying and distributed these on the backs of several willing dogs. Then Pelmen and Serphimera took three pyramids each, and mounted the waiting hounds.

The rest of the ride toward the mountain of the Power was hardly comfortable, and on more than one occasion the two humans had to fling themselves boldly off their mounts to get the pack to stop. But in due time, they arrived at the foot of that mountain that seemed so special to the Power. They were greeted there by a throng of dogs three times the size of the horde that accompanied them.

Serphimera stared at the sight, aghast. "How did Flayh have time to make them all!" she marveled.

Pelmen regarded the dogs stoically, and muttered, "I'm more concerned with why." He hopped off his steed, collected their belongings, and started up the mountain. Serphimera followed behind him. After a moment, she stopped and looked back. "They aren't following us." In fact, from this vantage point she could see that the army of dogs had started to ring the mountain, each facing outward, teeth bared as if defending it from attack. "It's odd," she murmured.

Pelmen didn't hear her. He didn't hear anything. He climbed the peak with a feverish haste, drawing upon reserves of energy he'd been unaware were there. He climbed as a man possessed.

Serphimera turned back to see he was already far above her. "Wait!" she shouted in annoyance. But he didn't wait. Then she realized that the process had already begun, and already it was taking Pelmen from her.

## CHAPTER SIXTEEN

# Alliances

ROSHA WOKE TO a cold, silent house. Puzzled, he rose and dressed, then went down to breakfast in the window-lined hall. He ate alone, served by a steward who seemed unusually subdued. They exchanged no words until the end of the meal. Rosha glanced up, caught the man's eye, and asked quietly, "Where's your master?"

The servant said nothing. He simply pointed out the window at a line of tracks in the snow. They led up the nearer of the island's twin peaks.

Wrapping himself in rare bear furs and donning a cap of the same precious pelt, Rosha started out after the lord of the island. The snow crunched under his boots and the hairs in his nostrils froze, but he kept up his quick pace and soon topped the hill. He saw Syth then, standing stiffly with his back to the wind, looking toward the gray skies of the north. The man must have heard him, but didn't turn around. "Syth?" Rosha called softly. In that still place his words seemed like a shout.

Syth didn't appear to be startled. He slowly turned to Rosha, and the young warrior saw a look of loss and despair in his host's face that wrenched his own stomach. "What is it?" he asked fearfully, awe creeping into his voice. "It's . . . not the dread returned, is it?"

Syth looked at the snow and breathed a long sigh. "Not any caused by magic. Or perhaps it is. I don't know. It's hard, these days, to put causes to things. Who can know what powers have been loosed upon us—or what powers we've loosed upon ourselves. Here. Read this." Syth thrust a note toward Rosha, and waited for the younger man to come and take it. "The flyer arrived this morning," he mumbled as Rosha took the letter from his hand.

TO LORD SERILIATH AND THE FELL LADY OF FALL—GREETINGS AND ADIEU. THE DOG UPON THE MOUNTAIN HAS SENT HIS BEASTS TO EAT ME—AND THEY WILL. MOMENTS AGO I WATCHED A HERD OF ENORMOUS HORNED MONSTERS UTTERLY DESTROY THE HOST OF BELRA, LORD GARNABEL, UPON THE PLAIN TO THE SOUTH. NOT ONE WARRIOR WHO STOOD TO FIGHT SURVIVED. THESE BEASTS CONSUMED THE CORPSES. THEY ARE GUIDED BY ADMON FAYE, AND THEY NOW SURROUND MY KEEP. MY WALLS ARE BREACHED. I GO TO DEFEND MY CHILDREN—AND TO FAIL. SO PASSES THE HOUSE OF KAM.

Rosha's eyes misted over as he read the last lines. He turned his angry, puzzled gaze up to Syth, whose face was hard. "I . . . I don't . . ."

"Magic beasts, do you think?" Syth asked sharply, though with no expectation that Rosha might know. "Mar-Yilot has been in her tower all morning—or rather her body has. She's abroad, seeking the answer to that question and the counterspell to these monsters. If such exists," Syth finished bitterly.

Rosha reread the message, still in shock from the incomprehensible savagery it described. "I . . . there were some huge horned beasts in Lamath, but—"

"What? Where?" Syth demanded.

"In Lamath. But I'd understood they were normally docile—"

"The dog rules Lamath now," Syth spat. "Any beast with half a brain can be pushed to hostility if the force applied is wicked enough. And Flayh is certainly that. Come on!" he barked, and he started for the palace.

"Where are we going?" Rosha shouted.

Syth wheeled swiftly to face him. "To war, lad. To war!"

The Lord of Seriliath spent the remainder of the morning sending messages to those few barons still living who stood with him. They were to rally to his side at dead Tuckad's keep—he would lead them to battle from there. He wrote swiftly, but took care to include every detail of his own recent experience and of Kam's end. The grim news would circulate quickly enough. It was best that his people hear it from him.

Like ripples rolling outward from the palace, the news spread to other parts of the island. Business on Sythia came to a halt. Cobblers, farmers, blacksmiths, and jewelers laid down the tools of their trades and took up those more ancient tools of combat. This was no longer a war for professionals. The life of their island had been threatened. They would march even against monsters to defend it.

Rosha sat in his apartment, struggling to control his thoughts. He was not afraid of his own death, and he'd caused the deaths of too many others to shrink from the coming battle. Two things, however, plagued his thoughts. The first was that he wished things were resolved between himself and Bronwynn. The second was that he didn't want to die wastefully. He heard the clamor all around him—men preparing to go to war out of loyalty to their lord. He liked Syth. He honored and respected Syth. But his loyalties were to others. Could this be his last summons to arms? To ride to a fruitless demise in the company of strangers, at the side of one of his father's old rivals?

There was a knock on his door. "Come in." It clacked open. He was surprised to see Syth himself step into the room. "You? My Lord, you have much to prepare—"

"And this is a part of those preparations," Syth answered quietly. He bore a shield and sword. The shield was angled away so that Rosha couldn't see the device on its face. The sword Syth laid upon Rosha's bed. "I understand your blade was 'borrowed' from a slaver. I can't judge its quality, but I can vouch for the temper of *this* weapon. It was forged for me—one of a pair. I can only carry one greatsword at a time. Will you bear its twin?"

Rosha grasped the sword and tested its balance. It was

beautifully made. Its blade gleamed, smiling with a bright ferocity. Its hilt was a work of art. Threads of gold, silver, and scarlet intertwined to form its grip, and its pommel was a brilliant diamond the size of a goose egg. Rosha gazed at it in wonder.

"A bit ostentatious, I realize." Syth smiled apologetically. "But I can assure you all that finery won't interfere with its effectiveness."

"It's beautiful," Rosha whispered, and Syth nodded in mute agreement. "What do these say?" the young warrior asked, running his fingers across a series of runes engraved on the blade and inlaid with gold.

"You'll have to ask the woman who gave them to me," Syth said; as Rosha met his gaze, he went on meaningfully, "They were a present from my wife."

"Powers?" Rosha asked soberly.

Syth shook his head. "I've never wanted to know." Then he looked down at the shield he still held. "My friend, you owe me nothing. While I have arms I'd be honored for you to wear, I see you as an ally, not a vassal. It would be inappropriate for you to wear my livery into the coming battle—if indeed that's where you choose to go. This shield . . . is false. It was carried by the ugliest man in the three lands as he impersonated one of the finest. It was taken from the hut where he discarded it—where my spellbound body lay in dread. False as it is, however, its colors are true. They're your father's, Rosha. Yours, now." Syth turned the shield around.

It was larger than his father's own battle shield, and much finer looking. The paint was new. Dorlyth had never worried much about that. But the colors were right—a field of tan, or "wheat-colored," as his father had always said, crossed by a single bar of forest green. Not flashy, but simple, and it was striking enough to be quickly recognizable on a battlefield, which was its primary purpose. Rosha took the shield proudly, and gazed down at it.

Syth paced the room and spoke. "We were warriors, your father and I. Ranged across the field or around the banquet table, we understood one another. You're just like me, so you'll understand, too. Ours are not the concerns of the shapers. They'll mold the events we'll only play a part in. They'll shape history, and thereby become legends. But those are things they'll do in solitary places. They'll do them *to* men, or *for* men, but they'll do them alone. Weak as we are, powerless as we are, it is our lot to lead the men they struggle in solitude to damn or to save. I find romance no longer in this task of war. What I once thought glorious I now find was only grim. But we do what we do because our puny weight might somehow tip the scales and because the people we lead must be *involved*, somehow, in their own redemption if it's to mean anything to them. I don't say war is the best way of involving them. I do say it's all I know. And now—today—it's necessary." Syth stopped walking and looked at his young guest. "Will you ride with me to Tuckad Castle?"

Rosha thought seriously before answering. He nodded finally. "To Tuckad Castle, yes. Beyond that, I don't know. You may have judged me wrongly, Syth. It's my wife who leads men, not I. As for my father—he was a leader, yes. But first he was a hero. He used to say that was a disease and that he feared I'd caught it from him. I did catch it. I believe, somehow, that a single individual can make a difference, and I want to be where I must be to make a difference in this conflict. Where that is, I don't know. Yes, I'll carry the twin of your sword, and I hope to do honor to it. And I thank you for this shield. But where I carry them, beyond Tuckad Castle, I really cannot say."

"That's fair." Syth started to leave the room. Then he stopped at the door. "But I haven't judged you wrongly, Rosha. If you think somehow we disagree, then *you* have misjudged *me*."

All available barges were pressed into service, but it still took several hours to get the army across the water to the North Coast. The minute the last citizen soldier stepped off into the snow, they left, riding as swiftly as possible to Seriliath under the coverage of Mar-Yilot's cloak. They spent the night there, but were up before dawn and gone, leaving the city empty of men and of horses. Bainer joined them that day on the road with his few warriors and began a tedious monologue that lasted a half hour before Syth interrupted.

"Bainer? Have you noticed anyone following us?" Syth asked, and he craned his head to look back along the column.

Bainer frowned. "I've not, no. But if you wish, I'll take my fellows and ride back there—"

"Wonderful idea!" Syth smiled. "Why don't you just establish a rear guard to insure that we're not surprised like the last time."

Bainer nodded importantly and reined his horse around to ride back down the column. Rosha frowned slightly and looked across at Syth. "I thought Mar-Yilot was covering us?"

"She is," Syth grunted.

"Then what's the need in that?"

Syth chuckled. "My ears need the rest. Don't yours? Besides, I'm trying to plan."

"Plan what?" Rosha asked.

Syth looked at him with a sly smile. "A task fit for a hero."

Rosha raised his eyebrows in surprise, then turned his eyes forward. They didn't speak again for the rest of the ride.

They reached Tuckad's keep by nightfall, and found that Cerdeb had already arrived. The man's face looked haunted. Few riders had accompanied him from his home far to the south in Downlands region, and the trip had been harrowing. "Dogs," he murmured. "Wicked beasts. They can talk! And slavers, of course. And now you speak of monsters . . ."

Much more in evidence were the burnt orange tunics of the merchant house of Hann. Syth had good relations with these traders and had harbored hopes that they might lure other trading houses to his cause. He quickly found the Hanni leaders and pressed them on the matter. "What about Blez or Uda? They hate Flayh's Ognadzu colors as much as you do, don't they?"

"We all despise Flayh," Laph mod Parem answered apologetically. "But no one else seems ready to fight him. Blez is a small house. The men of Wina are terrified. Uda is in a state of chaos. They lost their local leader last spring, a fellow named Tahli-Damen. The man went blind and then later lost his mind, and his family attributes all of this to Flayh. Now we have word that their ruling elder, Jagd, was assassinated in Chaomonous. Flayh is at the heart of all these doings." Laph and his brother merchants exchanged anxious looks. The trader went on, "You must remember, Syth. All of us watched Flayh display his power at the last meeting of the Council of Elders. We realize what we're facing. And now that he has tugoliths—"

"You know for certain they're tugoliths?" Rosha interrupted, and the merchant nodded grimly.

"They were stolen from Lamath when Flayh overthrew the religious governor there. They're malleable creatures that can easily be shaped to the personality of their handler. Rumor has it that their handler now is Admon Faye."

Syth nodded wearily and turned away. One could always trust the information of merchants. It was their business to know. He controlled his despair and looked back at Laph. "What can you tell me about new developments here?"

Laph sniffed and shuffled his feet. "Pahd mod Pahd-el has mustered the Mar. Or rather, his mother has in Pahd's name."

Syth raised his eyebrows. "I didn't receive that notice."

"Yes, well, you wouldn't, would you?" Laph said.

"I suppose not. Who stands with him?"

Laph snorted. "Everyone. Accept you and yours, us, and Ferlyth. Some are more active in their support than others, but only Carlog and your northern cities have resisted him."

"What about Garnabel?" Syth asked.

"If you know about the tugoliths, you surely know what happened to Belra, their citylord."

"Yes. Kam described it to me."

"Garnabel has totally surrendered. They've elected Pahd's cousin Janos as their new citylord and marched three thousand men to the capital."

Syth absorbed this news with a strained smile. "It's a wonder that *you* still stand with me, knowing all of this."

"We've come for only one reason. We've opposed Flayh too long for him to welcome us. He's a vindictive little man, and if he captures us, he'll kill us all—or worse. Our one hope is you and the Golden Throng."

"Bronwynn!" Rosha grunted. "Where *is* the Golden Throng?"

"Encamped on the Westmouth Plain. With the aid of Pelmen Dragonsbane, they routed the army of Lamath and passed through Dragonsgate."

"Ah-ha!" Syth cried, cheered at last. He grabbed Rosha's hand and gripped it hard. "Here is finally some good news!"

Laph mod Parem shrugged. "Perhaps. But if Lamath turns and closes the pass, their retreat will be blocked. And while I'm told it's a grand-looking army, they're untried in battle."

"You said they routed—"

"With Pelmen's aid," Laph said meaningfully. Then he asked with a raised eyebrow, "Can *we* count on Pelmen's aid?"

"That I don't know," Syth countered. "But we can count on Mar-Yilot."

"All Ngandib-Mar trembles before the Autumn Lady," Laph said politely, "but Flayh has proved himself darker and harder than even she. Joooms is with him, and so is the twin-killer."

"Yes, we know about Terril."

"Then if you will," Laph pleaded, "ask your lady if she can contact Pelmen and request his succor. Without it, we're lost. We *may* be lost *with* it."

Syth sighed, and patted mod Parem on the shoulder. "I'll ask her right now. Come on, Rosha." He started for the stairs that led to the chambers mod Tuckad had allotted them.

"You mean she's here?" Laph asked.

Syth smiled. "A part of her." They went up the stairs to find her.

Mar-Yilot glowed at the far end of their long, dark room. No tapers burned, nor were any needed, for the orange corona that ringed her transparent image provided all the illumination necessary. Her face was drawn with frustration and weariness, but that was her most common expression, so Syth felt no alarm. He walked confidently across the wooden floor to her, Rosha still trailing behind. "You've come." Syth smiled.

"I said I would," Mar-Yilot responded. "You are all safe?"

"We are."

"Did Cerdeb arrive safely?"

"Yes." Syth smiled wistfully. "But I can't say he brought much encouragement with him. Nor many warriors, either. He didn't have the luxury of coverage as he traveled. It looks to me like he's already making peace with defeat."

"He's a Downlander." Mar-Yilot shrugged as if that explained everything. Maris hailing from the Downlands did indeed have a reputation for faltering under pressure. "What of the House of Hann?"

"They're here with a full complement. But they, too, are worried. They've requested that you seek out Pelmen and plead for his succor."

Mar-Yilot snorted and propped a hand on a hip. "Did you tell them young Rosha here might have more influence with him than I?"

"I told them only that I would ask you. I said nothing of our contact with him, nor of his quest to reassemble this ancient weapon. Their information worried me more than Cerdeb's long face. Apparently Flayh has bent all the shapers save yourself and Pelmen to his will."

Mar-Yilot raised her eyebrows. "Joooms finally caved in?"

"Which we knew was inevitable." Syth nodded. "Now you're faced with a perilous army of opponents—"

"Pelmen battled many of us at once and won."

"That's true, my dear, and you're at least as talented as he. But the merchants credit Flayh's vindictive nature and unpredictability over your experience. Perhaps we do need to call Pelmen back after all. When he left Sythia he had very little hope of succeeding in finding the pieces—"

"He wouldn't have undertaken the journey if he had thought there was some other way." This was Rosha speaking. He lay back on a bed, peering up at the darkness, his hands clasped behind his neck.

"Yes, but if we move into shaper battle—"

"Flayh will defeat us," Rosha interrupted.

Mar-Yilot gazed at him caustically. "You sound very certain of that."

"I am," Rosha growled. Then he sat up, and his eyes glowed with light reflected from her aura. He looked into Syth's face and said, "You know it too."

"Do you have any suggestions?" Mar-Yilot snarled, but Syth held up a hand to silence her. Then he scratched his jaw and sighed.

"Rosha's right."

"Syth!" Mark-Yilot complained, frowning.

"He's right. The dog has the knowledge to counter any shaper attack on him. I'm sure that's what he's preparing himself to face. Perhaps if we sent someone he didn't fear against him—someone he thought he'd ensnared in dread—"

"You're thinking of going against him yourself?" Rosha asked.

"I forbid it!" the sorceress cried, and her halo of light flared up like a flame.

Syth smiled. "I couldn't go. I have an army to lead, small as it is, and besides—I'm not a hero." He looked around at Rosha. "You could go."

Rosha stared back silently.

This exchange of looks made Mar-Yilot impatient. "How

could he go? He's already been inside the fortress once and needed the help of two wizards to get out!"

"But he did get out," Syth murmured, eyes still on Rosha. "And he succeeded in bringing away what he went in after."

"You're suggesting we ask Pelmen to lay aside his task to help this boy get into the fortress again?"

"Not Pelmen."

"He'll need *some* powershaper to cover him." Mar-Yilot snarled. "And if you're thinking of his queen, remember: She's no shaper yet!"

"I was thinking of you, Mar-Yilot."

His wife stared at him. "Me! Where will *you* be during all this?"

"Outside on the plain with the Golden Throng, battling Pahd and our Mari brothers."

"No," Mar-Yilot said bluntly. "I'll not leave you uncovered."

"You can cover me all you choose, my Lady, but Flayh will penetrate your coverage and kill me if he pleases."

"Let him try! I'll battle him above the—"

"No," Syth barked, and his frown stopped her. "The key is the shaper. Eliminate Flayh and you eliminate the power that binds the other shapers. You also eliminate the need to murder countless Maris in Flayh's name."

"And you propose to send a boy to do a task that—"

"Not a boy, woman!" Syth roared. "A hero! One who's faced a bear, a dragon, Admon Faye, and most importantly of all, Flayh himself, and survived each encounter! Armed with a magic sword of your own design, protected and supported by your own vast experience, he could slip inside a castle he knows well and go straight to the source of our dilemma!"

"And what about the living fortress!" the Autumn Lady shouted.

"Create enough magic inside its belly and you'll incapacitate it! You told me so yourself!"

"And what of the other shapers during this time?" she snarled. "Joooms and Terril—where will they be?"

Syth smiled triumphantly and murmured, "Pelmen battled many at once, and you're as talented as he!" Then he frowned. "There'll be a battle going on below! That will attract Flayh's attention and that of his allied shapers as well."

"When he has battle beasts to chew you up and swallow you?" Mar-Yilot sneered. "Why should he trouble himself? He'll not even notice you!"

It was a strong argument, but Syth refused to heed it. "My Lady, listen! It's our only hope!"

"Then we're hopeless indeed, and perhaps should yield now!"

"Do you believe that?" Syth demanded accusingly, knowing full well what her answer would have to be.

Mar-Yilot pouted a moment before giving it. "No."

"Very well. Then we'll plan for—"

"But I don't believe this will succeed."

"Then let me convince you—"

"You'll *not* convince me, Syth! I'll do it, but I don't think it can possibly work!"

Syth threw up his hands in exasperation. "Of course you don't! Because there's one thing you always fail to take into consideration!"

"And that is?" she asked, cocking her head to one side.

"We are *right*. And Flayh is irrevocably in the wrong!"

She smiled, finally, but with cynicism, not amusement. "You think events will honor your moral vision?" she asked.

"I think we must live as if they will."

The sorceress shrugged. "And die with the same conviction."

"If need be, yes."

Mar-Yilot nodded, and looked at Rosha. "He fits very well with your Pelmen, doesn't he?"

Rosha had watched the argument unfold with a kind of awe. To be in such company, to hear his merits discussed so critically, and to measure the responsibility offered to him against his own self-esteem had challenged him to produce his best. He wanted to be wise, to be viewed as wise, and to justify Syth's confidence in him while winning Mar-Yilot's respect. When she aimed this comment at him, he responded immediately: "Of course. That's why they both impress you so deeply."

Mar-Yilot was stunned. She thought about it, then acknowledged the possibility with a nod. Her eyes suddenly darted at Rosha's face, gripping his attention. "And why I ought to be impressed by you, too?"

That startled Rosha. He could think of no quick retort. "I . . . don't know . . ."

"Well, it doesn't matter," Mar-Yilot said quietly. Melancholy crept into her voice as she continued, "My husband has made a decision, and I'll abide by it—even though I fear it will cost him his life. But I guess that's the way it is with moralists; they demand that the world be just, and then kill themselves proving it can be made a little more so." Without a good-bye, without any warning that she was leaving, Mar-Yilot disappeared.

The two warriors were left sitting in total darkness. It surprised Rosha to hear Syth chuckling. "She does love a good exit line," the lord of Seriliath murmured, and Rosha could almost hear the man's smile. He had no smile of his own. He reflected on the question Mar-Yilot had asked him. He'd never been much concerned with questions of morality, but her comment had truly stunned him. How could he be a hero and not have moral convictions?

"In any case, it's settled. Rest some—we've had a hard two days. But as soon as you're ready, you need to be on your way."

"To the High Fortress," Rosha murmured. Despite his efforts to keep them submerged, fears began to nibble on his confidence. "And when I'm there?"

"Just wait. She'll find you. Think, Rosha," Syth added, his voice rich with encouragement. "This is your opportunity to be who you must be."

Rosha stared into the darkness, swallowed, and nodded grimly.

It was inevitable that Erri should be recognized. He had, after all, been the head of the Lamathian government, and he hadn't hidden himself from his people as had the former king. As he shuffled along with the defeated army, listening, arguing, laughing, and encouraging, the whispers began around him. Soon the news traveled up to the head of the line, that while the upstart king had fled in fear, the prophet had rejoined his people in their hour of greatest need. Before long, a mounted contingent from the *ad hoc* leadership had raced back to greet him formally. Despite his protests, the prophet and the terrified Strahn were put on horseback and led to the head of the column.

As they passed, the warriors cheered joyfully, and Erri returned their waves with an ironic smile. It appeared leadership had little to do with one's ability and more with how many people recognized one's face.

The prophet hadn't planned on this. Politics was a nuisance, a headache he'd been happy to be rid of for a time. But by the time they arrived back in the capital, he'd decided that, if somebody had to lead Lamath for the next few critical weeks, it might as well be he—at least until other, more lasting arrangements could be made. Agarnalath had been right—Lamath needed someone like Asher, and that certainly wasn't Erri. He did, however, have someone in mind.

By the time they marched into the city square, there was already a sizable gathering of civic leaders waiting to greet him. Erri grimaced at their stiff, formal poses. Obviously they'd planned some sort of ceremony, and the small prophet hated the thought. There were so many things he needed to attend to. Why waste time standing around listening to pompous talk? Once again, the petty business of parochial politics interfered with his major concerns. He sighed inwardly and forced a smile of greeting for the tall dignitary who approached him.

"Lord Erri," the man began, and the prophet winced in pain. "We offer you a kingdom."

Erri nodded affably. "Fine," he said. He could have produced a far more flowery speech, but his attention remained elsewhere. He hoped to get this nonsense over quickly so that he could find some private place and tune his spirit to the movements of the Power.

"When shall we plan your coronation?" the man continued.

"My what?" the prophet grunted in shock, as he turned his head back to look up into the eyes of the official who towered over him. "I'm no king!"

"My dear prophet." The dignitary smiled condescendingly. "As I said, we offer you a *kingdom*. Our land has always been a kingdom. We're accustomed to that. And as we've all had the chance to sample your . . . *prophetic* . . . form of government—and, incidentally, to see where it leads us—we urge you to accept the throne we offer instead of returning us to that unstable circumstance. You shall be King Erri the first—or King Prophet, or whatever you might prefer—and at your death, the crown shall descend to your heirs."

Erri nodded thoughtfully and glanced around at the rest of the assembled leadership of Lamath. Their aims were rather transparent. They wanted someone to take on the difficult chore of binding the nation back together again—preferably someone they could disassociate themselves from when his policies became unpopular. Erri would serve nicely. And he had no heirs, which meant in all probability that the crown would eventually come to one of their heirs instead. By that time, the throne might be worth something again.

The prophet smiled, and said, "No."

A moment of shocked silence followed by his refusal; then the group buzzed with animated whisperings. Erri raised his voice to speak above them. "I'm not the king type! But you're right. Lamath does need a king." The gathered host hushed to listen to him. "We need a good ruler, a strong ruler. Someone a lot like Asher." Murmurs of agreement rippled through the crowd. The prophet had touched a nerve. That was it, exactly. "And I think I have just the man."

"Who?" someone blurted boldly, and there were several more cautious echos of the same question.

"I'd prefer not to announce that as yet. The time isn't right. Until that time comes, I'll accept your offer to rule Lamath as a regent. But let's not concern ourselves with the triviality of a coronation. Now if you don't mind, there are important matters that require my attention. Excuse me." Erri gathered up his robes and took off across the square.

This abrupt ending to their ceremony stunned the Lamathian leadership. They gazed around at one another in confusion and embarrassment. Strahn soon noticed that several people were looking expectantly at him. When others did the same, he found himself the focus of attention, and his face turned red. Not knowing what else to do, Strahn shrugged elaborately. Then he turned to race off after Erri, mentally berating the prophet for having so little respect for conventions.

Erri had already thrust the meeting from his mind and was wrapped in earnest conversation with the Power. He was pleading that his unannounced nominee for the crown of Lamath might survive the coming storm. Remembering Rosha's foolhardiness, Erri scowled. That was not a hopeful sign. Still, there came a time—sometimes in a moment—when foolhardiness was tempered by crisis into bravery, and ambition crystallized into destiny. "Perhaps," Erri mumbled, "that time is at hand for Rosha." Erri listened, but the Power did not respond.

Scouting parties from the two armies met and exchanged greetings long before the two armies came into view of one another. Nevertheless trumpets of alarm were sounded, and two lines drew up facing each other as if in preparation for a pitched battle. When the leaders rode out to parlay, all were smiling—all, that is, except Queen Bronwynn. She looked at Syth and addressed him sharply. "Where's Rosha?"

Syth's eyes widened, his only admission of surprise, but his smile stayed fixed and even grew warmer. "Your husband said you were direct—"

"Where is he?"

"That's a lengthy tale and a bit of a secret—"

"Tell it," Bronwynn snarled. She felt very much a queen this day and quite hostile. Syth looked around at his allies, then slowly turned back to face her. He got off his horse and started to walk away. "Where are you going?" Bronwynn called, her voice charged with annoyance.

"I said it was a secret. Come walking and I'll tell you."

Bronwynn looked at Joss, who gazed back impassively. She flung herself down from her saddle and walked quickly to Syth's side. Those left behind tried to appear disinterested as they strained to hear whatever bits of the conversation they might. They all heard Bronwynn emit a bark of outrage and saw her face turn red with rage. They heard nothing more.

"He's safe," Syth was whispering. "Much safer than either of us, at present."

"How do *you* know?" Bronwynn spat.

"Because it's my wife who's protecting him, that's why!" Syth growled back, mostly for show. He wasn't really angry. Rosha had anticipated Bronwynn's response and had tried to prepare him for it, but that had really been unnecessary. This was just like talking with Mar-Yilot. "And you can drive that jealousy right out of your head. It was my idea."

"Yours!"

"Our frontal assault will be suicidal unless they're successful. That is what you came for, isn't it? To aid Rosha in his cause?"

Bronwynn hesitated a moment at that, then snapped, "Of course."

"Good. Then why don't we map out our general strategy with the rest of the group? But keep quiet on Rosha's whereabouts. I trust my people and I'm sure you trust yours, but it's a treacherous age. Agreed?"

"Agreed." Bronwynn nodded, a little miffed at how easily he was handling her.

"One other thing before we join the others."

"Yes?"

"Is Pelmen with you?"

Bronwynn blinked. "No. He was, but we left him behind in Dragonsgate."

"Looking for the other pyramids." Syth nodded. He sounded dismayed.

"Why?" the queen asked.

"Oh. Just hoping."

"Riders!" someone in the ranks shouted, and a trumpet sounded the alarm again, this time in earnest. The two leaders whirled toward the south.

Bronwynn glanced at Syth's face and saw his disbelieving frown. She whipped out her sword and demanded, "Enemies?"

"I don't know!" Syth shouted in honest dismay. "It's either your husband returning far too soon or Admon Faye! Wait!" he called to his archers, who were nocking their arrows. "Wait until we know for certain who it is!"

The lead rider wore the colors of Dorlyth mod Karis. The rest were arrayed as freed men, in colors of their own choosing. They drew up some thirty yards distant, and the lead rider tore off his helmet and scowled at them. "What's the matter with you, Syth? Haven't we fought against one another enough for you to recognize me?"

Syth looked at Bronwynn in joyful surprise, but she was no longer beside him. She'd thrown her sword aside and was racing to greet her father-in-law with open arms. Dorlyth climbed painfully from his saddle, but he was still strong enough to grab her off her feet and swing her around like a child. The Golden Throng was perplexed beyond measure, but the army of the north greeted this sight with a loud huzzah. As Bronwynn and Dorlyth strolled arm-in-arm back to the beaming Syth, the

Throng, too, began cheering enthusiastically. They didn't know what, but evidently something wonderful had happened.

"Dorlyth!" Syth shouted above the din. "I thought you were dead!"

"So did your wife, apparently," Dorlyth said with a slight smile, and Syth covered his eyes in symbolic embarrassment.

"She was fooled," he offered apologetically as he pulled his hand away. "She thought Pelmen had put a spell on me."

"So she told us." Dorlyth nodded. "But here you are, so I judge she learned of her error, and here am I, so it wasn't quite as costly as you may have thought. And here *you* are as well!" Dorlyth grinned, hugging his daughter-in-law close.

Bronwynn smiled shyly, but didn't pull away. She felt none of that need to establish independence that had marred her last meeting with Pelmen, nor did she project any of her current ill-will toward her husband on Rosha's father. She'd not seen Dorlyth for years, but she'd loved him from a distance as a model of what her Rosha hoped to become, and as family. "Does Rosha know you're here?"

Dorlyth frowned. "I don't know the first thing about Rosha. Nor, for that matter, about you, or this army, or Syth, or what's been happening. I've been back at my castle trying to recover from a fire ring and I'm still not able to get around as well as I'd like."

"But how are you here at all?" Syth begged.

Dorlyth turned and pointed at his mount. "You see that horse? It used to be Pelmen's, and—"

"Minaliss?" Bronwynn asked, twirling out of Dorlyth's embrace and staring back at the horse. "It *is*!"

"Smart animal," Dorlyth said. "Came around through the fire, somehow, and found me. I managed to get up across his back and he carried me to my castle. I've been recuperating ever since then, but I got word from one of my people that an army was coming through Dragonsgate." Dorlyth propped his fists on his hips. "I am the Jorl of the Westmouth, you realize, sworn to defend the realm against intruders." He looked at Bronwynn.

She met his eyes evenly. "Am I an intruder?" she asked frankly.

"My Lady," Dorlyth said, "at this point I'm just glad there's someone around who's *willing* to come help us with this quarrel." He looked at Syth. "The Mar's been mustered on top of the High Plateau. Belra's been destroyed. I hear rumors that I can't make any sense of at *all*. I'm here to join you, although I can't offer much."

"You bring us a great deal, just by offering your presence," Syth responded warmly. "As to whether it will be enough—shall we all go and find out?"

Minutes later the allied armies were marching together toward the High Fortress. They hadn't a hope of conquering it—all of them knew that well. But if they didn't make the effort, there would be nothing left worth hoping for. At least, in this, they found purpose, and when hope was gone, purpose was a worthwhile substitute.

## CHAPTER SEVENTEEN

# The Baying Hounds

WITH THE fanatical courage that was sometimes born of terror, Terril drove his tiny body up the sheer face of the cliff. He had ridden the cold winter air currents all the way from Sythia and emotionally he was frozen. Suddenly he saw a window in the High Fortress looming up before him, and he shot through it with a triumphant buzz. His feet, human again at last, hit the floor.

Naturally, Flayh knew the moment Terril arrived. As the shivering wizard sat by a fire slurping soup straight from the bowl, a squat brigand tapped Terril on the shoulder. "The Lord Flayh wants to see you," he mumbled. "Follow me."

Terril didn't argue. He refilled his bowl from a steaming pot and followed the slaver down the hallway. The man ushered him into a room, then left. Terril took another draught of his soup before looking around. He suddenly noticed he wasn't alone. "Joooms?" he said, eyeing the hook-nosed man seated by the wall.

"Hello, Twin-killer," Joooms responded.

The lizard's superior tone of voice made Terril bristle. "What are you doing here?" he snapped angrily, annoyed at how swiftly Joooms could make him feel incompetent.

Jooom shrugged. "The same thing you are, I assume."

"Enlarging your treasury?" Terril sneered. Joooms's greediness was legendary.

"A little." The dark shaper nodded. "Though I'm more concerned with preserving the lives of my family. But of course, family ties don't matter much to you, do they, Twin-killer?"

Weary or not, an affront was an affront and not to be tolerated. Terril hurled a ball of flame at Joooms's head, only to have it bounce harmlessly away at a wave of the lizard's hand. "Come, Terril. Can't you be a little more creative?" Joooms stood and swivelled around to face his attacker. The two shapers would have begun then in earnest, had Flayh not appeared suddenly between them. They both leaped backward in shock. This was not an image, a projection thrown down by a shaper still above. This was the small sorcerer himself.

Flayh smiled gloatingly, and looked from one astonished wizard to the other. Then he shrugged, as if this feat were nothing. In fact, it was incredible.

"My Lord Flayh," Joooms said, bowing graciously with one knee to the floor. "You've taken us completely by surprise."

"Welcome, Lord Flayh," Terril muttered, imitating Jooom's polished charm.

"Hello, Terril. Welcome back. I hope you've brought me some usable information. I thought I'd pop down and hear it before you two kill each other."

"A minor misunderstanding," Joooms said smoothly, and Terril nodded vigorous agreement.

"I hope so. It matters little to me what you do to one another after the war is won; but until that time, try to stay out of each other's way. Otherwise, one of you will doubtless destroy the other, and I'd be forced to kill the survivor. That would all be a terrible waste."

"Surely you don't actually need us," Joooms suggested with a quiet smile. "With tugoliths to trample on the armies that attack you, and your own remarkable powers to counter shaper assaults, what good can we do you?"

"You think my powers formidable?" Flayh asked. He appeared genuinely pleased.

"Of course," Joooms answered, his dark eyes fixed unflinchingly on Flayh's disfigured countenance, his voice oily with charm. "Never have I beheld such a feat as I've just witnessed. Have you, Twin-killer?" He didn't wait for Terril's response but went quickly on, "Can you tell us how it's done?"

Flayh's eyes lidded slightly, and he gazed contemptuously at Joooms.

"Of course." Joooms nodded. "Trade secrets. But since your shaping is so demonstrably superior to ours, can't you release us from your service? Your victory is assured."

"Patience, Joooms," Flayh said. "Your children aren't far, and they aren't suffering. A few more days and, as you say, the victory will be assured. But it would make me nervous to think either of you were out there unattached, so to speak. Besides, I need your counsel. You've both battled Pelmen and Mar-Yilot, and I want to draw upon your experience."

Joooms chuckled. "I'll be little help to you there. While I've successfully eluded them both, I've never defeated either of them." The dark man frowned sharply and raised his voice. "Come, Lord Flayh, speak frankly! You know as well as we that what you've just done is impossible! The pair you battle are the best, and by their pairing are more frightful than any shaper force I ever faced, but surely they tremble before *you*, who can *be* anywhere you will!"

"Not anywhere. Not yet," Flayh muttered. "The range of my movement is small yet. But it should be sufficient, you think?"

"Without question," Joooms snorted.

Flayh looked at Terril. "And you? You agree?"

"My Lord Flayh," Terril answered wearily, "you know that I would surrender without a fight."

"Of course," Flayh snorted. "You already did. But Pelmen did not. Nor did Mar-Yilot. What news, man! What can I expect?"

Terril took a deep breath. "Syth has marched to Tuckad, where he gathers his armies. The son of Dorlyth rides with him. Mar-Yilot lingers in Sythia to cover her lover, and I doubt she'll venture anything save that. Your spell upon Syth terrified her."

"Yet that spell didn't hold. Syth raises an army against me! What about this woman with the healing touch?"

"You know about that?"

"Naturally I know!" Flayh barked. "Did you think yourself my only pair of eyes in the north? Where is she? If she travels with Syth, then magical attacks upon him would be useless, freeing Mar-Yilot to work her mischief! Speak!"

"She's gone!" Terril blurted out. "She left with Pelmen on some strange quest over a week ago!"

"What quest?" Flayh asked.

Terril trembled. "I could never obtain the details."

Flayh gazed at him a moment, somewhat disinterestedly, rather as a man might regard a chicken he's about to behead. "Where were they going?" he asked casually. "Or did you miss that as well?"

"I . . . don't know."

Flayh smiled slightly. "I know where Pelmen is. He travels with an army from Chaomonous that passed through Dragonsgate three days ago."

"With Queen Bronwynn?" Terril asked earnestly. "It's her army Syth plans to join!"

"Which means?" Flayh inquired in bored tones.

"That Pelmen and this witch healer will be together again with Syth . . ."

"Freeing Mar-Yilot to act." Flayh grunted. "And I believe you've told me something of this young queen, as well?"

"She's a shaper," Terril murmured, recalling the rolling inferno that ended his dream of dominating Chaomonous.

Flayh turned to the dark wizard. "You see, Joooms, why I need you. I have potentially three shapers aligned against me, two certainly. And while I may have superior power, I lack tactical training. I fear nothing from these armies. The tugoliths will demolish them on the plain. Should any warriors succeed by chance in eluding the beasts and getting up the Down Road, they'll face King Pahd and the rather colorful assemblage that continues to muster in the city—the cream of the Mar, I'm told?" He raised an inquiring eyebrow, and Joooms nodded:

"There are many good warriors among Pahd's supporters."

"Fine. Certainly no one could penetrate that cordon to face

my own castle guard and their hideous leader. Excepting, of course, a shaper. A shaper could neutralize my war beasts, perhaps even neutralize Pahd's army. We can't allow that to happen, Joooms. If that happens, I'm afraid your children will suffer. And we don't want that."

Joooms's brown eyes were expressionless—which in fact expressed a great deal. "No, Lord Flayh. We would not."

"Very well then. Suppose you tell me what I may expect?"

Joooms and Terril exchanged a quick look of mutual dismay. How could they teach a powerful novice to free his imagination? Joooms took a deep breath, but never got any farther. He was interrupted by a horrible sound that made all of them slam their hands over their ears and shut their eyes. It was like the baying of thousands of dogs. When it ceased at last and Joooms and Terril opened their eyes, Flayh had disappeared.

"What do you do next?" Serphimera asked.

"I don't know," Pelmen replied honestly. He had arranged the six pyramids in a hexagram on the cavern floor and now stepped back to survey them. Serphimera pulled her robe more tightly around her shoulders and shivered. The freezing wind only blew a little colder outside.

"You have no idea where to begin?"

"None." The word boomed through the cavern more loudly than he'd intended. Had he been more attentive to his wife, he might have noticed how this clipped utterance added to her chill. His attention remained fixed on the diamonds before him, however, as he sat quietly and waited.

Serphimera watched his face. She saw the intensity, the resolve in his clenched jaw, and the confident anticipation glittering in his eyes. While he didn't know the secret that would fuse these fragments into a single magnificent gem, he knew far more than had Sheth, that wondrous wizard of times past. He knew he couldn't do this by his own power and that he didn't need to try. Sheth's contribution was lodged within them, evidenced by their strange blue radiance. There was no need now for Pelmen's shaper skill—a good thing, since he'd always been a user of the shaper's craft, not a scholar of it. His contribution had nothing to do with magic. Rather, he was to furnish the one element the weapon had lacked when first it had been formed. Pelmen provided the faith.

He couldn't even say for sure what faith was. An attitude of mind? A method of interpreting events that saw patterns in random occurrences? A type of magic all its own? A gift? He favored the last view himself, believing that the gift of believing had been disclosed to him here on this very mountain by that Power who unified all things. He hadn't sought it—it had come unbidden. Yet it was there within him, irrefutably a part of him. He believed. And that belief had robbed him of his freedom, ripped away some measure of his own identity—and had given in their place the exhilaration of purpose.

His was not a false faith, some type of hypnosis, self-induced to escape the anxiety of living in an imperfect world. He had experienced the Power flooding through him and washing him clean as it rushed on to accomplish its own purposes through him. At the same time, his relationship with this mighty One remained a faith, and not a knowledge. Those moments of peak intensity, when he knew he was not the shaper but the one being shaped, fled swiftly. And there remained too many feathery brushes with the icy tendrils of doubt. It was not knowledge, but a faith—based in his own experience. Pelmen could do many things, but all were meaningless in contrast to his exercising of this gift. Pelmen's faith was a gateway. As Serphimera watched, it opened.

One moment he was Pelmen. The next he was something far, far more. The change dropped him to his knees, and he rolled back onto his heels, beaming with elation. Serphimera knew the feeling well. She also knew the sense of isolation it produced. She felt lonely, separated from her love by that very thing which linked them together. But Serphimera bore no jealousy. After all, she possessed a faith of her own. Like him, she waited.

Pelmen's face, already pale from the wintertime cold, began glowing, as if reflecting back the brilliance of some white-hot beam of light. He didn't shield his eyes, but opened them wide with wonder, as if he gazed, astonished, upon the landscape of a new world. At the same moment a tongue of blue flame erupted from the midst of the six pyramids, forming a seventh, larger pyramid of fire that engulfed the other six. Serphimera was forced at last to turn away and she faced the wall, where she watched her shadow dance and leap in the flickering of that bright blue light. Still she waited.

When at last her shadow disappeared and she dared to look again at Pelmen's face, she found his eyes were no longer fixed on forever, but on her. His face no longer glowed, but his smile had a radiance all its own. "Now," he murmured, "I know."

Through the cavern's mouth came a horrendous noise, which rose above the mournful wailing of the wind. It was the music of myriads of howling hounds, waiting impatiently for him to stop talking and start doing.

"I'll need your hands," he muttered, and Serphimera knelt beside him. They each took three of the objects and fitted them in place, then moved around to face each other and held the whole cluster together. Pelmen cleared his mind, and all expression faded from his face as he whispered, "In faith I plead that six be one, if so be the will of the Power." Slowly he pulled his hands away.

The pieces did not fall apart. They had melded into a single gem.

"Is it finished?" Serphimera whispered.

Pelmen turned the pointed object before his eyes, gazing into its sparkling depths. "It's fused together, at least."

"And ready to be used?"

"Yes." Although he only murmured the words, the howling outside suddenly grew louder.

Serphimera's head snapped around and she glared fiercely at the mouth of the cave. "Have you no patience?" she shouted, and though her human voice could scarcely have been heard above the supernatural cacophony, the myriads of beasts grew quiet.

Pelmen continued to stare into the crystal. "They've been waiting a long time, my love—"

"They can wait just a little bit longer."

Her passion surprised and pleased him. Fascinated as he was by this glowing thorn of gemstone, he set it aside and looked at her. He wished he could hide the melancholy in his eyes. For all his actor's skill, he could not. Besides, their love had been forged in integrity. He would not rob her of full participation in this, his final struggle.

She swivelled to face him with that fluid economy of motion that had so entranced the legions of Lamath. Far more regal than any queen, the former priestess of the Dragonfaith looked at him frankly and asked, "What happens next, my priest?"

Pelmen blinked. "Priest? I'm not the priest in this family. You are." He said it with a teasing chuckle.

Serphimera didn't smile. She folded her skirt under her as she sat on a rock. Then, with great gravity, she said, "I was never the priest. And you always were."

"What are you saying?" he asked, still trying to brush aside the subject with a smile. "I was the prophet, remember?"

"What is a prophet and what's a priest? There has been much confusion here, Pelmen. The prophet forth-tells, rebukes, and proclaims. You were never that type."

"That's right," Pelmen fervently agreed. "That's why I passed that task on to Erri as quickly as morally justifiable."

His continued levity annoyed her briefly. Then she subdued her own frustration and asked, "Why won't you be serious?"

The trace of a smile drained from his face, leaving behind only the grim lines of resolve. "Because I know where this discussion leads. And I suppose I'd like to play just a few moments longer."

"Do we have a few moments?" she asked pointedly.

"I don't know," he said sadly. "I guess not. Go ahead. I'm listening."

"The other aspect of the prophetic rôle is that of foretelling the future. Erri has some visionary sense. He is a true prophet. In fact, there are several who are beginning to discover the ability. That was always my foremost gift. *I* was the real prophet of Lamath." She paused then, to give him a chance to argue if he chose.

He nodded. "Continue." It seemed as if he had heard all this before, but it nevertheless needed to be voiced. Their conversation had taken on the texture of a ritual.

"I was called," she went on. "I responded. I obeyed. I interpreted events in the only way I could—and I was wrong. But through me, misguided though I was, the Power roused Lamath. It was the Power at work all along." Pelmen said nothing, for no response was necessary. "And when the time was right—when the opportunity arose—the intertwining of personalities and events was revealed and the pattern became visible. The Power is so creative! My contribution was not foreordained or predetermined. It was and is that the Power knows what the Power chooses to see and is creative enough to be able always to draw that pattern out of chaos."

"And my rôle, too, was revealed to you?"

"You are the priest, Pelmen. You have always been the priest."

"The Priest of Lamath," Pelmen murmured.

"Not of Lamath. The Priest of the One Land. The one standing between the Power and the people. The one who offers the sacrifice."

"Who *offers* the sacrifice?" Pelmen asked sharply. "Or the one who *is* the sacrifice?"

Outside, the dogs raised an enormous howl. Pelmen waved his hand toward the mouth of the cave. "You hear *their* opinion!"

"But do you understand my meaning?"

"Far better, I think, than you could appreciate." Pelmen sighed. He rose from his seat and paced around the cavern. "Call me whatever you choose—I've understood at least that much of my task since the day I first comprehended those strange symbols in the book Erri so treasures. I ran from it then. Later I realized the truth in what you've said—the Power is infinitely creative. The path I choose is the pathway to be chosen. I thought my past was to be ended with the dragon. Instead, it's to be ended here." He stooped and picked up the thorn-shaped crystal. "This weapon will absorb Flayh's power and leave him as he was before—a very greedy, very petty little man. It will take Mar-Yilot's power, as well as that of Joooms, Terril, and Mast, because it will free all these powers we shape to return to the Power at last. Many of them have been waiting eagerly for a long, long time." The baying outside began again and drew Pelmen's eyes back to the cave mouth. "They can hear every word we say," he murmured and he looked back at Serphimera. "It seems strange that, with so many powers enfleshed out there as dogs, there should remain so many that may still be shaped. They are all active now, Serphimera. They're stirred by the possibility of a gateway. They were disappointed when Sheth failed. Yet who can blame the man? The price of opening this gateway is the life force of a shaper, and nothing in Sheth's experience prepared him to make such a sacrifice."

"Unlike you," Serphimera breathed.

Pelmen nodded. "Unlike me." He gazed at her a long time in silence. "Did you know all of this?" he asked finally.

"Most of it," she admitted. "What wasn't revealed to me, I'd guessed."

"Then perhaps you realize that you still have a priestly task to perform."

"What task?" she said wearily.

"If I'm to be offered, who is to make the offering, if not you?"

Serphimera thought a long time before responding; then she shook her head. "I don't know if I can do that."

Pelmen sighed, turning the crystal before his eyes. "Somebody must. The point of this thing must be plunged into my—"

"I said I can't!" Serphimera flared, and a mournful howl arose from the distant dogs. She ignored them. "I love you, Pelmen Dragonsbane! I'll not be the one to take your life!"

Pelmen glanced up at her hopefully. "You know this?" he asked.

It took her a moment to understand what he was asking. When she did, she slumped against the cave wall. "Not by vision, no. I've seen nothing but our coming up here."

"Then it still could be," Pelmen said dreamily. "*Must* be."

"No!"

"There's no other way, Serphimera," he began, but she had slumped down into the dirt and turned her face to the rock wall. "Serphimera," he called, but she wouldn't speak. Pelmen went to crouch beside her and slipped his hands around her waist. "Later," he whispered. "We'll do it later."

She turned her tear-streaked face back to look at him and nodded. "Maybe, then—I'll be able. But there's time, still. There's still some time . . ."

The dogs, Flayh thought to himself. Those hellish dogs had been his undoing. They'd betrayed him! They'd used him to achieve fleshly form, all the while making him believe he was using them! But now they'd betrayed their own cause. Who could mistake that infernal racket!

Somehow, they'd managed to get the six pieces of the ancient weapons of Sheth reassembled. How? Flayh raged. Half of those pieces had been lost for a millennium! The thought of their reconstruction made him shiver. All powers fled! Flayh snarled a curse.

"Now they've actually found a shaper fool enough to reassemble it for them," he muttered. "Fool! What senseless dolt would not only sacrifice all his personal power, but his very life as well?" Of course, he knew the answer. Among the active shapers, only Pelmen had the peculiar turn of mind that would render martyrdom attractive. "Too long with those Lamathian dragon lovers. But where is he *now*?" Flayh demanded, pacing his tower cell. "If only these cursed hounds would quit their all-pervasive howling, perhaps I could—"

"In faith I plead that six be one, if so be the will of the Power."

The words stunned Flayh, setting him reeling. They were only a distant whisper, yet they echoed through his apartment. "Close!" he cried. "This Pelmen has to be nearby! Walls, did you hear?"

—of course! the High Fortress moaned. Humans may cover their ears, but this fortress has none! It must hear everything!

"Where does the sound come from?" Flayh demanded.

—Everywhere! the High Fortress wailed.

Flayh cursed the castle savagely and fetched out his atlas. While he hadn't traveled widely beyond the secured roads of the three lands, he was familiar with every feature of their topography. Like all merchants, he had excellent maps, and now he thumbed through the multicolored pages, studying the details of the Mar's physical features. No clues came from his search, however, and he slammed the book shut.

"Dogs, dogs," he muttered, walking toward a window. He flung aside a drape and stepped out onto a balcony, discovering with surprise that it was night. The sky above him was pitch black, overcast by clouds pregnant with snow, but the city below was alight with bonfires. The warriors of the Mar had congregated in its streets and were celebrating tomorrow's victory in advance.

"Meaningless," Flayh muttered to himself. That certain victory would be fruitless unless he could—

He heard something, something besides the agony of a castle or the moaning of excited dogs. Snatches of some private conversation echoed through his mind. Annoyed by the distracting laughter of the celebrants below, Flayh shouted, "Silence!" Then he ducked back into his castle.

He closed out the city sounds and bent his attention to listening. After a moment, he smiled quietly at the darkness. He could hear it clearly. He recognized one voice as that of Pelmen, and judged the other to be that of the shaper's woman by the nature of the intimate words they exchanged. They had remade the weapon, obviously, but had not yet put it to use. Flayh sat cross-legged upon his floor and propped his head in his hands. He would listen. Something they would say would give him the key to their whereabouts. Once given, he would be *there*, and they would experience a most unpleasant interruption of their intimacy!

If, that is, Flayh could hear them over that incessent baying! "Silence!" he shouted again, this time to the host of howling dogs. They were unlikely, however, to listen. Their baying was every bit as impatient as Flayh's—and every bit as ineffective.

## CHAPTER EIGHTEEN

# Into the Tower

ROSHA SHIVERED by an open window. The night was nearly gone, yet the Autumn Lady had still not made their appointed rendezvous. He glanced across the room to where the poor couple who owned this house huddled together under a quilt. Mar-Yilot had hidden Pelmen and himself in this same dwelling the night of their escape off of the High Plateau, and Rosha felt sure the couple had not been pleased to see him again. This, however, was where Mar-Yilot had sent him, and here he would remain until she came.

"Shut that thing," Mar-Yilot snapped, and Rosha grunted

with shock and whirled around to face her. Once he controlled the pounding of his heart, he reached up and closed the window.

"I didn't see you fly in," he whispered.

"Let's hope Flayh didn't, either," the shaper murmured. "Thank you, friends," she said to the city dwellers who peered up at her from under their blanket. "You'll be well rewarded. Come on!" she barked to Rosha as she unbolted the door.

Mar-Yilot had kept Rosha cloaked until he got into Ngandib, even as she'd ridden toward the city herself. Once he was hidden, she'd taken wing to join him. Now she covered them both as they glided down the alleyways. "Doesn't anybody here sleep?" she whispered as they encountered a rollicking outdoor party.

"It's been like this all night," Rosha muttered.

"Why not?" Mar-Yilot snarled. "*They* won't be fighting in the morning. They'll leave that to the tugoliths." She stopped suddenly and pointed.

Rosha looked up. The spires of the High Fortress loomed above them, glowing with the ruddy orange reflection of hundreds of bonfires. Dread came upon Rosha like a huge spider, slowly eating its way up through his stomach. He felt his gorge rising. He was sick with terror. Despite the frozen air, he was sweating heavily, and his heart squirmed within his chest as if frantic to escape.

They turned a corner and ran into yet another street party. A table had been moved out of one of the taverns, and a fat drunkard danced on top of it as it wobbled and rocked on the cobblestones. Mar-Yilot turned to move away, but Rosha reached out to grab her hand and hold her. She jerked around and glowered at him, then leaned up to his ear and snapped an inquiry in a fierce whisper.

Rosha pointed at the frolicking slob and sneered one word. "Pezi." The name meant nothing to the sorceress, but it obviously meant much to the young warrior, for she saw him grab for his dagger.

"No!" Mar-Yilot snorted, and she grabbed, too—not for a dagger but for two fistfuls of his wiry black hair. He nearly yelped aloud, but restrained himself as she pulled him swiftly back down the alleyway and jerked his head down to her mouth. "That's right," she spat savagely in his ear, "butcher the little pig. Announce to the whole city that we're here. Destroy Syth's plan with a wave of your blade. Nothing could please me more. Because then I could *leave* you here in good conscience and get myself back to Syth. Go ahead." She released him then, and he jumped back to stare at her, his eyes wide and white.

She glared up at him, paused for a moment to let her words soak in, then went on: "It's all temper with you, isn't it? Just like Dorlyth. Oh, you're all nobility and responsibility in the planning stages, but when the pressure starts mounting and the fear takes over, then impulse wins again, doesn't it? Well, go back and stick that little fat person, whoever he is. Then some of your fear might go away, and you can concentrate on how stupid you are!"

Rosha stood flatfooted and slightly stooped, his mouth open, his wide eyes blinking. When it seemed she'd finished, he closed his mouth and swallowed. Then he turned his back to one of the alley's walls and squatted against it. After a moment, Mar-Yilot repented of her ferocity and knelt beside him. She didn't apologize—after all, she'd only spoken the truth—but she did reach out to put a hand on his knee. "Are you all right now?"

It seemed a long time before he responded. When he did, he sounded remarkably controlled. "Yes, I believe I am." He turned his head then to look into her eyes. "My Lady," he breathed softly, "is there ever a time . . . do you ever grow out of responding to stress like a child?"

"I don't know," the Autumn Lady murmured; she gave him a slow, sly smile. "I'm not that old yet." She nodded down the alley. "Who was that?"

"Doesn't matter," Rosha said, and she was convinced he meant it. "Apparently your husband and my wife will be here by morning. We wait until Flayh marches out his tugoliths before we go in?"

"That seems wisest, doesn't it? Unless you want to get flattened against the flagstones? I'll drop my coverage of you as soon as we set foot inside. When that castle starts whining, we'll both be discovered immediately. You just sprint up the stairs. Get as high up as you can as quickly as you can. I expect to be otherwise engaged."

"What are you planning to do?"

The question surprised her. "Plan? I don't plan. You never plan a shaper battle. That's the easiest way to get killed."

"No plan?" Rosha frowned. "Then how do you fight?"

"By impulse—" Mar-Yilot started to say, then stopped herself as she saw his quick grin. Chagrined, she smiled too, then said, "All right. You fight like a child—all reflex and fury and imagination. As I said, I haven't grown out of it either." A raucous laugh rolled around the corner, and the auburn-haired woman turned her head lazily toward it. "Perhaps," she suggested, "we could lure him away. I'm sure he wouldn't be the only man murdered in this drunken city tonight."

"It isn't necessary," Rosha said shortly, putting Pezi out of his mind. "We're near the stable entrance. Shall we wait here until dawn?"

Mar-Yilot nodded. "That should be soon," she mumbled. Then she peeked around the corner. "Hmm," she grunted. "Your fat enemy just passed out beneath the table. Get back," she added quickly, then looked at Rosha to explain, "There are several slavers coming this way."

They hid and watched as three slavers approached the table where Pezi had danced.

Pezi was dimly aware of voices above him, but was feeling too relaxed to pay them any mind. He knew he really ought to get up, but it was just too comfortable here. He'd spent the night moving from one celebration to another, clearing each table of leftovers before moving on to the next. He couldn't remember when he'd had so much fun. There were no dogs out here in the city, no slavers in evidence—and, first and foremost, no cursed tugoliths. He'd been able to put his troubles behind him and simply enjoy himself. Now he wanted only to be left alone to sleep. The cobblestones beneath his head were hard, but they were far preferable to—

"There you are!" roared a boisterous slaver as a pair of his comrades tossed the table aside. Pezi's eyes flew open in time for him to see the bucketful of ice water dropping onto him, but not in time to jerk aside. His blue and lime tunic was soaked through. Moments later it was frozen. Pezi couldn't move. The three brigands each grabbed a part of him—one seized him by the nostrils as if intending to rip his nose off—and hoisted him onto his feet. They booted him in the backside, and he had the choice of moving his legs or diving face first into the cobblestones. He walked, his fat thighs flapping against the frozen material of his leggings. It was excruciating.

"Where were you, Pezi?" one slaver asked in mocking concern. "We were worried about you!"

"Especially your friend Admon Faye," a second man added. "He sent us out here to find you."

"It's a wonder you didn't freeze to death," the first man went on.

"How could he freeze?" the third asked. "He's pickled from the inside out!"

The three rogues each punctuated their comment with a shove; thus Pezi made quick progress toward the entrance of the stable. When he saw the large doorway yawning before him, he started resisting. "No!" he pleaded, shivering. "I don't want—"

"Afraid of the tugs? But they're your friends, Pezi."

"They'll eat me!"

"Not until you thaw out," the first slaver cackled as he kicked Pezi through the door. The fat merchant tumbled into the straw. He stumbled to his feet just as Thuganlitha raised his giant head and turned to look at him. Pezi squalled in terror. Despite his frozen legs, he outran the brigands to the staircase. He raced upward with amazing speed for a fat man. But when he reached the topmost stair, he stopped dead. Admon Faye was blocking his way.

"Hello, Pezi," the grotesque slaver said pleasantly. Then he clucked his tongue. "Where were you?" he scolded. "I thought I'd made it clear that all slavers were confined to the High Fortress?"

"I'm no slaver," Pezi rumbled, his teeth chattering.

"Ah, that's right. But you *are* a member of the castle security force, and a most important member of Lord Flayh's war cabinet. How could we make responsible decisions without our esteemed tugolith handler to advise us?"

*"Me?* You're the only one who can handle them!" the round-bellied merchant protested.

"Nonsense. Who brought them here? Who shepherded them through the wilderness? Who guided them past the dragon? Who led them into battle?"

"Please, Admon Faye, I'm freezing to death, can't you—"

"But of course, General Pezi. Go don your battle dress and get ready to lead your charges once more into the fray."

"What?" Pezi wailed.

"We missed your counsel, but we naturally needed to make some decisions. The slavers will remain here to protect the High Fortress. King Pahd will distribute his forces throughout the city. You will lead the battle beasts down the mountain and retrieve them for us when the carnage is done."

"But I can't do that! They'll go mad! They'll wind up trampling *me*!"

"There is that possibility," Admon Faye admitted sadly.

"No! I won't do it!"

"Be sensible, Pezi. Someone has to do it. The only people they know are you and me. Since I'm needed here in the High Fortress, that leaves only you to lead them."

"I'll—I'll get shot with an arrow!"

"Don't be ridiculous! These brave invaders will all be far too busy running to discharge any arrows."

"I'm *not* going to do it!"

Admon Faye sighed. "Very well." He gestured to the three slavers who had brought Pezi in. "Throw him over the rail."

"I've reconsidered!" Pezi said quickly as three pairs of hands grabbed him. "It's actually quite an honor . . ."

The ugly slaver smirked. "I knew I could count on you in our hour of need." Admon Faye turned his back and brushed past Tibb, who had stood quietly behind him watching this little drama unfold. Pezi's stricken gaze met Tibb's; hoping for some look of encouragement, he rolled his eyes meaningfully.

Tibb made no response. He just leaned casually against the castle wall, fingering the hilt of his dagger.

Rosha had never grown accustomed to waiting. He paced the alley, looking at the stable door frequently, working mentally to stifle his fears while preparing himself for victory.

"Can't you relax?" Mar-Yilot complained. "I've been working night and day trying to get us both right here and I'd like some rest before we go charging toward that door."

"You're charging in with me?"

"Of course. This way the castle will discover us both at once. If I can work fast enough, perhaps I can make the place too miserable for it to give a proper alarm."

"I don't understand. If the castle is conscious of magic all around it, why can't it sense your coverage of us?"

"Because I'm *not* covering us," Mar-Yilot said matter-of-factly. Rosha gasped in shock. "Why do you think I told you to get back when those slavers appeared? It's best that you understand this now: Once we get inside, you'll be on your own. Don't rely on me—I'll be busy. Hush—the tugoliths."

They heard the great beasts snorting and grumbling as Pezi and Chimolitha led them out of the stable. They sat motionless until the column was past; then they jumped up and ran for the stable door. The heavy, sweet scent of tugolith hide filled their nostrils as they burst inside. Rosha's gift sword flashed above his head, but he gave no other battle cry. No one blocked them.

The pair of slavers who had been assigned to guard this entrance had counted the task meaningless. They sat on the bottom step of the staircase, exchanging jokes, and were in the midst of a laugh as Rosha's blade scythed cleanly through both of them at one stroke. Before they toppled into each other's arms, he had bounded to the top of the staircase.

Mar-Yilot filled the vast room with fire. Everything combustible—stalls, straw, stairway, and bodies—burst into flame. She hoped this would prevent anyone outside from getting in to reinforce the castle garrison. Of course, it also cut off Rosha's escape, but she shrugged that off. If he lived that long, they would work something out.

Instantly she was a butterfly, winging her way up and out of the inferno she had created and trying to block out the anguished howling of the High Fortress. Reaching the stone corridor she transformed herself again, and murmured, "You sure complain a lot," to the wailing walls. Then she was off after Rosha, flinging fireballs in every direction and chuckling to herself. There was no question about it. She enjoyed this exercise of power.

Rosha moved faster than the shouts of alarm. He raced through intersecting corridors, stopping to do battle only if necessary. As a result, he gathered behind him a steadily growing train of startled slavers, buzzing like an aroused swarm of angry sugar-clawsps. He paid them no mind. Let the sorceress dispose of them. He had a more important task.

He whirled around a corner, intending to charge quickly up

a staircase. He couldn't reach it, though, for he faced his first real obstacle. His path was blocked by the most formidable swordsman in all the Mar—King Pahd mod Pahd-el had decided not to venture from his castle.

Pahd's flesh was a chill, ghastly white. Grief had drained him of every appearance of life. He looked bloodless and dead—but he wasn't. That same grief had charged him with a rage that demanded venting, and this onrushing warrior seemed the perfect target. Pahd's weapon was out. He was ready to fight. But Rosha suddenly wasn't. "Stand aside, Pahd," Rosha said. "I've no quarrel with you."

"But I have with you!" Pahd seethed. "This is my fortress! My home! You invade it and ask me to stand aside?"

"I've come after Flayh! Step aside!" The buzzing swarm was growing louder.

"After Flayh?" Pahd shrilled. "So that he can charge me with deserting him and torture her forever? Oh no!" Pahd whistled his weapon up and out. Only Rosha's quick leap backward saved his head from being severed from his neck. "Or maybe you *want* my Sarie to suffer?" Pahd screamed, and his sword sliced outward again.

"Mad," Rosha muttered as he danced aside again. It was too late. The murderous swarm was upon him.

The bellowing mob of slavers rounded the corner, howling obscenities and violent promises. Rosha hadn't time to raise his blade in self-defense. To his astonishment, he didn't need to. They raced right past him, and soon turned a corner at the other end of the gallery. Mar-Yilot! He wasn't *entirely* on his own.

The mob had passed between Rosha and Pahd. Now the crazed king squinted his eyes, searching for his disappeared foe. "Mod Dorlyth?" he grunted.

Rosha dodged to the side, hoping still to get up the staircase without battling Pahd. But although he couldn't be seen, he could be heard, and Pahd responded to the sound of his shuffling feet by jumping onto the staircase himself. "Cloaked, are you?" Pahd snarled. "Very well, then, come and slaughter me! I've no shaper to give me aid. I'm sick to death of shapers! And I'm tired, Rosha. Come on, boy, we used to be friends! Put me to bed at last! You know how I long for it!"

"Pahd, back off! Give us a chance and perhaps we can save her!"

"Save her?" Pahd moaned. "Only by death! Hack me down, Rosha, but promise me first you'll go slay her as well!"

"Pahd, will you please—"

Rosha again had to dive aside, for Pahd's eyes had suddenly caught sight of him and launched a savage strike. The cloak was gone. Mar-Yilot was otherwise engaged.

Pahd jumped down from the stairs and Rosha scooted back out of his way. The king's expression had changed. He no longer wore his grimace of grief. He smiled playfully instead, and beckoned at Rosha. "Fight, lad. Make it interesting."

There was no help for it. Rosha fought.

The hallway filled with the clang of sword on sword and the grunts and growls of men at exercise. In the manner of a master with his pupil, Pahd kept up a running critique: "Excellent. A little too late. Follow through, lad. Watch yourself." Despite the friendly words, the king's strokes whistled in with awesome wickedness, and Rosha was driven back to the wall. He battled not only with Pahd but with himself as well. He had no wish to harm this man. King Pahd was his own liege.

Time convinced him. It occurred to him abruptly just how much time he was wasting here. Hundreds, perhaps thousands would die today, sacrificing themselves to make his mission possible. Pahd would just have to join them.

Once the decision was made, it was over. Pahd had lost none of his excellence as a swordsman. Rosha was simply better. And with a parry, a slight feint and a dancing step to the side, Rosha freed himself and ran his sovereign through.

The king froze. Blood stained his tunic, then began to flow freely from the gash. "I'm sorry," Rosha whispered.

"I'm not," Pahd responded, and he crumbled slowly to the floor. "My pillow . . ." he murmured. Then he was gone.

Rosha was already on the next landing of the staircase.

Mar-Yilot worked quickly, and the howls of the High Fortress multiplied. But her attack had been expected. Terril and Joooms were lying in wait; as soon as the fires began in the stable, they were asking the walls for her whereabouts. They found her standing in the hallway twenty feet behind Rosha, overseeing his encounter with Pahd. They launched their first strike.

She felt a lizard scuttle across the top of her shoes at the same instant that a horrible burning struck the back of her neck and she knew the shaper battle had been joined. She took her altershape and glided frantically up the corridor, searching for a spot to stand and fight. She found an arrow slit which would be a convenient vent to the outside and took her human form beside it. Then she threw a wall of fire across the hallway, just in time to singe the wings of the onrushing sugar-clawsp slightly. Terril transformed himself and skidded along the floor of the corridor on his human bottom. He had the foresight to dodge aside immediately or he would have been engulfed by another gout of fire from the hand of the sorceress. Instantly, he bounced to his feet, and Mar-Yilot saw the rage in his eyes just before he disappeared. She put her back to the window to prevent his getting between her and her escape route, then she cast a glance at the ceiling. Joooms, she knew, preferred to drop from above when attacking in his lizard shape. She then threw all her energy into penetrating Terril's cloak. She saw them both, for Joooms had cloaked too, and they were evidently oblivious of each other, for they were about to bump together. Mar-Yilot didn't pause. She tossed herself backward, issuing from the arrow-slit in her butterfly shape. One opponent at a time was plenty, and Joooms, at least, could not pursue her out here.

He could hurl missiles, however, and he immediately rushed to the window slit and began dropping things on her. She expected fire, and dodged downward accordingly. But the lizard was a wily foe; he'd tossed a small ball of water instead, and it slammed down onto her with wing-crushing brutality. Mar-Yilot plummeted toward the pavement of the courtyard below, fluttering madly to regain control of her tiny body. She would have been easy prey in that moment to the burning acid of a clawsp attack. Given their relative sizes, one mere touch of Terril's chemically coated exoskeleton would have paralyzed her long enough for her two opponents to deliver the *coup de grâce*. But Terril and Joooms were not fighting in concert. They couldn't read one another's minds. Thus when Mar-Yilot dove out the window, Terril shot out afterward, and Joooms's water projectile had also knocked him from the sky.

Mar-Yilot managed to soften her fall enough to hit the cobblestones on her human feet. Not so, Terril. He struck the pavement hard enough to bounce twice. His hard shell withstood the shock, but it dazed him, and he lay there motionless for a moment. Mar-Yilot chanced to see him and raced over to try to crush him underfoot. Hearing her approach, he took his human shape. Mar-Yilot growled in frustration at the missed opportunity, but she did manage one well-placed kick before he disappeared. She kicked again at where he'd been, but he'd had the presence of mind to roll aside. She could remain no longer. Joooms *was* throwing down fire now, and flaming balls filled the air above her. Winged again, she soared upward, dodging his fireworks and flying past him to a higher level of the High Fortress. She wanted to check on Rosha.

She found him catching his breath on a stairway. "Are you all right?" she whispered. He just nodded. He hadn't the wind to tell her he'd just battled five slavers upon this stair; if she glanced around, she could see the evidence for herself. "Good," she grunted. "I don't know how much more I can help you. Both Joooms and Terril are onto me—" She paused, listening for a moment, then raced on. "Even now this fortress is telling them where to find me. Filthy mudgecurdle!" she screamed at the walls, and the corridors all around them filled with flames thrown from her hands. She was angry, and her fires burned hot.

Rosha could hear nothing save his own breathing; but from the satisfied sneer on Mar-Yilot's face, he gathered that the fortress was howling in agony. He felt none of her satisfaction. The castle's anguish merely saddened him. Like Pahd, it was but a helpless Drax piece in a game played by shapers. Rosha wondered idly if *he* was anything more?

"Must go," Mar-Yilot said. "They've traced me here. If I battle them in your presence, you'll get killed in the backwash. Good luck." Mar-Yilot disappeared.

A moment later Rosha heard something whistle by his head. He gave no thought to it. That was shaper's business, not his. He focused his attention on the battle to come; despite his weariness and the blood that coated his blade, these had been only the preliminary matches. The real fight remained above him.

He lunged up the stairway and rounded the corner that would lead him to Flayh's tower. There he skittered to a stop, struggling to control the nausea the sight of that face always stirred inside of him. His way was blocked by Admon Faye.

"Well." The slaver smiled. "When Lord Flayh sent me word you were on your way up, I'd hoped I might get the chance to renew old acquaintance. I'm sure the pleasure is all mine."

"I'm sure it must be, too," Rosha responded, controlling his stomach. "I can think of no one who might take pleasure at the sight of *you*."

Admon Faye chuckled deep in his throat. "Fine. Well, boy, let's get to the business of gutting you."

Ordinarily they would have been evenly matched, for the slaver was an excellent swordsman. Although Pahd had always held the reputation of the best in the land, he had never dueled Admon Faye, and the slaver's reputation with the blade spanned all three lands. Rosha had battled the slaver before; but at that time, he'd had the advantage. He'd surprised the burly brigand and had wounded him in the back before that clash had truly begun. Even at that, Rosha had been hard-pressed to beat the man.

This time Rosha was at a disadvantage. His combat with Pahd had drained him, emotionally as well as physically. Dispatching the five slavers on the staircase had winded him further. Then he'd had to dash up here. Admon Faye was fresh, and Rosha saw another slaver waiting behind to reinforce his ugly master. Rosha wished Mar-Yilot would make another brief appearance, but she did not. He awaited the slaver's attack, marshalling his strength.

Admon Faye sneered. "You see this lad, little Tibb? He's caused me no end of troubles. Even tore a hole in my back once, and I think he believed he'd killed me. Life is funny, Tibb. When you least expect it, life presents you with an opportunity for vengeance." The slaver danced lightly forward as he said this, and his sword tip came whistling upward. Rosha knocked it away with a jarring clang, and they were into it. The hallway echoed like a forge with the sounds of their hammering.

It was a narrow passageway, unsuited for swordplay. Here again Admon Faye had the advantage, for Rosha threw frequent glances behind him, expecting a new crowd of slavers to rush up at any moment. Admon Faye had the security of protected flanks. He also held a shorter, more maneuverable blade. A chuckle rumbled out of him. He was enjoying this.

Rosha kept Admon Faye back with short thrusts of his greatsword, but the slaver proved nimble. He dodged each of Rosha's jabs, and kept advancing, watching for an opening. He used his ugly smile as a psychological bludgeon, and his eyes bored into those of his young opponent. Rosha was obviously physically weary. Admon Faye sought ways to tire him mentally as well. His eyes darted over Rosha's shoulder, forcing Rosha to step backward and check behind him. When the young warrior's head snapped forward, Admon Faye had advanced another step, and was snickering. A moment later the slaver did this again, with the same result.

"Are you going to back all the way out of the castle?" The slaver grinned. Rosha answered by springing forward. Admon Faye dodged. At the same moment, he flicked his sword across Rosha's face. Only the warrior's quick reflexes saved the tip of his nose. But once more he'd lost ground. He was already feeling exhausted.

Admon Faye bobbed his head, glancing again over Rosha's shoulder. "There's no one there!" the young swordsman bellowed, refusing to be duped again.

"Good," Admon Faye soothed mockingly. "*Don't* look behind you. Why should there be any slavers behind you, responding to the sound of swords clashing in the heart of the fortress?"

Rosha took a chance. He lunged forward mightily, hoping to skewer his adversary. It was not a reasoned maneuver, nor did it prove successful. Admon Faye danced aside again, but this time he threw out a mailed hand to trap Rosha's sword against the wall. He also threw a devastating kick into Rosha's stomach, and the young warrior came loose from his weapon. Admon Faye let the trapped blade clatter to the floor, following up his kick with a diving tackle that knocked Rosha onto his back. They wrestled briefly, but Admon Faye clearly had the upper hand. Rosha felt the slaver's blade against his throat, and all the fight drained out of him. He'd done his best. He'd lost. He wished he'd had a chance to kiss Bronwynn good-bye and wondered briefly if she was even now being trampled by a tugolith . . .

Rosha waited, but the expected slash never came. The blade

lay across his neck, and the slaver's obscene smile remained fixed upon that loathsome face above him, but Admon Faye didn't kill him. Instead, the slaver toppled over.

Rosha wrestled himself away, grabbing for his dagger. By the time he got it out, he realized he didn't need it. He glanced up at the slaver's killer, his jaw sagging open in surprise.

"He's dead," Tibb explained, waving toward the body.

Rosha stared at Tibb in shock.

"I've been planning to kill him a long time, but this was my first chance. You see, he let my best friend die. My only friend." Rosha closed his mouth, but kept on staring. "He's right. Life gives you the opportunity for vengeance at the most unexpected times. And mine was double, because I got to rob him of his." Tibb looked up at Rosha and smiled slightly. "You remember me?"

"No," Rosha murmured.

"You kicked a sword out of my hand once. In Dragonsgate. Nah, you wouldn't remember. I know your wife, though. Nice lady."

Rosha stayed in his place, clutching his knife and watching Tibb's movements. Tibb gazed back at the slaver's body. "It went too fast, though. I wish I'd had time to make him suffer. I wish he'd died a little slower, so I could say, 'Remember Pinter? Well, this is little Tibb's revenge!' That's how I had it planned out in my mind. But then, if I'd done that, *you* wouldn't be alive now, would you?"

"No," Rosha murmured, still watching the weapon in Tibb's hand.

Tibb glanced back at him and suddenly understood. "Oh, no! Look, I'm not getting in your way. I know you're after the little wizard at the top of the stairs. I wish you luck—you're going to need it. I'm just standing here trying to figure out how you can work and plan and scheme for something so long, and then it's over so fast. It's not fair . . ."

Rosha didn't hear Tibb's ruminations. He had already scooped up his sword and bounded up the last stairway.

## CHAPTER NINETEEN

# A Feast Fit for a Tugolith

SYTH POINTED. Although dawn was still several hours away, the top of the High Plateau could be seen for miles, lighted as it was by huge bonfires.

"Is the city burning?" Joss asked.

"No," Dorlyth explained. "It's an old custom—burning the bonfires after victory. Only in this case, they're so certain of triumph that they're celebrating the night before."

"A psychological ploy?" the general suggested, and Syth snorted with grim amusement.

"Hardly. You don't realize yet, General, what a task we face."

"Perhaps that is true. I realize enough, however, to suggest once more that we withdraw." Joss leaned forward. "If there's no chance to win, why not fight another day?"

"Let's ride on," Bronwynn growled to Syth, ignoring her general yet again.

"One moment," Syth said, and he turned to look at Dorlyth. "You're hurting, my friend. I can tell by the way you sit in your saddle."

"You scald *your* backside and see how well you ride!" Dorlyth joked, but Syth would not return the smile. He kept his eyes on Dorlyth until the old warrior was forced to admit, "All right, so it hurts. You think that will keep me from this battle?"

"No," Syth murmured, "but I think it ought to slow your getting there. We must hurry, Dorlyth, if we're to reach the base of the plateau by dawn. You can't keep pace. Why not slacken your speed and lead our reinforcements?"

Dorlyth paused then nodded. "I'll not argue, although I'd like to."

Syth barked instructions to his allies, and a Mari contingent broke off from the main force to join Dorlyth. Then the united armies were off again, hastening toward the brightly lighted plateau.

They made good progress, reaching the High Plateau as dawn seeped slowly through the snow-laden clouds. The chill, somber light befitted the grim scene as Syth, Bronwynn and Joss rode through the wreckage of Kam's castle. Syth had thought himself prepared for the worst. He discovered that he wasn't. "Gone," he groaned in disbelief. "All of it! Everything's completely gone!"

Joss ventured no comment. His counsel had been rejected regularly. He doubted anyone cared to hear his opinion this time.

Bronwynn, too, held her peace. She gazed up the enormous walls of the plateau, trying to make out the High Fortress itself. There, somewhere, was Rosha. It was there she needed to go.

"Suicidal," Syth whispered softly.

Joss couldn't hold his tongue. "I believe I've made use of the same word," he muttered under his breath.

"What kind of evil beasts *do* such a thing?" the Lord Seriliath pleaded to the gray heavens.

"The beasts aren't evil. Their keepers are," Bronwynn said flatly. She felt nothing for this place nor for the grand family that had called it home. To her they were only names. But Syth felt much, and her passionless statement sparked his temper.

"You're an expert on these tugoliths?" he snapped.

Bronwynn looked at him. "I've offended you. I'm sorry. Pardon my callous manner, but I only stated a fact."

Syth ignored her apology and issued a brisk order. "Joss, prepare your people to flee at the first sign of these beasts. I'll go ready mine to do the same."

"I thought we had planned this frontal assault to distract Flayh's attention from his own fortress," the queen said quietly.

"When he has beasts who can do *this* to send against us? Look at this! There's not a wall standing! Not a single bone in sight! Consumed. The House of Kam has been consumed! You wish that fate upon your Golden Throng?"

"I thought *you* knew what we were facing, Syth."

"I thought I did, too," he mumbled. "In any case, we've done what we could. If we succeed in drawing Flayh's army out, perhaps that's something. I don't see how sacrificing our people to these monsters can lend any further aid."

"If by our standing we can win Rosha another—"

"Look!" Joss shouted, and his finger stabbed upward toward the top of the Down Road.

The beasts had begun their descent. They moved ponderously, as befitted animals of such enormous size. That was deceptive, however, for their strides were of tremendous length. Before any of the three could shake off the shock, the column was halfway down the mountain.

"Fly!" Syth cried, spurring his steed and wheeling toward his warriors.

Joss flicked his gaze to his queen. Despite Syth's order, he had not forgotten who commanded him. "Do it," Bronwynn grunted. Then she dug her heels into the flanks of her own war horse and rode hard—directly for the foot of the Down Road.

"Bronwynn!" Joss bellowed and, for the first time in his memory, he disobeyed his sworn ruler. He whipped his steed and galloped after her.

They raced across the plain, the tails of their horses streaming in the wind. Less than a hundred yards short of the road, Joss drew alongside Bronwynn and made a grab for her bridle. She reined in and whirled around to face him, her eyes wide with outrage. "What are you doing?" she demanded.

"What are *you* doing?" he shouted back.

"I gave you a command! Obey me!"

"My first duty is to save my queen! These beasts are going to eat you!"

"No, they're not!" she spat, and she spurred her horse forward, flicking her reins from his grasp.

"How do you know?" Joss cried, aghast.

"Because I'm going to talk them out of it!"

Joss sat stiffly in his saddle, watching helplessly as Bronwynn turned onto the Down Road and drew up face-to-face with the leading tugolith. He shook his head in grief. "Just like your father," he murmured mournfully.

* * *

By the time they got halfway down the mountain, Pezi felt rather proud of himself. In fact, he was even feeling kindly toward Admon Faye. After all, but for the slaver's insistence, Pezi would be missing this glorious moment. As it was, he had the best of seats for watching the final victory. He cackled as the warriors below caught sight of his descending beasts and broke ranks. The slaver had been right, of course. After the destruction of Kam's castle, no one would be fool enough to challenge Pezi's beasties. He would certainly receive an exalted place within Flayh's expansive dominion. After all, using tugoliths as battle beasts had been his idea! When the history of this time was written, Pezi felt sure he would loom large upon the pages.

What realm would he be awarded? Lamath, perhaps? He could imagine himself seated upon the throne of the grand old palace, surrounded by beautiful courtesans! Each of them would be holding trays piled high with the most succulent of victual delicacies. He could almost smell the mingling aromas of rare meats and subtle but substantial vegetables...

So lost was Pezi in this delicious daydream that he didn't notice the onrushing rider. Chimolitha had to point Bronwynn out to him.

"Man?" Chim called. Try as she might, Chimolitha simply could never remember Pezi's name—and her memory was exceptionally accurate. "One is coming toward us."

"What?" Pezi grunted, his eyes still closed. "One what?"

"A rider."

The startling thought caught Pezi off guard. "Ridiculous!" He snorted as he opened his eyes. Then he beheld the oncoming queen, and angrily shouted, "Absurd!" She refused to disappear. "Help!" Pezi squealed. He stood up on Chimolitha's head and scrambled around to look back over her tail in search of an escape route. All he saw was a column of gleaming horns. One of those, he knew, belonged to Thuganlitha.

"Man," Chimolitha complained with long-suffering patience. "You're standing in my eye."

"Sorry," Pezi said, and he sat down quickly and pivoted upon his huge rump to face forward again. Then he cringed in fear. Despite the fact that he sat atop what was currently the most powerful weapon in the world, over which he held at least nominal control, and the fact that the lone warrior he faced was a rather slightly built woman, Pezi's heart quailed. Gloom descended upon him. And when Bronwynn spat out her brisk challenge, he was too distraught to argue.

"Stand still!" Bronwynn commanded the tugolith. When the beast heard no countering command from above, Chimolitha obeyed. "Where are you going?" the queen of Chaomonous demanded.

When Pezi still didn't answer, Chimolitha decided she must. "Down," the tugolith replied.

"Why?" Bronwynn asked sharply.

"To kill those people," the tugolith said, waving her horn toward the plain.

Once again, Bronwynn demanded to know, "Why?"

Chimolitha, while quite bright for a tugolith, was hardly quick by human standards. Nevertheless, the greatest genius among generals could not have given a more intelligent reply. "I don't know."

"Did someone tell you to?" Bronwynn asked.

"Someone was going to," the tugolith answered.

"Who?" Bronwynn inquired, and the huge animal rolled her eyes upward to indicate the mass of quivering flesh that trembled atop her skull.

"Pezi!" Bronwynn spat, as if his name was a piece of sewage. "So it's you, is it?"

"What are you going to do with me?" he implored.

"What am I going to do with you? *You* appear to hold the reins of power, seated as you are astride this massive living weapon. What do you intend to do to me?"

Her question jogged Pezi somehow, reminding him what enormous power he did indeed possess. "Eat her!" he shouted to Chimolitha. "Eat her now!"

Chimolitha again rolled her eyes up to look at him. "Why? I like her."

A great deal of suffering and bloodshed might have been averted then had certain tugoliths up the hill exhibited a tiny bit of patience. But tugoliths were not a patient breed, being short on understanding and long on means of expressing irritation. Fifteen tugoliths up the road, Thuganlitha expressed his by horning the beast in front of him. A chain reaction of hornings ensued.

When the tug behind Chimolitha rammed its single gleaming

tusk into her hind quarters, she reacted instinctively. She jumped forward several paces. Her huge body landed only a couple of feet in front of Bronwynn's horse—or rather, where Bronwynn's horse had stood.

At the sight of that monster hurtling toward him, Bronwynn's steed turned tail and raced back down the Down Road. The queen could not control him, which was perhaps a good thing. Thuganlitha had not been content with horning his predecessor just once. As the gored flanks multiplied, the herd of tugoliths stampeded down the remainder of the incline. Bronwynn would surely have been tossed aside or crushed, had her terrified horse not carried her out of the danger.

They broke onto the battlefield, a phalanx of rampaging, wounded monsters. They fanned out across the plain, some running aimlessly, others with deadly purpose. They drove before them a long wave of fleeing warriors warned to run. Some had nevertheless hesitated to watch Bronwynn's conference with the beasts. Those who had delayed too long now paid with their lives.

Oblivious to the thunderlike pounding of tugolith hooves around him, General Joss flogged his war horse toward Bronwynn's side. He avoided being trampled in the same manner he'd avoided being skewered by an arrow in times past—by ignoring the danger and attending to duty. He rode with the fatalistic assurance that when it was time for him to die he would die, and no sooner. He reached his queen's side just as she managed to regain control of her spooked animal. "My Lady, we must—"

"Get to the leader!" Bronwynn screamed, cutting him off. "That's the only way to turn them!"

Joss craned around to look. "Which one?" he cried.

"There!" the queen shouted, spurring her horse forward. "The one with a fat lump on its head!"

Pezi clung to Chimolitha's scaly hide by every means available—arms, legs, toes, fingers, and teeth. He'd even buried his nose in a crevice between two scales. He heard the wind swishing around him, but he didn't feel it. He was in shock. He wondered where they were, but dared not raise his head to look. For a while, he feared that they would race on forever, but soon he felt the beast below him slowing down. He pleaded around teeth clenched upon a bony projection that she not stop suddenly.

Chimolitha came at last to a standstill, and the fat merchant warily raised his head and looked around. What he saw made him weep with frustration. The interfering woman was riding toward them again! He wasted no time in getting down from his perch. He didn't know what Bronwynn's intentions might be, but they certainly could include nothing advantageous to himself. He'd been fortunate enough to survive one headlong charge across this battlefield. He wouldn't subject his overworked heart to another. It took only a moment for him to establish the quickest route back to the Down Road. Then Pezi started running.

Chimolitha seemed rather embarrassed as Bronwynn raced up to greet her. "They stuck me," she started to explain.

"No time for that!" the queen cried breathlessly. She threw up her hand and pointed at those tugoliths who were gleefully mauling warriors. "Can you stop that?" she cried.

Chimolitha swivelled her head to look, then turned back to the queen and shrugged her enormous shoulders. "I will try."

For a beast that appeared so clumsy and slow, Chimolitha moved with amazing speed. Bronwynn charged along in the tugoliths' wake with Joss in frantic pursuit. The animal obviously took her commitments seriously. One by one, she chased down her peers, got their attention with a quick prick of the flanks, then demanded they stop squashing people. Only one gave her any real objection. Not surprisingly, that one was Thuganlitha.

"Stop!" Chimolitha shouted as she rumbled up beside him.

Thug was busily goring a supply wagon. He'd already consumed its contents, including the unfortunate driver. At first he pretended not to understand. "What?"

"Stop!" Chimolitha repeated.

Thug looked around, surveyng all the wonderful people and wagons remaining to be demolished. "Why?" he whined.

This was a question Chimolitha had not yet faced. She turned to look at Bronwynn, who stood in her stirrups watching this confrontation with wide eyes. "Why?" Chimolitha asked the young queen.

"Why! Because it's so dreadfully wrong! It's senseless

slaughter! It's . . ." she paused, searching for the proper words. "It's bad!" Bronwynn blurted, and left it at that.

The tugolith brightened, and turned back to Thuganlitha. "It's bad," Chimolitha explained.

Thuganlitha frowned. Then a wicked little smile curled the corners of his leathery lips. "I *like* bad."

That shocked Chimolitha. "What?" she demanded, and the recalcitrant tug repeated more forcefully, "I *like* bad!"

"No!" Chimolitha growled.

"Yes!" Thug roared back.

"No!" Chim bellowed.

"Yes!" Thuganlitha thundered. To emphasize his point, he rammed his horn through the heavy wagon and flipped it over as effortlessly as if it had been a dried leaf.

Chimolitha lowered her head and stabbed. The sharp tip of her horn pierced deeply into Thuganlitha's hindquarters.

Thug screamed and bolted forward, crashing through the remains of the wagon and dashing onward another fifty feet before turning back to face his nemesis. His giant eyes were bloody with rage, and his voice tore the sky like a trumpet as he shouted at Chimolitha, "I'll kill you!" Evidently, however, he wasn't ready to do that immediately. He wheeled around and shot off across the field, heading for the road up the cliff face. He would go back up to the top of the mountain. There, he remembered, were men who would let him play.

Chimolitha looked back at Bronwynn. "He's going up," she explained.

Bronwynn seized the opportunity. "I want to go up, too. Will you lead me there?"

With a curt nod of assent Chimolitha started off across the field, and Bronwynn swiftly followed her. Joss turned back at last toward his fleeing army, scanning the retreating line in search of a trumpeter. Moments later he'd found one, and the horns of Chaomonous echoed across the bloodstained, trampled snow.

"I'm safe!" Pezi cried aloud as he reached the foot of Down Road. There he fell on his face in the snow and thanked whatever powers had given him the strength to waddle across that vast field of battle. He'd not believed he would make it, what with tugoliths whizzing here and there around him and bodies and equipment tripping him up. His whole life had passed before him—several times, in fact, for it took Pezi a lot longer to cover that wasteland of half-eaten carcasses than it might have a man who was in shape. But he'd made it! His tugoliths were busy doing their nasty work, but there were still plenty of warriors left out on the plain to eat, so they would not finish up until long after he was back inside the High Fortress. Then he could sit back, enjoy a well-deserved victory feast, and start planning how he would rule his new kingdom.

As he got to his feet and started his climb, he wore a smile almost as broad as his belly. He'd come a long way from his days as a petty merchant in Chaomonous. Yes, sir, there was still room at the top for the tough few who were willing to *work* to make their dreams come true.

He heard a rumble behind him. He couldn't believe it. He jerked around in astonishment and froze in place. Thuganlitha! It was Thuganlitha! And he had nowhere to run!

Thug was still snorting with rage when he turned up the road. When he saw Pezi standing there waiting for him, Thug, too, froze in astonishment. This was incredibly good fortune! Thuganlitha smiled and started slowly toward the tubby little merchant.

"Chimolitha?" Pezi croaked, but his voice had been stolen away by terror. "Help?" he whispered again. He finally got his legs to move and started backing away up the road. Although his voice was gone, his mind remained quite active. It had been right here that Queen Bronwynn had talked Chimolitha out of attacking her. If she could do it, perhaps he could do the same! He summoned his courage, found his voice, and shouted, "You'd better not eat me!"

Thuganlitha stopped moving and frowned. "Why not?" he asked.

"Because I'd be dead!" Pezi explained crossly.

"You would?" Thug replied and he puzzled over that a moment. He knew about eating and he knew about dead, but he'd really not connected those two things in his mind.

"That's right," Pezi went on, gaining confidence. "And that would be most unpleasant."

Thuganlitha looked at him. "Un-plea . . ."

"Unpleasant," Pezi reiterated.

"What's that?" the tugolith demanded belligerently.

"Unpleasant? Why, you know. Terrible! Horrible! Bad!"

"Bad?" said Thuganlitha, perking up.

"Yes," Pezi affirmed. *"Bad."*

Pezi had said the wrong word. Thuganlitha's naughty smile returned. "I *like* bad," he said, and he started toward Pezi, his great jaws sagging open.

"You—" Pezi choked "—you what?"

"I like to *do* bad!" Thuganlitha smiled wickedly.

"Wait!" Pezi cried, backing away earnestly. "Let me figure this out! You—you like to do bad things, so if eating me is bad then you—" Pezi suddenly stood his ground and announced, "You cannot eat me!" His new confidence made Thuganlitha pause.

"Why not?" the tugolith snorted.

"Because! I am a *bad* man. To eat me would be a *good* act. Therefore, since you *like* to do bad, you *don't* want to eat me, because that would be good! It's a moral issue, you see."

Thuganlitha was confused. "I don't understand," he complained, and Pezi's spirits brightened.

"Ah, yes, but you don't want to understand. Understanding is *good*, and since you want to do bad, then understanding is not for you at all." As he said this Pezi casually resumed backing away. It was impractical, he knew, to expect that he could hold the beast in check until he could back all the way up the road. His only hope rested on so confusing the tugolith that it would be forced to sit down and think. Then he could escape—or so he hoped!

Thuganlitha plodded up the hill after Pezi, his huge forehead furrowed in thought. "I can't eat you . . ." he said.

"That's right!" Pezi prompted.

". . . because you are bad."

"I am!" Pezi agreed enthusiastically. "Yes, indeed, I am!"

"I'm confused!" Thuganlitha bellowed.

"Good!" Pezi called, looking over his shoulder.

"Confused is good?" Thuganlitha grinned, his sharp teeth gleaming. He gazed at Pezi hungrily. "You confuse me!"

Something in the monster's tone made Pezi turn around and face the beast again. Thuganlitha was salivating, and Pezi's anxiety level shot up. "Yes?" he whined.

"So you're good!" the tugolith trumpeted happily and he went on merrily, "I can eat you!"

"No . . . !" the fat merchant whined plaintively, but it was too late. He suddenly visualized what his own mouth had looked like to his fork all these years—

Then he was gone. Thuganlitha ate Pezi in two huge bites. The merchant who'd devoted a lifetime to gobbling goodies had become a goody himself—and got gobbled.

Lord Syth heard the horns of Chaomonous and swung his charger around. He couldn't imagine what had happened, but he spent no time pondering it. He gave a quick order and Mari trumpets answered those of their southern counterparts. The army of the north wheeled and galloped for the High Plateau.

Syth's retreat had been more orderly than that of the Golden Throng. As a result, there had been fewer Mari casualties. Though they had further to come, his warriors were better prepared for battle. A couple of hundred Chaons preceded them up the road, eagerly following the lead of their queen. Syth honored their courage, but feared for them. If Pahd had properly marshalled his forces in the streets of the city above, these undisciplined Chaons stood little chance of surviving. Perhaps it was prejudice, but Syth thought it only reasonable that it would be his own force, skilled and experienced in the Mari way of battle, who would make the difference—assuming, of course, they were not all swept off the Down Road by some new act of sorcery.

Rocks and garbage began dropping from the cliffs. "Shields up!" Syth ordered, but most of his men had already had the good sense to cover themsleves. No boiling oil or burning pitch fell yet. That made sense. King Pahd had never expected them to advance this far, and had not prepared for such. Syth smiled grimly and raised his own shield against the fusillade of refuse.

There was now as much confusion on top of the plateau as there had been on the plain below less than an hour before. The destruction of the enemy by the tugolith had been so certain that no one had established any defensive strategy. Since there had never been any previous assault upon the city itself, the jorls and shurls loyal to Pahd were uncertain what its weak points would be. There were many things that could be done, of course, and not one of them thought for a moment that Syth and his allies would actually succeed in taking Ngandib. But decisions needed to be made immediately—and King Pahd was not to be found.

There was no shortage of leaders shouting orders. Most prominent among them was Janos, Pahd's cousin, who had long been Jorl of the Nethermar and was also the newly elected Citylord of Carlog. His contingent was the largest, aside from that from the capital city itself, and his intimacy with the king demanded respect. But Janos was arrogant and rude, and the men of the High City had never liked him. Despite this present threat, they chose to wait for Pahd to lead them. A messenger was dispatched to the fortress to inform the king of these developments.

Thuganlitha had already reached the top of the road when the rider returned with startling news. He couldn't get into the castle, but those on the walls had shouted down that King Pahd was dead. It was rumored that he'd been slain by traitors among his own palace guard. As the tugolith churned toward them, the men of the city quailed and fled. In its moment of crisis, the Mar was leaderless.

Janos was enraged, both by their cowardice and their unwillingness to accept his leadership. He barked an order, and those who served him lined up across the main thoroughfare, facing the Down Road. They didn't have long to wait.

Chimolitha rumbled up onto the High Plateau. Not two steps behind the huge beast came Queen Bronwynn. Janos was shocked. He'd expected warriors, not a woman. Yet this woman was evidently a warrior as well. Her visage was fierce, and her tawny hair streamed from beneath a golden helmet. Her sword was out, and now she waved it toward the High Fortress and shrieked a savage battle cry. Gilded soldiers were spilling onto the plateau behind her. Janos raised his weapon and gave the command to charge.

Only a few obeyed him, for obvious reasons. Chimolitha was lumbering toward them, the golden queen at her side. Suddenly the beast stopped.

"Thug has gone back," the tug explained apologetically to Bronwynn.

"Then go find him!" Bronwynn shouted, adrenaline coursing through her in anticipation of battle. "I'll follow you there!"

"I can't," the tugolith told her.

"Why not?"

"There are men in the way."

It took Bronwynn a moment to comprehend the problem. She glanced at Janos's line, then cried, "Just run them down!"

Chimolitha gave the queen her most puzzled look. "I can't," she whined again, and Bronwynn demanded to know why. "It's bad," Chimolitha explained, and her huge eyes pleaded with Bronwynn for understanding. Chimolitha had two great virtues—a moral sense and a memory. If it was wrong to squash men on the field below, it was wrong to do so now. The young queen suddenly understood.

"You're right, my friend. This is our battle. Stay here." Bronwynn wheeled her horse back toward the High Fortress and screamed the command to attack. It was lost in the noises of warfare, for already the flanks had clashed together. She spurred her horse forward and closed the gap in the middle, riding hard for Janos. Her subjects swarmed in behind her, giving the watching tugolith a wide berth. As this wave broke on the defensive wall, the Mari warriors had to give ground. They were quickly reinforced, however, by the men of the city. Despite their hatred for Flayh and mistrust for Janos, they hated foreigners more. Those Chaons were invading their home!

Janos smirked as the woman rode toward him, expecting easy prey. He was unprepared for her shrewd handling of a blade. He had no way of knowing she'd been schooled in the arts of war by Admon Faye himself. Eventually his superior size and strength prevailed, and he was able to drive her back. He couldn't manage to wound her, however, nor to knock her from her steed.

Bronwynn broke off and moved further down the line. Her concern was not to win individual duals, but to get through this wall of Maris and closer to Rosha. She was not a strategist. She could provide little leadership for her valiant cohorts, excepting that of example. So believing, she whirled toward a new opponent and attacked him. This man was less fortunate than Janos. He dropped from his saddle, gushing blood.

Syth and his warriors had finally reached the top of the road. A plan had already formed in his mind, and a quick glance at the situation assured him it had a chance of working. He broke off toward the right, leading his riders around the northern rim of the plateau.

Janos saw the maneuver. "Qirl! Ngarl!" he shouted to a pair

of his lords still in the rear. "Mod Syth is circling! Cut him off!" Men sprang quickly to obey. The battle for Ngandib had started to radiate outward through the city.

In the midst of the struggle, Chimolitha stood calmly in her place. She gave little heed to the confusion all around her. She didn't understand any of it, but she was used to not understanding the things that mankind did. She had done what she'd been told by a lady that she liked. That was good. And the lady had told her to wait here. She gazed placidly over the heads of the combatants at the high-gabled townhouses along the street and waited.

"Why me?" Joooms asked quietly. "Why not you?"

"Because Lord Flayh put me in charge, and I'm commanding *you* to do it!" Terril thundered.

"The man must be beside himself," the dark wizard said dryly. "And so must you, to choose to battle Mar-Yilot on your own and let me play with the armies. But fair enough. I'll be in the city, if you need me."

"I can handle her by myself!" the twin-killer shouted, and Joooms's only response was a chuckle that disappeared as he took his altershape. An instant later the lizard had skittered down a stairwell and was gone.

—She's behind you, the High Fortress warned.

Terril instinctively cloaked himself and dodged aside. A sword that would certainly have impaled him whizzed on down the corridor, and Mar-Yilot muttered a new string of curses at the castle. Terril pinpointed the source of the sound. He dropped his cloak long enough to shoot a thought at a beam right above her invisible form. It ripped out of the wall and crashed to the floor, bringing a large chunk of the floor above with it. Through the dust, Terril made out a butterfly gliding upward. It escaped through the newly made hole in the ceiling into the next level, and it was Terril's turn to swear.

—You pair of foul insects! The High Fortress protested. Is it not enough to torment this house? Must you wreck its structure as well?

Terril had no time to argue. Trapped by his own choosing in a singlehanded struggle for his life, he had time only to respond to attacks. And he was terrified by the possibilities.

Joooms had already started down the stable stairs when he

discovered they were no longer there. They had been burned away by Mar-Yilot's fire. He fell into the ashes. It was a long drop, but his lizard form absorbed such shocks well. He rolled onto his four legs with a flick of his tail and looked around.

He'd come in search of a horse. There were none. What he did see was a tugolith, who appeared to be cowering in a charred corner. "Hello there," he said, taking his human shape right in Thuganlitha's face. The tug grunted in surprise, and backed further into the corner. "Aren't you supposed to be mauling people out on the battlefield?"

The tugolith seemed chagrined. "I can't," Thuganlitha answered.

"Why not?"

"Chimolitha stuck me."

"I see." Joooms nodded. "Well I happen to need a mount and there are no horses available. Would you be willing to carry me?"

Thuganlitha didn't know how to respond. He didn't much like the idea of going back out to face Chimolitha, however. "I'll eat you!" he threatened, hoping to chase the man away.

"No, you won't," Joooms said and he climbed onto Thug's head. "Let's go," he ordered.

"I won't," Thug grumbled. A moment later a ball of flame exploded under his belly, and Thuganlitha bolted out of the stables, content that here, at last, was a man who could enforce his directives.

As they rumbled down the main street, Joooms studied the action. He saw Ngarl and Qirl leading a group of warriors toward the north and decided to follow them. "That way," he told Thuganlitha, and the beast dutifully turned the corner. When they turned westward again on the next major artery, they barrelled into the thick of a battle. Syth mod Syth-el had made good progress toward the castle, and the city's defenders were going to be hard-pressed to stop them. The tugolith's appearance turned the tide immediately.

It surprised Joooms to see Syth. He had never before seen him in battle. Although they'd been on opposite sides many times, Mar-Yilot had always had Syth carefully cloaked. But Mar-Yilot was busy, Joooms remembered with some satisfaction. He bore no animosity toward Syth. But Joooms had battled Mar-Yilot all morning, and this was merely an extension of that same struggle. His purpose was to do injury to the Autumn Lady, and nothing could injure her more than the death of this warrior. "That man," Joooms said to Thuganlitha as he pointed. "Trample him." The tugolith gave a happy trumpet, and charged.

Syth saw the monster coming. He glanced around for some route of escape, but his way was blocked on all sides by horses and riders. Then he saw Joooms on the tugolith's back and realized there was no chance. Other men were being trampled, but only because they happened to be in the way. The beast was coming for him. Syth glanced up at the High Fortress, bidding a bittersweet good-bye to his lady. When he looked back, monster and magician had disappeared—just as he'd known they would. But he could still hear the rumble of the heavy beast's horrible hooves.

Mar-Yilot was ducking around a corner when it struck her that Joooms was gone. An inexplicable fear clutched her. She dove recklessly for the nearest window, and beat the air with her wings, seeking a breeze that would carry her over the battlefield.

"Where is she?" Terril demanded a moment later.

—She has left. Good riddance! The High Fortress replied.

Terril, too, found a window, and flew out in pursuit. He had more speed than Mar-Yilot; but if she caught a wind, those widespread wings would carry her off like a sail. If he could only brush her butterfly body, he could stun her to the ground, but first he had to catch her.

The city lay spread out below her, and she marveled at what she beheld. The allied attackers had reached the plateau! She sought out the banner of Sythia Isle and dropped toward them. Suddenly Terril buzzed before her, cutting her off. She dodged around him—an easy trick, since her own form of flight was so erratic in contrast to his. The sugar-clawsp moved quickly, though, and he blocked her again. He swooped toward her, trying desperately to brush her with his purple shell. Again she fluttered aside.

When Terril buzzed toward her again, she was ready. She timed her transformation perfectly. There, in midair, she took her human shape and clapped the insect between her two palms. "Got you!" she shouted as again she donned her altershape. Then she glided onward toward the pennants of Syth. The body of Terril the twin-killer plummeted from the sky and smashed through a housetop. He was already dead, however. He'd thought his last thought within the stinking body he despised and died as a squashed insect.

Mar-Yilot soared above the skirmish, frantically scanning the faces of the living. Things were going badly for Syth's men. The city's defenders were driving them back toward the edge of the cliff. Mar-Yilot made no effort to protect them. She had other concerns that drove her desperately on, fluttering back and forth above the heads of the battlers. Her hope was fading fast. Then she saw his body and dived toward it.

She alighted beside him, a woman again, and knelt to touch his face. "Syth," she called quietly. "Syth." The battle still swirled around her, but she was oblivious to it as she called his name over and over and stroked his thick black hair. Only a tugolith could have so utterly crushed and ruined his handsome body. And she'd not been here to protect him! She dropped her head to his chest to listen. Was it wishful thinking, or was there a faint rhythm still to his heart?

"My Lady!" pleaded a voice nearby, and she glanced up to see a warrior from the Isle reaching out his free hand in supplication. "Autumn Lady, defend us!" he cried as a pair of Ngarl's swordsmen fell upon him.

Mar-Yilot blinked. She knew what Syth would do. Syth would help. But she was not Syth. She was Mar-Yilot, and her first and only concern was preserving her husband's fragile hold on life. Ignoring the warrior's pleas, she pulled a magic cloak around Syth and herself. Then she bent her head across his chest and wept with mingled fear and relief.

It snowed. Large, fluffy flakes drifted out of the sky. On the plain below, the tugoliths frolicked in excitement. Gerrig could have seen them if he'd looked over his shoulder. He and those with him had been driven near to the edge of the cliff. He had no time, though, to look at anything save the weapons that sliced toward him.

The snow made the cobbled streets slick. Between parries, he shifted his feet in search of more secure footing. All around him men were slipping. Some never had the chance to get back up. Others had already taken too many steps backward and fallen off the High Plateau. Gerrig certainly would have panicked if he'd had a chance to think about it, but he was too busy surviving to think at all. He could see Bronwynn about thirty feet in front of him. She was still mounted and still dealing misery to anyone with the temerity to challenge her. But the burst of power, the magical explosion that Gerrig and his comrades kept expecting, had still not materialized. She was proving to be a wonderful warrior, but at the moment they needed her to be much more.

Syth's flanking attack had evidently collapsed. Mari defenders swarmed in from the right side. The top of the Down Road was also to Gerrig's right, and a quick glance that way told him that soon the enemy would control it, cutting off any possibility of retreat. He longed for an intermission, but none was forthcoming. Suddenly the screams behind him took on a very different quality, and he looked around to see what caused the change.

He saw, yet didn't see. Something huge and very noisy was coming around the northern rim, but it was also completely invisible. Gerrig could see the terrified warriors it was knocking over the cliff, as well as those it trampled underfoot. But he couldn't see the beast itself. "Magic," he gasped, and the Mari he'd been fighting grunted agreement. Gerrig glanced around to see that his opponent, too, was staring at the spectacle. He brought his sword scything around across the other man's unprotected belly, chopping a deep gash there. Soon the cobbled street was even more slippery; but, at least for a moment, he was free. He stepped carefully toward his right to get a better view.

It had to be a tugolith. Gerrig didn't know much about them, other than what he'd learned today. But he *had* heard the story of how Pelmen was almost pulled apart by a pair of these beasts and how quick wits and a smooth tongue got him free. Gerrig believed himself to be at least as quick-witted as his old acting partner, and even more loquacious. Perhaps he could turn that talent to advantage?

Certainly somebody had to do something. The cloaked monster was drawing very near. Gerrig realized he'd taken refuge in the shadow of another tugolith, the beast that had led Bronwynn up the Down Road. With a boldness born of years of facing potentially hostile audiences, Gerrig tapped Chimolitha on the hind leg. "Excuse me?" he called.

Chimolitha had been at peace until she felt this annoying tapping. She turned around to see what was causing it, very nearly crushing Gerrig in the process. "What?" she demanded, dropping one enormous eyes down to stare the player in the face.

Gerrig swallowed. Despite his own rather large size, this eye alone stretched from his waist to several inches above his head. It was impressive, to say the least. He smiled. "Hello."

"Hello," Chimolitha answered politely.

"Ah . . . are you on our side?" Gerrig asked.

The tugolith was puzzled. "What side?"

"The side that Queen Bronwynn is on," Gerrig explained quickly.

"Who?"

"Queen Bronwynn! That lady there." Gerrig pointed.

Chimolitha looked over her shoulder. "I like that lady," she said gravely.

"Good!" Gerrig said enthusiastically. "That's great to hear! You see that thing coming toward us?" he continued, pointing now at the invisible Thuganlitha.

Chimolitha looked in that direction. "No," she replied honestly.

"That's right. Of course, you don't see *it*, but can't you see what it's doing?"

"What's *it*?" Chimolitha asked, frowning. Already this conversation was well beyond her, but she kept struggling to comprehend.

"I think it's a tugolith," Gerrig murmured quietly. "Cloaked, of course, so there's a powershaper involved. But it's destroying our side! You've got to do something!" Indeed, the invisible beast was coming closer by the second. Gerrig's voice reflected a trace of panic.

"What side?" the bewildered tugolith asked. She still hadn't figured out that concept, yet this strange man kept on using it anyway.

"*Our* side! The friends of Queen Bronwynn! Look, that tugolith is right there! Do something!"

"Where?" Chimolitha asked, dancing with anxiety.

"Right there!" Gerrig pointed, moving away from her giant feet with no little anxiety of his own.

"I don't see!" Chimolitha cried frantically. This stress had unnerved her.

"No! It's invisible! But look where it's squashing those men!"

Chimolitha stopped jumping and frowned. "That's bad," she grunted.

"You better believe it," Gerrig earnestly agreed.

Chimolitha understood almost nothing of what was going on. This was a perplexing climax to what had already been a most confusing day. But one thing did make sense. Where there was bad, there was usually Thuganlitha. That was something she could deal with. "Thuganlitha?" Chimolitha trumpeted. "Are you there?"

"Yes," came a petulant reply out of nowhere.

"Don't talk," another disembodied voice commanded, and the sound of it caused Gerrig to quake in terror. Granted, he'd recognized this as the handiwork of a shaper, but what little he knew about shaping had convinced him that the magician himself would be somewhere miles away. This voice had clearly come from the hidden tugolith's head! Gerrig swung around behind Chimolitha's hindquarters in the hopes of not being noticed. He had courage to spare, but no one ever accused him of being foolhardy.

"Why can't I see you?" Chim asked Thug.

"I don't know," Thuganlitha replied, and once again the sorcerer's voice said:

"I told you not to talk!"

"But she asked me," Thuganlitha explained, despite the magician's shooshing whisper.

What Gerrig knew of magic he had learned from Yona Parmi, who'd gotten his information from Pelmen. One thing Yona had emphasized stuck now in Gerrig's mind. A power-shaper could only do one thing at a time. Whoever sat on the back of that beast was shielding himself and the tugolith from view. As long as the shaper was busy doing that, Gerrig could feel relatively safe. That gave the player an idea.

"Thuganlitha, you are bad," Chimolitha announced.

"I like bad," Thug agreed pugnaciously.

"I'm going to horn you."

"I'll horn you first!"

"Be quiet, both of you!" Joooms shouted. "Neither of you

shall horn the other! You must cease this arguing and trample the remainder of these golden-mailed warriors!"

"What's golden?" Thuganlitha asked.

"Trampling men is bad!" Chimolitha shouted, frowning reprovingly.

"Only if you trample on the wrong men!" Joooms instructed. "It's good if you trample on the—augh!"

"Man?" Thuganlitha said, "something is climbing on me." But the tugolith's warning came too late. Gerrig's blind sword thrust had struck soft flesh, and Joooms was wearing no armor. The shaper fell from his perch, clutching his rump, and immediately magician and tugolith alike became visible to all. Gerrig never saw the dark-skinned wizard alter his shape and skitter away, leaving a piece of his tail behind to thrash in the snow. The actor was too busy rolling across the cobblestones, away from those stamping hooves.

At the sight of Thuganlitha before her, Chimolitha had trumpeted and charged.

They crossed horns. Those mighty tusks clacked together with the jarring impact of a pair of tree trunks. Up the street, where Bronwynn fought on, the battle raged unabated. But the combatants who were clustered around the top of the Down Road stopped fighting and searched for a place to hide while this battle of behemoths unfolded.

The horns clacked together again, the sound accompanied by a pair of tugolith bellows. The two beasts began circling one another, their huge eyes bloodshot with rage. This was an old grudge, and the battle had long been delayed. They'd never liked each other from the day their mother calfed them, and all toleration had vanished in the violent events of the morning. They circled. Then Thug lunged forward. He'd always been impulsive, and never as bright as his sister. She'd stepped aside, turning her head to gore him as he thundered past. He wheeled about, screaming in pain and frustration, and launched another charge at her. When she tried to skip away again he moved with her. He buried his horn three feet into her fore-quarters, and it was Chim's turn now to cry.

Thug backed up and took aim again. Chim was wounded now, and moving more slowly. He darted for her side, and only her quick leap forward prevented Chim from taking another devastating puncture. As it was, he didn't miss her completely. A new streak of blood marked her hindquarters. But she gave something back in return. Angled as she was, Chim couldn't get her horn into him, but she could swing her head. She slung it around, slamming it into his hind leg. Thug wasn't cut, but he was bruised, an Chimolitha swung back to face him head on. They trumpeted their challenges, and once more Thuganlitha charged. Chimolitha wisely stepped to the other side this time. Thuganlitha raced past her unchecked, and launched himself out into space. He'd run off the top of the High Plateau.

Chimolitha whirled around to face him. She was greatly surprised when he wasn't there. "Thuganlitha? Thuganlitha! Why can't I see you? Are you there? Thuganlitha!" Certain that her antagonist was once again playing tricks on her vision, she wandered off around the northern rim, calling the name of an adversary who could no longer hear at all.

Behind her, the interrupted battle resumed. Now, however, things were worse than ever for Bronwynn's beleaguered band. They were completely encircled, and Janos was tightening the noose.

## CHAPTER TWENTY

# The Opening Gate

ROSHA PAUSED before the door, battling his memory and his fear. The last time he'd stood here, he'd been an arrogant fool. Was he any different now? He and Mar-Yilot had never discussed what they would do if he got this far—perhaps because neither of them expected he would. Was she covering him at this moment? He wished he could understand the speech of the walls.

He was but a plaything of powers, he thought to himself, but he felt no bitterness at that—only an aching pain that he had managed to come so far but was so unequal to the task. If Pelmen were only here, he would—

What would Pelmen do? The answer hit Rosha with a shock of realization. Pelmen would do nothing. Pelmen would let the Power do it.

Suddenly the young warrior felt new strength in his arms and new breath in his lungs. He charged forward. He slammed through Flayh's door and leaped to the center of the room, swinging his great sword before him in a grand arc. Anyone seated there would have been decapitated immediately. Of course, no one was.

"Was that your entire plan?" a voice asked from the corner, and Rosha whirled to face Flayh once again. Then he froze as he watched a beautiful ball of green flame explode before him. His sword slipped from his fingers. A chill crawled up his body, starting in his toes and numbing him slowly from the floor up. As it touched his throat it choked off his voice; as it touched his mind it erased all possible options of escape. It left only a portion of his thought processes free—enough for him to recognize what was happening to him.

Then he began to see the fears and miseries of all mankind become a vivid part of his own experience. Failure, hatred, disappointment, disease, grief—he participated vicariously in every horror. The most telling burden of all was his realization that he was powerless to change it, and that he was just as lost as all of those whose cries of misery he had heard. This was the dread, the *true* dread that had condemned Lord Syth to days of hell. Now it consumed Rosha. He wanted to scream, but that release was denied him. There was no release available.

"That was it?" Flayh asked pleasantly. "To rush in here, whirling a sword about? What foolishness. What waste! Oh, not for me. Those bodies you left on the stairs are no concern of mine. But what a waste for you. All that effort, with not a thing to show for it." Flayh paced around Rosha and picked his book up off the lectern. "I was just about to depart when the castle told me of how the little slaver had knifed his master in the back. Such treachery intrigued me. Then I grew curious, wondering just how you planned to challenge me. I thought you must certainly have some other stratagem besides the one that failed so miserably the last time you came leaping into this room. How anticlimactic. I'm disappointed. On the other hand, you've never impressed me as a man of subtle thought."

The sorcerer walked to the black drapes and threw them aside. He winced at the bright light that streamed in the window. Down in the city it was still snowing; but here above the clouds, the sun burned brilliantly.

"Your friend Pelmen has just revealed his location to me, so I must be off. And you, my insistent young gadfly, must be off as well. Of course, you left by air the last time, too," Flayh said as he opened the door to the balcony. "But that was through the back window, and you fell into the reservoir. Remarkable, how you managed to clear the wall. Perhaps you'll clear the front battlements today! Of course, there's no lake on the front side of this fortress. Only cobbled streets." Flayh turned back to Rosha and summoned him with a wave of his hand. "Come along," he said. "Jump off."

Rosha had no control over his muscles. They now took all orders directly from the powershaper. His legs walked obediently to the opened door and onto the balcony. There they climbed the small balustrade.

Like the frantic flutterings of a trapped bird, Rosha's mind sought some means of survival. Abruptly, however, a calm settled upon him, a peace the young warrior could not account for. He was in dread, yet he was also in the presence of the Power, for the Power was present in him. In that moment Rosha tossed his need for self-control aside and surrendered to the future. Come what might, he suddenly understood the shaping of the Power. Everything was all right. He watched disinterestedly as Flayh caused his legs to throw him off the tower. Then he was falling . . .

Try as she might, Bronwynn couldn't make the magic come. She vented her frustration on a string of foes, yet she made no more progress toward her goal. As her warriors dwindled in number, she began to look behind more than she looked ahead, hoping for some sign of reinforcements coming up the Down Road. Only a fraction of her army had made it up the hill, and she'd not seen General Joss since he turned aside to regroup for the first assault. But the men of the Mar now held the top of the road, and Mari supporters lined the cliffs. Without a tugolith to lead Joss up, any attempt to scale the heights would be senseless—in the general's own words, suicidal.

The queen had started applying that same description to her own situation. Hopelessness stole its way into her spirit, and her arm felt the immediate effects. Suddenly it lost the elasticity, the wiry toughness that had allowed her to sling the sword from side to side all day. She reined her horse away from the fight, seeking refuge in the midst of her faltering force. Her arm dangled limply as she sucked in air, wishing she had some new inspiration to suck in along with it. A moment later, a new wave of sound deepened her despair—the Maris who stood along the cliff were all looking downward and were cheering wildly.

"The tugoliths have returned to their bloody business," she mumbled to herself. That's why Joss hadn't come. The beasts were nothing but huge children. Left to their own devices, they would behave as any group of unsupervised children might—with utmost cruelty. And she could do nothing about it.

The cheers swelled in volume. Bronwynn hung her head in defeat. Then her defiant spirit surged back, and she jerked up to glare savagely at the Mari warriors clustered around the top of the Down Road. Suddenly they were falling back before the object of their adulation, and Bronwynn saw a new troop of warriors gallop onto the High Plateau. Leading that charge was Dorlyth mod Karis, riding upon the steel shoulders of Pelmen's old horse.

Dorlyth had long been a Mari hero. Since leading his people to victory in the Battle of Westmouth, his story had taken on the proportions of a legend. The rumors of his death had traveled widely, but many had disbelieved. Now those who'd scorned the story crowed aloud in their triumph. King Pahd had fallen, and golden-mailed invaders fought in the very heart of the High City. But here was Dorlyth mod Karis, come to lead the Mar to victory once again! Little wonder the people of the city cheered. They were perplexed, however, to see golden warriors riding up behind him. Side by side with Ferlyth came a tall, grim-faced soldier in armor the color of sun!

"General Joss," Bronwynn breathed, and she swung her weary horse and rode wildly out to meet them. All around her, the battle ceased as Mari eyes turned expectantly to watch Dorlyth cut this woman from her saddle. The watchers were astonished when Bronwynn and Dorlyth saluted each other and reined their mounts around to face the fortress.

"You're just in time!" she cried in relief.

"Maybe," he grunted. "Maybe not. Where's Rosha?"

"There!" she shouted, flinging her arm around to point toward the castle.

"Then let's go!" Dorlyth shouted, and Minaliss sprang forward. The ranks of puzzled Maris parted to let them fly past, and soon the great war horse led the invaders to the foot of the High Fortress.

Bronwynn gazed upward, trying to penetrate the mist. The instant she saw the body dropping, she knew who it was. "Rosha!" she screamed in terror and grief. Suddenly Bronwynn leaped into the sky.

She was aware of the wings on her back and the scales on her flanks, but she paid them no heed. The exultation over at last finding her altershape would have to wait. At this moment, she was a golden dragon with a single purpose—to catch her lover before he struck the ground.

As quickly as she thought it, it was done. Rosha landed between her shoulder blades—right between her wings. The impact knocked the breath out of her and nearly slammed her to the ground. She screamed again, in pain this time—a raucous, shrill cry unintelligible in human speech. Then she was rising again, soaring upward, and Rosha was safely with her at last.

"A dragon!" she thought to herself. "My altershape is a dragon!" And the joy of that thought carried her up through the cloud and out of it, into the sunlight above. She glanced down at herself and marveled. She wasn't a very big dragon, true, but she was a dragon just the same. And what other powershaper in all the world could boast such an altershape! She glided in a lazy curve around the castle's uppermost spires and uttered a screech of total joy. Then she dropped back into the clouds, flying with an expertise born of instinct down to rejoin Dorlyth and Joss on the ground.

It was fortunate that she'd chosen that moment to descend. An instant before she touched down, her dragon-form disappeared, and the young queen and her lover bounced unceremoniously across the pavement.

Bronwynn quickly got up onto her skinned knees and looked at Dorlyth in shock. "What happened?" she gasped.

In somber silence, Pelmen and Serphimera had built an altar. It wasn't much—just a pile of rocks stacked against a stone shelf that jutted up from the cave floor. But as they stood beside it, their shadows thrown across it by the radiant object that glowed at their backs, this poor altar seemed to them the holiest spot in the universe. Here they would sacrifice their love and their future in order to redeem the past.

In that moment, it seemed worth it all to both of them. They were, after all, believers, and the Power in which they trusted had cleansed their spirits through an ecstatic experience of its presence. Purity hung in the air like acrid smoke. Nothing about the world outside the cave seemed real any longer; true reality had localized in this place and focused upon this rough, rocky ground.

"It's time," Pelmen said. He climbed onto the altar and stretched out on his back. Serphimera glided wordlessly to her feet. She pivoted around, and her eyes fixed intently on the pointed crystal object. She stepped to it and lifted it gently in her hands, thrilling to its touch. Then she spun again and walked gracefully back to Pelmen's side. "In the heart," he said. She turned the crystal point downward and raised it over her head to strike.

"Stop!" commanded a voice behind her, and Serphimera whirled around in surprise. For one brief instant, hope flared within her. Nothing would please her more than a stay of execution. But the sight of the figure standing in the cave's mouth caused her expression to harden. She felt a chill tingle through her toes. She ignored it, and turned back to her ritual task.

Pelmen was gone. The altar was empty. She gasped in surprise and gasped again when his voice cried up from the altar, "Strike!" By the time it registered with her that, while she couldn't see him, he still was there, she no longer held the crystal thorn. A ball of blazing fire had knocked it from her grasp. She scrambled after it.

"Leave it!" Flayh cried, as he jumped across the cave. When the woman would not obey, he exploded another ball of flame in her face, setting her back on her heels. He couldn't fathom how she'd deflected his spell of dread, but it didn't matter. She was obviously responsive to simple fire. He raced to the gleaming object and grabbed for it. Other, invisible hands closed on it at the same moment and struggled to jerk it away. Flayh won the contest, but only briefly. A fist cracked across his jaw and sent him spinning to the ground. Once again the object bounced away. Another fist struck him, and Flayh roared with anger. This was foolishness. He cloaked himself and bounded after the glistening object. It shot into the air, and Flayh tackled the empty space below it. His arms closed around Pelmen's legs, tripping him to the floor.

Pelmen landed heavily on several sharp rocks projecting from the cave floor and he groaned in pain. He couldn't hold onto the large gem. It flew away and lodged against the wall. Flayh vaulted toward it. Pelmen couldn't see his opponent, but he heard and felt Flayh's movements. He responded by twisting onto his back and throwing his legs into the air. They tangled together with Flayh's, and Pelmen heard the crunch as his opponent took a heavy tumble.

Serphimera crouched beside the altar. Her face and hands burned horribly, but what most concerned her were her eyes. She could hear the shapers struggling but couldn't see them. The afterimage of the flash still partially blinded her, and she worried about permanent damage. She and her lover were in the midst of a struggle. She needed her sight to aid him.

The two shapers rolled apart. Both kept themselves cloaked. Both plotted their shortest route to the magical object, while each tried to outguess the other.

Flayh acted first. Pelmen saw the other wizard briefly appear and immediately disappear again. He lunged for Flayh and grabbed only air. Recovering quickly, he dodged to the side and fastened his gaze on the glowing jewel.

"Here, Pelmen," a voice said from the cave's mouth, and Pelmen jerked his head around to look.

"And here," it spoke again, this time from beyond the altar.

"And here," it said a third time, now from a corner of the cave not three feet from where Pelmen stood. Pelmen was still cloaked in invisibility and had no wish to give himself away. He swivelled his head slowly, to keep the collar of his robe from rustling. He saw Flayh standing next to him, smiling grotesquely toward the center of the cavern, light reflecting off his bald, blue pate.

"You see I can be anywhere—" Flayh began, but he was soon interrupted. A fist split his blue-tinted lip and bloodied his mouth. He howled with rage and leaped magically to the far side of the room, terribly incensed that bad luck had positioned him within Pelmen's striking distance. "I can be anywhere I choose in a moment!" Flayh finished, his smile gone. He bolted out of that spot into another and continued, "That's how I came to be here, Pelmen. Moments ago I was in my tower in Ngandib." Flayh cloaked himself and put up his fists to shield his face. He listened carefully, but Pelmen made no reply.

Flayh turned his attention toward the treasure and watched it a moment. It didn't move. He tiptoed out of that spot, expecting at any moment to collide with his invisible foe. So this was shaper battle, Flayh thought to himself. He wasn't sure he liked it.

Serphimera was up on her knees, staring around at the empty cavern. She could see now. The patterns of light and shadow were different, since the source of their light had shifted over to the wall. She'd come to realize that it was through no fault of her vision that she couldn't see the shapers. They were hidden from one another and from her. At the moment, there was little she could do to help Pelmen except keep quiet. The shapers were using silence as a weapon. She didn't know what effect it might be having on them, but to her it was tortuous.

Flayh broke the tension. "You are skilled, Pelmen, in forcing others to play your game. But isn't it rather childish? You've bloodied my lip like a schoolboy. Doesn't it strike you as silly for the two foremost powershapers in the world to resort to bare knuckles?"

As Flayh spoke, Serphimera felt a reassuring hand on her shoulder. She almost reached up to pat it. Such a gesture would surely draw Flayh's eye. She fought the temptation as Flayh continued. "Very well. If you so choose, follow my voice and strike me again. Come ahead. I've chosen to battle you on *my* terms."

The hand remained on Serphimera's shoulder. Pelmen was not responding to this challenge. Flayh's image flickered into view and abruptly disappeared again. The voice continued from another part of the cave. "I know why you're here. Those poor, howling beasts outside have given you away. They wanted me to free them, you realize. When I wouldn't, they sought out you. And you, replete with moral obligation and ethical sensibility, naturally have agreed."

"It had nothing to do with the dogs," Serphimera said, and Pelmen's invisible hand clenched slightly on her shoulder. She assumed he was trying to silence her, but she saw no need to be quiet now. After all, Flayh could see her clearly.

"Ah," Flayh said. "The woman with the healing touch, I assume? None other than our crazed, dragon-loving priestess. What an unlikely couple! The two of you make a formidable alliance. You realize, of course, that if you follow through with your use of this object, your partnership will be permanently dissolved?"

"We think it's worth the price," the woman responded serenely. She wondered why Pelmen didn't act.

Flayh chuckled. "Serphimera, you're so transparent. Keep me talking while your lover prepares to subdue me, isn't that your intention? But I'm talking to *him*. Pelmen, is it worthwhile to you? Certainly you'll be killed; you've already accepted that sacrifice. But do you want to see her killed, too? She will be, you know. Think of it—all those powers my artistry has rendered into canine form, along with all the other powers who choose to go, departing in a single instant through that little crystal object. Why, the power vacuum that creates will lift the top off this mountain. It will take us *all*. And tell me now, is all this necessary just to defeat me?"

Pelmen spoke. "Your ego is enormous, Flayh."

"Ah-ha!" Flayh crowed. "So he does have a voice."

"I'm not surprised that you believe history revolves around you. It's a common fault of man. And you, Flayh, for all your power, are certainly common."

Flayh's laughter rang out of another section of the cave. Pelmen's hand left Serphimera's shoulder. She immediately felt lonely.

"So you're doing all this out of purer, grander motives, is that it?" Flayh asked. "Would you like to tell me what you hope to achieve?"

"We'd like to change man."

Flayh laughed again. This time he seemed genuinely amused.

"Now who's being egocentric? History revolves not around Flayh, oh no. It centers instead on Pelmen the Player!" When Pelmen did not respond, Flayh went on scornfully, "You think this act of yours will accomplish that?"

"We believe so."

"How? A few words muttered in darkness, a ritual bloodletting, an explosion on a distant mountain peak? Why should that change man? It will please those hounds out there, no question about that. It will suck away my power and Mar-Yilot's and your own. But it won't change man. Most people pay no attention at all to the powers. Magic won't be missed. And power will revert back to where it resided before your interference—to the hands of the Merchant League. You won't change man, Pelmen. You'll only exalt mediocrity. There'll no longer be means for a man to soar to the heights."

"You're wrong, Flayh. Quite wrong. But I doubt you could comprehend the joys of soaring under the Power's control."

"Ridiculous," Flayh grunted. "Meaningless words. Your powers are great, Pelmen, but greatest of all is your power of self-delusion. Your time in Lamath affected your mind. You've been influenced by those fanatics who hungered only to be swallowed by the dragon. What a fool you are, Pelmen, to have had such power and wasted it in foiling me! You could have been king over three lands at once! Now *I* will be, instead. Because, while you've agonized over the responsibilities of power, I've learned how to use it."

"As you see," he finished, and once again his voice had shifted over a wide space in an instant. "You surely understand by now that I could, at any moment, dart over to that beautiful object you've labored so hard to assemble, snatch it up, and begone with it back to my tower."

"Why don't you?" Pelmen asked.

"Because it seems evident I must kill you first. Otherwise I should have to contend with your repeated attempts to overthrow me. Is that not so? And I must remove dear Serphimera from the picture as well, for who can say? She may have the power in her fingertips to resurrect the dead. While I have you here together, it would be inefficient of me not to dispose of you both. Inefficient and dangerous to the new state."

"Meaning yourself," Pelmen said.

"Of course. But don't fear too much for the land's future,

Pelmen. I will be a benevolent despot. I can be a good ruler when my authority is not being regularly challenged."

"But that's just the problem, isn't it, Flayh?"

"What do you mean?"

"There will always be someone to threaten you."

"You think so?" Flayh asked. Then the light disappeared.

While the two men had argued, Serphimera had decided to act. She was tired of being the only participant in this confrontation who could be seen. She'd remedied that, creeping unnoticed to the glowing object, snatching it up and hiding it beneath her voluminous robes. She kept her grip on it, though, so she was ready to wield it as a weapon.

Pelmen and Flayh both shouted in surprise and dashed toward the spot where the jewel had glowed. Serphimera had turned her body toward the source of Flayh's voice, and now she felt Flayh brush against her. How did she know it was he? Smell, perhaps? The boniness of his body, so different from that of her lover? Somehow she knew, and she stabbed upward with the object, burying its point deeply and drawing a scream from the pierced shaper. She jerked it free and stabbed again, this time toward what she thought was his throat.

Flayh's death rattle both relieved and terrified her. The life force of a shaper had been expended, and she had not been obliged to kill her love!

She was certain, however, that neither she nor Pelmen would survive the aftermath. The mountain rumbled and the dogs howled. For one horrible instant, she feared she'd be forced to witness the cataclysmic events she'd set in motion. It was blessedly brief, however. She passed away into darkness.

Noise and light sundered the mountain. The bodies of thousands of dogs dropped lifeless into the snow. The proud, ancient firs of the forest fell prostrate in obeisance. The earth trembled with excitement, the clouds parted, and the sun and stars chorused together in jubilation. Myriads of powers, long lost and lonely, were in that moment reunited with their Maker. And in the process, that fabulous jewel wrought from six perfect diamonds was smashed into powder. The Power's gateway had opened and closed.

The world of men experienced a slight tremor. It was quickly forgotten.

* * *

Rosha sat up and looked at Bronwynn. "It's over," he said.

She'd expected him to be dazed and shaken, but he was alert and very much in control of himself. His eyes troubled her, however, as they met hers. They showed unspeakable suffering and great calm at the same time. "What happened?" she asked again.

"Didn't you feel it?" Rosha asked. "The magic passed. That's why you lost your altershape and why I lost the dread."

"The dread!" Bronwynn gasped in horror. "Flayh laid a dread spell on you?"

"He did—at the same moment the Power took me. And I was aware of all that happened while I lay on your back."

Bronwynn studied him doubtfully. This wasn't the Rosha she'd known. He was different. As he climbed to his feet, there was an attitude of confidence and certainty about his movements. Somehow, he'd finally found himself, and she wasn't sure she liked the change.

But as he reached out to pull her to him and kiss her soundly, she decided she did like it. This was the Rosha she'd always wanted.

"I hate to interrupt . . ." Dorlyth spoke beside them, and Rosha whirled around, delighted shock on his face.

"Father!" he shouted. Holding Bronwynn in his left arm, he reached out with his right to return Dorlyth's embrace. "They told me you were dead!"

"I thought I was, too. But you know how these shapers are, flying off to a new thing before they've finished the old. Rosha, what is all this business? I don't understand at all."

Rosha sighed. "Pelmen and Serphimera remade the ancient weapon that was designed to kill the dragon. And just before he made me jump, Flayh said he was going there to the Mount of Power. With the Power in me, I was aware of the struggle of the three of them for the weapon. Serphimera got it and sacrificed Flayh. Magic departed at that instant, and the top of the mountain blew off. We'll search, of course, but I'm certain all three were destroyed."

Silence greeted his words. Then Dorlyth whispered, "Pelmen gone!"

"And all magic departed," Bronwynn murmured, her gaze far away.

Rosha gave his wife a quick squeeze and then turned to the

crowd clustered around them—Maris mingled with the invaders who had been locked with them in a deadly struggle only minutes before. "Mar-Yilot," he barked. "Has anyone seen Mar-Yilot?"

"I saw her briefly," a Mari warrior volunteered. "Lord Syth was trampled by a tugolith, and she covered them both—"

"Where was this?" Rosha asked. The man pointed. "You, you, and you," Rosha commanded members of the crowd. "Go with this man, find them, and bring them to the castle. You others, start looking among the fallen. We'll bury the dead later, but the wounded must be treated *now*."

He didn't wait to see if his orders were obeyed, but turned to look up at the High Fortress. "Mar-Yilot burned away the stairway," he muttered to himself. "But there must be someone inside." He marched toward the stable entrance, and people parted to let him pass.

The stable was filled with ashes. Rosha stepped over them to gaze up through the castle's open floor. "Anyone up there?" he called.

"I'm here," a voice answered, and the slaver who'd stabbed Admon Faye tossed a rope down through the hole.

"A slaver!" someone who'd followed Rosha snarled.

Rosha smiled grimly. "One who saved my life. Are there other slavers still there?"

"None to give you trouble," Tibb answered. "I let the slaves out of the pit and armed them. They took a bit of vengeance. There's a winch here. Shall I draw you up?"

"In a moment," Rosha called. Then he turned to set the crowd to cleaning the stables and to finding wood to rebuild the staircase. Minutes later, the group he'd sent to find Syth returned, carrying the Lord of Seriliath on an improvised stretcher. Mar-Yilot followed.

"Is he alive?" Rosha asked.

"Barely," she muttered, her eyes averted. There was a sob in her voice as she looked down at her unconscious husband. "And this time, there's no Serphimera to help him with her healing touch!"

"There's one here who can help him," a voice called from above. They all looked up to see a woman peeking through the hole in the ceiling.

"Sarie?" Rosha asked. "Sarie lan Pahd?"

"That's right," Sarie answered. "Let me send you the man who healed me."

A man came sliding down the rope to kneel quickly beside Syth.

"Wait!" Mar-Yilot ordered suspiciously, blocking the man's hands away from Syth. "Who are you?"

"My name is Tahli-Damen," he told her brightly. Clear eyes, freed from the blue haze with the end of magic and spells, locked onto those of Mar-Yilot. "I'm from the Power."

There was the sound of massive feet pounding the ground outside, and the crowd cleared away from the door. Chimolitha stepped carefully inside, with Gerrig sitting gingerly astride her horn.

"Gerrig!" Bronwynn shouted, clapping her hands. "You survived!"

"Yes, your Highness, thanks to this beast. I found her wandering around the streets. I thought she might be able to help us in cleaning up."

"An excellent idea," Rosha said. Then, at someone's cry, he turned to see Syth mod Syth-el's eyes fluttering open.

Syth tried to move his head, found he couldn't, and lay back. He peered curiously up into Rosha's face. "Did we win?"

"We won," Rosha replied, his voice at once sad and proud. "But it cost us."

He looked around and saw that the crowd continued to grow as people from the city shoved their way inside the stable. He raised his hands to get their attention and addressed them all:

"King Pahd is dead. He died honorably, defending his fortress and his family. The intruder who bewitched his family is gone for good. These golden-mailed warriors are merely guests in our city who will soon be returning to their own land.

"Ngandib is once again a free city of the Mari confederacy and will remain so. Your contributions to her defense will long be remembered. Let it be proclaimed through all the streets that the battle is over. Tonight there is a *true* cause for celebration."

Dorlyth beamed with pride. Less than two years before, his son couldn't say a single sentence without stumbling over his own tongue. Now he made speeches in the palace!

Rosha raised his gaze to the entrance to the palace. He nodded. "Perhaps we should get on with the business . . ."

But the murmurs of approval from the crowd were turn to cheers. Then someone raised a shout: "Rosha for citylo... of Ngandib!"

"Rosha for king," another voice cried. "Hail King Rosha, who drove out the evil wizard!" More voices picked it up, giving Rosha no time to correct the idea. Then it was a clamor from all.

By night, it was official. The new king stood with his queen at a palace window, watching the celebrating crowds below. It was then a messenger bird arrived from Lamath.

"What does it say?" Bronwynn asked as Rosha stood frowning over the note.

"It's from Erri," he told her. "He wants us to be king and queen of Lamath. He says it was his idea and that it has finally been voted on. Oh, he also congratulates us on the victory."

Bronwynn nodded. "We'll have to accept. It was always Pelmen's dream to unite the One Land again. But with three capitals, where will we live?"

"Dragonsgate," Rosha told her. "We won't have to reside there all the time, but it's the logical center of the lands. That's why the dragon chose it."

## CHAPTER TWENTY-ONE

# Crowns

SPRING HAD come by the time the crowning of the new king and queen of the One Land could be arranged. But the months before had been busy ones.

The wreckage of the brief war had to be repaired, wounded required healing, and the tugoliths had to be returned to Dolna. Above all, a search for the bodies of Pelmen and Serphimera had to be undertaken.

They were never discovered. The searchers found that the

top of the mountain had been blown off, and the bodies must have been blown to bits or buried under the wreckage. But the remains of Flayh had been tossed to the bottom of the mountain, entangled with the bodies of an immense pack of midnight black dogs. They left it where they'd found it.

Pahd's body was accorded full honors. Along with two empty coffins for Pelmen and Serphimera, his casket was dropped from the top of the Rock of Tombs. Pahd slept at last where he could never be disturbed.

It was left to Kherda to plan the coronation, and the Prime Minister gloried in the task. He was disappointed when Bronwynn vetoed his elaborate plans for a great scaffolding and platform, telling him that the ledge of the dragon's cave was the right place. Hope revived briefly when he visited the place and discovered its condition and the nauseating odor. But Bronwynn was adamant.

"It can be cleaned," she told him. "See to it."

Hordes of workmen were organized and induced to work at immense task. Kherda watched from a safe distance. He soon discovered that, even allowing for some theft by the workers, the jewels mixed among the muck would pay for the labor many times over. And he consoled himself with thoughts of the grand palace he would design for the royal couple.

Even that plan collapsed when the great throne room inside the cave was discovered. In the end, Kherda had to content himself with the building of an impressive stairway up to the cave.

But at last the day arrived.

The parades began, streaming into the Central Gate from each of the three mouths, with musicians from each of the three lands struggling to outdo one another.

Lord Joss led the Golden Throng from Chaomonous. Kherda watched as the general climbed the stairway to the entrance. His face registered only a slight shock as the remaining odor struck his nose, but he took his place stoically.

Dorlyth, mounted on a strangely agitated Minaliss and accompanied by Ferlyth and Bainer, led the Mari lords. Syth was recovering, but still not strong enough for the journey. And Mar-Yilot, slowly learning to cope with her loss of power, elected to remain with him. Even Janos put in an appearance. Maris and Chaons regarded each other cautiously, but both were glad hostilities were ended. New markets and trade were in all minds, now that the old merchant monopolies had collapsed.

The arrival of the Lamathians caused barely a ripple of excitement. The ubiquitous pale blue robes were a common sight now. But when the tugoliths advanced into the pass, Chaon and Mari alike took notice. These were the newest wonders of the world. The huge beasts wore enormous smiles; with Thuganlitha gone, there was much less quarreling.

Last of all, Rosha, Bronwynn, and Erri entered the pass at the same moment, each through a separate mouth. They rode to the center of Dragonsgate, where they dismounted and embraced. Then Erri led the two young sovereigns up the stairway. Loud fanfares greeted their ascent.

"What is *that*?" Erri muttered as he turned to smile and wave at the wildly cheering throng.

"*That* is dragon," Bronwynn said cheerfully. "Just a ghost of what it smelled like when I was here before. Kherda promises it will all be gone after the final washing."

There were solemn vows to be made and oaths to be sworn. Then Erri took up one of the two identical crowns and raised it above his head. Bronwynn knelt.

"I wonder what they think we're saying down there?" Rosha muttered.

Bronwynn chuckled. "The wisest words ever uttered, probably."

"Very well then, let's say them. Remember the Power. All wisdom proceeds from that." Erri smiled and placed the crown on her head.

Bronwynn got to her feet and waved, while the assembled nations cheered loudly. Then Erri picked up the other crown and turned to Rosha. "Do you still feel pain from the memories of the dread?" he asked.

"Some," Rosha murmured as he knelt.

Erri nodded and pressed the crown down on Rosha's thick curls. "That may be good. Some dread may be desirable in a leader. A long memory certainly must be."

Rosha stood to receive the adulation of the crowd. As he gazed down at the sea of faces, he murmured, "Now can we go?"

"Not without saying good-bye," an unexpected voice said from behind them.

The three figures high above the crowd turned their backs on the throng in such precise unison that everyone assumed it had been planned. Suddenly they disappeared into the cave. A moment later, Erri emerged to step quickly down the stairs to the Prime Minister. "Kherda, what's next on the program?"

Kherda was flabbergasted. "Why, the recessional, of course—"

"Not yet. Do something else."

"But—what?"

"Just stall. You know how, I'm sure." Erri started back up the stairs.

"Wait!" Kherda cried. "What are you discussing?"

Erri smiled mysteriously. "Secrets. Matters of faith," he said. Then he popped back inside the cave.

Kherda sighed, wishing they'd let him know before they changed the ritual. But he had the coronation to control and little time for resentment. He called upon years of experience as a professional courtling and stalled.

Erri found Pelmen embracing Bronwynn and Serphimera in a crushing hug from Rosha. "Where have you been?" the new king of the One Land was demanding.

"On our way here," Serphimera answered. "At least, we've been for the last two weeks. Before that we were—sleeping."

Bronwynn peered at Pelmen. "Where?"

"Underneath the mountain."

"How did you survive?" Erri asked.

"In your own words, remember the Power!" Pelmen looked at the three, smiling. "I assume that the Power saved us."

"And the explosion?"

"I never heard the explosion. I woke in darkness with Serphimera beside me. It took us a while to convince ourselves that we weren't some kind of shades, but then we started looking for a way out."

"We were in a tunnel of some kind," Serphimera added. "When we reached the end of it, we found ourselves climbing out in the middle of the Great North Fir. Then we heard of the coronation and came here to wait. We couldn't miss that."

"But how did you see to get out?" Rosha asked.

Pelmen shrugged. "We had light." He stretched out his hand

before him, and suddenly a globe of blue flame burst into life above his palm.

"Shaping!" Rosha whispered in shocked surprise. "Then magic isn't gone! Some of the powers haven't left?"

"Some apparently never leave. They're just not ready for new discoverers."

Rosha and Bronwynn stared at their friends in surprised delight. Erri stood to one side, chuckling.

"We buried you," Rosha remembered suddenly. "We've got to tell the people you're alive!" He started for the cave mouth. Pelmen grabbed his wrist and pulled him back.

"Please," Pelmen said quietly. "Don't do that."

"Why not?"

Pelmen looked at Serphimera. "It's very pleasant for us now—a welcome rest. Give us that. Then, after you've moved into this underground castle, we'll find you from time to time. There are corridors that lead to other entrances, and we can come and go without being noticed."

Rosha looked back and forth between them, then nodded slowly. "So be it," he said. He glanced at his wife. "That's all right with you?"

Bronwynn smiled. "It is indeed."

"Good," Rosha said. he grabbed his wife and the prophet by their hands. "Come on. We've a coronation to conclude." They started for the mouth of the old twi-beast's lair, but there Rosha paused and looked over his shoulder.

"We'll see you later," he said firmly.

Pelmen the powershaper smiled. "We'll come."

Then the new King and Queen of the One Land stepped back into the sunshine to accept the rights and responsibilities of their realm. As he smiled down at his new subjects, Rosha permitted himself a quick glance over the shoulder. But Pelman and Serphimera had already gone. His throat ached with a touch of sorrow, but he quickly overcame it. This was a day of joy. He raised his hand high above his head, and waved.

# Glossary

Admon Faye: An obscenely ugly slaver and outlaw, chosen by Flayh to be head of security in the High Fortress.

Agarnalath: A warrior of Lamath.

Asher: Once Chieftain of Defense and Expansion of Lamath, he was eaten by Vicia-Heinox while helping Pelmen to kill the beast.

Bainer: A Mari warrior allied to Syth and Mar-Yilot.

Barleb: Operator of the barge between the North Coast and Sythia Isle and a servant of Syth.

Belra: A Mari warrior, Citylord of Garnabel and Shurl of the Upper Coast, allied with Dorlyth against Pahd mod Pahd-el.

Blez: One of the ancient trading houses participating in the Council of Elders, the merchant monopoly.

Blue flyer: A magical breed of bird used to carry messages over long distances.

Bronwynn: Queen of Chaomonous, wife to Rosha mod Dorlyth, and long a friend of Pelmen Dragonsbane.

Carlog: One of the larger cities of Ngandib-Mar, located in the Furrowmar region.

Cerdeb: A Mari leader from the Downlands region allied to Syth mod Syth-el.

Chanos: A lord of Ngandib-Mar loyal to King Pahd with a long personal grudge against Tuckad.

Chaomonous: "The Golden Land," the largest of the three nations clustered around Dragonsgate, ruled by Queen Bronwynn.

Chimolitha: "Chim," a pleasant-tempered tugolith who was involved in the near execution of Pelmen and who helped him survive.

Chogi lan Pahd-el: Mother of King Pahd mod Pahd-el and a powerful force in the administration of Ngandib-Mar.

Clawsp: *See* Sugar-clawsp.

Danyilyn: A professional actress in Chaomonous and a close friend of Pelmen.

Dolna: Official handler of tugoliths in Lamath.

Downlands: One of the six regions of Ngandib-Mar, located far to the south in the area of Arl Lake.

Dorlyth mod Karis: Warrior, hero, father to Rosha mod Dorlyth and friend to Pelmen Dragonsbane. He was made Jorl of the Westmouth by Pahd mod Pahd-el for his victory over Chaomonous.

Dragonfaith: The ancient religion of Lamath, centered on worship of the two-headed dragon.

Dragonsgate: The central mountain pass connecting Lamath, Chaomonous and Ngandib-Mar, formerly the home of Vicia-Heinox.

Drax: A three-sided table game played throughout the three lands, usually with wagers on the outcome.

Erri: The Prophet of Lamath and chief architect of the growth of the skyfaith, as well as the potential ruler of Lamath.

Ferlyth mod Kerlyth: Cousin and ally of Dorlyth mod Karis and Jorl of the Furrowmar.

Flayh: Once the ruling elder of the trading house of Ognadzu, now an immensely powerful wizard residing in the High Fortress of Ngandib. His altershape is the dog.

Furrowmar: One of the six regions of Ngandib-Mar composed of the highland farmlands in the central west.

Garnabel: A large city in Ngandib-Mar, located in the Furrowmar.

Gerrig: A professional actor in Chaomonous and close friend of Pelmen.

Golden Throng: The army of Chaomonous.

Hann: One of the merchant families participating in the Council of Elders, the merchant monopoly.

High Fortress of Ngandib: The ancient castle situated on a spur jutting from the High Plateau that was the home of Pahd, which was brought magically to life by Flayh.

High Plateau: The outcropping of rock in central Ngandib-Mar upon which the city of Ngandib was built.

Imperial House of Chaomonous: The royal palace of the ruling family of Chaomonous, brought to life before the making of the dragon by the wizard Nobalog.

The Isles: One of the six regions in Ngandib-Mar, composed of all the islands off the North Coast in the far north of the land.

Jagd: Ruling Elder of the trading family of Uda, residing in Chaomonous.

Janos mod Jerrid: Cousin to Pahd mod Pahd-el, Jorl of the Nethermar, and ally with Pahd against the rebels of the North Coast.

Joooms: A Mari powershaper of dark complexion and secretive nature, known for his greed. His altershape is the lizard.

Jorl: Administrative head of one of the six regions of Ngandib-Mar and a hereditary title. Upon the death of a Jorl without an heir, the title is conferred upon an individual of the King's choice.

Joss: General of the Golden Throng, long-time Lord of War for Chaomonous, appointed Ambassador to Lamath by Queen Bronwynn.

Kam: A lord of Ngandib-Mar whose lands touch the base of the High Plateau, and who is allied with Syth against Pahd.

Kherda: Prime Minister of the land of Chaomonous.

Lamath: The large coastal kingdom north of Dragonsgate, long ruled by a weak king in consultation with the leaders of the Dragonfaith, now ruled by the Prophet of Lamath.

Laph mod Parem: Ruling Elder of the merchant house of Hann in Ngandib-Mar and an ally of Syth mod Syth-el.

Maliff: Falconer to Queen Bronwynn in the Imperial House of Chaomonous.

Maris: People of Ngandib-Mar.

Mar-Yilot: "The Autumn Lady," a sorceress of Ngandib-Mar and wife of Syth mod Syth-el. Her altershape is the butterfly.

Mast: A squat, somewhat cowardly wizard of Ngandib-Mar. His altershape is the frog.

Minaliss: A powerful war horse once belonging to Pezi, later ridden by Pelmen and Bronwynn.

Mudgecurdle: A small furry creature looking much like a pleasant bunny but ejecting a horrible stench when startled. Used as an epithet meaning "traitor" or "betrayer."

Naquin: Formerly the High Priest of the Dragonfaith (by heredity, not conviction), later an initiate of the skyfaith and a missionary sent by Erri to Chaomonous.

Nethermar: The rich, diamond-producing region of Ngandib-

Mar stretching from the Garnabel Bridge to the North Coast.

Ngandib: The capital city of Ngandib-Mar, sitting upon a high plateau in the center of the land. The citylord is considered to be King of Ngandib-Mar.

Ngandib-Mar: The warlike, highland country to the west of Dragonsgate, rich in jewels and martial tradition, and the land of magic. Also called simply "The Mar."

Ngarl: A Mari lord loyal to Pahd and his cousin Janos.

Nobalog: An ancient wizard from the time before the making of the dragon who brought the Imperial House to life and wrote the spell-book that became the source of Flayh's knowledge.

Ognadzu: One of the two premier trading houses in the three lands and a leading participant in the Council of Elders, the merchant monopoly. Its ruling elder is Flayh.

Pahd mod Pahd-el: Citylord of Ngandib and King of Ngandib-Mar, a formidable swordsman. His chief interest is in sleeping, allowing Flayh to usurp his power.

The Parks: One of the six regions of Ngandib-Mar, a heavily wooded area stretching northeastward from the High Plateau to the Great North Fir.

Pelmen Dragonsbane: Formerly Pelmen the player and the Prophet of Lamath, renewer of the skyfaith and killer of the dragon. A powershaper when in the Mar. His altershape is a falcon.

Pezi: An obese merchant of the House of Ognadzu, nephew to Flayh. An earnest, unprincipled incompetent.

Pinter: Once a slaver and an outlaw, he died after the battle beneath the Imperial House of Chaomonous in the arms of his companion, Tibb.

Pleclypsa: The largest city in the southern region of Chaomonous and the site of an annual dramatic festival.

Powershaper: Anyone gifted with the ability to shape the powers, but classically only those who, among other talents, can change into an altershape.

Qirl: A Mari warrior loyal to King Pahd made Jorl of the Isles by Pahd's command.

Riganlitha: A curious but unassertive tugolith frequently harassed by Thuganlitha.

Rosha mod Dorlyth: The son of Dorlyth, friend of Pelmen,

and husband to Queen Bronwynn of Chaomonous. Hero and bear's-bane.

Seriliath: One of the largest cities of Ngandib-Mar located in the Nethermar region on the North Coast. Its citylord is Syth mod Syth-el.

Serphimera: The former priestess of the Dragonfaith, blessed with ecstatic visions and healing power. The love of Pelmen Dragonsbane.

Sheth: An ancient powershaper from the time of the making of the dragon who failed in his attempt to use the Power's gateway to kill the beast and was himself killed in the process.

Shurl: An office conferred by the king of Ngandib-Mar upon favored supporters.

Skyfaith: A renewal of the ancient, pre-dragon faith based on dependence upon the Power.

Strahn: A young Lamathian initiate of the skyfaith and the aide to Erri the prophet.

Sugar-clawsp: A small, purple-shelled, flying insect that exudes a chemical harmful to human skin whenever it is aroused.

Syth mod Syth-el: Lord of Sythia Isle, his family home; Citylord of Seriliath, and husband to Mar-Yilot, he became the leader of a group of northern lords opposed to the nepotism of King Pahd. A wise leader and a good husband.

Tahli-Damen: Once the ruling elder of the trading house of Uda in Ngandib-Mar, now a blind initiate of the skyfaith.

Terril: "The twin-killer," a Mari powershaper. A crafty, treacherous man whose altershape is a sugar-clawsp.

Thuganlitha: a mean-spirited, violent tugolith given to horning anyone or anything that displeases him.

Tibb: A small but nimble slaver and brigand from Lamath with a deep sense of personal loyalty.

Tuckad mod Pak: A Mari lord allied with Syth mod Syth-el and the Citylord of Drabeld.

Tugolith: An enormous horned creature from the far north of Lamath who can carry on human conversation at the level of a toddler.

Uda: One of the premier trading houses participating in the Council of Elders, the merchant monopoly.

Vicia-Heinox: "The twi-beast," a two-headed dragon created in ancient times, who dominated the three lands for a millennium from his home in Dragonsgate. He could talk intelligently, and loved diamonds.

Wayleeth: Devoted wife of the merchant Tahli-Damen.

Westmouth: One of the six regions of Ngandib-Mar stretching eastward from the High Plateau to Dragonsgate. A sparsely settled, hilly country with no major cities.

Yona Parmi: A professional actor and a close friend of Pelmen.

# About the Author

Robert Don Hughes was born in Ventura, California, the son of a Baptist pastor. He grew up in Long Beach, and was educated in Redlands, Riverside, and Mill Valley, gaining degrees in theater arts and divinity. That education continued and he finished a Ph.D. in Missions, Religions and Philosophy in Louisville, Kentucky.

He has been a pastor, a playwright, a teacher, a filmmaker, and a missionary, and considers all those roles fulfilling. He has published several short plays, and presently teaches drama. He spent two years in Zambia, and while there was bitten by the Africa bug. His two passions are writing and football—not necessarily in that order, especially in October. He is married to Gail, a beautiful South Alabama woman who loves rainbows, and fills his life with them. They lived in Africa for several years where he did missionary work. They now live in Louisville, Kentucky, with their daughter Bronwynn, who was born in Africa.

Most of all, Bob likes people. The infinite variety of personalities and opinions makes life interesting. The sharing of self makes it worthwhile.

*From the award-winning master of both Science Fiction and Fantasy...*

# PIERS ANTHONY

**Available at your bookstore or use this coupon.**

____**JUXTAPOSITION** 28215 2.95
The exciting conclusion to The Apprentice Adept trilogy. Both science and magic fuse as Stile carries on a desperate war to restore the balance and prevent the destruction of the alternate worlds.

____**SPLIT INFINITY** 30761 2.95
Two alternate worlds, one ruled by science... one ruled by magic. Stile is caught in a desperate game of survival between the two.

____**BLUE ADEPT** 28214 2.75
Book two in this exciting series. Stile continues to compete in the games between the two worlds for his very survival as each round becomes more and more difficult.

## plus more of the magic of Xanth...

____**NIGHT MARE** 30456 2.95
While barbarians were invading from the north, Mare Imbrium had problems of her own as she was exiled to the day world with the ominous message "Beware the Horseman."

____**OGRE, OGRE** 30187 2.95
Ogres were stupid, ugly, could hardly speak and spent all their time fighting and eating young girls. But not Smash. He was ugly, but full of high flown conversation and surrounded by young girls who trusted him implicitly.

BB **BALLANTINE MAIL SALES**
**Dept. TA, 201 E. 50th St., New York, N.Y. 10022**

Please send me the BALLANTINE or DEL REY BOOKS I have checked above. I am enclosing $ ............ (add 50¢ per copy to cover postage and handling). Send check or money order — no cash or C.O.D.'s please. Prices and numbers are subject to change without notice.

Name____________________

Address____________________

City__________ State__________ Zip Code__________

08 Allow at least 4 weeks for delivery. TA-64